STROKE OF LUCK

LILAH LANCE

TITAN SECURITY BOOK I

To the girl who dreamed of her superman...

but didn't wait for him to rescue her

COPYRIGHT

AUTHORS NOTE

This novel contains mature themes and explicit content intended for adult readers only. It includes:

• Strong sexual content and detailed intimate scenes
• Violence and intense emotional situations
• Mature language
• References to traumatic experiences

MISSION BRIEFING

Welcome to Titan...

You are now a part of a team of security professionals working on saving face, saving lives, and sometimes saving their enemies.

Your objective, if you choose to accept it, *is to uncover a secret.*

Your team consists of:

Agent Reed Whittaker & Miss Alisha Malhotra

Together, you and your team will uncover secrets in the interconnected web of lies that Titan exists within.

I wish you the best of luck with Reed and Alisha.

CHAPTER 1
ALISHA

I WAS GOING TO THROW MY DRINK AT THE SLEAZY SUIT AND TIE WITH A cocky smirk, his wedding ring glinting under the club lights.

"Let me take you home tonight."

Biting back a comment, I tried not to let it grate on my nerves that it was because of men like Suit and Tie over here that I was bringing in my twenty-fifth birthday today, a virgin.

Instead of blaming it on life, a tiny dating pool filled with arseholes, and the responsibilities that consumed me?

My frustrations were on this idiot.

I had come to Teasers, one of New York's premier burlesque clubs, intending to escape.

Around me, the 1920's style decor, with floating multi-colored parasol umbrellas and lush, warm lighting, created a wonderland for seduction.

Scantily-clad performers in colorful wings, lingerie meant to be torn off with guests, and feather boas wrapped around their necks—I would have been in girl heaven.

The scent of white sage and flowers from the live plants mingled in the air, usually a comfort—now tainted by Suit and Tie's cheap cologne. Fidgeting with the vines dangling near my shoulder, I leaned back against the plush velvet barstool, trying to maintain distance.

"No, thank you," I replied firmly, but his eyes only widened, his smirk growing.

"Goddamn, your accent is sexy," he was undeterred.

1

"I'm waiting for someone." *Anyone. But you.*

As he reached out, I scooted further back, but before I could react, a figure in black obstructed my view.

The unmistakable scent of sea and spice filled my senses, and for a moment, I shifted in my seat, my heart pounding.

Reed Whittaker, CEO of Titan Security and the source of all my sexual frustration for the last three years, blocked my view. Broad shoulders. Chocolate hair.

The kind of look that made a woman think twice about her late-night decisions.

"Not gonna happen," Reed rumbled, his rich, velvety baritone laced with quiet menace.

The Suit and Tie sounded offended, his bravado deflating. "Who the fuck are you?"

"Don't even think about it," Reed said in a voice I heard over the music. "Turn around, go back to your friends."

Reed cut an intimidatingly rugged figure even among the common masses, exuding an undercurrent of raw power usually reserved for archangels strolling among humans.

The aura of intensity radiated from him.

Reed liked to make the occasional unannounced visit to Teasers, and by some stroke of luck, I seemed to be there on those nights.

His focus remained fixed on me the nights he was here, ensuring my safety even when I hadn't realized I needed protection.

But I figured that was his job. I told myself it wasn't a big deal. He'd usher me into cabs, steadying me with those large, calloused hands.

Except for that one night months ago when a friend's early departure prompted my exit shortly after.

As I approached the entrance, Reed materialized from the shadows.

Is everything all right? Is there anyone taking you home?...I can.

Why? I can catch a cab...

I just want to make sure you get home safe. Can I do that?

Sure...

Reed walked me to my doorstep, remaining in the hall until I was safely inside.

The entire interaction burned itself into my consciousness. Just a man ensuring a woman's safe passage home. Even though I hadn't so much as touched a drop at the club that night, the memory alone intoxicated me for weeks afterward.

He wanted to make sure I was safe. Without touching me. He never pushed for more.

Almost like he waited until I was comfortable.

A warm heat blossomed within me that had nothing to do with filling any empty space. Just his mere existence was enough to set me alight.

Because I wanted Reed. Lara confided that she trusted him implicitly to protect everyone.

Reed took that responsibility seriously.

I didn't hear what Suit and Tie said to Reed.

He was sputtering before Reed, and even surrounded by the dancers, every eye around me in the club seemed inexplicably drawn to this. Suit and Tie grumbled something under his breath.

The taut line of Reed's shoulders tensed like he was physically restraining himself.

"I'm not going to repeat myself. Get out. Or you can get kicked out."

"Yeah, and who the fuck are you?"

I saw the way Reed's entire body stiffened. *Drat.*

Before I could overthink it, I reacted on sheer instinct. I don't know what possessed me then, but I felt the dangerous shift as Reed tipped his head, his body coiling.

On instinct, I reached out, and my hand found its way into his. "Reed."

The instant we made contact, he looked over his shoulder at me, those storm-cloud eyes flashing with an untamed intensity that stole my breath.

I shook my head slightly, silently pleading. Unspeakable emotions lingered in his gaze as it raked over me with heat.

I injected some tease into my voice. "Where have you been? I've been waiting for you." *In more ways than one.*

His brow furrowed a fraction, and I willed him with my eyes to just go along with it.

Please, just play along. He searched my face intently.

When his head swung back towards the hapless suit, Reed was every inch the merciless predator, catching the attention of the rest of the club's security.

One of them, Nate Wyatt, a blonde Viking of a man, emerged soundlessly to stand at Reed's side.

Unlike Reed, Nate wore a shirt that said "Security" on the back.

Though not as massively built as Reed's, Nate's broad shoulders and navy eyes radiated an equal aura of threat.

He took one look at the slime ball, not hesitating in the slightest to reach out and lift him bodily from his seat.

I was too stunned to speak, unconsciously gripping Reed's hand.

A silent look passed between Nate and Reed, and whatever he saw in his boss's eyes made Nate shake his head at the suit, almost sympathetically.

I held my breath as the man squawked indignantly about harassment and lawsuits.

Nate all but growled, flanked by two other immense security guards, forcibly ejecting not just Suit and Tie, but his entire friend group. All because of me.

Embarrassment flooded me as I tried to tug my hand back from Reed's grip.

But he wouldn't release me, as his eyes followed his men until they disappeared from view, seemingly oblivious to the murmuring crowd we had attracted.

Reed loosened his grip, though his fingers remained tangled with mine.

"Don't feel bad," he said evenly, as though dealing with such confrontations was all in a night's work for him.

Tousled chocolate hair, just messy enough to tempt wandering fingers. A jawline perpetually tense.

Clean-shaven and smelling like the sea, Reed Whittaker was the kind of man who made women rethink their decisions. Several times.

He towered over my frame, forcing me to tip my head back to meet that stormy gaze head-on from where I sat.

Reed fit the dark, seductive aesthetic of the club like he was born to it.

He ran Teasers security with an iron fist, yet he moved through the crowd with an ease, a comfort of knowing he was in charge.

Everyone yielded to him.

He didn't dress the part of a CEO, his classic bomber jacket over a white shirt.

Powerfully built, the loose material hinted at the sinewy muscles beneath.

My imagination ran wild with visions of him making love to me beneath the cascading waterfall installation or near the canopy of pink cherry blossoms draped over the mezzanine.

He made me feel a little unhinged, untamed.

A little out of it.

Growing up with a Bengali-English mother and an English father, my baby sister Avani and I had inherited a blend of mannerisms and cultural practices from our parents.

Once, I landed in Reed's arms when I nearly took a spill months ago.

Reed had materialized by my side with lightning-fast reflexes, one broad palm across the small of my back, catching me against his solid chest before I could fall.

I still remember covering my burning face with a hand and murmuring an embarrassed thanks, unconsciously dipping into a tiny, deferential bow of gratitude.

A habit ingrained from my Mum.

When I finally peeked up at him through my lashes, Reed's lips curved into an amused smile that set my olive skin ablaze with a crimson flush.

My friends loved to tease me about my not-so-subtle fixation on Reed, which I staunchly denied.

After all, I had an obligation to Avani to not parade a revolving cast of potential lovers before her.

To my sister, I was already unconventional as a pseudo-parent.

Being a successful social media influencer, I'd been so focused on raising Avani and running my business that I neglected my own needs and desires.

Dating was one realm of life I had no experience navigating. Men were a no-go.

The influencer life was less glamorous than people thought, and it had left me feeling emptier than I wanted to feel. Which led me to Teasers tonight. Desperate to no longer feel so stuck.

Privately dreaming of Reed showing me what I'd been missing. Wondering if the reality could possibly live up to the fantasies.

"Are you all right?" The rough timbre of Reed's voice dragged me from my wandering thoughts.

That familiar clench of his jaw, the storm brewing in his eyes.

It paralyzed me every time our paths crossed.

I had barely exchanged words with him, yet the charged silence crackled, threatening to consume me if he so much as brushed against me.

I blamed it on the pent-up energy and not because Reed was well...Reed.

"You didn't have to do all that," I managed, shaking my head minutely. "I didn't want to make a scene."

"You didn't make a scene," Reed's deep voice washed over me as he stated the obvious with maddening calm. "I did."

Reed was a looming storm.

The stillness before the lightning cracked through the sky. I told myself the fluttering in my ribcage was simply the effects of too many mojitos consumed too quickly on an empty stomach.

"Does that happen to you often?"

It did. More than he knew.

The overzealous fans at meet and greets. The creepy comments on my Instagram and social media in general.

Pinned by the weight of his stare, I didn't know how to answer him. Something lurked under his surface, something that told me he hadn't stopped thinking about what he'd like to do to Suit and Tie.

"It's all right."

"It's not alright. He shouldn't have tried to put his hands on you," Reed's eyes darkened as he bit out the words. He raked over the slinky dress, hugging my curves before snagging on my heels.

"He didn't—"

"He was going to," Reed stated. "That was enough."

"Enough?" I repeated.

Reed's face remained impassive. "Why did you hold me back?" Storm cloud eyes took me in.

"I don't want you getting into a fight."

Over me. Even I didn't have enough ego to voice it.

Reed's eyes intensified as though confused.

"I don't like the idea of...people getting hurt over..." *Oh, drat, I am floundering.* "I don't want you to get hurt over something so..."

Seeing me struggle, Reed leaned in, halting my rambling. "You don't want me to fight for you?"

Did he want to fight?

I couldn't think with him this close. I had the biggest crush on Reed.

"Why would you?" I managed to whisper.

His brows rose fractionally as though incredulous I'd even ask such a thing.

I could only murmur. "I don't understand. I just didn't want to see you hurt."

Something unguarded flickered in Reed's eyes as they softened momentarily. He clearly hadn't expected that response. His hand

6

shifted to cup the side of my neck, thumb brushing the dangle of my earring.

A hint of wry amusement filled his expression, though he found my concern for his well-being laughable.

"What are you doing here tonight?"

I lifted my chin at his censuring tone, taking in the press of his full lips, drawing into a slight frown, brows furrowed. How did I even begin to answer that?

"You haven't been here in a while," Reed murmured.

I want to get laid.

Preferably by a man who looks and smells like you. Do you have a brother?

I deflected. "A girl's not allowed to have a drink and enjoy her Friday night?" *Or her birthday.*

His head tipped in that subtle way that really shouldn't have looked effortless. "It's Sunday."

Drat. His hand fell from my neck to brace against the back of the chair, and I immediately missed the contact.

Keeping track of the date often proved challenging in my unconventional lifestyle—the not-so-glamorous hustle of an influencer rarely adhered to regular business hours or anything resembling a routine.

He dipped his head, brushing my ear.

"How much have you had to drink?"

I clenched my thighs instinctively, my palm lifting to press against the firm wall of his jacketed chest. Instead of pushing him away, I seemed to anchor myself to his solid presence.

"I'm fine, I just—"

"How much?" His dubious expression made it clear he didn't believe me for a second.

Avoiding his searing stare, I glanced toward the remnants of my drinks. "Three?"

Reed's mouth ticked up at the corners, a rueful amusement dancing in his eyes.

"If you plan on staying here all night, lightweight, you'll have me for company."

My eyes widened, bristling at the gentle jab as a frisson of heated awareness licked through me at the implication of him staying by my side all night.

"Lightweight?" I echoed, indignant.

Reed grinned, his tongue darting out a little between his teeth as he leaned against the bar top.

"You're like Bambi on ice when you drink," he murmured, eyes dancing with mirth. I could only see his tongue and felt my entire body respond to that.

I could hear my governess in my head. Ladies do not daydream of being taken like a wild woman by a man like this.

I gasped, affronted. "I'm appalled by your candor. I can absolutely hold my weight—"

"Even when you're offended, you're still so..." His achingly sensual smile only widened as I sputtered.

"Articulate?" I supplied, arching a brow.

"Proper," Reed countered, that Northeastern accent rendering the simple word into something indecently sensual as it rolled off his tongue.

A weighted beat stretched between us, the air thrumming with unvoiced tension. Reed's gaze seemed to search my face, his brow furrowing slightly as if piecing together a puzzle.

"How long did your family move you guys around?" he asked abruptly. "Kids usually have accents if they've been around another language until about thirteen or so."

I blinked, startled by his astute observation.

Memories of my childhood flashed through my mind.

The familiar streets of Chiswick, the rolling hills of Oxfordshire, occasional stints in America, and trips to Calcutta, which my parents took us on to preserve Mum's culture. My Mum's voice echoed in my ears, her soft accent a constant backdrop to our lives. A life I no longer had.

"I was a teenager..."

Reed nodded, his eyes never leaving mine. It was as if he was absorbing the information, tucking it away for future reference.

Reed tipped his head back, looking behind me, his eyes darkening.

"Are you going to do that cute little bow again when you thank me for saving you this time?"

My heart stuttered at the word "cute".

I fought to keep my composure, willing myself not to visibly react.

Do not combust. Do not move.

As his words fully registered, confusion swept through me." Save me from what?"

CHAPTER 2
ALISHA

A SUDDEN SHOVE SENT ME FORWARD INTO REED, WHOSE ARMS BANDED around me, pulling me flush against his chest.

Raw masculine heat with his scent enveloped me as he settled us onto a vacated barstool.

Reed's body an unmoving shield against the swelling crowd cheering for whoever was performing.

I didn't look. All I felt was him.

Reed's stormy eyes locked onto mine, a flicker of something simmering in their depths.

"You okay?" His gruff words cut through my daze.

"I'm fine," I managed, acutely aware of how my body pressed against his. Every nerve ending sparked to life in a way only Reed could ignite.

"I do apologize," I prattled on, terribly conscious of him. "I'm certain you have far more pressing matters to attend to than rescuing me from sudden death on a Sunday evening. Surely someone is awaiting your return at home, and I don't want to keep you—"

Reed's intoxicating scent wrapped around me, making me want to curl into him.

A low chuckle rumbled through his chest, the vibrations echoing into my own. I swore I felt his nose graze the top of my head, almost as if he were inhaling the scent of my hair.

He didn't say a word, just held me securely in his embrace as he waited for the jostling crowd to subside.

Reed's expression darkened as he surveyed the crowd, eyes scanning each person.

It gave me a rare opportunity to study him unobserved.

"I have no one at home."

Reed is single.

Lara, who knew him better than I did, often teased that he frequented the club because he knew I would be there. But I couldn't bring myself to believe in that kind of luck.

I had discreetly asked Lara about Reed's personal life once, and her eyes had sparkled with mischief as she gushed about him.

She had confided that even Nate, Reed's second-in-command, couldn't quite match Reed's uncanny ability to control everything with an iron fist while still retaining his sense of compassion.

I don't want to bring someone home to Avani only to have it not work out. I feel so much pressure to do right by her. What if Reed can't handle that?

Reluctantly, I pulled myself back to the present, savoring the sensation of resting against Reed.

I could feel my curves molding to his strength, his body a solid wall of muscle beneath me.

Reed's fingers threaded through my hair, gently toying with the strands.

"Reed."

His attention turned to me. "You don't have to do this," I murmured. "I know you have more important things to attend to."

Amusement laced his tone as he spoke. "There is nothing else I'd rather be doing."

His words ignited a fire in my core.

My fingers danced over his collar, electricity sparking beneath my skin at the barest contact.

I slid my other hand under his jacket, feeling the hard planes of his chest.

Mortification burned in my cheeks as I tried to pull back, but Reed's hand shot out, capturing mine and pressing it firmly against his heart.

"I've heard you've been asking about me," he rumbled, his deep voice sending tremors through my body. His large hand splayed over mine, his heat seeping into my skin. "What did Lara tell you?"

"Nothing," I squeaked, my voice betraying my nerves. His masculine chuckle only deepened the flush in my cheeks.

"I've asked about you, too," he confessed. My heart all but sputtered. *He had?*

His lips, the bottom one slightly fuller than the top, looked so soft and inviting.

Before I could stop myself, visions of Reed moving over me, inside me, his lips trailing open-mouthed kisses along my throat as he drove deep flooded my mind.

My fingers drifted lower on his chest, and I heard his breath catch.

"Angel," he warned, and I froze at the unexpected endearment. "At least buy a man a drink first."

His eyes darkened as if he could read the wanton thoughts swirling in my head. "What's gotten into you tonight?"

"I could say the same for you," I countered, incredulity coloring my tone. "You've barely spoken to me for so long, and now you—" I broke off, unable to find the words.

"Do you want me to take you somewhere?" His question ignited a flurry of ideas that had my entire body nodding.

Breathe.

I wanted to be anywhere but here, the noises around us fading away until all that existed was the pair of eyes watching me with undisguised hunger.

When I licked my lips, his gaze zeroed in on the movement.

I had been touching him wherever I could reach.

"This dress," Reed murmured, his voice low and husky. "I fucking hate it and love it at the same time."

"Why do you hate it?" I asked, my voice embarrassingly breathless.

"I don't think you want the answer. Not here, at least."

His eyes darkened with appreciation as they raked over my curves, lingering on my ample breasts and thicker thighs.

"Is that why you like it?" I couldn't believe I dared to ask.

His hands drifted to the bare expanse of my back, sending shivers down my spine. "Yes."

His eyes darkened further as he realized how little fabric there was.

"I never got close enough to take you in until today. I saw you sitting there alone for the first time and..." Reed trailed off, his gaze intense. "Your eyes looked different tonight."

I *felt* different tonight, but how could I not with Reed flirting with me?

My body thrummed with arousal, and I was acutely aware of how my nipples might be visible if I moved just so.

11

"What did they look like?" I asked, not wanting to reveal my secrets.

As he considered the question, myriad emotions played across his handsome face.

"Something I didn't like." At my expression, he smiled. "Any more questions you'd like answered, Angel?"

He looked like he wanted to devour me whole.

"Why do you call me that?"

"Because I think you are...inherently good."

Warmth blossomed in my stomach. I didn't know why I was avoiding his flirtation. I wanted him. Reed would never hurt me. I knew that much. But my heart?

Negotiable.

"You don't know that," I argued. "What if I have parking tickets? Or was I mean to an animal?"

I didn't, and I wasn't.

"Or maybe I ran over an old lady today."

"Did you?" Reed's smirk was playful. He was humoring me, and I liked that.

"Well, no, but I could have. You can't possibly tell I'm good." I breathed. "Why are you looking at me like that?"

He shook his head. "Just thinking about how I missed out on three years of you and your little self."

Three years. That's when we met.

We'd danced around each other since then. My smile faltered.

"I didn't realize—"

But I *had*. It was a lie.

Familial obligations and nerves had held me back from talking to him. I'd chickened out every time. And Reed...he looked like he knew.

Then I registered his words.

"I am not little," I tried to inject a hint of indignation into my voice. "I'm five-three. That's average height."

Reed grinned, canines flashing and his tongue darting out past his teeth in the sexiest thing I had ever seen him do.

"I'm over a foot taller than you. Trust me, you're the perfect size."

Good Lord.

The deep, rich double entendre sank low in my belly.

He dipped his head. "And if you wanted to leave, you could...but since you liked sitting on my lap so much, I figured I'd let you stay here."

I felt my soaked undergarments on his lap, no doubt leaving a complete mess.

"You look like you'd rather be anywhere else than here, doing anything else than this."

I got the feeling that if I budged an inch, Reed would see his opportunity and take it. So I gave him one.

"And what does it look like I'd rather be doing?"

CHAPTER 3
REED

You look like you'd rather be doing me.

It was on the tip of my tongue to say it.

But I held back, not wanting to completely overwhelm the beautiful woman who had haunted my dreams for the last few years, now perched on my lap.

No, I was a patient hunter, and three years had been a long time. But I didn't want anyone else.

Her sweet, fuck-me stare told me everything I needed to know.

I'd known from the moment I introduced myself.

Her soft dusky hazel eyes dilating, her breath hitching, those pretty pink lips parting slightly in awe.

Her hand had lingered in mine just a moment too long.

One thought had drifted into my mind as the darker parts of me became utterly enamored with this soft, sweet woman exuding the kind of effortless sex appeal that others paid fortunes to achieve.

I had other obligations tonight, but the moment Lara's text came through, nothing else mattered.

> Alisha is coming tonight! Avani just left for college.
> Empty Nest = Opportunity. Woot! Woot!

I'd been tinkering with a new motherboard in my room, texting Evie about system implementations, and strategizing team assignments for new hires. The Devereaux family situation loomed large, and my

14

mental laundry list of potential fuck-ups grew by the minute. I couldn't afford this, and yet here I was.

Like Pavlov's dog, I reacted to her presence. *To Alisha.*

I'd asked Lara about her the moment I first saw her.

Information was my currency, and Lara had been a stellar wingman ever since, tipping me off whenever Alisha graced the club.

Tonight, she was a vision straight out of my darkest fantasies.

Red silk and gold jewels adorned her body, begging to be stripped away.

She looked ethereal under the fake tree, vines trailing across her shoulder.

Raven hair cascaded in waves to her shoulder blades, her petite frame perched on the barstool, an unwitting temptress. Olive skin glowing under the lights as her eyes took me in.

"Hang on," she said, tipping her head adorably. "What do you think you are if I'm inherently good?"

I bit back a laugh, drinking in the sight of her on my lap, desperately trying to ignore my obvious arousal.

She's so fucking beautiful.

Her nails glided down my shirt, coming to rest near my heart. Her other hand found its way to my nape, sending shivers down my spine.

"No, I don't think I'm inherently good," I admitted. Instead of being alarmed, her eyes softened.

"What if I knew whether you were inherently good or not?"

A genuine smile tugged at my lips.

In mere moments, Alisha had coaxed more laughter from me than I'd experienced in an entire month.

Desire coursed through my veins as I watched her tilt her head, studying me intently.

Her slightly rosy, rounded cheeks contrasted beautifully with her dark, lush hazel eyes. Utterly sexy yet somehow innocent.

It was her eyes that stopped me in my tracks. Playful, with a hint of something more.

A light burned within them, a flame of warmth and compassion that thawed places in me I thought had long surrendered to darkness and ice.

In her presence, I felt a warmth I'd forgotten existed, and a hunger I'd never known.

I'd fantasized about seeing those locks splayed across my thighs. Spread out on my pillow.

Alisha was the kind of woman that didn't come around often. She was the kind you pounced on, dragged back to your cave, and kept there.

Oh, I'd wanted to do just that. But I wasn't a complete idiot. Or a shit hunter.

The irony was that I had come to Teasers, one of the most renowned burlesque clubs with no shortage of women.

Yet, not a single one had captured my interest.

In my head, I'd had her so many times, imagining her pouty lips wrapped around my cock, her perfect hourglass figure working as she took me.

Visions of her beneath me while I fucked into her until she moaned for me to *not stop* in that accent of hers, husky, pleading, begging.

No matter how hard I tried, I couldn't erase her image from my brain, the way she looked.

I'd had few interactions with her over the years, and I knew why she wasn't available.

Her baby sister. Avani.

Even with the occasional hookups to blow off steam, any thought of her sent me to the gym, working out for hours until it calmed down.

Case in point? *Now.*

Seeing that son of a bitch next to her, motioning to his friends that he could take her. I immediately reacted.

Not her. Not my girl.

"You don't know me, Angel."

She rolled her eyes, a playful smile tugging at her lips," And yet you seem to know me so well, huh?"

More than she realized.

More than she understood how fucked she was for staying on my lap.

She could've gotten up at any time. Instead, she lingered, touched my heat, and leaned into me. I could move her dress a little, shove my dick in her, and let her squirm over me all night right here.

I inhaled her scent. Roses, honey...it was cardamom...

Something different.

It was something a little spicy and sweet at the same time, and it was addicting.

"I don't think you want the answer to that," I picked my words carefully. "I don't need you tipsy and thinking things."

I genuinely wanted to just make sure she got home safe and sound. *In those fucking heels.*

My gaze lingered on the mojito she'd been nursing, the condensation pooling at the bottom of the artfully crafted glass.

But as much as my body screamed at me to take what I'd craved for so long, a flicker of doubt held me back.

Alisha tilted her head, her hazel eyes glinting with a challenge. "And if I said I wanted to know?"

I bit back a groan, images of throwing her over my shoulder and finger-fucking her until she screamed my name, flooding my mind.

This wasn't working. I needed a different tactic.

One that didn't involve me thinking with my dick.

I racked my brain for a fucking solution.

"Lish, it's Sunday. You don't usually come alone. Tell me what's wrong."

CHAPTER 4
REED

"How did you know?" Her eyes widened, genuine surprise coloring her features.

"I pay attention." *Boy, did I ever.*

That anxious look from earlier tonight was back in her eyes, tugging at something deep within my chest.

"You won't judge me?" Alisha whispered, her voice small and vulnerable as she held out her pinky.

I blinked, momentarily stunned by the innocent gesture.

This was why I was so drawn to her.

Despite her confident exterior, Alisha had these endearing little quirks that slipped beneath my armor, melting into my bloodstream like cotton candy dissolving in water.

I locked my pinky with hers, and the contact sent a jolt through me. "I promise."

Her tongue darted out, wetting her lips.

"Avani started school," Alisha continued, oblivious to my level of knowledge.

Her voice had a note of pride, even as it wavered with emotion. "I just don't feel good about it..."

"Are you worried about her leaving?" I asked, my thumb stroking the delicate skin of her wrist in a soothing pattern.

"Not exactly," Alisha's gaze dropped to our still-joined pinkies. I wanted to draw her closer, to offer comfort.

Alisha shifted, her shoulder pressing into my chest.

"She's just Downtown. She comes home sometimes, but no—" Her words poured out in a rush, revealing more to me than she ever had.

I drank in every detail, committing it to memory.

"I think we both didn't get the life we wanted. Avani was twelve when Mum and Dad died—"

Two years before I met her, Alisha had lost her parents. I knew so much about this woman.

"She didn't get to be a normal teenager," Alisha continued, her voice thick with emotion. "And I didn't get to be a normal twenty-year-old girl."

The vulnerability in her voice stirred something within me.

"I bet." My chest tightened with empathy. Avani was Alisha's last remaining link to her family.

I couldn't fully understand what she was going through, but Gabriel, my best friend, pseudo-brother, and someone who ran Titan from the shadows, had become the guardian of his teenage sister, Evie, seven years ago.

As long as I had been at Titan, Gabriel had taken care of Evie. So had I.

"I feel horrible," Alisha whispered, her eyes shimmering. "On the one hand, I miss my sister, but on the other hand, I'm grateful for my own time."

"Where is everyone?" I asked, glancing around the club. Alisha never came to Teasers alone. "I thought Gemma was free from her usual duties."

Gemma was a leggy blonde heiress who'd turned her back on her family, scandalizing the world in the process. She'd landed on my radar when she'd requested a bodyguard from Titan Security after parting ways with her previous one. There *was* Lara, but she was busy tonight, winking at me when she saw me with Alisha.

"No one but Lara knows I'm here."

My pulse quickened at the implication.

"I just wanted to be...not alone, per se. Just..." Alisha trailed off, her gaze distant.

"Not attached to anything," I finished for her. Her eyes met mine, a flicker of surprise passing over her features.

"Yes," She worried her bottom lip between her teeth. "Do you ever think about leaving it all behind? Going somewhere far away...to some remote island where no one knows you, just for a bit?"

A humorless laugh escaped me. "Every fucking day." *If only she knew.*

19

"Not many vacations when you're CEO?" she asked, a hint of curiosity coloring her tone.

More like CO. Being in command was a far cry from being a soldier in the trenches. I didn't want to delve into that tonight.

Couldn't, even if I wanted to.

The majority of our work at Titan was classified as the kind of black ops missions that never saw the light of day.

"Why were you upset about your sister?" I pivoted, steering the conversation back to safer waters.

Alisha's brows knitted together, a flicker of annoyance passing over her face at my evasion.

"I didn't know if I made the right choices with Avani. If I should've taken her back to Chiswick. I don't know if I want to keep doing my job—"

She shook her head, her lush waves cascading over her shoulders.

"I'm tired of pretending. Like I'm wearing a mask, I don't feel for what I do anymore, like I'm changing and straddling two worlds, and I have to pick which one I want."

Half the time, I didn't even know who I was. But one thing stood out to me, a truth that lodged itself in my ribcage and refused to budge.

Alisha's family isn't from here.

The idea of never having met Alisha, of her not existing at all...it wasn't something I was willing to contemplate.

I just got you.

She continued, oblivious to the way her words had tilted my world on its axis.

"Avani wanted to stay with me, and I was doing really well with my brand deals. It's just...over the last few years, it's lost some of that sparkle it used to have. I'm not sure who I am anymore," Alisha glanced down, and I realized our fingers were interlaced.

"I feel like I'm stuck between two parts of my life that I want, but if I pick one, I might lose the other."

"And if both parts could exist?" I asked, my voice low and rough with an emotion I didn't dare name.

She met my gaze, her hazel eyes searching mine for answers I wasn't sure I possessed.

"How?"

"You find a balance," I said, the words tasting like ashes on my tongue. "And you try every day to make sure you can honor both."

Or something like that. Alisha studied me, her head tilted in a way

20

that made me feel like she was seeing past my carefully constructed walls.

"Speaking from experience, Reed?"

My name from her lips made my chest clench.

"I think you should be proud of yourself. You raised a teenager on your own without your parents. You worked a full-time job, if not longer. What's that saying? You can work nine-to-five for someone else or—"

"You can work twenty-four hours for yourself?" Alisha finished, a soft laugh escaping her lips.

I didn't understand her struggle, not really. I didn't have a relationship with my half-brother, Adam, nor did I care to. Life had brought me better connections, ones I'd chosen for myself.

Or, as my therapist had put it, I didn't have to settle for shit when I could have the best.

I leaned in closer, my breath mingling with hers. "What do you want to do?"

Somehow, despite the undeniable want coursing through my veins, the conversation had shifted to something deeper, something that tugged at the hidden corners of my heart.

She pondered my question, her teeth sinking into her plump lower lip again, turning it a shade of dark pink that had me clenching my jaw.

"Well, now that you mention it, the only thing I didn't really get to do was date much."

The words hit me, a swell of irrational jealousy rising in my chest at the thought of my girl in the arms of another man. I had no right to feel this way, to care about her romantic history, but the possessive beast within me snarled at the idea.

"I prioritized Avani. She became my entire world for the longest time, with a full-time job on top of that. Dating wasn't even possible."

"I can imagine." I forced myself to focus on her words, shoving aside the thought of Alisha with anyone else.

I told her about Gabriel and how Evie was his whole world. That was putting it lightly.

If Gabriel had his way, Evie would never have left his side, but she was a woman now, and I suspected she shared Alisha's desire to forge her own path in life. "But it sounds like you're doing a good job."

An easy smile graced Alisha's lips, the sight making my heart stutter in my chest.

"Such confidence. What makes you say that?"

The truth? She radiated warmth and compassion, the kind of light that drew people into her orbit. I couldn't tell her that or reveal the depths of my fascination for the last three years.

So, I switched gears, steering the conversation away from the darkness that cloaked my work life, especially anything involving Gabriel.

"I can just tell," I said simply.

Steering the conversation back to safer waters, I quipped. "You don't miss out on much by not dating. Besides married businessmen..."

I'd deal with him later.

When I wasn't distracted by the expanse of all that golden skin in my arms.

"I think you're trying to make me feel better about being a hermit," she teased, her voice like honey and sin. I wanted to tell her that I was a hermit, too, when I could be. And that she was welcome to join me in my den anytime.

"In all the conversations I imagined us having, this wasn't one of them," Alisha admitted, a pretty flush staining her cheeks.

"What did you imagine?" I asked desire coating my tongue. The thought of her fantasizing about me, about us, was enough to make my blood run hot. She chewed on her lip, a nervous habit that only made me want to soothe the abused flesh with my own.

"I don't know...but not this."

She was closing up again, the walls coming back brick by brick.

"Does this conversation mean you want to go on a date?" I blurted out, the words escaping before I could second-guess myself.

Alisha's eyes widened in surprise, and something else—hope, maybe —flickering in their hazel depths.

"Are you...?" She trailed off, her unspoken question hanging in the air between us. *Asking me out?* I tipped my head. Her eyes widened a little. "I would love to."

Alisha said slowly as if testing the words on her tongue. My chest clenched a little at her admission.

"But I like to keep my life private regarding that stuff. If that's all right with you..."

Damn straight it was. It was the most important thing to me. And when she'd answered, it made me ask another question.

"Were you on a date tonight?" My heart pounded a little in expectation. The question fell from my lips before I could stop it, a hint of desperation coloring my tone.

"I think so."

For a moment, jealousy burned through me like wildfire until I caught the soft smile playing at the corners of her mouth, her eyes sparkling with mischief.

"And I think it's going rather well."

Well, shit. "But I didn't buy you dinner."

"Who said I wanted any?" She countered, her voice dropping to a husky whisper. A slow smile stretched my lips.

"What's your favorite kind of food?" I asked, genuinely curious.

"Greek." Her answer was immediate, with no hesitation. She laughed at my surprised expression. "Did you think it would be my culture's food?"

I nodded, a sheepish grin tugging at my lips.

"I do like it, but my ancestors are probably rolling in their graves right now," Alisha tipped her head, her hair spilling over her shoulder in a cascade of dark silk. "You?"

"Greek."

"Favorite color?"

She threw her head back, her laughter musical. "I cannot believe you. Pink. Your turn."

Anything you wear. "Red." My gaze drifted down her dress. Her lashes fluttered in a tiny bit of shy embarrassment. And that was cute as fuck.

"Favorite place in the world?"

"Underwater." Her brow arched in silent question. "It's quiet down there. You?"

"Anywhere in Ubud."

Now, it was my turn to be surprised. "Bali?"

"You've been?" She sounded impressed, and I felt a swell of pride in my chest.

"It was one trip. A complete accident."

Gabriel and I had gotten into some trouble in Jakarta, but he'd managed to finesse our way out of it. Needing a breather, we'd flown to Bali. Gabriel, who couldn't relax for shit, had finally let his guard down when a raven-haired woman appeared on the beach.

She'd been just his type. *Like Alisha is mine.*

"Fine, one last question," Alisha said, pulling me from my thoughts.

"We aren't making it to twenty?"

She glanced around the club, her smile soft and secret.

"Not here, at least." Her smile faltered, uncertainty clouding her features. "I...I don't know why I said that."

I squeezed her hand, a silent reassurance. "You'll get no judgment from me," I promised, my voice low and earnest.

"Thank you." The way she said it as if I was doing her a favor, simply by being kind, made me want to hunt down everyone who had ever made her feel unworthy.

"Maybe you're right. I'm probably not missing out on much. Makes me glad I've never—" She stopped.

Just outright stopped.

Part of her looked terrified at what she was about to say when she was talking. I was hooked.

It was too quick. *She's hiding something.*

She chewed her lip with that look on her face again, like she was afraid of something. Or embarrassed.

"Part of me wants to ask you to finish your sentence." My intuition knew something was off about how she said it.

She squirmed, trying to get out of my lap. "It's not important." I pulled her back. *She likes to run.* I liked to chase. That was fine by me.

"I think it is." Oh, now I was focused. "Don't run from me, Angel." *If I catch you, I'll fuck you.*

I dipped closer. "Finish the sentence."

Her mouth formed a little O as she leaned back an inch. "I don't think that's a good idea."

"It sounds like a fantastic idea." *Because now I was sure of it.*

Her eyes widened a little, her body leaning a little back, letting me lean in more. Trapping her between the bar top and me.

I raised a brow, watching her throat work. "I don't think I should say it with the way you're looking at me."

"How's that, Angel?" I wasn't expecting that to slide off my tongue.

She drew her bottom lip into her mouth. It was a whisper. "Like you know my secrets."

Did I? "Which is?" I was so close I could kiss her right now. If I wanted to, I could have her right now.

"I think you've surpassed your twenty questions."

"I haven't. We're only on eight," I'd counted everyone I'd asked her in between.

A rueful smile came to her lips. "You're wicked."

Carefully persistent.

"I've never been with...someone like you."

Fuucck.

Did she know what I was?

Did she know what I liked?

And why did that make my chest swell?

Elation wasn't the right word for the blast of heat coursing through my body and possessiveness surging through me.

I wanted to take her back to my home and protect her. Be my submissive.

I wanted to devour her for myself and keep her there. The idea of anyone else having her made me growl.

"Someone like me?" Rough around the edges, but still shiny enough for her to be with? Or a fucking monster in her bedroom.

She licked her lips. "Is that nine?"

I only had one. "Why did you come here?" I bet I had a good idea why now that it all added up.

"Tonight?"

That's eleven.

Before I could say anything, Alisha whispered it low. "I mean, it's my birthday; the least I could do is—"

Any rational thought in my brain screeched to a halt.

"Wait, what?" I had to calm down. I just about yelled at her. Even the mental voice in my head telling me to kiss her screeched to a halt. "It's your *birthday?*"

Idiot, you have an entire dossier and miss her birthday? How had I not remembered that?

"What about the girls, you didn't tell them?" I was incredulous. This needed to be fixed.

"I think you just got to your fifteenth."

Oh fuck, the damn questions.

"I didn't want to do anything but celebrate tonight. And not with a woman."

I couldn't look at her.

I didn't.

Afraid I had no restraint if those eyes bat at me one more time as she said that. Her golden skin, dark hair, those eyes.

I couldn't think.

I raked my hand through my hair, messing it up even more.

The way she said it, I knew exactly what she was implying. I couldn't pace while holding her but damned if I couldn't try. Put her on my dick, that would help me think straight.

But I stayed still. My brain worked overtime.

My voice dropped as I drew closer, aware of prying eyes despite the show going on. I got to her close enough to drop my head to her ear.

"You needed a man tonight, Angel?"

Her breathy gasp in my ear confirmed what made my blood heat. Her. With another man. Touching her. Making her moan in his ear while she came.

"Sixteen."

I'm putting you over my knees, Angel.

I couldn't even fathom allowing her to go home alone. "Is that what you needed?"

Do you need it from me?

I couldn't stop myself from finding the spot behind her ear as she gripped my arm, and I realized I'd asked the question out loud.

"That's eighteen."

"Reed."

Oh fuck, that's how she'd sound in bed.

That breathy, husky moan of my name. I hadn't even touched her yet, and she was driving me out of it.

"Yes." *Fuck.*

"You want me to take you home?" I felt my heart clench and arousal pulse through me. My cock had been thick with arousal since she'd sat on my lap.

Twenty.

"Are you sure?"

"Yes."

CHAPTER 5
ALISHA

I COULDN'T BREATHE.

I wanted Reed.

That's why I'd shown up at Teasers on my birthday.

I craved something more than just being a sister, more than the life I'd carved out for myself.

The journey to my apartment passed in a blur, anticipation crackling between us like electricity.

Reed's deep blue Maserati purred through the night, its sleek contours reflecting the city lights.

My heart raced, a mix of excitement and nerves coursing through me.

As we pulled into the garage, Reed wordlessly emerged and strode to my side. Before I could protest, he swept me into his arms.

"I can walk," I whispered, still reeling from the intensity of his earlier reactions.

"I know." But his voice was taut with emotions I couldn't identify right now.

Warmth bloomed across my cheeks as I nestled my face into the crook of his neck, my body trembling with a heady mix of nerves and desire. His heat seeping into my skin.

I was acutely aware that I had just asked *Reed*, the man I'd secretly longed for so long, to sleep with me for the first time.

The elevator doors dinged open on my floor, and the night guard stepped in as Reed and I exited.

This felt familiar, yet entirely new—Reed had never come inside before.

He set me down gently in front of my door, and with trembling fingers, I fumbled with the keys, acutely aware of his presence behind me.

As the door clicked open, a wave of lush roses and honey scent enveloped us, instantly calming me.

Reed stepped into the entryway, his eyes methodically scanning every detail.

I watched him, curious about his reaction, suddenly feeling shy despite my earlier boldness.

My apartment, an upscale high-rise, reflected a blend of luxury and practicality.

My upbringing had instilled in me a resistance to ostentatious displays of wealth, despite my considerable means.

The open-plan living area flowed seamlessly into the kitchen, dominated by an enormous cream sofa that we spent hours curled up in.

Reed's gaze swept over the space, taking in the colors that diverged from minimalism.

Feminine artwork adorned the walls, fresh flowers, the odd stacks of Avani's books that were artfully arranged. It is my home.

"You live in a home," Reed mused, his voice tinged with admiration. "It's beautiful."

"Thank you." A satisfied smile tugged at my lips. I'd worked hard to make this space a sanctuary for Avani and me. If I expected Reed to simply pounce, I was wrong. He didn't move, simply taking in my space.

His eyes landed on the refrigerator, covered in an eclectic mix of items—report cards, postcards, and colorful alphabet magnets spelling out messages.

As Reed removed his shoes, I glanced down at the plush slippers I'd instinctively slipped into.

A fleeting thought of getting him a pair flickered through my mind before I swiftly dismissed it. He might not want to stay.

I slowly padded up beside him, watching as his gaze drifted over the fridge.

Reed absorbed every intimate detail. I felt shy sharing everything with him now.

His fingertips grazed over a photo of Avani in her oversized bunny costume with big floppy ears from last Halloween.

Her infectious smile radiated pure joy, and I felt a warmth spread through my chest at the memory. I'd raised *her*.

"This is Avani," Reed said softly, his voice filled with a tenderness I hadn't expected.

"It is," I replied, a fond smile tugging at my lips. "When she said she was going as a bunny, I expected something different. But she showed up all the kids were begging for photos."

As I spoke, I noticed Reed's eyes drift to another snapshot behind it. My heart rate spiked, and I instinctively moved to divert his attention, but I was too late.

Drat!

"I, on the other hand, did not get the proper bunny memo," I admitted, biting my lip self-consciously. I braced myself for his reaction, heat rising to my cheeks.

In the photo, I wore a micro-skirt that left little to the imagination, paired with fishnet stockings and thigh-high boots.

The bustier clung too tight, my cleavage threatening to spill free.

Long bunny ears completed the look, and I grinned into the camera with a sexual confidence that felt alien to me now.

Reed's thumb brushed over the bottom of my skirt in the photo, and I felt a shiver run down my spine.

His eyes met mine, dark and intense, and suddenly the air between us felt charged with electricity.

"You look..." Reed's voice was low and husky, trailing off as his gaze raked over me. I swallowed hard, hyper-aware of his proximity.

Reed took a step closer, closing the distance between us. I could feel the heat radiating from his body.

"Come here, Lish."

"Why?" I asked, even as my body instinctively leaned towards him. My heart pounded in my chest, a mix of anticipation and nerves making my breath catch.

Reed's lips curved into a wicked grin that made my knees weak.

"Because I've been wanting to do this since the moment I saw you."

Reed stamped his mouth over mine.

CHAPTER 6
ALISHA

REED DIDN'T KISS. NO, HE DEVOURED ME.

I moaned as his tongue thrust into my mouth, and I tasted Reed.

I clung to him, my knees weak with the sheer force of my need. His strong arms banded around me.

I'm kissing Reed.

One hand behind my neck, he kept me steady as he plundered my mouth.

Years of pent-up frustration, unsatisfied orgasms, and the thrill of finally having him had me returning his kisses with equal fervor. My hands clawed at his jacket, desperate to feel his skin against mine.

"Lish, I plan on doing more than just kissing you," he growled, his voice low and rough with desire. "But I need to set some ground rules first."

He shrugged off his jacket, tossing it carelessly onto the marble island, and my eyes widened at the sight of his tattooed arms.

Good lord, I had no idea he looked like that underneath.

His classic white shirt stretched tight across his chest, leaving nothing to the imagination.

"Angel, you keep staring at me like that, and all my plans are gonna get thrown out the window."

Reed's mouth fell to my lips, and he pulled me close.

"I need you to understand a few things before I take you," he murmured against my lips.

"Nod if you hear me, Angel."

He demonstrated a nod, and I followed suit.

"Let me be your Dom, Lish. I can take care of you."

"A what?" I breathed, my mind reeling. He blinked, realization dawning in his stormcloud eyes.

"You've never been with someone like...me. I thought when you said that, you meant you'd never—"

Quick, think fast.

"I haven't," I admitted, my cheeks flushing with heat. "But I mean...I've seen and heard things. I'm not completely inexperienced."

You little liar.

"I'm not going to tie you up with a ball gag and light up your clit, Lish." *Set my what on fire?*

"But I'm in charge the entire time." Reed's gaze locked with mine, intense and unwavering. I instinctively tried to back away a little, nervousness fluttering in my stomach at the thought of giving him everything. But he pulled me back with a soft growl, his grip unyielding.

"Don't run from me, ever. If you do, I will catch you and spank your ass so red, you won't be able to sit all prim and proper."

I flushed deeply, heat coursing through my veins at the thought of his hand connecting with my bare skin.

"If it ever gets uncomfortable, I want you to tell me."

I nodded, my breath coming in short, shallow gasps as he mimicked the gesture.

What about setting anyone's clit on fire?

Did I want to try that?

I licked my lips, a thrill of excitement mingling with the nerves in my belly.

"How do I let you know it's too much?"

His eyes flashed with heat at my question, a predatory gleam that sent a shiver down my spine.

"You want a safe word?" he murmured, his lips brushing against mine in a teasing caress. I nodded, my body strung tight with anticipation.

"Or you want colors? Red for stop, yellow for uneasy, green for *don't stop*." I gasped as he nipped at my lower lip, a sharp sting that only heightened my arousal.

"Both," I breathed, my mind racing to find the perfect word. "Storm." *It seemed fitting.*

"And what color are you, Angel?" His lips moved against mine.

"Green, Reed," I whispered, opening my mouth in acceptance. *"Green."*

"I'll be the first to admit, I'm an opportunist," he growled, his hands roaming over my breasts. "When you came to me tonight, I wanted to fuck you right then and there, where everyone could see."

Good Lord.

My pussy clenched at his words.

"Would you have liked that?" he asked his voice a low purr that sent a shiver down my spine. I knew what he was asking, and in that moment, I was completely his.

"Yes," I admitted, the words slipping past my lips before I could stop them. "I've wanted you for the longest time."

His lips pressed against the side of my neck, trailing fire along my sensitive skin.

"Especially tonight, hm?" I moaned as he sucked a spot on my neck I didn't know was sensitive. "Tonight, you needed me to fuck you, didn't you, Angel?"

He said it as he squeezed my breasts, and I arched into him. I was utterly lost as he pressed wet kisses down my neck, parts of me clenching in response to his words.

All the while, my hips worked.

"Yes." I cried out as he picked me up, grinding my hips down on his length. I gasped as I clutched him tightly. *"Yes, please."*

I was aware of how forward this was.

The desperation in both of us to simply...be. I'd wanted Reed for so long. I was starving for him, my core clenching, my womb tightening as the sensations ratcheted up inside of me.

He gasped as I bounced on him. It gave me an idea of how rough he was. I *liked that.*

Sensations skittered up my body at the sheer want of Reed.

"Yes." I couldn't stop. I was so close. "Reed, please—"

I closed my eyes and groaned as he stopped.

"Not like this, not now." He whispered, his mouth capturing mine. "My first time with you can't be on the kitchen counter."

My heart clenched at that statement. He didn't know. *He couldn't know.*

"Why not?" I couldn't breathe. I wanted Reed with desperation. *Nothing but him.* Consuming me.

With a groan, he carried me further into the apartment.

"I need somewhere soft. I won't hurt you."

The words made me clench internally while something warm settled in my heart. The duality of Reed never left my mind. Cold and reserved while burning hot for me. Rough and deadly while soft and considerate.

"I've been patient for three years. I don't care who you've been with," he whispered. "I'll make you forget every last one of them tonight."

I tried not to tell him there was no one else. I couldn't get my lips to form the words. *Tell him.* He walked into my room, setting me down and tugging at my dress, his eyes dark at seeing I wore nothing else but panties.

Tell him.

When could I have?

I couldn't get out of it fast enough as I flung it on the floor.

Standing tall and still in his clothes, I felt like I had just emerged from the sea in front of this man.

A curious mix of boldness and shyness washed over me.

Reed's presence was overwhelming, like standing before a force of nature.

He reached for me, fingers threading through my hair as he removed the clip.

The soft thud as it hit the carpet seemed to echo in the charged silence between us.

His eyes roamed over me, dark with desire, and I felt my body respond to his gaze.

A flush crept across my skin, and I fought the urge to cover myself.

Reed's eyes were dark as he took me in, coasting over my body, nipples hard and breasts aching, my stomach slightly rounded and then lower.

Hungry. *Dark.*

His hair mussed from my fingers, fell over his eyes making him look like a dark king.

His hands came to the sides of my head, brushing my hair back as he took me in.

"The first time I saw you, I thought you were the most beautiful woman I'd ever seen. I wanted to take you home that night. With your big fuck me eyes, taking me like a good girl."

I all but glowed at the words, *good girl.*

His words sent a thrill through me.

"Why didn't you?" I asked, barely recognizing my own voice, husky with desire.

33

"You weren't ready," he replied softly, his lips brushing against my ear. "You wouldn't have let me."

He didn't spare a single moment as he reached for me again, kissing his way down my neck and tugging at my panties, sinking in front of me.

If I could've ever imagined Reed, it wouldn't have been on his *knees*.

"You have to feel safe, don't you? And you felt safe with me tonight."

He knelt before me, his head bowed to me, and my heart skipped a beat.

I felt his breath against my most intimate parts.

His whisper against my stomach made me weak. He pushed me back.

In a slow topple, I fell on the bed, my back pressed into the mattress, legs falling open of their own accord.

Reed sank between my thighs to the floor.

"I've dreamed of you like this…Let me taste you…"

I opened my mouth to say he could, but with the first stroke of his tongue, all thoughts left my brain.

Everything centered on his tongue inside of me, warm, wet, and hungry.

Oh, that's different.

I gasped at the assault on my most sensitive flesh, the sensations leaving me breathless. I had *never* had this.

I'd only dreamed of his stormy eyes gazing up at me as he worked his mouth all over me.

"Oh, God, Reed."

I clutched at the sheets, bucking my hips up as he ate at me with the same fervor he took my mouth in.

Reed did *nothing* in half measures.

His mouth sucked on my clit, as two fingers dipped into my entrance teasing me.

Rubbing gently, firmly, until he slid them in, the slight stretch leaving me sobbing for more.

Deeper. *Curling.*

I was squirming, crying, sobbing his name as he drove me to the brink.

It felt almost embarrassing how much noise left me as he moved his fingers then against that spot, curling every time, pressing into it with enough pressure as he sucked.

"*Reed.*" My orgasm was building, pooling low in my belly, rising, burning me alive, as his hands moved along the side of my body.

The *last* thing I was expecting was how strong he was holding me down.

I squeezed my eyes shut, my back leaving the bed as I cried out, the sensations unfurling in my body.

He didn't stop as I said it. His fingers worked rougher, curling into that spot hard. I felt myself soaking them.

I felt his growl against my clit, and I snapped. When it crashed into me with no mercy, raking through my body, my back arching as I clutched the sheets.

A low growl came from between my legs as his tongue worked my clit before plunging into my core.

I screamed as it prolonged my orgasm while he slid it into me. The image of him alone sent micro shocks through me, my thighs shaking around his head.

"Reed, please, I need—" He rose up swiftly then, tearing his shirt off, followed by his pants.

I had been right from his arms that Reed worked out.

Every inch of him was roped in muscle, toned like a fighter, his wide-set shoulders leading down to his pecs and a tapered waist.

I didn't know what he did, but no way he sat behind a desk.

Speckled with scars and cuts and tattoos, Reed's body made my breath catch.

His hand dropped to his pants, and I was helpless to stare as he eyed my body.

I didn't want to move as I watched him.

"Do you think about me when you touch yourself in your bed?"

His hands went to his belt, his dark head bent as he watched me, eyes bright as he took me in.

I did. "*Yes.*"

Shaking, trembling, I breathed in and out hard, watching him taking off his clothes.

I heard Lara mention over the years about how she thought Reed walked around with *big dick energy.*

She wasn't wrong. Not that I had much experience, but there was no way.

I was a virgin. *Tell him.*

"I don't think you're going to fit."

CHAPTER 7
REED

SHE'S SO FUCKING SWEET.

"Have some faith, Angel. I think we'll fit just fine."

I dropped my mouth over hers, holding nothing back. Kissing Alisha was a dream.

I'd imagined it so many fucking times. I felt my cock throb at the taste of her, mint and sugar on her lips, and the scent of her invading my body.

"I knew you'd be like this," I growled in her ear, nipping that sensitive spot where I knew she'd squirm. Adorable and sexy at the same time.

Lush.

Pulling her farther back on the bed with my arm under her, I crawled on top of her.

Sheets bunching between my fingers as I felt her soft form under me.

Dragging my fingers up her thighs.

She was so *soft*, her skin so supple underneath the press of my fingers. I braced my arms against the sides of her head, letting her feel my cock pressing against her core.

"I *wanted* you," I found myself saying. "For the *longest* time."

With her legs spread open to accept me, her head thrown back in a moan, it was everything I could've dreamed of. I dropped my mouth down to her neck, sucking and biting and leaving marks for tomorrow so she wouldn't forget.

Locking eyes with her, I needed to be sure she was ready.

"Tell me what color."

"Green," she gasped out. "So green. *Please, take me...*"

I felt like I was dreaming when she said that. *Years. I've waited years.*

I pressed into her slowly, watching her eyes widen. "Tell me you're on something?"

"I'm on the pill," she gasped out. Relief flooded through me as I kissed her, the head of my cock nudging against her entrance.

The wet heat nearly undid me right then and there.

"I'm not gentle, I can't be. Hold onto me," I warned, my voice strained.

With that, I plunged forward, her wild scream mingling with my guttural groan.

"Oh fuck..."

I didn't get far.

Even with how wet she was.

"You're so fucking tight, Angel."

I kept my knees planted on the bed as my dick speared into her with a growl.

I looked at her face and stilled, eyes closed tight and expression pained. I was instantly still. I didn't move.

Her eyes opened a little, and I wanted to hurt myself at the sight of her tears. *Why was she—*

"*Alisha*," I didn't recognize my voice. "What's wrong?"

"I'm okay." She didn't look it. The tears slipping from beneath her lashes said otherwise. "Please tell me that's all of you."

It wasn't, not even close.

But she wasn't okay.

I looked down where we were joined, my heart dropping to my stomach at the idea of hurting her, making me pull out with concern, just enough to see—

"*Fuck*." Blood.

That was blood. *I knew it.*

Even under the warm lights. How was that even possible? Combined with her pain...She was twenty-five.

There was no way—

"*You're a virgin?*" I knew my expression must've freaked her out since hot tears ran down her eyes.

"Please don't be mad," she pleaded, voice breaking. "I didn't want to tell you. I *just*—I wanted you."

Oh, Angel. Soft hazel met my eyes, and I realized how uncomfortable she was.

I felt like a lance had been driven through my chest.

She's never done this before.

It dug in, unveiling a bevy of emotions cloaked in arousal, possessiveness, and sheer awe at being the man she chose to be with flooded me.

Even then, the darker parts of me felt nothing but the need to now mark her, bite her, fuck her with my cum.

I captured her apologies on my own tongue.

"I got you. It's all right. I'm the one who should be sorry." Emotions battered at me from all sides.

My brain was running miles, unable to comprehend how she was a virgin. How she'd wanted to give herself to *me.*

Another wave of emotions crested.

"A—are you angry?" she asked timidly, shattering my heart.

"Are you kidding?" I braced myself above her on my elbows, fighting to focus past the rhythmic clenching of her body around my cock. "*Why?*"

Her voice was a whisper. "Because I didn't tell you."

I silenced her with my mouth, pouring every ounce of my devotion into the brush of my lips on hers.

"No, I'm not. Angel, just let me..." I pressed into her again, reveling in her gasp. "I'll take my time. We'll go slow."

Not like this. Her first.

Her *only.* I slid in deeper, loving the way her mouth opened in a silent O.

"That's it, let me in. Spread your legs just a bit, Angel. Just *like-*" Oh *fuck.*

My hands reached under and lifted one of her legs higher and fucking *finally*, I bottomed out.

An animal noise left her lips. Long moments went by and I felt the rhythmic squeezing of her body wrapping around mine.

I bent my head finding her throat, kissing down, licking and sucking until soft moans left her.

Lower, finding her nipples beaded and taut. I took one in my mouth, toying with it on my tongue, my teeth.

Until she rocked her hips up.

"I can feel that Angel, I can feel you easing. *Fuck*, that's so sexy."

"Reed, you feel so good."

All thoughts of fucking her so hard left me for a different reason. Out of concern for her.

I slowly dragged my dick out every nerve ending sensitized to this woman.

This gorgeous woman who trusted *me*.

"Does it still hurt?"

Wet eyes batted up at me as I smoothed her hair back. "A little...but I like it."

My body absorbed her statement, it sinking in somewhere where the depravity of my own sexual needs met it with warmth.

Fuck. Heat pulsed inside of me.

Centering where I was buried in her. *Perfection.* That's what she felt like. Depraved thoughts flooded me again.

Trailing my fingers down her throat, I gripped gently, testing out if she liked that.

I was a monster for pushing her so hard, but she liked it. I slid back into her slowly.

Testing the waters. Testing her limits.

Oh, she's gorgeous. Her eyelids fluttered as her pussy clenched tightly around me. Her soft exhale told me she liked it.

"It's so deep."

I watched her eyes roll back as I squeezed. "Do you know what happens to good girls who like a little pain?"

She shook her head, her eyes squeezing shut, tears streaming down them. I wanted to lick at them. "They get *fucked.*"

All my resolve completely shattered at her admission. She liked it. "Is that what you need, Angel?"

"*Yes.*" *I've waited years for you. For this.*

I continued the slow drag of my cock out of her. "I'm going to destroy this little pussy, *ruin* you for anybody else."

There will be no one else. She had no idea what I wanted with her.

I won't ever think straight about you ever again. But fuck, she was so pretty when she whimpered. "*Yes, Reed.*"

Oh, fuck.

"*Say it.*" Oh, she *liked* that. I felt her pussy clench around me as I said it.

She licked her lips, her eyes hazy and cheeks flushed red. "I want you to r—ruin m—me." *God, she's so pretty.*

I swallowed her moan as I nudged in. I wanted to sink into her body forever. Darkness cloaked my vision. I couldn't think. She was struggling, which pleased my inner monsters.

"F—for *anybody*—" She squealed as I plunged in harder than all the other times.

I growled into her lips. "There won't be anyone else. *Ever*. You're mine. Always have been."

I looked into her eyes, wet and delirious with pleasure. Knowing there was no other way, I'd rather have her.

"Now let me *lay my fucking claim*." I gripped her shoulders, keeping her still under me, as I began to *fuck*.

"Scream for me, little virgin." My tongue tasted her tears as she obeyed while I worked my hips. I felt her tits bouncing under me as I fucked.

"*Reed.*"

A litany of filth left my lips. "Teasing me with that tiny pussy in my face for hours. *The things.*" Thrust. "*I'm going to do*" Thrust. "*To you.*" Thrust.

I snapped my hips in over and over, feeling the wet clenching, pulsing around me.

Gasping into her mouth, loving the way she squealed and whimpered every thrust, making her eyes hazy.

"Don't stop," she begged. "*Don't stop.*"

I had no intention of stoping.

"You feel so good. You're so tight around me. Just need to get you broken in a little bit more huh? Then I can ride it whenever I need to?"

I was a depraved monster taking her like this. And then she surprised me even more.

"*Yesyesyes.*" She was *incredible.*

"Harder," she pleaded, nails digging deliciously into my skin as she urged me on. "Please, baby."

Something primal unfurled in my chest at her words. That she wanted me, needed me, just as desperately as I needed her.

Our mouths were desperate, hungry, as I thrust my tongue in her mouth letting her suck. The rhythmic clenching of her mouth and pussy were driving both of us so close.

"*Harder?* Feels like *my fucking birthday* fucking you like this."

I didn't recognize my voice. "The next time you show up in that sad excuse of a dress, I'm going to sit you on this cock. All *night*. Let you *take* what you need."

40

"*Oh God, Reed.*" I felt her getting tighter until it felt like a fucking fight to get in her.

"I'm so close," she cried into my mouth. "Don't stop, please." I gritted my teeth against the urge to let go, determined to bring her with me over the edge.

"Such a good girl," I praised, never ceasing the relentless drive of my body into hers.

"I can feel how close you are, Angel."

I need to be deeper.

I rose up above her quickly, lifting one leg to my shoulder before settling back down while driving my hips into her. A wild scream left her mouth.

"Any minute now, I'm going to blow my fucking load into that little hole of yours. And you're going to take it, aren't you?" I was a beast inside of her.

"Tell me," I demanded, punctuating each word with a hard snap of my hips. "Tell me who you belong to."

"You," she gasped out immediately. "Only you, Reed. I'm yours."

Damn, that sounded good.

"Such a *good girl*. Come for me."

I pounded into her then with a series of strokes even I couldn't hold back, gripping her ankles tight, aware of my position, and grinding deep into her with every thrust. The sensations were so intense I knew I was going to blow inside of her, dimly aware of her screaming my name.

Watching Alisha come would be engraved in my memory until it replayed on a loop.

Arching with pleasure as she exploded, nearly strangling my cock in her. I squeezed her throat as she bucked, and I let go so she could scream. I would've grinned had I not been in rapture.

Oh fuck, she's stunning.

I fucked her through it, gritting my teeth and letting myself fall over her. Listening to her screams spurred me on.

"Say my name...*just...like...that*," I punctuated my words to the time of my thrusts. "Gonna come inside this little pussy. Fill you with my come."

She was wild under me, sensitized from her earlier orgasm, and depraved enough to do whatever I asked her.

"Come inside of me, *please*. Oh God, Reed, I— I—"

41

I exploded with a groan, gripping her body close and plunging so deep I lost my breath.

"Oh, fuck, fuck, *fuck*." Under me, she was sobbing in pleasure, fucking thanking me for my orgasm over and over.

Oh, she was fucking *perfection*.

I shook and collapsed fully on her, dropping my weight down, my hips working still as I pumped every bit of my seed into her.

Dimly I realized Alisha was undulating, her pussy clenching wild.

I groaned into her neck, kissing every inch I could touch. Dropping her legs slowly and stroked her hair back.

She trembled, legs shaking and back arching as my lips found her heart.

I pressed my lips right above it, holding her tight and steady as she shook.

I waited years for you. Years.

And every bit of you is worth it.

CHAPTER 8
REED

I woke up before my alarm.

Alisha's scent filled my nose.

Roses and cardamom, mixed with the hazelnut coffee drifting in from the kitchen.

I remembered setting the automatic coffee maker last night, a small gesture to make her morning a little easier.

I knew it was barely five since it was still dark with creeping rays of sunlight coming through.

I woke up at that time long enough to know I'd missed a morning workout and that I was going to be late if I stayed in bed any longer.

But this wasn't my place.

No, there was feminine décor, artful pieces of color thrown everywhere, a closet brimming with clothing.

It was an expansive room decorated with parts of the woman in my arms. My place looked like a high-end hotel.

And that's what it felt like some days, but this? This was a home.

Alisha.

She'd been a virgin. And had offered herself up to me on a fucking platter.

My head had run wild as I'd kissed her so long after taking her, I felt harder than steel within moments minutes after making love to her.

No, *fucking* her.

Alisha hadn't wanted a gentle lover.

Deep down inside, I fucking knew she'd fulfill every craving I had for her.

And then some. I hadn't asked her *why*.

Given what I knew about her, that would keep her one.

I had kissed her while my brain worked feeling like her mouth was the best release as I thought about her.

This morning, there was a slight bit of frosting on her cheek, and I grinned easily.

My cheeks hurt from smiling.

Last night, I had a moment to get on my phone, thankfully, while Alisha lay there breathing from her orgasm, nobody blowing it up for once. I'd let her catch her breath and ordered a cake.

Thank fuck for the city that never slept.

And then, like a depraved monster, I'd turned and seen her thighs part, seen the blood on them, on the sheets, and I'd lost all semblance of sanity.

Every rational thought was obliterated, and I had mounted her so fast, my face between her legs again, cleaning her up with my tongue.

Alisha had been sensitized, and she'd sobbed, grabbing my hair, tugging until I relented, backing off enough.

I'd tasted every part of her I could get my tongue into.

Her blood on my tongue felt *right*, sinking into the depths of my demons, comforting them as well.

Then I lit her candles on her cake and wiped her eyes as she'd cried a little, cuddling her close to me.

Happy Birthday, Angel. I'm sorry I didn't come sooner.

And then she'd swiped a little bit of the frosting on my nose. And I'd eaten the rest of it off her body.

It had been a good fucking birthday.

Now, with the soft rays of sun seeping in through the large windows, I took in Alisha as no discomfort came at a change in my schedule for once.

All I did was inhale the scent of roses and Alisha lying in my arms after passing out a few hours ago.

Part of me wanted to ask her. Part of me didn't have the ability to ask since it felt like I already knew the answer.

I want this. More than today.

That thought sprouted the moment I opened my eyes. I wanted to take her out like I promised. I didn't care.

We started it in bed.

I didn't care *where* it started.

Just that it did.

Memories of the previous night floated into my consciousness as I felt my body wake up.

As the clock ticked by, I drowsily lay next to her letting her take as much from me as she wanted. As she needed.

Gratitude washed over me as I made a mental note to send Lara a token of appreciation for her matchmaking efforts.

Teasers had always been my excuse to catch a glimpse of Alisha, and now here she was, nestled against me. *Finally.*

As she stirred, I realized I needed to get to my phone before my alarm went off. It was somewhere on the floor.

I didn't want Alisha to function without enough sleep.

I couldn't resist brushing my lips gently over hers, marveling at how her body responded even in sleep.

Her legs fell open slightly, her lips parting. The intimacy of the moment wasn't lost on me.

One day, I'll stay longer.

Even with everyone counting on me, I'd drop the world for this woman. I'd wanted her for so long.

It felt like a fucking crime sneaking out.

I haven't waited this long to let her go so soon.

I dipped my head, keeping my voice low, whispering promises to her.

I wish I had time to make her breakfast.

I made a mental note to order her something in a few hours and send her flowers.

I couldn't leave her anymore.

Now that I had her?

I wasn't going anywhere this time.

CHAPTER 9
ALISHA

REED HADN'T RETURNED.

Two days had passed since he'd left.

The silence of my phone was deafening, unbroken by texts or calls.

Instead, I found myself surrounded by an aroma of freshly baked bagels and pastries, a breakfast spread fit for a small army, courtesy of Reed.

Morning light filtered through the sheer curtains, casting a soft glow on my girlfriends gathered in my cozy living room.

"Que!" Lara Ford's dark eyes flashed as she erupted in Spanish from her spot on my living room floor. "He didn't come back, and you finally slept with him?!"

She sat cross-legged on the plush carpet, her sequined top catching the light with every movement.

I nodded slowly, bracing myself as a cushion hit my body.

Lara stood, looking like an angry pixie in all those sequins. The cushion's impact hurt less than the ache Reed had left when I'd woken to an empty bed.

Hours after I'd posted on my story, a courier had delivered breakfast, asking if my name was Reed. I nodded, confused.

Lara pounced, her messy bun toppling as she playfully attacked me with a pillow. "Aliiishaaaaaa!"

She peppered me with rapid-fire questions, each more outrageous than the last.

"How was he? Is his cock long and thick? Did he destroy your cookie? How's it doing after the beating it got? Oh my God!"

Her energy was astounding for someone who'd been up all night.

She shrieked as she caught my expression. "What did I say about Big Dick Energy?"

I thought I'd heard Reed distantly, but it felt like a dream.

I hate doing this to you, but I have to go to work this week. I'll be back, I promise.

Gemma and Lara had arrived days later when I'd texted them, bringing snacks, pastries, plastic tiaras, and in Lara's case—vibrators. Now, my tiara was knocked askew, and Lara's was lost under the couch.

As Lara pressed biscuits into my body like an overgrown cat, I called out. "Help, Gemma. She's killed me."

My best friend, Gemma Marchand, emerged from the kitchen carrying a tray laden with drinks and food, her musical laughter filling the air.

Gemma moved with quiet grace despite her statuesque five-eight frames.

Her blonde hair was perfectly styled in a chignon, and her ankle-length dress whispered against her skin as she set the tray on the coffee table.

The scent of freshly brewed tea mingled with the aroma of blueberry lemon muffins, making my stomach growl in anticipation.

I met Gemma a few years ago at a charity function. When I started the Poppy Project, she'd expressed the desire to step in from time to time and help out.

Recently, she'd left her family behind to be closer to her friends in New York.

Now, she looked as if she'd stepped off a magazine cover, polished and regal.

"Gemma can't save you from these paws, chica," Lara teased, her eyes sparkling with mischief.

"It was just one night," I said, feeling the words sink in. The sting was palpable.

As days passed, I'd been tempted to ask Lara for Reed's number, but pride held me back. I refused to be the lovesick puppy, running to him for affection.

"It is not! Reed likes you!" Lara exclaimed, flopping her body weight on me.

"He does not," I mumbled, unable to process her words.

Lara pulled back, eyes wide. "¿Estas loca?" she exclaimed, switching to rapid-fire Spanish. "Por supuesto que le gustas..."

"Let me translate," Gemma interjected, her light accent cutting through the air. "Lara asked if you were insane because Reed likes you. He stares at you and hovers protectively at the club. She says he's crazy about you and has asked about you before. Hang on—"

Gemma paused, listening as Lara erupted in more Spanish.

"She says she told him you were single, but he said—" Gemma's eyes widened in surprise. "I did not realize Reed was that connected."

"What did she say?" I asked, my interest piqued. "You guys can't keep your language a secret from me."

"It's not a secret, Alisha," Lara replied playfully. "You're just bad at learning languages."

"She's not bad," Gemma countered diplomatically. "She just needs practice." Lara looked skeptical.

"Alisha doesn't have a hot motorcycle-riding surfer bro to help her learn Spanish," Lara quipped.

"He was a kite surfer," she clarified, turning pink. "And I learned a lot in Miami, but...I learned more from him."

Her eyes sparkled with mischief, a hint of a smile playing on her lips.

Life had certainly been exciting for Gemma since leaving her family behind.

Even now, paparazzi seemed to lurk around every corner, trying to capture Gemma's human moments.

I marveled at the interaction between my two friends—their personalities were so different, yet they got along well.

A few years ago, I'd never imagined them getting along like this.

Lara, a bubbly Mexican with her long, dark hair piled into a messy bun, wore costume makeup sans costume.

She'd been a happy accident, a chance encounter when she'd tagged me on social media to promote the club.

I'd been intrigued and found myself falling in love with the place.

Together, Lara and I had selected feminine, elegant details to make it more upscale.

On the other hand, Gemma was a former French heiress from a family that invented old money.

Even now, she sat with her legs primly crossed, her back straight as a rod, the picture of elegance and refinement.

Lara's excitement broke through my thoughts, her voice rising. "Reed's been interested in you for a long time—"

Gemma sipped her tea, the delicate porcelain cup clinking softly against the saucer as she set it down. "He has asked about you too, Lara."

I heard you've asked about me...

"I can't believe you kept this from me," I said, my mind reeling. "Reed was interested years ago? Why didn't you—"

"Because you weren't ready," Lara interjected. "You'd just lost your... and Avani needed you. He was building his company. Now look at you —a successful influencer dating a millionaire."

I felt my cheeks burn, throwing a pillow at her.

Lara's dark eyes glittered with amusement. "Reed even said if you didn't want him naturally, it wouldn't matter. He needs to feel like you want him to."

Lara pretended to play the violin and croon. "A match made in romance history..."

But I had. I did. My eyes watered as I admitted. "He hasn't called or texted in days. He just...left."

Lara's expression softened, dropping her invisible violin. "Didn't you say he promised to come back?"

I nodded, my heart clenching at the memory.

"Then trust him. Reed keeps his word," Lara assured me, her eyes twinkling mischievously. "Besides, Reed's like one of those animals—"

"A wolf," Gemma added. "He reminds us of a patient wolf."

"Yeaaaahh," Lara agreed, her fingers curling into claws. "Like he was watching you through the club's foliage, waiting to catch you like a bunny. And he went gr—"

She mimicked a wolf snatching its prey, her teeth bared in a playful growl.

Gemma laughed at Lara's imitation, and I couldn't stop myself from joining in.

The sound of it filled the room as Lara all but tipped over with her actions.

She topped out at maybe five feet. *Maybe.*

"Now that he has you in his den—or your den—he's not letting his meal go easily. I know men. I am the Dick Whisperer," she said, her voice dropping to a conspiratorial whisper.

She closed her eyes, hands coming together in a Namaste gesture, looking like a wise sage.

I shook my head, laughter bubbling up. "I'll never get used to you," Gemma said, smiling.

"You can loiter with me and be defiled with—what was that word?" Lara asked playfully.

"*Debauchery*," Gemma replied, hiding her smile behind her teacup.

Lara frowned, struggling with the word. "Debu—Deba—*Dabuchery*."

"Good effort," Gemma said, blue eyes twinkling.

"Thanks, I try," Lara grinned before turning back to me. "Reed and Gabriel never bother coming to a client's place *just* because. And Reed isn't upgrading the security system *that* often when he's admitted he could do it from home."

The knowledge that Reed came to Teasers for me eased my anxiety.

"Have I met Gabriel?" I was curious since Reed had mentioned him a few times.

Gemma frowned. "Is he the gentleman who comes around occasionally?"

"Yeah, but Alisha hasn't met him, and he isn't a gentleman," Lara's cheeks turned an uncharacteristic chase of pink. "The point is, Reed's good to *you*."

Lara shifted in her seat as she talked about Gabriel.

"They work in cybersecurity, you know?" Gemma said, bursting my thoughts. "He can help you with the issues you have with all those creeps and those weird DMs you get."

I did get a lot of creepy direct messages. I ignored most of them, but lately, I have been getting several accounts that are bothering me. Reed would handle it. If he were here.

"He confuses me," I shook my head. "I can't figure him out. It's not because he's a mystery. I feel like I can't get a grip on him. He said he wanted to be my Dom. I don't even know what that means."

Gemma's eyes widened, her teacup pausing midway to her lips. "Like he wants you as his sub?"

Lara's head swiveled towards Gemma, a mischievous glint in her eye. "Not so prim and proper, are ya, Duchess?"

Gemma blushed as Lara slyly called her a filthy slut.

I liked that, too.

She was utterly devious with her grin as she looked back at me. "I fucking knew it. You have to ask him what he wants from you. Not every Dom wants a contract and to chain you up to the wall. Maybe Reed just wants you to be submissive in bed. Figures he'd want to tie you up and toy around with you." *What?*

"I don't understand what that means."

Lara pretended to play her invisible violin. "Did you like the night he was with you?"

I turned beet red. "Um, yeah."

She shrugged, dropping the act. "Then you're halfway there." Her smirk landed on me again. "I'll give you a heads up. Just do what Reed says."

"Why? What would he do if I didn't?"

"Gurl. You *don't* want to find out." She looked at the floor wide-eyed in an expression that told me it terrified her.

I looked at Gemma for an explanation, and she whispered. *"Dick Whisperer."*

Gemma looked empathetic. "I don't think you have to figure him out. I think the biggest thing we both wanted to know is if he was kind to you."

She then turned to Lara, noting the time.

"It's ten in the morning," She handed Lara a wine glass from the tray of drinks, adding with a hint of exasperation. "I thought we talked about this."

Lara raised a brow, her voice thick with exhaustion. "For you, it's morning. For me, it's almost bedtime. And Mama needs some sleepy juice to pass out."

The life of a performer was nocturnal, the late nights and early mornings blending together in a haze of sequins and spotlights.

Gemma pulled a quilt over her hand-stitched white dress, watching Lara with a dubious expression.

"I will say, my last bodyguard, I still keep in touch with him and his wife. I asked him about Reed after you told us a few days ago," Gemma started.

She absently played with the intricate designs on her skirt.

"Reed worked for the government for a bit. He couldn't say for whom, but he mentioned a few nasty things that happened to him. So *Gabriel—*" she nodded at Lara, who turned an attractive shade of pink. "Began Titan around seven years ago. I understand that they both have a stake in it, but Reed stepped in as acting CEO. He still has a lot of work cut out for him. The company grew thanks to Gabriel's reputation, but Reed is the brains behind making it work."

He must've been really young.

Gemma handed Lara another glass of wine, the deep red liquid swirling hypnotically.

"From what I gathered, Reed is ruthless. My bodyguard liked him but said he would think twice before questioning him. Reed runs the company differently. He has only a few people in his corner he even remotely trusts, and those people run smaller operations with other agents in the company. So he's busy."

A shadow of unease crossed Gemma's face, her brow furrowing as she added. "But they both said Reed will do whatever it takes to get what he wants. It's part of why he's been so successful.

"But he's completely different from me," I whispered.

Lara said in a matter-of-fact tone. "*That's* because he loves you. I've watched him moon over you for years."

My mind reeled at the contradiction. "But you guys just implied he's dangerous!"

"He's both sides of the same coin," Gemma said softly, her eyes meeting mine. "I've seen how he looks at you. At first, I admit I was worried. But after hearing about your tryst, I don't think he's the type to hurt you. I think Reed has wanted you for a long time. You just needed to be in the right place."

Gemma's expression shifted, her eyes growing distant as she continued. "Lara's right. You need to talk to Reed about what he wants from you in bed when he's back. If you're his sub, it's important that he explains it to you."

She paused, her voice softening. "You've had a tough few years trying to be perfect for Avani—"

Gemma knew about my desire to make my parents and Avani proud. This weight had settled on my shoulders, and I refused to budge.

"We left that night because Avani asked if you could bring back some heating pads for her cramps, and you took off. Lish, you had a full-time job being a mom to your sister for the last five years. And Reed knew that."

"A man who is that patient won't let you go," her voice was low.

What changed was when I told him Avani had left for college and that I had been willing to reach out to him.

"Yeah, the horizontal tango. The banana split. A mating dance in the night," Lara chimed in, her showgirl voice cutting through the tension.

"And now you're his boo thaaaang," she added, her voice dripping with suggestiveness.

I burst into laughter. "*Do you sing during sex?*"

Lara blinked, her expression thoughtful. "I'm celibate. Have been for years," she shrugged, handing Gemma her wine glass. "*Por favor.*"

Gemma wordlessly served Lara more wine, her expression a mix of amusement and disbelief.

"I cannot believe you're celibate," Gemma mock-whispered.

"Why? Because everyone has seen my tits?" Lara joked her voice light but with uncharacteristic darkness in her eyes. "It takes all the fun out of sex. He can't be amazed. He's already seen it before."

I had always wondered about Lara's lack of a sex life, remembering her mentioning how she hated being used in bed.

"I have no clue what I'm doing," I whispered.

Gemma finished her tea, the delicate china clinking softly.

"Darling, none of us do. Last year, I was having tea with the prime minister of a foreign country. Now, I'm currently a plain Jane who serves tea to my best friends."

She was anything but a plain Jane, and though she hadn't talked much about why she'd given up her life, she looked happier than ever.

Lara yawned, stretching wide.

"Love you, *chicas*, but I am exhausted. I need to head back to my...what did you call it?"

"Den of debauchery?" Gemma offered, her voice laced with playful teasing.

"No."

"Hovel of Whoredom," Gemma suggested, making me giggle at the contrast between her refined appearance and the crude phrase.

"No," Lara repeated firmly, though amusement danced in her eyes.

"Sanctum of Sin?" Gemma proposed, eyebrows raised suggestively.

"Oh, that's a good one," Lara grinned. "I'm gonna catch a cab, I'll see you chicas later."

"Hang on," Gemma interrupted. "I'll drive."

"You don't have a license," I frowned, confused by the image of the former heiress driving. Twin shades of pink emerged on Gemma's cheeks.

"No, but just because I'm no longer...doesn't mean I don't have adequate funds to take in a driver," she said, her voice lowering. Lara's eyes widened, realization dawning on her face.

"Nigel, here I come," she squealed, her voice high—pitched with excitement, her feet already carrying her into the entryway to put on her shoes. "Let's stop and get cake!"

Gemma looked at me apologetically, her expression softening with vulnerability.

"I would like to start gaining weight," she said, her voice above a whisper, eyes downcast.

As I took in her waif-thin frame, the sharp angles of her collarbones, and the delicate curve of her wrists, I realized that a lifetime of struggling to fit in with a family that didn't like her had led to far more issues than Gemma ever discussed.

Both of us had grappled with our public image and the toll it took on our mental health.

The constant pressure to be perfect, to fit into society's mold, had been a shared burden.

Our body dysmorphia had become a bonding point, highlighted by a memory of a dinner function where we'd been served a mere morsel of risotto.

This is dinner? This isn't enough to feed Avani.

Do you want to go grab real food after this?

That night at a diner, we'd talked for hours, our different backgrounds fading away as we discovered how much we had in common.

Despite our contrasting upbringings, Gemma and I had been close for years.

"She's been making me eat more," Gemma said, slipping into her shoes.

"*Yeah*, so you can be *juicy* like my booty," Lara chimed in. I laughed, remembering how Lara, barely topping five feet, had a curvy figure one could envy. As she liked to say, she was *grabbable*.

On cue, Lara spouted. "*Grabbable*, bay-bee." Before taking off outside.

"I need to go make sure she doesn't accost him again," Gemma said, her voice tinged with amusement and exasperation. "Poor Nigel, Lara tried to give him a lap dance last time, but he just about died."

Nigel was an older gentleman, and I could imagine.

As she slipped on her coat, Gemma's tone turned serious.

"I'm not saying Reed isn't a kind man. But he didn't get to where he is today by being a *nice* man."

I knew she was right.

I was under no illusion that Reed wasn't cloaked in darkness, his edges sharp, and his past a mystery.

But memories of him teasing me, making me laugh, and kissing me so tenderly before he left contrasted sharply with the image he presented to the world.

My heart and mind were at war, unsure what to make of him.

"I want you to know if you ever need anywhere at all, my home is still your home," Gemma added softly before leaving.

As the door closed behind her, memories of the last few nights came rushing back, flooding my senses.

Reed was *everywhere*.

His presence lingered in every corner of my apartment, his scent on my sheets, his touch branded onto my skin.

The ache inside me grew, a heavy feeling settling in my heart.

I was left alone with my thoughts, trying to reconcile the different facets of Reed and my own conflicting emotions about our budding relationship.

And despite all the reassurances—I had no idea if I'd ever see him again.

CHAPTER 10
REED

"Reed! You've been at this for an hour!"

I was lost in thought, the world around me fading away until a familiar voice cut through my reverie.

As the treadmill hummed beneath my feet, the rhythmic pounding of my strides filled the air.

Sweat glistened on my brow, my heart racing with each step.

Evie Monroe's slender form stood to my right, her dark auburn hair cascading around her blue cloud print pajamas.

She looked more like a teenager than the brilliant twenty-three-year-old cybersecurity expert I knew her to be.

My mind had been working during my entire run.

The woman I've been crushing on for three years just slept with me. I left her. I'm not trying to take out my rage on your brother for keeping me here longer than I wanted to be.

I didn't say that. Any of that. I kept those thoughts to myself, focusing instead on Evie's words.

"She's just a girl, not a honey badger," she said, her tone laced with concern.

I didn't need to ask what she meant.

Evie had become like a little sister to me, thanks to my friendship with Gabriel.

While I wasn't as close to Evie as Gabriel was, I still felt a sense of responsibility towards her, a desire to be the sensible big brother who wouldn't go ballistic at the sight of her with a boyfriend.

In turn, Evie would peer over my shoulder whenever I had browsed Alisha's photos for the last three years.

"Don't you have an exam you have to study for?" I asked, trying to change the subject.

Evie rolled her big brown eyes. "Who needs a cert when you already hacked into government secrets?"

I grinned, the familiar sensation of my tongue darting out between my teeth, something Evie looked delighted over. Pride swelled in my chest. I had taught her well, molding her into the go-to expert for all things cybersecurity. She was brilliant, even if she lacked confidence at times.

"Back to your *girlfriend*," Evie said, her eyes glinting with mischief. *That sounded good.* "Nate told us. Well, he told Selena. Who told me. And I told Gabriel. He's surprised that you took this long."

I shook my head, not wanting to discuss my love life with my pseudo-sister. "Evie—"

"I can't believe you're avoiding her. She's so pretty," she interrupted, her voice rising with excitement.

"I'm not avoiding Lish—"

"You've liked her for years, Reed." I know.

"I can't do this with you," I said, pumping my arms harder as I pushed myself to the limit. "You're my sister."

"Am *not*—I'm Gabriel's sister. You're his best friend. I know things."

I huffed out a laugh despite the burning in my lungs. "Jesus, kid. You're going to cling to me…all day."

"You haven't left in two days and I'm losing my mind with both you and Gabriel helicopter parenting."

Guilt twisted in my gut. I knew I had been neglecting my responsibilities, but that wasn't the only reason I'd been here since Monday morning. Since Alisha. Since I promised her I'd come back soon. Fuck.

As I continued to run, my feet pounding against the treadmill, Evie's words echoed in my mind.

The sweat poured down my face, my lungs burning with each breath.

"I'm not a helicopter parent," I managed to say between puffs of air. "Are you dating someone?" Evie's cheeks turned red.

"No. *You are*," Evie crossed her arms over her chest, a knowing look in her eyes. "I can see you stalking your girlfriend's Instagram feed. I know you miss her."

Ah, hell. I had hoped to see if Alisha had posted anything since our night together.

Other than her usual breakfast and hazelnut coffee two days ago, she had only posted a photo with her girlfriends this morning.

Seeing Lara in the picture had surprised me, given her nocturnal tendencies.

But it was the sight of Gemma that had me scrambling to assign someone I trusted to watch over her.

Someone Gemma would trust too.

I had even asked Evie to keep an eye on Alisha's online presence.

As a social celebrity, she was bound to attract some overzealous fans. I needed to make sure she was safe, even when I couldn't be there myself.

Alisha wouldn't like it, but she didn't need to know.

I huffed, my words punctuated by my labored breathing. "I am not avoiding my—Alisha."

Evie's face lit up with a beaming smile. "So you're staying to make sure Gabriel doesn't scare away the new hires?"

Correct.

Gabriel had a reputation for intimidating everyone. But that didn't mean I was using work as an excuse to avoid Alisha.

No, I just needed to knock some sense into him.

I couldn't go home and touch her again, only to leave once more.

It had taken every ounce of my willpower to pull away that Monday morning.

I didn't want to admit to Evie how much I was struggling. Three years of pining, one incredible night together, and now I was utterly hooked.

As I continued to run, my mind raced with thoughts of Alisha and the mess I had left behind at work.

I had planned to come to the office, sort out the chaos, and then return to her side, ready to dedicate myself fully.

But the timing of our first night together had been far from perfect.

Doubts crept into my mind, gnawing at me.

What if she regretted it?

What if she hated me now?

I hadn't even sent her a proper text.

What would I say?

Sorry, I left in the morning. I have messes to clean up at work, a man to kill, and I almost forgot about the whole expansion, hiring new people, and branching out our contracts.

Oh, but I'm definitely buying you an entire flower store to make up for it.

No, I couldn't say that to Alisha.

I did send her breakfast, though.

Should I have sent flowers for every day I was gone?

I didn't know.

My last relationship had been as cold as ice.

I hadn't called. I didn't know how to talk to Alisha, how to explain what I did for a living.

The club had been one night.

One night after countless evenings of silently watching over her, ensuring her safety.

She would look at me sometimes, but she never truly saw me.

Until that night when she'd sat on my lap and smiled like I was the moon.

I had no hesitation about taking her.

I didn't believe in rules. I believed in claiming what was mine.

If Alisha wanted a twelve-course dinner and demanded I wear a suit, I would. But if she told me she wanted to climb me like a tree and let me fuck her senseless? I would.

I had long ago decided that the dating game wasn't worth my time. I wanted it straight. I hated playing games.

And she hadn't either.

I wanted nothing but her.

I didn't need to get to know her over a candlelit dinner.

I already knew I liked her.

Flowers and sweet nothings wouldn't change that.

I realized, though, that those things would still matter to her, and I wanted to give her everything.

I just didn't know how to convey that through a text.

I fucking hated doing anything over technology. It was *impersonal*.

Aside from the occasional work related texts, I absolutely hated being on my phone for personal matters.

The irony of working in security, yet struggling to articulate to my woman how much I missed her, did not escape me.

I craved Alisha. Even now.

Hence, the treadmill.

I wanted to kiss her awake and swallow her smiles. Normally, walking into Titan filled me with a sense of ease, but today, I was itching for a fight.

With one particular person.

The last set of men had quit after their first day, thanks to Gabriel.

I had two new guys downstairs now who I felt would meet all of Gabriel's impossible criteria.

The last set, he had kicked their asses, telling them that if he could take them down, they were fair game for anyone else.

Privately, I knew he was right.

All of us could stand toe to toe with each other. Except for Evie. She was support, and she was Gabriel's entire world.

It wasn't like the company was struggling.

We needed shadows to take over, to give the original Titans a break.

We needed a way forward that didn't involve one of us getting hurt or ending up half-dead in a ditch. And I had one problem.

A six-foot-five asshole of a problem who would use the new recruits as target practice if he could.

Lately, he'd been crazier than usual, and he wasn't telling anyone else why, which got on my ever-loving nerve.

Because I knew.

I fucking knew why.

Gabriel walked around like a great white shark, ready to tear into anyone. And he did.

He was currently downstairs. *Somewhere.*

I fucking knew what he was doing.

And I didn't care anymore. He was becoming intolerable, his edge setting off everyone else.

Save for with Evie. I didn't know how Evie dealt with him, but the interactions between them were so polarizing it had thrown me for a loop.

She was the only person he ever smiled with, even though she was his pseudo-daughter.

I was twenty-nine, and I couldn't imagine having a kid right now.

But Gabriel wasn't much older than me, and he'd already taken in Evie years ago.

Probably around Alisha's age.

"When I'm done, I want to talk to you about a few things." At her expression, I corrected myself. "*Not* Alisha."

She pouted. "But she looks so *nice*, and it's been forever since we had a girl around here besides Selena…"

I felt even guiltier now.

Alisha would be good for Evie.

Selena was always out on assignments, but the Cuban had been hired not just for her skills but also because Gabriel hoped she'd be a good influence on Evie.

A potential big sister figure.

Gabriel was mildly regretting letting Evie try on Selena's clothing, though.

Evie batted her big brown eyes at me. I would've stopped right then at the concern in her gaze.

But any mention of Alisha and my fucking dick lost its mind. It stirred up feelings in me that had been forgotten for so long.

I wanted her. God, how I wanted her.

I thought that *maybe* if I had just one night with her, the craving would subside.But it hadn't. If anything, it had only intensified.

A part of me wanted nothing more than to spend my days in bed with her, exploring every inch of her body.

But I had a life, too.

And Alisha wasn't just *any* woman.

She's been mine for a long time.

I'd shamelessly snooped whatever I could about her a long time ago. She had been pretty fucking popular then.

Even more so now, even if her social media was filled with her posts about her charity work and less photos of herself.

She was my opposite and daunting in every way on her own. She had four million followers on social media and men who panted after her every step they could.

Alisha had no shortage of men who wanted her.

I read some of the comments on her photos ranging from men giving her their number or promising her wealth beyond her imagination.

How many princes were there really in Dubai?

She was *gorgeous,* and I had expected someone shallow with no personality.

Alisha had been *far* from it when I'd seen her helping her friends and turning down every man in the club who approached her.

I'd gone up to Lara once to ask her what her deal was. I couldn't figure her out.

As I continued to run, my feet pounding, my mind raced with thoughts of Alisha.

Over the last few years, after compiling and analyzing everything I knew about her, I had come to realize that she was warm-natured and kind-hearted to the point where she'd given up her own life for Avani.

It was a fact I understood well, thanks to my time spent with Gabriel.

And when I fully grasped that?

I had nearly caved. *Nearly.*

Except, Alisha wasn't looking for someone to save her, and she didn't need me. She had her own life.

Until she'd shown up this week, looking lost and, for once, unsure of herself.

Vulnerable and shy, she seemed so far away from the woman I'd known.

That's when I stepped in.

But did she just want me for one night? If I showed up at her door again, would she thank me for my service and kick me out?

What if she couldn't understand my lifestyle? My job?

My team?

And then there was the glaring truth that we were polar opposites. I never thought the Bambi-eyed golden goddess would get under my skin.

Me, who lived among spies and death and missions where I could die on any of them.

Alisha worked with women's shelters, and I worked to eliminate the men who threatened them. We were so far apart that I wasn't sure if I could ever let her see that part of me.

My lungs burned as I pushed myself harder, the sweat dripping down my face.

The rhythmic thud of my feet against the treadmill echoed the pounding of my heart.

The life I led was dangerous, and the thought of exposing her to that world filled me with dread.

But the memory of her smile, the way she looked at me that night, kept pulling me back.

I wanted to be the man she saw in me, the one who could make her feel safe.

I just didn't know if I could be that man while still being true to who I was.

I had tirelessly spent the last few days getting everything together. I did my job.

I served Gabriel.

Titan was now a huge company.

It had grown over the last few years.

I'd been young putting it together with Gabriel reeling from his life. I knew he needed me then, but it had been *years*.

And now whether he liked it or not—we needed to move in a different direction.

I needed to move in a different direction. One towards a future instead of the past.

Which meant I needed to confront Gabriel.

CHAPTER 11
REED

I was staring at Evie, my mind still racing with thoughts of Alisha, when a sharp-taloned hand I didn't see coming reached out and tugged the emergency brake on the treadmill.

The machine halted so abruptly that I had to brace myself to keep from falling.

I glared at the person responsible, and vibrant green eyes met mine in a challenge.

"That's not funny, Selena."

Next to Evie stood the statuesque form of Selena Taveres, a perfectly manicured hand holding the red emergency cord.

Out of everyone in Titan, Selena was, in my opinion, the most dangerous. Because she was deceptive as fuck.

The Cuban bombshell was dressed to the nines, her model figure even at five-feet five-inches, accentuated by her signature thigh-high boots with razor-like heels that made her tower over Evie.

She flipped her deep brown hair over her shoulders, her emerald eyes glittered as she gave me a look that said, *what are you going to do about it?*

Gabriel had hired Selena years ago after me. A young and beautiful spy trained by Agency operatives in Cuba.

She hadn't spoken a word of English, regarded all men with suspicion, and had kicked Nate's ass on the spot.

I'd hired Nate, her soon-to-be former partner in crime at work. Gabriel didn't let me live it down for a year.

Nate and Selena had been inseparable ever since once Selena realized that nobody on the team wanted to sleep with her. We just wanted to protect her.

I'd seen her in action, wearing nothing but a sparkly bra and panties while taking out people. Lethal.

Until she got around Evie.

Who had been banned from ever going to the club with Selena.

She was sisterly with Evie, regarding her with warmth as the two women said I was being silly in Spanish back and forth.

Her expression ranged from annoyed to downright wicked, and she smirked when Evie answered her question.

"*¿Tienes una novia?*" Selena asked with utter shock and delight. *You have a girlfriend?*

Evie told her in Spanish who it was, and Selena looked awed.

Another deep voice joined them, Nate walking in with an easy grin matching Selena's. "Are you ladies talking about Reed's crush?"

"She's so freaking gorgeous," Evie said, holding up a tablet with no doubt a freaking presentation on Alisha on there. "Everyone, this is Alisha Malhotra, the model."

A collective exaggerated "*wooooow*" went off in the room from Nate and Selena, who humored Evie.

Nate winked at me, playing it up for Evie, who he didn't want to disappoint. Everyone had adopted Evie.

Evie's fingers swiped over the tablet. "I made a little slideshow. I picked the best photos, but if I can be honest, I don't think she has a bad angle."

As Selena oh'd and ah'd, Nate grinned at their expressions.

His eyes met mine, and his smile dropped at the look on my face.

I stepped off the treadmill, my chest heaving as I tried to catch my breath.

The sweat dripped down my face, my muscles aching.

While grabbing a towel and wiping my face, I was trying to compose myself. The duo gathered around Evie.

Evie rambled on about Alisha's awards and animated movies while Nate took the distraction and walked up to me.

I didn't miss the look in his eyes and the way his shoulders tensed.

"You took her home." I didn't kiss and tell. Especially about Alisha.

Out of everyone who knew about my obsession with Alisha, Nate had seen it firsthand, and he wouldn't bullshit me.

I didn't say a word to him, just giving him a look that said, *don't even think about talking about her.*

"I cleared up your man. He won't be saying shit."

I'd hired Nate after working with him while he'd been another three-letter agency's bitch. Nate often served as a bridge, softening the edges of Gabriel's icy ruthlessness.

Despite his six foot two Viking-esque demeanor and ever-present leather jacket, Nate had been instrumental in the organization's growth and success.

The former sniper with a penchant for following orders without question.

Something I had needed.

When I say jump, you jump.

You do not ask how high.

Despite bearing witness to the darker aspects of humanity; Nate was protective of Selena and Evie, followed my orders to a T, and tolerated Gabriel well enough.

Nate was one of the few people who could take Gabriel in a fight. But when the conversation turned to Alisha, the exterior melted away, revealing the genuine warmth in his eyes.

It sent irritation up my spine at him looking at me with an easy smile. If he saw it, he cut it out.

"Gabriel's busy," Nate said, changing the subject. "You want me to look into it for you?" I did. If there was anyone with enough finesse in the world, it was Nate.

"Get Lucy." He would know where she was.

Nate raised a brow, his navy eyes impressed. "Jewel thief is the route you're taking?"

Insurance appraiser. Archaeologist. Tomb raider.

Nothing she did was legal, so it was right up his alley.

"She's hot as fuck." Nate had his priorities together.

I kept my voice low. "I sent you details. But I doubt she's in the city. Get in touch with her."

I didn't know about the details, but judging by the smirk on his lips Nate knew her a lot more than me. My phone pinged, and I looked down, seeing if it was Alisha. It wasn't.

Instead, my screen lit up. I had taken a photo of her two mornings ago when I'd left, as a reminder of what was important to me. To remind myself not to get swept into the ice that was the world I lived in.

66

On the outside, I worked for Titan, and underneath, the underbelly, the shadow of Titan, was an iceberg, one that was currently working downstairs.

Alisha's hair had fanned out in the photo.

She was naked under the covers, her shoulder visible, the sun just teasing enough over her skin to make her glow again.

Immediately, warmth rushed over me.

She didn't know, but I'd made it my background so every single time I forgot myself, I'd be able to anchor and center myself. I knew even before I put it away that Nate had seen it.

"You got it bad," he was quiet, his usually playful eyes serious, as Evie chattered in the background. "You gonna break every man's hand who tries her?"

Suit and Tie was lucky he had his arm left. He didn't try her. He tried me. I looked at Nate hard eyes as he gauged me.

The very thought of another man touching Alisha sent a surge of possessive rage through my veins.

I knew I had to keep it in check, but the urge to protect her, to claim her as mine, was overwhelming.

I'd had Nate take him to a satellite office we had in Midtown strictly for Gabriel's shits and giggles after I'd left Alisha's.

I'd wasted no time in teaching him what not to do.

I didn't tolerate disrespect under my roof.

I didn't tolerate it from my staff or the idiots who drank too much and tried to flex on me and what was mine. I just made sure to send enough of a message to anyone else around him.

Suddenly locked in a room with me, the bravado had been replaced with nothing but another grown man nearly shitting himself because he was so afraid.

My only regret was not putting a bullet in him. I speared Nate with a look that said, *What do you think?*

Nate held up his hands, his voice low. "I'm not judging you. I just need you to realize she isn't a part of our world. When it comes back to her? She's going to wonder who she's with." He was no stranger to doing the same for Selena or Evie.

I knew that. I know that every fucking day.

"I'm taking advice from you now?" I didn't give a shit. "Do you remember who you took home this time? Or are they just blank faces?"

Unlike me, Nate didn't have discernment.

His eyes shifted away uncomfortably, and I was briefly distracted by Selena praising Evie.

Evie continued her appraisal of my Alisha. "...She runs a charity that helps women's shelters and her sister helps her with it. Avani's also really pretty as you can see..." Evie sighed.

Evie wanted to be around other girls.

Alisha would be good for her.

Selena smiled and brushed back Evie's waves behind her ear, in a maternal gesture, as Evie was excitedly talking about my girl.

And Evie continued, to my own torture and Nate's amusement.

"She was the face of EllaBeauty two years ago. The CEO of Roadsters, whose mother owns EllaBeauty said in a video he had a huge crush on Alisha—"

"Who is that?"

Nate shot me a look at my tone and the look in my eyes. "You can't kill Matteo DuPont."

I wasn't going to. I was just going to talk. Evie looked up at that, a small "wuh" coming out of her mouth. Nate smirked behind her, tossing his leather jacket onto the back of a chair as he sat down, blue eyes in utter delight, looking every bit the biker he was.

Nate grinned at me. "Andrei DuPont's younger brother is the CEO of Roadsters."

Andrei DuPont ran the company over Roadsters, Durand, and I didn't work with often, but enough to know, I couldn't kill his baby brother.

Evie turned the tablet around, and all I saw was a fresh-faced pretty boy in a navy suit, dark hair falling over his eyes.

Alien aqua blue eyes with pupils rimmed in black, grinning as he held my Alisha a little too close.

Her cheeks were pink as she smiled into the camera. In the second shot, he kissed her cheek, and she was red in the face. I saw red.

I know those eyes. Blue, eerie and alien in his pretty boy face. Phillipe DuPont's eyes.

The entire family has them.

"Ohhhh, Evie put the slideshow away," Selena smirked as she said it. "Reed is going to kill him."

Nate snorted. "If there's anything he wants to kill, it's his woman's pussy."

I practically growled at Nate. Evie flushed beet red. Selena laughed in agreement.

Both didn't care Evie was in the room.

I did.

"Don't worry Reed, I just ignore them when they start," Evie said in a sing-song voice, closing the tablet on the young man's face.

I took a deep breath, trying to calm the rage that had begun to simmer in my veins.

I knew I had to keep my emotions in check, but the thought of another man, especially one as powerful and influential as Matteo DuPont, having any interest in Alisha made my blood boil.

It shouldn't have made me so fucking jealous to know the level of reach Alisha had.

Except the thought of her dating some spoiled, pretentious French CEO of a luxury car company made my jaw work.

I chugged from my water bottle to distract myself from how the team teased me.

Nate grinned as he put his arm around Selena and Evie's shoulders, both women having the opposite reaction.

Selena looked at Nate with a look that could skewer a man while Evie grinned, but neither moved his arms.

"You've been pining after Lish for years, and you finally took her home, only to end up at work?" Nate was pushing it.

"Don't call her Lish," I growled. It came out harder than intended, and now I had three sets of eyes blinking at me. Two of those people now wore a smirk. "Don't talk about her."

"You like her." It was all he had to say for his counterpart to smirk with him. Selena said something rapidly in Spanish, and even Evie giggled.

"I know she's too pretty for me, Selena."

Selena's eyes met mine with an unimpressed look.

Out of all the women who didn't fall for bullshit, Selena sat at numero uno. I could hear her in her head asking me.

Why are you still acting like a stupid idiot?

"I do like her. But it isn't serious." *Bullshit.* It had been pretty fucking serious. But I didn't need the team gossiping or placing bets on when I'd marry her. *Not if.*

Both Nate and Selena exchanged a look, and then they burst into laughter. Evie turned away.

"What?"

Nate laughed so hard that he turned red. "Are you fucking kidding me? When was the last time you took anyone home?"

Another reason why I wanted to leave with her.

Selena said something about me being a stalker.

"You haven't had a good woman in forever, Por eso eres un estúpido idiota," Selena said.

That's why you're a stupid idiot.

There it was. Nate grinned with both of the girls tickled in his arms.

"Not since the banshee from Hell." The last person I'd expect to pitch in was Evie.

"*Evie.*"

Nate laughed loudly at my reaction to little Evie, out of all people.

"What?" My counterpart shrugged. "She was awful. She was mean, and she said Selena was a whore and I was fat. Remember when I gained those ten pounds during freshman year?"

"She did what?" Nate and I said simultaneously as Selena pretended to mime sawing up someone.

Nate's smirk dropped the moment Evie mentioned someone had said anything against the girls. Now I felt like shit.

"Evie, I'm sor—" I didn't know.

"It's okay," Evie brushed it off, visibly looking uncomfortable since she was already petite to begin with.

I couldn't remember why I had ever picked Kelly as my ex-girlfriend.

At the time, she'd been perfectly what everyone in my life wanted.

She was as cold as me and gave me the emotional distance I needed.

Gabriel and I had gone the same route, just with different institutions.

I was done working for another three-letter agency and had gotten royally fucked in every way, shape, and form possible. Gabriel and I had taken both of our asses out at the same time after an assignment of his had gone south.

He'd quit and offered me a job at starting Titan as old friends coming together. I accepted.

"The ladies have spoken," Nate said in a feigned regal voice. "I say we have a verdict. *Reed is whipped.*"

A noise came from behind them, and every head in the room turned.

Icy pale blue eyes crinkled in amusement as he took us in. The temperature in the room dropped ten degrees the moment he walked in.

A whisper of my pent-up rage ran through me. I was ready to throttle him.

Evie launched herself a full burst at the reason why we even existed at Titan. Gabriel.

Dressed in his shark suit, as he called it, the all-gray designer shit hid the powerful martial artist he was.

At six-five, Gabriel Monroe was bigger than me without being bulky.

His broad-set shoulders built powerfully along with the way he moved. Trained, precise, and silent.

I opted not to wear stuffy clothing. I hated ties around my neck.

He lifted up Evie's tiny frame with ease in his arms and smiled with an uncharacteristic warmth he only saved for her.

Evie had once said if Gabriel had been a tad nicer or even friendlier, women would lose their shit over him since, most of the time, he reminded every one of a pissed-off Angel.

But he scared everyone.

Save for us.

Which is why it was harder to find people who wanted to work here. Gabriel set Evie down, and she beamed as he gently brushed her hair back.

His voice was a murmur as pale blue eyes took her in, a frown creasing his eyebrows. "You look tired."

"Reed has a girlfriend," she chirped. I saw Nate and Selena find opposite directions to stare at.

Gabriel held Evie close, his icy eyes narrowed at me, and the room seemed to plummet into a frigid chill.

If it got any colder, Nate would start feigning shivers just to lighten the mood.

Gabriel's expression smoothed into one of bored indifference as he inquired. "Any luck with the fresh meat?"

He knew full well there were two of them in their rooms.

I had been purposefully keeping the third one away from Gabriel's scrutiny, handling his paperwork myself.

"Depends. Are you going to let them live?"

"Did you warn them about..." Nate trailed off, his eyes darting towards Gabriel.

"I did."

Gabriel looked mildly amused at Nate while he held Evie at his side. I swear the fucker got off on terrorizing everyone who set foot in Titan. I finished wiping the sweat from my neck.

"I can't have you grilling them anymore. They're all good enough."

"Good enough gets people killed," Gabriel's voice was low, his eyes deadly. "I don't need to lose anyone on this team."

"Then you hire the next batch. And no, they cannot be affiliated with the mob. Alexei scared Evie the last time he came with the O'Hara's."

The smirk on Gabriel's face vanished at the mention of that incident.

He looked like he was mentally adding Alexei to his hit list for daring to upset Evie. She squirmed in his arms, and Nate and Selena shared a knowing smirk.

There was *one* surefire way to get under Gabriel's skin. And she was currently hugging him. His eyes darkened as I spoke, his entire demeanor shifting.

Evie, sensing the tension, went into full soothing mode. "He was friendly after I got to know him. He brings cupcakes now when he comes by."

Gabriel's mouth curled with displeasure, his eyes flashing as he fixed me with an accusatory glare.

Nate laughed quietly at how quickly Gabriel's temper flared.

"Why did you *let* Evie eat cupcakes with an Enforcer?" Gabriel's eyes were eerily bright as he set her down.

Let her? "You *let him* into the house. I told you to meet them in Midtown."

"Aidan showed up unannounced." Gabriel's focus was elsewhere. *"You let Evie around Alexei?"*

This *motherfucker*. Evie had seen worse than Alexei.

"We are *not* fighting about Evie right now."

Evie huffed, pushing out of Gabriel's arms. "Gabriel, he didn't *let* me do anything. I'm an adult."

And here we fucking went.

I couldn't believe we were having this conversation again. Nate watched silently, his eyes ping-ponging back and forth while Selena studied her boots, clearly wishing she were anywhere else.

We can't do this here.

"I need to talk to you," I was trying to keep my frustration in check.

"Mom and Dad are going to fight," Nate quipped, earning a withering look from Gabriel.

Despite being a former spy, Nate was still a hundred percent an asshole.

He held up his hands and ducked behind Selena, who scowled at him, obviously not appreciating being used as a human shield.

The tension in the room was palpable, the air thick with unspoken anger and frustration.

I could feel the weight of Gabriel's gaze on me, the silent accusation in his eyes.

"Come on." I motioned as I walked out, ignoring the team watching me.

~

As we moved through the hallways, heading downstairs to the gym, I couldn't resist voicing my thoughts.

"She's growing up, Gabriel. You gotta let her breathe." It was like talking to a brick wall sometimes.

"Says who." Gabriel's stubbornness was infuriating.

"Says me." I shot back, my patience wearing thin.

"I don't care what you want. She's never stepped foot outside of this house, never shot anyone. She doesn't know pain." The look on Gabriel's face made it clear that he intended to keep it that way.

For all his finesse, Gabriel sounded like a man discussing paint. "I trained her to not be a field agent."

I didn't bother telling him I'd been discreetly training Evie for the field.

It would only make matters worse. Gabriel trusted me with Evie, so I sometimes knew her better than him. She'd expressed her willingness to learn, and for a few weeks, I'd kicked her ass, and then she'd started fighting back.

I was proud of Evie for slowly building her confidence, but Gabriel seemed determined to stifle her growth.

"Even I can see you're suffocating her," I said as we entered the gym. I needed to hit something before I lost my cool completely. "You know she's dating, and she can't tell you because she knows you'll kill him."

I fucking suspected Evie had been seeing someone.

I just didn't know who, not because I didn't care or was unable to find out, but because—she was a fucking kid.

"I don't give a shit who he is, he won't get anywhere near her," Gabriel growled. "Don't act like you give a shit and understand how I feel."

He didn't even wait until we got on the mats.

The moment my foot touched it, Gabriel's fist connected with my face, pain radiating through my jaw. "I can't believe you, son of a—"

"Wait until you get invested," Gabriel interrupted, his tone dark and even more pissed off. "Evie said she has a younger sister."

He paused, letting the words sink in. "You're already attached to the older one. You're going to lose your shit when you—"

He didn't get to finish his thought before I moved faster than him, squaring off.

I didn't hold back, going straight for his stomach with all the force I could muster.

"At least take off the fucking suit, you man Barbie," I spat, my frustration reaching a boiling point.

I was sick of his games, sick of his secrets, and sick of being left in the dark. If he wanted a fight, I was ready to give him one.

"Don't you fucking start," Gabriel growled something in him, unleashing whenever he fought.

He shoved me off a few feet and hauled his suit jacket off, revealing a shirt straining against cords of muscle underneath.

We circled each other in his massive gym, the tension palpable.

This was why we couldn't talk in front of the team.

Because the team couldn't see their parents fighting.

It was my house rules.

And this was the only way we could communicate. We sparred all the fucking time to work out our issues.

It probably wasn't healthy, but it worked for us.

"Stop fucking with me," I snarled, closing in on him.

Gabriel didn't listen to normal conversations.

No, if you wanted him to respect you, you had to earn it. The motherfucker was an entitled snob.

He was also my best friend, even if he'd never admit it.

He didn't let me finish, and I ended up flat on my back from one of his fucking kicks, the breath knocked out of me.

Fucking Kyokushin.

Gabriel was a beast whenever he fought, moving quicker than anyone I knew.

Too bad I'd been working off all my misery at the gym. I was on him in a flash, taking him down with a flip.

I grunted as I felt his weight over my head before he landed with a groan.

The sound of our heavy breathing filled the gym as we both scrambled to our feet, our eyes locked on each other.

I could see the anger burning in Gabriel's gaze, the frustration that mirrored my own.

"You *motherfucker*," I barked a humorless laugh. "You need to let Evie grow up. You need to stop fucking things up with every recruit we get. You're tearing apart the team all for some fucking heirloom?"

I whipped myself up, my frustration reaching a boiling point. That set him off.

Every time I brought it up after he'd told me he was searching for some fucking artifact, I had been astounded.

"Don't start—"

I snarled, cutting him off. "You spent days looking for it with the O'Hara's. I fucking knew that was Aidan's town car. You already finished your business with him years ago. You want me to fix the shit you don't have time to do, but you won't tell me where he's going to find it?" Gabriel's eyes went dark, his jaw tight with anger.

"I know you want to keep the family together. But you can't keep doing this."

That was why I came back to Titan for the last few days. I'd left my girl safe at home, covered in my scent. I knew she was good.

But *this*? He was why I was needed *here*.

"I can't keep doing this," I said, my voice low. I was done being left in the dark, done being a pawn in Gabriel's games.

It was time for him to start trusting me, or I was out.

He scoffed. "One night with your crush, and you can't function? *Is her pussy that—*"

I saw red. I launched myself at him, slamming my fist into his mouth with a satisfying crunch.

"Not one fucking word about her," I growled, holding him down. "Not one. I don't give a fuck what you do. You are the only reason I'm still here. So here's what's going to happen."

I pressed my arm against his throat, my rage boiling over. I knew he could fight back anytime, but I also saw the shock in his eyes at my ferocity.

"You are going to tell me why the mob boss of a crime syndicate still shows up here. And if the heirloom is, in fact, in Cape Verde. The new hires are going to acclimate to Titan. And before you get your fucking panties in a twist, I never got someone for you."

Or me. I was dead serious.

"You are the only reason I lurked. I respect your time with the O'Ha-ras, but I run this shit. You need to trust me as your fucking teammate to do the right things. You're losing the team. I'm trying to keep things together."

His eyes were unholy bright.

We'd done well for ourselves in the last few years, getting our name out and sub-contracting smaller groups and units to be a part of Titan.

But recently, the itch in my body to get a replacement crew for us or to double the original Titans had occurred to me. The team was struggling. Selena refused to take a break over her loyalty to Gabriel.

And because he was Gabriel, he said. "It's not Cape Verde." I resisted the urge to roll my eyes. Gabriel used my small moment of distraction to flip me over his head. I groaned, knowing I wasn't going to be able to fuck Alisha the way I wanted to without icing my back after this.

"Where do you learn this shit?"

He wasn't smiling anymore. I wasn't as good as him, but I was good. He was pissed. And so was I. I was tired of this. I didn't want to fight my best friend, but he didn't want to admit his destructive tendencies. Someone had to fix it.

He scrambled back, and so did I.

I waited, bracing for the next hit, for anything. He was bleeding from his mouth. Alisha would have questions if I showed up this messed up.

"I didn't know you were still training while you were fangirling over Alisha?" Her name on his lips had me lunging. Gabriel laughed without humor, moving out of the way. "Good to know Nate's still useful."

I sparred with Nate all the time, and despite his laid-back demeanor, the motherfucker could fight.

Wiping the sweat from my brow, my chest heaved as I tried to catch my breath.

Gabriel and I had always had a good relationship, but this was new.

We were both on edge, pushing each other's buttons in all the wrong ways.

When Gabriel moved, I saw a word tattooed on his left pec, revealed by a cut in his shirt. Before I could determine it, he quickly shoved the fabric closed and wiped his mouth.

"Is this why you've been lurking around here?" He spat out blood. "You could be with your girl."

"Tell me something I don't know."

That, and I was processing my emotions away from the one thing

76

that threw all of them to shit. I panted for a hard minute, feeling the weight of my years catching up to me.

"I know you want to make sure you don't lose your family. But do you remember why you put me in charge of making these calls?"

He grumbled something, so I said it out loud.

"Because I want the greater benefit for the team. I would be *devastated* if anything happened to any of them. If you keep working them this hard and do not cut them any slack, you will lose everyone. *Including Evie.*" His expression was mutinous as he listened, which he never fucking did, so this was a fucking miracle.

Hell was freezing over.

"I'm not going to let anyone in that would dare threaten what we've built. But you gotta let me do my fucking job." For a moment, he said nothing, simply processing. He remained silent so long that I almost braced for the next hit.

"I'm not losing Evie," he finally said. I sighed. At least something got through to him.

"You keep going, and you will." *I knew her.* "I'm her brother too."

His eyes watched me, and I could never tell anymore what was behind them. Something haunting him, something so different than I had ever seen. And then he tipped his head. I exhaled. That was one for the books.

"You've been lingering here instead of going home to your girl so you could school me?" He raised an eyebrow. I had.

"Are you asking me for reassurance as my work wife?" Nate always joked about how Gabriel was just a needy work wife. I got it now. I ripped my shirt off, now that it was filthy. I needed a shower and a change of clothes.

"You avoided me for the last forty-eight hours."

He scowled, loosening his tie as though it hurt to breathe. "I have a lead."

That's what I was afraid of.

Whenever Gabriel disappeared into his den and didn't emerge, he was on a small bender.

"Where?" First, it was Cape Verde.

"Senegal."

I didn't tell Gabriel, so I asked Nate to do some digging for me.

I was getting tired of the secrets myself.

Only because the longer it went without him getting his peace, the more of a dick Gabriel was to everyone around us.

"Senegal." He had tried misleading me before and tried to keep it from me. So I'd resorted to asking Lucy, my personal con artist. "Gabriel, I can't help you if you don't let me in."

A beat passed between us.

"It's my necklace," he said, shaking his head. "I can't tell you right now. I need confirmation."

"You fucking have to. You're going to send in a team for –"

"No," he stopped me. "This isn't the job for a team. If there's anyone who's going to go get it, it's me."

I couldn't believe what I was hearing.

"Are you out of your mind?" I was losing my shit. "You're not going there alone."

And then there was the one subject I didn't touch.

"Does Aidan need you to kill someone else?" Gabriel had done one tiny favor for the eldest son of the O'Hara clan a long time ago. To murder his father. "Why else was he here?"

No love was lost there.

Cormac O'Hara had been a bastard, and Aidan wanted a clean slate to turn his kingdom around.

Now, as the current mafioso of the crime syndicate in Chicago, Aidan would drop in from time to time, discreetly seeking time with Gabriel for whatever he needed.

Initially, I didn't understand why Gabriel did business with him until I realized how useful his guys were.

He wiped his mouth. "Aidan's youngest brother, Kieran, is in New York. He wanted me to keep an eye out. Aidan wants to keep Killian as the spare, and Kieran wants nothing to do with it."

Aidan O'Hara had two younger brothers, Killian, second in command, and Kieran. Who was now...not in the mafia? I raised a brow.

Gabriel's expression furrowed. "It's not like that. Kieran's close to Aidan. He's just nothing like his family." Gabriel wiped his hands. "Kieran wanted out. Aidan gave it to him."

"Just like that?" Aidan O'Hara let his baby brother walk?

Gabriel shrugged. "Killian's better." The second oldest. He grinned at my expression.

"Maybe you have a new recruit after all."

"I'm not hiring Aidan O'Hara's brother. I don't have a fucking death wish."

If a single hair on Kieran's head got messed up? I would lose operatives to the Irish mob.

"He's a good kid. Insane fighter," Gabriel countered.

"I don't give a shit if he fights better than you. I'm not stupid enough to let him in. And you shouldn't either."

Besides, if anything happened to him, we'd have more issues than we do now. But I knew Gabriel was leaving something out.

"Aidan didn't come out here just to ask you to take care of his brother," He didn't say a word. "I'm going to Africa with you. When you go."

Not if. Because if Lucy didn't find his fucking necklace, we would go together.

His eyes went dark. "You don't know what you're signing up for."

Yes, I did.

"In the words of Selena, don't be a stupid idiot. We're family. We always have been. Don't fucking try it. And let me do my fucking job," I paused. "I'm taking a few days off. I can't keep…this up for everyone. It's time to let everyone lead without training wheels."

He looked impassive. "Family, huh?" I nodded.

"Speaking of family…" He started. "James is dead. Adam keeps emailing us. And since I find the little shit annoying, I think you should talk to him."

Only Gabriel could deliver death like a weather report.

I stopped moving. Before I could say a word, Gabriel wiped his face with a towel. "Evie pulled it as soon as she saw it."

That's why Evie had been hanging around me like glue the last two days.

My stepfather James Russell dying was not news to me.

Why Adam wanted to reach out after years of silence was beyond me. I hadn't seen my half-brother since he was thirteen.

He'd be maybe twenty-five now.

We hadn't spoken. I wasn't sure what he wanted, but I didn't want to find out.

My stepfather, who had made my childhood a living hell, was gone. I should have felt something, anything, but all I felt was a hollow emptiness in the pit of my stomach.

And then there was Adam.

The golden child who could do no wrong in James' eyes.

I felt Gabriel's eyes taking me in.

I shook my head, trying to clear my thoughts. I couldn't deal with this, not now. Not when I had so much else on my plate.

"When you find this fucking buried treasure, I want to be the first to see it."

For some fucking reason, some family heirloom had haunted him with nights of no sleep and constant bad moods. Gabriel's smile lacked humor.

"You ever going to tell me why you need to find your necklace so bad?"

He was silent.

"You ever going to tell me why you keep *almost* killing people and destroying their company for touching your new girl?" *Touché.*

One side of his lip quirked up in the closest thing to a genuine smile. "It's almost convincing, you know, you walking around trying to blend in with the *normies*. Like you're just like everyone else."

Instead of being a full-on monster? Yeah, I got that.

"I'm not doing this." I walked away, giving him the finger.

"Who did you hire to replace you?" The one person I was keeping away from the rest of the team.

"Some guy named Liam Sullivan!"

I didn't wait.

CHAPTER 12
REED

I COULDN'T LEAVE WITHOUT GETTING THE REST OF THE TEAM ON THE same page.

I made my way back upstairs, showered, and changed into clean clothes, walking through the halls of the manor.

The eerie atmosphere of Gabriel's home never failed to unsettle me.

Despite its elegant French design, the massive white residence gave me the creeps, as if it was haunted.

Gabriel refused to call it a mansion, but its sheer size and custom-made features were enough to make my stomach churn.

And then there were the hallways, winding and seemingly endless, leading to places I didn't want to think about.

As I walked, I made a mental note that if I ever brought Alisha here, I would never let her out of my sight.

The sound of hushed voices caught my attention, and I paused outside one of the conference rooms.

Through the slightly ajar door, I caught a glimpse of Nate with Selena perched on his shoulders, Selena peering into the adjoining room through a window.

"Can you see them?" Nate whispered, his voice strained.

"Shh," Selena hissed, her fingers digging into his hair. Dark bangs covered her eyes. "You're making too much noise."

"Says you." He growled, shifting beneath her weight. "Your heel is digging into my pec."

I pushed the door open, my eyebrows raised in a mix of amusement and exasperation. "What are you two doing?"

They didn't spare me a glance, Selena craning her neck to get a better view while Nate grumbled under his breath.

Selena told him to shut the fuck up and lift since he brags about lifting heavy all the time. "I lift weights, woman, not you—"

"Shut up—" She gripped his hair. "*Do it.*"

Nate groaned, straightening with Selena on his shoulders, her green eyes focused now.

"Evie has a meeting with the new hires," Nate explained, glancing over at me and holding Selena's knees. "They didn't know that Evie was a woman. They kept calling Monroe a guy until they realized it was her."

Which meant Gabriel hadn't sunk his fangs into them...yet.

"Why are you spying on her from the library?" I bit back another laugh as Selena's heels dug into Nate's chest.

He hissed, grimacing. "*Lena, that's my—*"

"*Shut up, pendejo—*"

I snorted. "Did you forget about the security cameras?" Both of them looked at me, neither one fazed by the cut on my brow or my lip.

That would need ice.

I bit my tongue as Nate looked up at Selena, who looked down at him at the same time.

He let Selena down, both of them trying to maintain an air of dignity while trying to straighten themselves.

Nate ran a hand through his messy blond hair, the epitome of a disheveled biker. "Comm room?"

Yes, the fucking comm room.

I hadn't been entirely truthful with Gabriel. I had hired Liam Sullivan to help Evie, in a sense.

That was the only capacity in which he would be taking on any responsibility. Gabriel and I were irreplaceable.

Even if I craved a break *sometimes*, I liked what I did.

"I am passing most, if not all, of my paperwork to Liam," I instructed Nate. "Go through him for that. He'll be working with Evie on the cybersecurity angle for a while, picking up all my projects. Let him know I can't afford another PR nightmare at Teasers, so I set up a meeting with him and Lara. Evie will train under him."

Liam Sullivan was better than me at half of the stuff I did.

I looked at Selena. "Kellan's your shadow for now. If I need anything, he'll be the first one I pull, so be flexible. And Garrett's going to be Gabriel's."

Garrett Fuller, a former Green Beret topping out at six feet six, was built like a tank and checked all the boxes.

I had no doubt Gabriel, who had yet to meet him, would be thrilled. As thrilled as he would be, I had a specific job in mind for Nate once I realized he would be the perfect fit.

Selena's man-eater personality would crush a weak man. Somehow, I didn't think Kellan Watts fell into that category.

"You picked him up from the airport the other day. Is he good?" She huffed out a breath, nodding. "With his jacket." I fought back a smile.

I had specifically asked Kellan to wear that jacket.

Kellan was scary smart. He spoke close to ten languages, and he was whiplash smart and adaptable, so I told him he couldn't show up looking like who he was. He'd bristled, but I told him it would help.

Deception was our middle name. He'd shown up looking like he played college football with a goofy grin. And the entire team hadn't batted an eye.

I needed a way to keep people and cater to everyone without giving too much away.

"He's good to balance you out," I said instead. "You can practice your Spanish with him when he helps you kill all those men who hit on you in Paloma."

Few things were precious to Selena, and one of those was parked outside in its Cherry Challenger glory. I watched her turn a little pink at that.

"Nate, I sent you a gig as a bodyguard."

"Fuck," he groaned, mirroring Selena's expression. "Please let it be a sexy young divorcée this time."

The last time a woman had wanted him, it had been a sixty-year-old heiress with a penchant for being a little too handsy.

"Close, she's important."

Gemma wasn't my type, but she was pretty and elegant. His eyes lit up.

"She just needs you whenever she goes to work events, so it shouldn't be bad at all. Enough for you to get back and do what you need with Selena and the lost boys. Gemma is Alisha's best friend. Try not to fuck this one up."

For me or her. Alisha would never let me live it down if her best friend was fucked over by my guy.

Nate's grin fell, and his hard, navy eyes met mine. "Gemma Marchand?"

Selena frowned. "Are you sure you don't want me to do it? Nate will end up on the news."

That was the one.

"No, you're with Kellan. He's good for you. Nate, can you overlook your bias to help her or not?"

He looked like he'd rather do anything else. But he nodded, still looking upset.

"I need you guys to make sure Evie doesn't do anything that will make Gabriel kill everyone. Selena, I've sent you everything for the new guys. In the event, you guys can't reach me–"

Because I had a girlfriend to go and win over again.

"You're in charge. *Entiendes?*"

I gave her a warm smile at the show of pride in her eyes.

"Sí, *entiendes.*"

"Why is she in charge?" Nate started. "No offense, Selena, you're overqualified for everything you do. What the fuck happened to Gabriel?"

I knew they'd think this way.

I paused. "Gabriel and I are still running everything–"

"You're hiring more than three guys, aren't you?" Nate's eyes looked wary.

I was.

"I'm hiring way more than three guys. The two in there are just a start."

Liam counted, but...he was a special case. Both of their eyes widened like saucers. I wanted people under them. A team. We were the roots, but we needed...support.

"You're replacing us?" I knew she was serious when she said it in English.

"Put the knife away, Selena. I'm not replacing you. We just can't keep pushing like this. I'm trying to find a middle ground."

She sheathed her knife into somewhere on her body I didn't want to try and figure out.

"Play nice."

I was only human.

And just because we had something good didn't mean we couldn't run it to the ground.

"I sent you everything you needed going forward. I'm leaving now."

"You are going to your *novia?*"

I gave a curt nod. It always took time when I came up here.

Yes, I'm going to my girlfriend.

CHAPTER 13
ALISHA

I NEEDED TO GET SOME AIR.

I was losing my mind, cooped up in my room, inhaling the scent of Reed from my sheets.

Gemma had texted me that she had hired a bodyguard from Titan, and he had shown up this week.

While she was going over her plans with him, she couldn't go over our plans for the charity I had.

Gemma liked managing the Poppy Project and running things through me.

She enjoyed helping, and I appreciated her expertise.

We'd started it just as a women's help center to get out information about menstruation and college books.

Recently, I had an idea to start packing parcels specifically for women in local homeless shelters. That had been the entire concept: to bring something more to the table with all the good we had.

My Mum instilled in me the value of appreciating what you had and making sure you gave back.

When she'd lived in Calcutta as a little girl, she'd told me her mother had told her that there were girls out there less fortunate than I was, women who couldn't go to school, get a backpack, or even pursue their dreams.

She hadn't wanted the same for her girls. So when I'd picked a career she hadn't approved of, it had disappointed her. After my parents passed, the project became a way for me to honor her values.

And because I needed a reminder of who I was, I went to lunch with my sister on one of her rare days off.

Avani went to a private college Downtown that cost me an arm and a leg to send her. I had the money but never realized how expensive college was.

It was criminal.

Even with my success, I recognized I was also working to make sure I never had to doubt how I would take care of Avani.

I threw myself into my work, and I was reminded of why every time I saw her.

She was in my arms, hugging me, when I entered the familiar diner.

"*Didi.*" I warmed at the sound of her calling me sister in Hindi.

The scent of honey and vanilla clung to her, mingled with something indefinably *Avani*.

One day, I wanted to take Avani and myself back to Calcutta to explore, sightsee, and taste the things our Mum had growing up.

It wasn't our usual brunch day, but I'd asked her if she wanted to get together, and we had. I brushed her cinnamon locks back, her eyes dark and bright as she beamed. Avani was a few inches taller than me.

"You've gotten so big," I teased, knowing I was still shorter than her five feet six. She giggled, and I felt like we were little girls again for a moment. Memories of when I'd braid her hair or she'd steal my hair pins and our Mum would urge us to get along.

"It's only been three days I've been gone," she beamed. But I missed her. I did. After our parents had passed, I never let her go. Never let her stray.

Memories of our father corralling the both of us to get along after a fight in our childhood were now a distant dream.

It still hurt in a dull ache that I'd never see my parents again. It was partially why I was so careful when I drank, and I liked that Reed wanted to take care of me when I was vulnerable.

The drunk driver that killed my parents had *not* been considerate.

"Three days, no," I waved my hand. "It feels like forever." She giggled as I asked her about how it was going for her.

I still saw her as the twelve-year-old I had to take care of.

I had gotten the news about our parents from her when she'd been on the phone with our Mum.

We'd been frantic until someone had answered. It had been a horrible few months after. I'd watched her flourish over the last few years since then.

Despite her shy and reserved nature, she opened up with me, and I always made it my prerogative to be a safe space for her to turn to.

Avani never fought with me, never caught an attitude, and was an anomaly among little sisters I heard could have an attitude.

I wondered somehow if she worried I wouldn't love her the same way once our parents had died if she did complain.

I wondered if she felt guilty if she did like I felt guilty for living my life without her.

Before our parents' accident, Avani and I hadn't been close.

I was not the perfect daughter like she was.

I had distanced myself a bit from my family. That winter, she had been visiting during holiday.

Now, I was glad she had.

I hadn't let her go since.

Losing Mum changed me and her. Avani popped a strawberry from her pancake into her mouth.

"What about you?" she asked softly. "Are you all right?"

As my sister spoke, I realized what I sounded like to Reed. *Proper.* Avani had a stronger accent than I did. Only on her, it sounded crisp and sweet. Effervescent. She smiled at me despite her concern. I think he'd like her.

"I think my social media manager just wanted to build suspense for the new project I'm working on." *Liar.*

In response I took a quick photo of her munching on her strawberry which she mock frowned at. She wiped the corner of her mouth all dainty, and I grinned.

"I was thinking about actually partnering with EllaBeauty's clothing brand line and creating a pajama and lingerie line that was a lot more affordable. I think it would be cool to have sexy but comfortable pieces."

I had dreamed of doing this, and Maxine DuPont, the CEO, had loved the concept for their brand. As Avani's eyes grew wide and she made a noise of happiness, I laughed and had an idea.

"Are you free for the rest of the day?"

At the look in my eyes, she clapped her hands. She knew exactly where I was going with this.

Just because we were mature young women didn't mean we didn't believe in a little retail therapy. Hours later, I practically collapsed in my apartment, giggling with my sister. We'd gone to thrift stores, and I'd taken so many photos.

My stories were blowing up, and I had made it home with Avani as the sun was going down.

The best part about having a sister was also being her best friend.

Avani had found a cute bookstore, and we'd hauled up bags of those for her, which she'd no doubt add to her collection. I ended up purchasing so much. As she tried on different outfits, I was munching on mochi donuts.

For a moment, a sensation went through my heart at a memory of Avani trying on one of my mother's sarees as a kid.

"*Didi*, do you remember when we used to steal Mum's clothes?"

"All the time. She had a wardrobe to die for."

"Do you remember when Mum was upset that morning when she left for work about her pin?" I did.

Avani looked sheepish. "It was me. I was the hairpin bandit."

I mock gasped. "We all knew you were the hairpin bandit."

Now, she really gasped, and I laughed.

"I felt so guilty," she cried. "That's not fair."

I laughed harder as she tossed a pillow at me.

"That is so cruel, *Didi*. You knew it hurt me."

I didn't get a chance to respond. The doorbell rang. I frowned as I stood and walked up. It was late. Who on Earth–I slowed my steps. There was a white note inside my door.

Peering through my peephole, I saw no one. I picked up the letter without thinking. Who slid notes under people's doors anyway? My heart beat quickly. I could've sworn I picked up the mail on the way in.

Had I forgotten it, and someone was letting me know?

Sometimes, I left my keys outside, and someone knocked or rang my doorbell to let me know. It was a safe building.

I wanted to open it as a chill went down my spine. But something stopped me.

"Is everything all right?" I spun around, hiding the note.

"Yes, I think it was the post," I pasted on a smile. "Goodness, would you look at the time? It's nearly eight. And a school night, darling."

She shook her head with a smile.

"It's fine, Lish, I'm with you. I don't care about going to bed late."

"Perhaps," I slid the letter onto the kitchen island. "Nevertheless, I'm afraid you can either stay here in your room or head back to your cozy closet."

I knew why Avani wanted to stay in the dorms. It gave her a sense of everyday life as much as it did for me.

As uneasy as it made me think about her growing up, I knew sometimes she had to. As I hugged her, my eyes drifted to the note. A chill ran down my spine, and unease bloomed in my stomach for some reason.

I waited until Avani called her taxi, and I made sure she got in safe before coming upstairs and stepping back into my apartment.

Without my sister, the temperature had gotten chillier, and I was back to my solitude. The white piece of paper on the kitchen island practically screamed for me to go pick it up.

I slid my outside shoes off and into my slippers as I padded to the kitchen.

You didn't wait for me, Alisha.

THAT CHILL SPREAD TO MY BONES AS MY HANDS SHOOK WHILE READING the note. Slivers of cold nerves slid down my spine.

Was this some sort of joke? I needed to call the police. The fact that I'd slept with Reed a few days ago, and then the note? It was too weird. Holding the note, I scrambled to grab my cell phone with shaking fingers.

What was this?

Sure, I got hate mail sometimes and the occasional handsy fan, but this was...someone knew where I lived?

I felt the anxiety take over, the fog take over my head, bile in my throat, and suddenly, I couldn't breathe. My eyes looked around my apartment, feeling shaken up. Whoever it was, they knew where I lived. I needed to do something. To get up. Anything but be here.

For some reason, I couldn't think straight. When my parents had passed away, something had changed in me. I was more...alert. Call it years of being anxious at having a teenager who stayed out late studying, so you went to go pick her up, had driven me here.

The fear of not being good enough. Constantly having to pretend. The dysmorphia of hating yourself and your image and revamping your style for the public eye. Hearing negative things said about you, you constantly have to fight against that.

It was why I never posted the bad because I had seen people commenting horrific things on Gemma's posts, saying things that she deserved to die. After all, she'd abandoned her family, as awful as they were. It was gut-wrenchingly painful. I couldn't even imagine how she felt.

I didn't even know what to do.

Would someone tell me to laugh it off?

Say this was just another idiot?

Would another cop tell me I should be flattered men were paying attention to me?

Being a woman could suck.

And there came the guilt.

The guilt and the fear from the first night I'd taken Reed home returned. The guilt and shame of living my life?

And then anger right on the back end of that, as though this person could make me hate myself for choosing to live. To experience Reed.

Even if just for *one* night of pleasure.

As hurt as I had felt, I didn't want to continue feeling that way forever. Almost held back with my life. *Because of sex?*

A sickening thought occurred to me just then, like a twist at my insides. *Oh God, what if...something happened to Avani?*

That thought made my blood run cold. My heart dropped as I'd just dropped my sister off in a cab.

This reeked of a man's jealousy.

I wondered about the men I'd gone on a date with. None of them knew where I lived in the past, and that had been years ago.

But what if one of them had followed me home? And now they knew where I lived?

A cold feeling slithered down my spine, and my stomach wrenched. The panic at losing my sister clogged my throat as my vision blurred.

She was all I had. My family.

What if by being selfish and seeking out companionship with someone who couldn't text or call me, I'd put her in danger? *I'm a horrible sister.*

I had to protect her. And I had to call the police. Somewhere, the doorbell rang, and my head whipped around. My heart rate escalated.

He was back. He came back. He knew my sister left, and now he was back. I couldn't stop.

I didn't think.

I screamed as loud as I could and shrieked, grabbing for a knife. Anything. My fingers fumbled.

Fear clogged every cell in my body. I didn't think. It flowed through my body.

Distantly, I realized I was loud. Bloody. Murder. *Loud.*

A second later, I heard a slam, the door breaking open on its hinges, and I couldn't stop screaming.

An animal noise left me, and I hadn't realized I'd sunk to the floor behind the kitchen island. At the sight of a dark figure holding a gun, I shrieked, covering my face with my hands.

Something crashed to the floor, and items toppled around me as I scrambled back behind the kitchen island.

I caught a glimpse of stormy eyes in shock as he approached me.

"Lish! It's me." He was repeating it over and over, but I was drowning. "What's wrong? Did something happen?"

Dimly, I registered it as Reed, but my brain freaked out. *He came back...*

I stopped screaming as I saw his concern. Reed. He had a gun in his hands.

His eyes were a storm of focus and alert as he scanned the room for any threats, landing on the piece of paper in my hand.

The letter fell out of my hand as he quickly tucked his gun away and held his hands up to show me he was clear.

"Let me come to you. Easy. Easy, Angel. I won't hurt you. Breathe for me," he took in a deep breath, miming that I should do the same. I did. I tried.

But I couldn't breathe.

When he got close, I was in his arms, hyperventilating. *Reed's here. He's here.*

It felt wrong how my body responded to him, as though I was home in his arms.

He wrapped me tight and kissed my temple, and I all but melted into him.

Inhaling his scent, his familiar cologne, the hint of the sea, I exhaled.

He was saying something. To breathe. *Slowly.*

He was counting to four.

I obeyed, unable to focus on anything but his voice in my ear.

"Good girl, one more time...again. God, you're freezing."

He held me tight for long moments as I calmed down. "What happened?"

He was scanning the apartment.

"The note," I gasped. "The note."

I couldn't stop shaking. Reed momentarily assuaged the icy fear in my heart.

He turned his head while holding me, and I clung to him as he grabbed the note.

I heard the rustle of paper.

Nothing came out of him as he sat there on the floor, holding me to him.

"You don't know who sent this." It was a statement, not a question.

I didn't. I shook my head. "They know where I live."

I felt hot tears in my eyes as my vision blurred. *Reed is here.*

"My sister...He was here...He was here."

I couldn't think as he was holding me again, tighter. I trembled as I told him what had happened before he showed up.

The note. My sister. The doorbell.

He rubbed circles on my back as his lips pressed against my temple.

"Pack your stuff," he said after a long moment. "You're coming home with me tonight."

CHAPTER 14
ALISHA

"What?"

I yanked my body away from him. As terrified as I was, I could acknowledge how forward that was. I backed up a little on the floor.

Despite the panic, even I admitted I didn't know Reed well enough *to move in with him.*

"Hang on a bloody second," I could barely speak. If possible, Reed looked even angrier as my throat worked. "You cannot just show up after..."

I couldn't fathom how he could appear after days of radio silence, a bouquet of flowers lying on the counter like a peace offering. The floral scent mingled with the adrenaline pumping through my veins.

"I—you—I'm not going anywhere with you," I insisted, hating the tremor in my words. "There's got to be another option."

Oh, there was. I saw it in his expression. Like he knew it as well. I swallowed again, my fingers unwillingly going to my throat.

In a few strides, Reed was at my fridge. He paused. I knew what he was seeing.

"Why is there nothing but donuts and coconut water?"

He grabbed some coconut water and brought it to me, helping me to my feet and onto one of the barstools.

I gratefully chugged, eyeing him as I did.

The moment I finished, Reed cornered me again, bringing both of his hands to either side of the kitchen island. Trapped, I tried not to let my body get the best of me this time, the heat in me sinking low at his gaze.

I just sipped my coconut water again, shyly glancing up at him. And then I noticed the cut on his brow.

The bruised cheek. Concern filled me.

"What happened to you?" I'd let him into my body. Into my home. Into my life. And yet, I felt like I knew nothing about him. "Were you in a fight?"

The darkness in his eyes was unfathomable. His jaw was tight. Right now, he didn't look anything like the safe Reed I knew. He looked like the man underneath, the other side. A storm.

"It's not safe here."

The words made my gut clench.

I knew that much. But I looked into his eyes.

"Reed, I don't want to leave my home. I'm not trying to sound spoiled, but—"

All I felt was agony at the idea of leaving this place behind. It wasn't just *my* home.

"This is where my sister and I grew up the last few years. All my memories—"

The photos on our fridge, her books on the coffee table. Everything. This was the apartment I bought when I earned my EllaBeauty brand deal. This is was my home.

"Avani was just here."

I felt Reed's hands come up, holding my face tight. He looked like he was struggling with himself for a moment.

It took him a while. I imagined he wanted to carry me bodily out of my house but warred with himself.

"Fine, you can stay," sheer relief coursed through me, and my heart calmed down until he added. "But I'm staying with you." I recognized that as the CEO, he had employees who could've stayed with me. It didn't have to be him.

"And I'm setting up security measures so nothing happens to you."

"Why?" I didn't get it. "Why are you here?"

Pain lanced through his expression. "If you have to ask that, I guess I really fucked up."

I bit back a response. He hadn't let me go.

"Lish," he looked pained. "I'm so sorry—"

"It's all right," I whispered.

"No," Reed shook his head, his lips brushing over mine for a moment. "It's not. I fucked up. I'm sorry, *I'll make it up—*"

I wanted to melt into him, but my brain kept throwing up warning signs.

"It was one time," I argued weakly.

"It was your first time." I stilled in his arms as he pulled me tight to him. "Several times."

I struggled to get any air into my lungs with how close he was, the dark locks over his eyes, his all-black attire with the touch of white underneath.

It broke my heart to see his face bruised enough for me to know he was busy doing something I didn't want to know.

I remembered when I had been with him before he knew I was inexperienced, he almost believed what the world did. That I was a confident woman. A burning flame.

"That doesn't…it doesn't change anything."

I pushed on despite being scant inches from him and him being displeased.

"You can't possibly want me more just because you found out I was…I hadn't been with anyone else."

"Oh, but I do." He was wicked.

His voice was a dark caress against my body. I felt his arousal through his clothes, through mine, fueling mine.

"I've wanted you for the longest time. And I waited patiently." His voice dropped to a whisper. "You think I'm going to let you go after you told me the same thing with no words?"

You told me the same thing with no words.

I needed to take a step back. My body was responding to his every move.

"I can't—" I pushed at his chest, and he didn't budge.

"Stop running from me." He looked even more upset that I would try.

"I can't think with you."

"That's the point."

I couldn't think straight. "I want you to let me help you." But how did I do that? At the loss in my expression, he moved back just a scant, his hand moving to the back of my neck.

"Because you want me to be your—?" *I didn't even know.*

"Because I care about you," Reed said fiercely, his eyes blazing with

96

sincerity. "I'm sorry for letting you down. I promise it won't happen again. I had to take care of some things, but I'm here now. For you."

As my lips parted, Reed seized the moment, his tongue delving into my mouth with a fervor that left me breathless.

His hands roamed my body. "I'll make sure nothing happens. I'll take care of you. Just let me, Lish…Let me."

It was *right* there, within reach.

And while I knew there was nothing wrong with sleeping with him, doubt crept in.

What if the note was just a scare tactic? What if I was blowing things out of proportion?

Reed pressed into me, invading my senses and thoughts.

"I know you're scared," he murmured, rubbing my back. "You're so tense, Angel."

But my mind was racing with a million thoughts.

"I need a minute," I whispered, my voice barely audible amidst the chaos swirling within me. "I need to process what you've already had days to figure out."

I took a shaky breath, my heart pounding in my chest. "I don't believe you. I'm confused. You say you want me for years, but after you have me, you leave me for days—"

"I can explain—"

"And now this—"

We both fell silent, the weight of the moment hanging heavy in the air.

I exhaled heavily, the words struggling to escape my lips. "It was one time. That's all it was."

The admission gutted me, leaving a hollow ache in its wake.

Unable to meet his gaze, I focused on a point on his black jacket, reading the designer name on the zipper—a brand I recognized.

If he could afford that and his car, Reed was wealthier than I'd realized.

Lara had mentioned he was a millionaire, but I could never tell.

There were so many shadows and secrets layering him, and it felt overwhelming to process.

"One time?" The bite in his voice made me wince, but I still didn't dare look at his expression. "That's what I was, one time?"

No. I want you so badly I ache for you.

I bit my cheek to keep from screaming the words.

Because he had left, no matter the reason. A simple courtesy text would've been the kind thing to do.

I couldn't bring myself to believe him, the doubt and fear clawing at my heart.

A part of me knew he could've been gone for work, but another part of me was terrified of heartbreak.

Not when I was already under this immense pressure to let him stay with me, to protect me.

"You didn't call or text—"

"I can explain—"

"I don't care!" I felt it leave me then, almost like a physical force willing to hurt him. I didn't know where it came from.

I felt disoriented. From him.

From the unknown specter now haunting me.

The note was seared into my mind, leaving me uneasy, and with Reed around, I couldn't think straight.

I was scared, the fear seeping into my bones and clouding my judgment.

Deep down, a cold, painful sensation filled me, reminiscent of losing my parents and feeling like I was losing Avani, the only constant in my life.

I wasn't sure if Reed's desire for me was consistent if his intentions were true.

I couldn't look at him.

"You can stay here," I forced out, my breath shaky. "But I can't be with you. I don't want a relationship."

Each word sliced into my heart, leaving me raw and bleeding. But maybe I needed him to feel a fraction of the pain he'd inflicted on me.

"It was just one night, and I think we should see other people. It's obvious we are not suitable for each other."

We were too different. I didn't understand his world. My fingers dug into my chest, a futile attempt to steady my racing heart. I couldn't meet his gaze, focusing on anything else. The fabric of my slippers and my dark hair cascaded around my face like a flimsy shield.

Reed had offered to stay, and yet here I was, pushing him away. The irony wasn't lost on me.

The hurt pulsed through me like a living thing. I felt exposed.

"Other people?" His voice was a low growl, his head dipping closer. "You want to see other men."

It wasn't a question.

He didn't say it. He didn't have to.

"I need to live my life," I paused, my eyes daring to meet his for once.

I didn't like what I saw there at all. Reed's eyes were the window into his emotions and his heart. In the past, he'd always appeared calm before the storm. Now, he was the storm.

"You plan on moving on, Lish? From me? From this?" He was so close I had to gasp at the pressure on my stomach. "I was just *one* night to you."

"Yes." Liar. But this was the reason why I never brought men around Avani. I wanted to be a good example for her. She was my parents' baby.

His lips turned cruel in a twist I wasn't expecting to break my heart, but it also sent a shiver down my spine.

"Did I make it memorable for you? Or do you need another lesson from me to convince you it wasn't one night for me?"

I tried to turn away, unable to look at him, and that seemed to upset him more.

But deep down, a part of me wanted to see how far he would go, how much he truly wanted me.

I felt him grip my neck, my breath leaving in a gasp. *Now you've done it.*

I felt lust shoot into my core, my body growing wetter by the second experiencing this side of him.

Was that why I had said those things?

At the look in my eyes and my nipples hardening to points, his eyes were cruel, but there was a glimmer of satisfaction in them.

His lips moved over my throat. "You think after I tasted your blood on my tongue, I was going to let anyone else have you?"

My heart raced, my body trembling with a mixture of fear and desire. I was torn between wanting to push him away and craving his touch.

The intensity of his gaze and the possessiveness in his voice all stirred something primal within me.

Heat flared through me at the words, dark and rich, coming from him. "Let anyone take what was mine?"

Words from nights prior I'd memorized whispered in my head. I felt my eyelids flutter shut, my body responding to his possessive tone despite the conflict raging within me.

I will ruin you for anybody else.

His dark velvet whisper in my ear sent bolts of lust straight through me. "I should edge you for the rest of the night for even thinking you could threaten me with other men."

Why did this feel so good?

I was torn between the desire to push him away and the overwhelming need to *surrender*.

"I don't think you'd like being edged to insanity, would you, Angel?" I didn't know what edging was. But it did not sound fun.

Do what Reed says. I think I was about to find out why Lara had warned me.

The low laugh that came from my squirming made me even more wet, my body betraying the words I had spoken earlier.

"No, I don't think you have. But I can. I can drive you to madness with my cock in you. Silence all those thoughts in your head, Angel. And you'd let me, wouldn't you?"

I would shamelessly, I would.

I felt drugged, my mind clouded with lust and the overwhelming desire to submit to him.

His hands cupped my breasts and then rolled my nipples, sending shockwaves of pleasure through my body.

A moan left my throat as I closed my eyes, tipping my head back as his mouth whispered over my neck.

"Look at you, so fucking worked up over me. Even your lies won't save you from me."

There it was. The darkness he lived in, the intensity that both terrified and thrilled me.

He cupped my breasts, tugging on my nipples. Hard.

"Reed," I gasped, grabbing at the kitchen island so I wouldn't grab him.

A vicious swear left him as he picked me up over his shoulder. A hard slap on my ass made me cry out as his fingers worked at my stockings.

"*These fucking tights,*" he growled as he ripped them easily.

For a moment, I gasped as the cool air touched my exposed skin as he shoved my panties to the side.

A second later, I was crying out for another reason.

Two fingers shoved into me with little grace as a groan left both of our lips. I was overwhelmed and blissfully stretched.

Nothing but hot, wet pulses and *Reed*.

"You're *dripping*," He worked them deep and settled as I pulsed and wriggled. "This is what I would've done to you that night."

Disoriented, I clung to him as he strode purposefully through my apartment, his strides eating up the distance to the living room. The world tilted and blurred, the furniture and walls bleeding together in a haze of adrenaline and need.

I cried out as it drove his fingers deeper when I tried to wriggle away.

The dark, low chuckle that came from him was nothing but a wicked promise.

A few hard slaps landed on me, and when he finally came and let me down, turning me over the back of my couch, grateful for the soft press of fabric against my belly.

I heard the clink of his belt as I tried to scramble up. I didn't make it far.

In another second, he was tying my wrists with the belt together as I gasped with the knowledge that Reed was bigger and stronger and manhandling me. And I loved it.

"Tell me your safe word."

I loved this. "*Storm.*"

He pressed a kiss to my neck. "What color are you?"

Gone were my earlier thoughts about anything. *I'm safe with Reed.*

"Green." His expression was dark when I looked over my shoulder as he stroked his cock. God, nothing would look so erotic.

Now, in the light of the warm lighting, Reed looked like a fierce warrior behind me, taking his claim.

Taking *me.*

"I don't have it in me to take my time anymore."

I didn't recognize his arousal-laced voice, a deep growl that let me know Reed was done playing with me.

His hand reached for my throat, squeezing gently as he looked down between my legs.

"Don't worry, Angel, I'll give you what you need. Just bend over and arch that pretty pussy for me."

I barely got a second to feel the tip of him before I cried out, turning around and grabbing the couch. I obeyed. At the first plunge of his cock, an animal noise left my lips, with Reed following.

"*Fuccck.*" His booted feet spread my legs wider.

I clutched the back of the couch with my manacled hands and held on as he sank even deeper.

"This is what it's going to be like every single time with you, isn't it?"

I struggled to get a breath in. To feel anything other than Reed invading my every sense, every thought. I felt like I was drowning, my hands gripping for purchase.

"That wasn't so hard, was it?" he growled, his hand moving, pressing on my swollen clit.

"*Reed.*" I shrieked as my legs shook wildly with that. "Oh God. It stings..."

A dark laugh left him as he hit pay dirt, bottoming out in me. I struggled to take it. A strangled cry left my mouth as he split me wide.

"That's it. *Scream* for me."

"*Too much,*" I croaked as he hit somewhere so sweet. I was trembling like a leaf, held up by his arm around my hips. The fingers on my clit circled, driving me insane.

His lips were at my ear. "It's just enough for you. That little pussy can take all of it. I know it can."

He bit down on my earlobe while pressing so deep I felt my feet leave the floor only held up by him. Closing my eyes with a blissful groan. Sighing and melting into him.

"What color, Angel?"

"*Green.*" It was a squeak. He hummed in approval.

"*Now,*" he growled. "Let's have a conversation."

My eyes popped open. *Oh God, I'm going to come.*

He held deep inside of me, making it hard to even think, to formulate words other than pleas.

"I guess I didn't make it clear enough when I took you the first time that you." *Thrust.* "Are." *Thrust.* "*Mine.*"

He ground in deep with the next thrust. I cried out.

"Mine to take. To *fuck.* To protect. *Mine.* Let me make that *very* clear now, Lish. There will be no one else who tastes you, feels this tight little pussy clench down every time I hit your back wall. No one else who hears how sweet your screams sound every time I get so deep you see stars."

I couldn't breathe as whimpers and sobs left me as his pace on my clit increased.

"*Oh God, Reed,*" I chanted, I was so close just from that alone. Reduced to tears with pleasure, I trembled beneath Reed's touch, my body a live wire of sensation.

His dark chuckle shot bolts of pleasure down to where he was driving me insane, every thrust pushing me closer to the edge of oblivion. Arching back to receive more, I was wriggling in a futile attempt to escape the overwhelming intensity.

Reed, knowing me so well, simply shoved deep, his movements precise and unrelenting. I shrieked, feeling the beginnings of my orgasm crest, teetering on the brink of ecstasy.

"Reed, I'm *close*—"

The words barely left my lips before he stopped abruptly, leaving me teetering on the precipice of release.

I gasped at the sensation of having my pleasure ripped away, my body aching for the completion it craved.

"I told you," he growled, his lips grazing my neck, his breath hot against my skin. "I don't do well with ultimatums. Or being threatened. So tonight, I'm going to teach you a lesson."

His words barely penetrated my fogged brain, each syllable dripping with dark promise and unspoken desire.

"I'm going to drive you crazy all night long. If I'm staying here, I want to be buried so deep inside you that you're not going to think straight."

He gently brushed his fingers over my clit, the feather-light touch sending shockwaves through my body. I gasped, my hips bucking involuntarily, seeking more of his touch.

"When you're begging for mercy, *maybe* I'll let you come."

Who was this man? Why was he so naughty?

I could feel his smile, a wicked curve of his lips against my skin. "I won't stop until you're limp with pleasure, fuck drunk with my cum, Lish. You'll think twice about *threatening* me with another man."

I was wriggling like a worm on a hook, the pressure inside of me increasing with every word he uttered. Tied up, pinned, and being edged until I thought I might die from the sheer intensity of it all.

"Reed, *please*." I didn't sound like myself, my voice a desperate plea, barely recognizable amidst the haze of lust that consumed me.

It was too much, the sensation of being stretched so wide I could feel him swell, combined with the deep nudges he gave somewhere delicious within me.

"*Please*, I'm sorry."

I sobbed, my fingers clutching the couch, my knuckles turning white from the force of my grip.

I couldn't think, couldn't breathe, couldn't focus on anything but the overwhelming need that coursed through my veins.

"Are you, Angel?"

He was a monster who held me captive with his touch, his words, his very presence.

"Are you sorry or just desperate to come? Don't even get me started on trying to run away from me."

A low laugh slipped out of him, the sound sending shivers down my spine. "I haven't even gotten started on *that*."

I was going to die. I was certain of it.

Die from the pleasure, the torture, the exquisite agony of being pushed to the brink again and again, only to be denied the release I so desperately craved.

And yet, even as I trembled and begged, a part of me reveled in the intensity, in the raw, primal power that emanated from him.

I was lost, utterly *lost*.

I felt like his doll as he played with my clit, working me up to a frenzy, my body a mere plaything in his skilled hands.

"*You are not allowed to come,*" he growled, his voice a dark caress against my skin.

I squirmed, only to realize that every twist and turn pushed him deeper inside me, the sensation both torturous and exquisite.

"*Not until you learn your lesson.*"

CHAPTER 15
ALISHA

INTENSE PLEASURE BLOSSOMED AT THE PINPRICKS OF PAIN CAUSED BY Reed's sheer size.

He played me like his personal toy, and I quickly approached the edge once more, on the brink of ecstasy.

Unable to stop it, I was *begging*, my voice a desperate plea for mercy.

A broken sound escaped my throat at the agony of being so close, *right there*, only to have it ripped away.

The noise that emerged from me as he chuckled, backing off, was one of frustration.

"Why are you doing this?" I knew why, but the question fell from my lips nonetheless. My thighs were *shaking*.

"Have you learned your lesson?" It was a whisper, a dark promise, as he returned to my clit, his touch electric, searing. "Am I just one night, Angel?"

I screamed as he rubbed in circles, the pleasure building, building, *building* until I thought I might break.

It was so good, so *good*. And then he stopped, leaving me teetering on the edge once more.

"Yes! I learned my lesson!" I was a mess, my words tumbling out in a desperate rush. *"You're not one night. You're more than one night! Happy?"*

At this point, I would say whatever it took, promise him anything, just to end this sweet, agonizing torment.

"Very." He didn't thrust, his body still, a cruel contrast to the chaos that raged within me. "But see, I don't believe you. Not yet."

Ohhhhh God.

And then he began a pounding, relentless assault inside of me with his hips that I knew I'd never *not* come.

I closed my eyes, unable to escape the sensations of how deep he went, how hot I burned for this man.

My voice raw, my body on the verge of shattering.

Godthatssogood.

"Don't you fucking come. You are not allowed to come."

A broken noise left my lips at that growl, a sound of pure desperation and need. I struggled then, my body fighting against the inevitable, not wanting to discover what Reed would do if I *did* come. I gasped as I clenched tighter, the effort to hold back my impending orgasm almost impossible.

"No!" I cried, my voice a ragged plea. "I can't—I *can't*— Reed!"

Oh God, *right* there, right *there*.

He stopped, leaving me gasping, groaning with the effort to keep myself from tumbling over the edge.

A few seconds passed, an eternity in the haze of my desire before Reed pulled back from me slowly.

I knew what was coming, what he had in store for me.

He did it *again*, and I lost focus, my mind a blank canvas of pure sensation.

The third time he did it, an animal noise left my lips, a primal cry of pleasure and pain.

I started crying, great big waves of tears flowing from me, my body and mind pushed to the very limits of what I could endure.

Reed's lips were at my ear, his hands gripping my chin, crooning softly. "I think my girl learned her lesson, didn't she?"

I couldn't speak. Just nod, feeling the wave of emotions coursing through me.

The weight lifted off my chest, giving away, the emotions fighting inside of me aware there was no reason to fight. I was still sobbing, unable to wipe my tears from being tied up. I felt him tip my head back, his tongue lick at my tears, and I cried more.

Completely at his mercy.

Slowly, his hand went to my clit and stroked. I lit up. He just nudged into me just enough to let me know he was still there. In that sweet spot.

"Come for me, Angel."

I came down. *Hard*. Those nudges that kept hitting right where I felt tender. *Ohhhh, God.*

When I fell from the edge of my orgasm, I saw dark spots. I was shaking so hard that Reed pressed into me and held me tight. Warmth rushed from my womb and I clenched down on him screaming in delight.

"Oh fuck, you're so *sweet*." I bit my lip to not lose my voice, a metallic taste in my mouth from the force of biting down.

All the while giving me those little nudges.

I was falling hard and fast and unable to catch my breath as he rubbed and worked me through it.

I'm not going to make it. "Reed."

"It's all right...I got you, I always have you...Let go for me, baby."

Slowly, Reed brought me back down.

Kissing my neck, my shoulders.

Dimly, I realized he was still hard.

He was *huge*, thick, throbbing inside of me, and that made it even more decadent. I was a sobbing mess.

"I need...I need more, please."

I didn't even know how I'd already come once, and yet I felt like something was being kept from me.

Like he'd gone easy with me.

Even though he'd held up my orgasm, something was right there.

How could it feel like that?

"I don't think you can take it anymore, Angel. I'll break you."

And maybe I wanted that.

I wanted to break and shatter and be reassembled into pieces that no longer made me feel the way I did. I gripped the couch and pushed myself back on him, pleading with my body for more.

That earned me more slaps to my ass. I cried out.

"*Please, Reed.*" Tears streamed down my cheek. I wriggled in his hold, it was too much, too big, too intense.

I was squirming on his length, and it just took up so much space.

"Only you make me like this, I learned my lesson. I learned—"

I couldn't form words anymore; I just *shook*.

Only once, and I was breaking apart.

I felt him reaching for my clit again, and this time, I did my best to wriggle *away* from it. It was too intense.

"Are you *trying* to *run* from me?" A growl escaped Reed. "*While* I'm balls *deep* in you?"

He spread my legs wider and shoved into me with a ruthless pump. *"Now you've fucking done it."*

He let my clit go, and I wanted to sigh in blissful relief. Only then did I realize what I'd done.

Reed didn't fuck me so much as split me open, and as he began a brutal rhythm inside of me, his hips pumping so hard and the grip changing from my hip to gripping my hair tight as he fucked into me with a ferocity that I *loved.*

My feet never touched the ground with the intensity of his thrusts combined with the way he *pounded* into me.

"You're going to drive me *insane.* " he snarled. "I've dreamt of fucking you like this."

He was *relentless,* and I was shaking for a different reason. After being taken to the edge already, my orgasm was fast approaching, and I would never survive it.

"Is this what you needed?" He bottomed out with every thrust. "Is this what my bad girl needed while I was gone? Her pussy stretched and filled with my cock until she didn't have to think." *Gods, yes.*

"Giving me rules? When I'm done with you, the only rule you'll have is that you are going to be naked in bed for days until you've satisfied me."

Slamslamslam.

"Reed."

He pressed down, rubbing circles on my clit. I exploded. It felt like a supernova had gone off in my womb.

I felt Reed struggle behind me as he swore, and my back all but arched off the couch as he gripped me with an arm around my waist.

I sucked in the air, but I just saw light in my vision.

Distantly, I was aware I was *screaming.*

The orgasm crashed into me with the grace of a hurricane as Reed pumped into me faster, working me through it pounding it out of me.

Each stroke hit somewhere so sweet. I couldn't hold back my cries. His strokes, long and deep as he promised in my ear, would help me ride it out.

Tears streamed down my cheeks.

"That's my girl, easy...grind that pussy on me and take what you need..."

This is what I wanted.

This is what I needed.

My legs shook wildly until it felt like I would collapse from it.

"This is the only way you'll listen, hm?" His soft, velvet voice soothed my nerves. "With my cock so deep inside of you, you can't think of anything else."

I wasn't even ashamed to admit it. It was.

"Anyone else." Something thrummed in my blood, in my veins with Reed. A hunger I had never experienced before. "I'm not done with you yet."

And I knew he was going to live up to every promise he'd made to me. I had no chance of surviving Reed. He would make sure it. He did nothing in half measures.

"This isn't just one night for me," his calm voice was at odds with his ferocious thrusts.

The kind that made my teeth clink and my breasts bounce.

"You are more than one night to me."

Sensitized and deliciously wet for him, I felt my heart ache at what he'd said.

"Reed," I begged. "Don't stop. *Please* make it hurt."

With a growl, he obliged, slamming into me so hard and yanking at my hair that my eyes rolled back.

Just like that.

"You're so fucking perfect," he groaned. "That little pussy can take me, can't it? *Say it.*"

"Ahh—m—my l—l—little pussy can—" I shrieked as my back arched, and he gripped one hip and *pounded.* God, this was filthy, and I reveled in it. *"I can take you."*

"Fuck yes, you can. Come for me, Angel," Reed was working like a beast inside of my body. Sensitized from my orgasms, this one felt like it would destroy me.

"Ah—Reed, I—" I squeezed my eyes shut as the sensations exploded. I gasped with the intensity and screamed as it got too much to hold back.

I heard his moans as I worked myself on him in tandem with his thrusts.

I wasn't just coming anymore.

It was just one drawn-out orgasm.

Tears tracked down my eyes, and I couldn't even scream anymore.

At some point, Reed let my hair go.

I felt both of his hands grip my hips and began to snap his hips so hard that my eyes rolled back in pleasure.

Something was *released* from me. It slammed into me, the intensity of orgasm making my eyes roll back.

"*Yesyesyesyesfuckme.*" I was *wild*. "*God, Reed, oh God.*"

The ferocity of his thrusts didn't let the pleasure ebb but build.

I was gone as he pumped with savage growls, and his fingers worked around my hip to find my clit.

"There you fucking go—" he was unhinged behind me. "*Let me have it.*"

As he pounded, I felt his fingers press against the nub of flesh, and my mouth opened in a silent scream as my belly clenched tight.

It was *nothing* I had felt before. I *heard* it.

"Oh fuck, that's *it*...I fucking *knew* it was right *there*. Squirt all over my cock—"

I felt the animal scream in the back of my throat as I buried my head in the cushions, and *even* then, it hurt my ears as I felt whatever this was as something akin to a tsunami ripped through my body.

Everything centered right where Reed was drilling into me.

Oh God, I'm dying.

Reed caught me from falling as he kept my legs wide open with brutally relentless thrusts as I convulsed around him, the slick evidence of pleasure wet. Filthy.

The obscene slaps of flesh against flesh.

He drove into me with single-minded focus, as though determined to wring every last drop from me.

I shrieked again, convulsing and clenching down on him. Unrelenting waves of release flowed from me.

The world faded.

Distantly I was registering Reed's encouragement, praise, awe. Words left me. Nonsensical noises.

The sound of my orgasm rushed from me.

I felt myself scrambling to grab onto *something*, Reed's arms locking around me tight.

Noises tore from my throat, primal and uninhibited, mingling with Reed's own grunts of satisfaction.

My fingers grabbed empty air, desperate to anchor myself amidst the ecstasy.

My vision went dark. Heat flooded me, and I heard his praises as he bent over me as.

I felt my orgasm dripping down to my ankles. I was shaking like a leaf as Reed kissed my back.

My body quaked and convulsed, my orgasm down my thighs as Reed held me steady.

Oh god, what was that?

How did he—what did I—

For long moments, he stayed buried in me, kissing my neck and pressing his lips all over me.

"I got you…it's all right. You're okay."

An unintelligible noise left me as I felt Reed slowly straighten me.

As he slid out, I winced at the sensation of him leaving my body, combined with the orgasm that coated my legs. If I wasn't so exhausted I would've been mortified.

His arms were wrapped tight around me.

Reed wasn't small or gentle, and I wouldn't have it any other way. I couldn't even stand leaning on him as he wiped my eyes, kissing me gently.

Reed gently undid the belt and let it drop.

I was a mess. I couldn't think at all. I felt limp as a rag as he lifted me into his arms, carrying me into my bathroom.

Once there, he set me on my feet letting me lean against him as he began turning on the shower.

Holding me against his chest, I avoided the look on his face as he took in my wet thighs. Covering him.

We were both panting. Heat burned in them as he kicked his pants off, and I blushed furiously.

I didn't know I could do that.

"I'll do it again," his voice was deep and rich like heat sinking into the nooks and crannies of my last reserves of resolve.

I didn't realize I said it out loud.

"I'm going to clean you up," he pressed his forehead to mine. "Get you into bed. Fuck you until you realize who I am. I'm staying with you. By your side. And I'll explain everything."

~

"I CAN'T–" MY VOICE WAS HOARSE FROM SCREAMING AS I SHOOK MY HEAD unable to move from Reed's arm around me as he held up another bite of food to my lips.

"I'm stuffed."

His eyes heated as I blushed at the double entendre after what he'd done to me. He took the bite for himself instead.

I laid in Reed's arms after he'd cleaned us both up and fed me until I was satiated, and then he took it for himself.

"I got you groceries, too," he murmured, breath ruffling my hair. "I just have to put them away."

My mind drifted as Reed ate.

I could see him taking me in occasionally, but I laid back against him, drifting.

The sheets pooled at my waist, the cool air on my nipples causing them to pebble, but the initial embarrassment had faded when Reed had seen and felt every part of me.

Especially after what he'd made me do in the shower again.

I had a feeling. You're so sensitive after you come.

I figured if I pushed against that spot hard enough, over and over, it would make you squirt like that.

My mind had gone blank, my senses overloaded by the sheer magnitude of the release.

It was as if every nerve ending in my body was on fire, the pleasure so acute that it bordered on pain. Now, I felt myself floating.

He had driven me crazy in the process as he'd cleaned my sensitized flesh and whispered endless praises against my skin, trying to break down all my defenses.

I'd felt consumed by him underneath the water when he'd slid his fingers inside my tender body and proceeded to do to me what he'd done earlier.

He'd angled his fingers into a part of me that I felt was too sensitive. And then he proceeded to keep his promises.

I'd screamed so loud I was worried people thought I'd be dying.

I had been squirming in his hold, and it had only made the orgasm more intense.

Made him growl and hold me down, fucking into me using his fingers curled against that spot. I died a little then.

Under the spray of the showers, I felt it coming out of me as Reed had all but growled his pleasure at watching me do it.

Just like that, Angel. Squirt all over me.

Before turning me around in the middle of it, sliding into me, and slamming into that spot, prolonging the sensations.

This is the position that does it for you, isn't it, Angel? The one that hits it so deep you lose your mind. It was.

I'd never come like that in my life.

I was grateful for the wet sprays washing it away, but I felt it gushing. I'd almost passed out with the intensity of it if he hadn't held me up.

Now I was sore. So sore it hurt to walk. Reed had hummed his pleasure, letting me know he'd love for me to stay in bed all day with him.

Where he'd tongue his apologies into my skin.

After drying me off, he'd made himself comfortable in nothing but a towel, tapping on his phone while I applied products. Lotions, serums, scents.

His tattoos flexed as he tapped away on his phone, the soft glow of the screen illuminating his chiseled features.

Reed had been comfortable with his nudity and had taken a look at the pajamas in my hand after and shaken his head.

For the first time in my life, I leaned against a man in my bed, and my mind was blank as I focused on solely the moment.

Not the tasks that needed to come.

I was completely mush.

Reed's gentle voice broke the comfortable silence. "Penny for your thoughts?"

"I can't think."

His lips brushed against my exposed shoulder. "Good. I gotta get some work done after you get some sleep, so don't let me keep you."

My gaze drifted to the pink bedside digital clock, its soft glow illuminating the late hour. Nearly three am.

Which meant we'd been at it for *hours.*

Avani had left at around eight, and then the note...

The thought of the threatening message brought me back to reality.

"What are you going to do about the note?" I asked, my voice soft but laced with concern. Reed was silent for a bit.

"I'll run it through fingerprint scans, see if it holds anything. I'll also go through the cameras outside your door down to the street. See if anyone looks suspicious. I need to install some extra security cameras and doorbell cameras, and then make sure the note is where it stops," He paused, his tone becoming more serious. "And you're getting a bodyguard. Before you give me that look, that's non-negotiable."

I pressed my lips together, knowing there was no room for argument. Not with the look in his eyes.

His brain had processed all of that, and I knew it was his job, but it was completely over my mind. I could see him thinking. I knew there was more, but there was another question burning on my tongue, bigger than the note.

"Where did you get that scar?" I asked, my curiosity getting the better of me.

When Reed had been on his phone while drying himself off, I had been distracted by his body.

I had known he had a sleeve of tattoos on one arm, but I didn't know about the scar on his back the first night. It was a long, ugly gash between his shoulder blades, and it looked...painful. Like someone had tried to cut something out of him.

Even now, I wondered who had done that to him.

"Which one?" he asked, but the hint of darkness in his voice told me he knew exactly which scar I meant.

I gave him a pointed look, and he took a swig of water as if steeling himself.

For a moment, I thought he wouldn't tell me.

"My stepfather."

I didn't know much about Reed, but I absorbed this new piece of knowledge like a sponge.

His revelation about his stepfather left me with more questions, and I couldn't help but ask. "And your Mum?"

Reed fell silent, his gaze distant and his expression unreadable.

The seconds ticked by, and just as I thought he might not answer, one side of his mouth quirked up in a bitter smile.

"Who do you think handed him the knife?"

CHAPTER 16
REED

WATCHING ALISHA, I CHEWED ON MY GYRO CAREFULLY.

Her eyes, usually bright and expressive, were now wide with a mix of emotions I couldn't quite decipher.

The usual rosy glow that adorned her cheeks had faded, replaced by a pale complexion as she processed my presence.

From the very first instant, I laid eyes on her, one thing about Alisha had been absolutely certain: her warmth.

It radiated from her like the sun.

Her presence alone had the power to dispel any lingering darkness, filling the space around her with a glow that drew me in.

Sitting on Alisha's bed against her tufted headboard, I had my legs spread open and her form resting against me.

It was a dream, or it would be if I didn't have my therapist's voice in my head.

Let yourself out to let them in.

I just wasn't expecting Alisha's eyes to grow wet as I watched her absorb what I had said.

"What?" Her whisper cut through my thoughts.

As though she couldn't fathom a mother hurting her child.

Because Alisha wouldn't.

She nurtured Avani and her home. I saw it in the colors around her, the warmth in every space, the occasional plants, and mismatched books. Signs of femininity that spoke of love and lush laughter.

I shook my head as though I didn't know what she meant. I did know. I just didn't want to dig any further than this.

"What did you do after?" Her voice quivered as the tears now flowed freely. "W-who took care of you?"

In the aftermath, I had driven myself to urgent care, unable to afford the ER, leaving my mother and half-brother, Adam, distantly shouting in my ears.

That night, I slept in my car, parked in a twenty-four-hour diner.

I'd *never* forget those moments. That night was engraved into my memory. The driving motivation for me being so successful now. The following day, I enlisted in the military. Gabriel had already been serving for two years.

I recounted the story to Alisha, omitting the details she didn't need to know.

"You're killing me," I murmured, my heart aching at the sight of Alisha's tears. Seeing her cry, especially over me, was unbearable. I dipped my head to her neck. "It's all right."

"Why would someone do that to their child?" she mumbled against my temple. "It's barbaric."

"In a way, it made me better," I admitted into her skin, surprised at my own willingness to admit it. "It taught me about people and their motivations."

The experience showed me that even though my mother loved me as a boy, her love wasn't strong enough to overcome the threat I posed to her family and happiness.

It set me on a path of intelligence, honing my skills in people and dissecting their intentions within moments of meeting them. Few people could get through my analysis with their true character undetected.

Gabriel. The team.

It didn't matter if people didn't pick me. I picked people and created my world. I was good at reading people.

I'd picked her. I just needed her to pick me.

It was her kindness, above all, and the warmth she exhibited that had attracted me.

On top of Alisha's determination to do right by her sister and not allowing anyone to come into her life until *she* had been ready for it. She gave Avani the grace no one ever gave me.

I wanted to know every little thing about her and absorb her until I got to the center.

I found myself letting her in a little more at the sound of her sobs.

I didn't know why I thought sharing my past would help, but as I sat there with Alisha, the words began to pour out of me.

"I don't hate her," I found myself saying. "My mom came from a well-off family. She had me as a teenager and married my stepfather when her parents refused to support her. She barely finished high school, and he was older than her."

It wasn't ideal.

But she did it for me.

I didn't know what happened to my biological father.

I told Alisha the story that I knew.

Alisha's sobs gradually faded as she listened intently to my story.

The room fell silent, save for the sound of our breathing and the distant hum of the city beyond the walls.

"He wasn't always a monster. Not until my mom had my younger brother, Adam. He was the spitting image of my father, while I...I looked too much like mine."

A reminder of what he didn't want.

As time passed, the difference in treatment became more apparent.

I was an outcast. I went to a different school, denied the things Adam had.

While he focused on his schoolwork, I was left to do the housework after school, eating scraps, and feeling like a stranger in my own home.

I watched Adam get all the things I didn't, and he had no clue.

Or he didn't care. I didn't know.

There was nothing for me.

I did what I had to do to survive, learning to exist somewhere in the middle.

At least I had it better than Gabriel. We'd been friends since high school. Until him, I had been alone, but from that loneliness, I learned to succeed. I didn't share all the details with Alisha.

"As I got older, things got worse. Until it all shattered that night. I left and never looked back." A humorless smile tugged at my lips.

"It's not a sad story, Lish. I found a family at Titan. I have a home now. I have everything I could want." Almost.

"But it also hurt you. It left you vulnerable," she whispered, her breath hitching. "And your brother..."

Her eyes were horrified about me and Adam.

I didn't tell her about his emails.

I hadn't responded to them.

117

"You shouldn't have had to go through that. Sometimes the things that don't kill us still leave us scarred. I can't imagine what you felt like as a child. I am so very proud of you for overcoming all that." She shook her head in disbelief, her eyes wet and shining with admiration. "You're incredible."

Unfamiliar sensations blossomed in my chest at her praise.

I'd been commended by the military and government officials for my work, but never...like this. I never told anyone.

Maybe Gabriel.

A part of me acknowledged the broken pieces, the vulnerable young man I'd been, bleeding and scraping by with a bruised sense of self as I started anew.

Yet, another part of me was grateful, for it was that young man's hunger for more, for better, that had led me here. To being a Titan.

"You've done a lot of incredible things," I said softly. "You've built an entire empire."

A bashful smile graced her lips as she ducked her head, her hair falling forward around her face. "I take photos for a living. It's hardly labor."

"Don't sell yourself short," I insisted, knowing that many of my guys had harbored admiration for her ever since Nate had teasingly brought her up to me. "I know you've worked tirelessly to get where you are. To support your sister, who I always knew was your top priority."

Alisha's achievements spoke for themselves.

She'd started young and taken the world by storm in her early twenties, all while caring for her sister.

My admiration for her ran deeper than she could imagine. Her eyes widened at my words, surprise etched across her delicate features.

"Why do you think I didn't ask you the moment I laid eyes on you? I wouldn't have gone after you unless you were ready."

Had she been willing, I would have made her mine years ago. But I was a patient hunter.

It was a trait Gabriel and I shared, an understanding that the chase was always worth it.

Because when I finally had her, she would belong to me.

She would think of no one else.

"I waited," I whispered. "Just like you did." I kept my tone low and soothing, as if speaking too loudly might startle her.

"That's how I know you try to run from me. Because I'm aware that I scare you."

"Not because of what you want in bed..." Her words trailed off, a hint of reassurance in her tone.

No, I knew that aspect didn't scare her. "No, I didn't think so."

I loved the delightful flush that colored her cheeks.

Even now, she swallowed hard, looking as if she might bolt at any moment.

But I held her close. I had no intention of letting her go anywhere without me by her side.

"I think you try to test me, to see if I'll stay with you," I murmured, my voice low and filled with conviction. "You try to push me away out of fear, thinking that if you push hard enough, I'll walk away from you."

I leaned closer, my lips hovering just above her parted lips.

"I don't scare easily, Angel. I've made up my mind that I like you."

The warmth of her breath mingled with mine as I continued. "I can assuage every fear you have and then some. I've waited years for you. A few words aren't enough to push me away."

She exhaled shakily, her body trembling slightly beneath my touch as the weight of my words sank deep into her very being.

The room seemed to hold its breath, the air heavy.

"Let me in, Lish. I won't let you down."

I wondered if I had said too much, too soon, but the need to express my feelings overrode any hesitation.

Let her in.

"W-why are you doing this?" Her voice was barely a whisper, hazel eyes wide with a mix of wonder and vulnerability.

I felt the corners of my lips tug upward in a gentle smile.

"Because I know you've been abandoned too, and I have no intention of doing the same to you. Because I see something in you that's worth fighting for."

And I'm not going to stop until I have you.

I paused, my gaze locking with hers. "Because I know that I am more than one night to you, just as you are to me."

I needed her to understand, to believe in the truth of my words. "And I am not going anywhere."

CHAPTER 17
ALISHA

HE WASN'T GOING ANYWHERE.

At the moment, he sat across from me at the kitchen island, working on his laptop while I focused on my own.

He had decided to work from my place, spending more time with me.

During a conference call with Maxine DuPont, the CEO of EllaBeauty, and the marketing manager, I pitched my ideas for the spring campaign, complete with sketches, fabric swatches, and photoshoot concepts.

Maxine and I had a relationship, largely because since she hired me as a spokesperson for her brand five years ago, their sales had reached an all-time high in their seventy-two-year history.

I worked with them for about three years before doing my own thing.

Maxine was a hands-on leader who believed in maintaining a personal connection with her brand. Countless influencers and models fought to work with EllaBeauty. I was surprised I'd even been picked up for their campaign. It had changed my life in the nick of time for me to support Avani.

As always, Maxine jokingly brought up her son, Matteo, a good friend. I couldn't help but laugh it off despite her recurring attempts to set us up.

"...Teo is showcasing his new cars at the F1 race if you're interested." Maxine mentioned, her eyebrows raised suggestively.

Even the marketing manager grinned at Maxine's not-so-subtle approach to playing matchmaker.

However, there were a few reasons why I couldn't fully engage with Matteo.

One reason was currently frowning at my laptop from across the kitchen island, looking devastating in a hoodie, making it difficult for me to concentrate as I pressed my thighs together.

Biting my lip.

Squirming.

"I would love to go," I forced a polite laugh, breathless under the intensity of Reed's gaze." But I'm afraid Avani has an event at her college."

Although I didn't want to insult Maxine or imply that I wasn't interested in dating Matteo.

But I wasn't sure if Reed considered me his girlfriend yet.

Despite his constant presence over the past week since the note incident, I refrained from mentioning him. We didn't label it. I didn't think we knew how to.

Maxine assured me they would be in touch, encouraging me to email her my ideas. I planned to collaborate with them, staying loyal to my established fan base and the crowd that already adored me and my products.

My gaze drifted to Reed, who had returned to quietly working on his laptop.

Earlier that afternoon, a tall blonde man with crystalline blue eyes and an eager-to-please demeanor had stopped by my apartment, introducing himself as Kellan Watts. Towering over me at six-two, he wore a charming letterman jacket and a wide, infectious grin that matched the gleam in his eyes as he took me in.

As he diligently followed Reed, I resisted the urge to ruffle his messy blond hair.

He looks like he just graduated college.

Kellan dropped off two duffels for Reed and asked me if I needed anything. Reed had introduced us, stating that Kellan would be my point of contact when Reed wasn't here if I needed anything. Because even if Reed did want to be my full-time bodyguard, he had a company to run. Kellan would help me with anything else.

When he left, I looked at Reed. "He's absolutely adorable. Like a golden retriever."

Reed's tongue darted out between his teeth as he grinned. "Would you believe me if I told you he's a sniper who speaks ten languages?"

I discovered that Reed worked for a company where most of the people were former military or CIA personnel. It was a little insane for me to comprehend that Reed had been as well.

"I would not have guessed that." Kellan looked like a poster child for an Ivy League school. As I said it out loud, a deep laugh came from Reed.

"I'll be sure to tell him."

Reed warned me the doorbell would go off several times during the day, and it had.

From more groceries to food delivery, Reed had placed the flowers he'd gotten me from last night on my kitchen island and made himself comfortable.

His creature comforts in my home. And it felt like our home.

As I watched Reed and Kellan work, I couldn't help but feel a mix of emotions.

On one hand, I was grateful for their presence and their protection.

On the other hand, the fact that I needed protection was unsettling, and I couldn't shake the feeling of unease that had taken root in the pit of my stomach.

Just a few days ago, my life was normal.

And now this?

I tried to focus on the positive, on the fact that Reed was here.

In the past few days since he'd been here, Reed had established himself in my home, sleeping in my bed and making morning coffee for himself and me before he worked from home.

I thought I would be driven crazy by now, but Reed had a way of calming me down and easing me into things in his way.

My body felt sore and bruised but mended and healed.

The dichotomy could only exist with Reed, who took me every night until I had simply tapped out last night, being too sore to continue.

It didn't feel like I could get enough.

I felt starved.

Longing for him even now when I should've been focusing on Maxine, who was talking with her marketing manager about the timing of the release of the clothing line.

"Alisha—" I heard. "I think the camera froze."

No, I was just gaping at the hot hunk sitting across from me.

Who was currently sporting a smirk since he knew the camera did not freeze.

"I think April would be good," I said breathlessly. "I'm sorry, internet connection's not always reliable."

At that, I bit back a smile when Reed frowned.

He got up and checked to ensure the internet was fine.

Reed upgraded my internet and added a few devices to my home.

He'd spent the week setting them up through my home.

One of them was called a raspberry pie, as he called it. A doorbell camera, a camera that faced my apartment door. I chatted a bit longer before they had to go.

"I'm so excited," I said before I could stop myself to Reed when it was over. "I have always wanted to launch a collection for women to have nice things to wear to bed that are still affordable products."

I looked up and saw him smiling. "Do you want to see the concept?"

He didn't say a word as he walked over and pulled up the barstool beside me, nodding.

As I explained, Reed listened intently, and I explained to him the idea behind the Poppy Project and wanting to ensure every woman had clothes, period products, and things to make herself feel good but also a feeling of comfort for herself.

"I felt inspired by how I had grown up, with this concept of comfort, but style still embedded in every piece. It's just a rough draft..." I continued to tell him about different style concepts. I showed him lingerie and pajamas and beautiful dresses.

He repeated it back. "You wanted a fairy core meets dark seduction, and you thought these looks would balance it out?"

Hearing words like that fall out of Reed's mouth shouldn't have given me so much pleasure.

Especially when said with such seriousness. "Because that's where your style has evolved to."

I nodded, my cheeks hurting from my smile. "I thought I could offer extremely flattering clothes around each theme separately. I don't always feel like wearing one or the other, so I thought of combining them." I pulled up the sketches.

"It would be the best of both worlds. I want to give it themes, too. I thought calling the first one, 'Lost in the Glen,' would be super cute."

It was so feminine and pretty, and I could see women loving it. Which was the point.

I explained to him about the textures of fabric, sparkles, and pieces that would make any woman feel feminine at an affordable price point.

"I want to make women feel good about themselves," I said calmly. "I think Avani and I had that growing up. I feel like it contributed to my success."

As I spoke, I noticed Reed gave me the space to be me.

I didn't have to pretend to be dumb or pretend like I didn't know things or make myself smaller.

I spoke to him like I did at my meetings, and he listened.

At one point, he wrote something down, and I felt my heart sputter at the intent and focus in his eyes.

A little smile played on his lips as I continued.

When I finished, he echoed a lot of it back to me, asking follow-up questions.

"Have you thought about perfume or skincare with it?"

A burst of pleasure went through me at his perception, and at my smile, he grinned.

"It's funny you should mention that," I hadn't brought this up with *anyone* yet.

"I have been talking to a small shop I found to design a few natural scents. It's run by women. I wanted to know if I could combine my charity with them to help employ survivors of domestic violence to give them a source of income, purpose, a safe place to go, and internships..."

I told him about how Avani was a volunteer for me, and it helped to educate people on the less-pretty side of life.

"I want to pitch it when the scents are ready, and each one will complement the looks in tandem, but you can still mix and match. Because where's the fun if you can't?"

I told Reed about a book series Avani had loved that inspired me with their aesthetic. I grew excited to tell him about my blog, all the makeup, and all the styles. Reed sat with me, asking questions and never once making me feel like it was silly.

His smile grew. "When we picked our call signs for assignments, Gabriel wanted us to stick to a theme. The company is Titan, so we stuck to that theme. I'm Jupiter, and he's Apollo."

I was delighted. "Like nicknames?"

Reed explained to me it was to be able to talk to each other in short-hand without people knowing. "That's so neat, I want one."

"You have one, you're Angel," Reed kissed my cheek. "Tell me about where you're launching this. Internet only? I can build your site securely. Did you want one or two separate ones..." I blinked at Reed, who looked at my screen and then at me.

I didn't even understand what he was saying. "...should pay DuPont a visit to see their server racks...." *What?*

He looked at my expression and paused. "I lost ya."

"A little...but I think you're asking to make sure the site and my project are secure." He smiled and nodded. It was interesting navigating each other's jobs.

Reed and I both tried to ask each other things to warm up to it. "Is that why you set up the dessert?"

His brow furrowed. "The dessert...."

"The pie?"

"Oh, you mean the raspberry *pi?*" I nodded. A breathless smile came over his face. "It's p-i, not p-i-e." He spelled out. "It's to...never mind."

"Why did we need the pi?" I couldn't figure out where it was. "Did you hide it in the apartment?"

He was grinning ear to ear. "Come here, Angel. I'll build your site for you."

I didn't know what he found amusing, but he kissed me soundly. "You juggled this with your sister in your life?"

I had. An odd look entered his eyes.

"I mean, Avani's all grown up," I said, and then I caught myself.

Reed had told me earlier this week he wanted me to practice accepting when I received praise. "But yes, I did."

His smile was worth it.

"It sounds incredible, Angel. I'm looking forward to going with you when you launch it."

He grinned at my expression.

My heart rate escalated. "You want to come?"

I was surprised. Reed did not look like the type to enter girly stores with me and watch me take photos with fans.

"Yeah, don't I look like I belong in a feminine clothing store?" I could get used to laughing with Reed.

CHAPTER 18
ALISHA

One evening, I recognized the dark shadows under Reed's eyes from staying with me.

"I'm worried about you," I whispered as he cuddled me close after making me come over and over again.

Rising over him, I held his face in my other hand, taking him in. "You're not sleeping. I can feel you getting up all night."

Worry entered his eyes. "I'm sorry, am I keeping you up?"

"*No*, Reed. But you need to go back to your place and get some sleep. Didn't you say Kellan could come by to switch with you if I needed it?" I added. "It's not that I don't want you to stay. I also feel tremendously guilty watching you live like this."

Because it was because of *me*.

Part of me acknowledged I was being selfish by not moving in with Reed. I don't know why I felt frozen with fear at leaving my space for his. Why? I felt *paralyzed*.

Reed wasn't sleeping well because he kept one eye open at night for me.

For a long moment, he was quiet. "Please, I'll be okay. If Kellan can get you a day off, I'd rather you be okay as well." I could see the shadows under his eyes. "I'll still see you, but you have to sleep."

He closed his eyes for a moment and tipped his head. I kissed him. I didn't tell him how it felt like all this was happening because of me. And it hurt me to see him like this. Reed hadn't figured anything out over the last few days, and I knew he was burning out when I watched him today.

He hadn't left.

I could never forgive myself if something happened to Reed because of me, and I needed him to take care of himself as well. Something I knew he'd neglected because of me.

"I'll still come back to you every night."

He cut me off as I opened my mouth to protest. "Just to kiss you, make love to you, I can do that."

I smiled softly. "Nothing would make me happier."

I couldn't believe I had said I didn't want anything serious with this man. Even guilt at what was happening hadn't stopped me from offering myself to him.

I whispered it into his lips. "I like that you didn't play games with me."

"I like that you gave me a chance."

As his gaze shifted, I trailed my fingers down his body, feeling the tension building beneath my touch. He had pleasured me only moments ago, yet the hunger in his eyes told me he desired more. And this time, I wanted to be daring.

Give me a chance, beautiful girl.

With determination, I rose up, straddling him. I relished the way he drank in my every move, his hands gripping my hips possessively.

"Lean forward," his dark whisper sank into my pores as I obeyed, and he captured my lips, his hand working between my legs to position himself at my tender entrance, still soaking and wet. I moaned around his tongue as he slowly sank into me, just the tip. I pulled back and pushed my hips down, taking more of him.

"I'll never get used to how beautiful you look right there," Reed looked at me with such emotion I'd never forget it. "The moment you take me, struggling just a little bit, enough to make me lose it." I *was* struggling.

"Just…a…little bit," I panted, taking him deeper, pressing my hips down and rising up a little.

He arched his head back with a groan. "That's it, Angel. Keep going." I was. I was squirming, stopping for a moment to catch my breath.

"Lish," his growl made me clench harder. "Lean forward."

I did as his hands gripped my hips.

Reed gently eased out of me a few inches as though testing me out before shoving his entire length in me.

My scream mingled with his groan of approval as he bottomed out.

Reed always gave me a moment to adjust.

His hand pressed into the back of my neck, drawing my lips to his. For long, searing moments, all I felt was his tongue stroking my mouth while his length pulsed inside of me.

"I can't believe I let you run for years."

I smiled into his mouth. "*Let* me?"

The delicious stretch of him sliding into me, filling me while I clamped down, made me lose focus.

Hips grinding of their own accord taking my pleasure, every dip brushing my clit as I moaned into Reed's mouth.

He held my face in his hands as I whimpered.

"Take what you need from me."

Tears of relief mingled with desire streamed down my cheeks as the waves of ecstasy crashed over me, leaving me vulnerable and alive. Wanting.

His touch was coaxing, guiding me through the storm, his other hand firmly gripping my hip, grounding me in the moment.

His mouth claimed mine, responding to his every touch with a hunger that consumed me.

I surrendered to the sensation, clinging to him as though my very life depended on it.

At that moment, I wanted nothing else, nobody else, no one ever.

But him.

Breathless, I whispered against his lips. "I feel like I've known you my whole life. I want you so much."

He inhaled shakily. "Just give me a chance, beautiful girl."

A moan left my mouth as his hands gripped my hips, grinding against me to the time of his tongue thrusting back in.

I couldn't think as Reed held me and adjusted me before thrusting back into me. I gasped in delight.

"That's the spot, isn't it?" Dark seduction rolled off him in waves. "Right there."

And then he proceeded to reduce me to a mess as he held me tight to him while bucking his hips up and into me.

No longer grinding but repeatedly slamming into me until I screamed. I was a sensitized mess as he pressed his lips to my temple and licked my tears.

He swore as I sobbed into his neck, every thrust grinding my clit into him.

"*Oh, God, yes, yes, yes, Reed.*"

"*Tell me who you belong to.*"

I was losing it.

I felt my orgasm brewing so quickly after the first one.

"*You,*" my abdomen tightened, and my legs shook around his hips as the slap of him against me became one continuous noise. "Only you."

My orgasm took my breath away as I bit down on his shoulder to keep from releasing a shrill scream as I came.

I whimpered and quivered, pulling his own orgasm as he growled his release into my skin, hot puffs of breath between us as I hungrily reached for his kisses.

There were always kisses.

And I realized I could get used to Reed manhandling me.

CHAPTER 19
REED

I DIDN'T WANT TO GO.

Existing with Alisha felt like home.

Finding her quirks only made me crave her more. I fucking liked being around her.

From her morning grumpiness to waking up with her, her hazelnut coffee with milk, her tendency to scatter socks across the floor, the chaos of her closet, and the way she left her belongings strewn about.

Open mail, letters, forgotten books for Avani—it was all part of *her*.

It became my mission to be around her, locking doors, securing her windows before bed, gently nudging her to take care of herself.

Her doing the same for me. She wasn't wrong. I needed to go back to the Titan manor. Or Midtown.

I needed to focus on my life too. Sometimes at her place, we worked around each other.

I worked into the night, fell asleep after her, and woke up before her. But I liked pushing myself.

Eventually, Alisha started pulling me to bed.

Only after pleasing both of us, did she finally ask me questions. She'd been confused adorably, and asked me about why I was a dominant partner who didn't mind certain things.

I told her, while I liked the idea of a submissive, I didn't have the desire to pin a woman to a St Andrew cross for hours and demolish her.

Younger me had wanted all that, but I wanted something different now. I liked Alisha for all that she was.

Minus Alisha wearing a ring, someday, I'd never ask for a slave. I didn't want one. Her submission in bed, as was our entire relationship, was a choice. She didn't have to worry about other women or me controlling her.

It went against everything in my body to walk away from her. But she wasn't wrong. I switched with Kellan earlier on in the day, so he could go home in the evening. Out of all the newbies I'd taken to Kellan because he reminded me of what Gabriel could've been had the world not ripped his heart out.

Try as he might, Gabriel reminded me of someone who'd fallen into the darkness. He relished it.

They were similar in build, Gabriel being taller, but where one was a walking glacier, Kellan was in fact a golden retriever.

It was exactly why I'd hired someone who had also done really well at deception. He looked harmless.

Until he killed for her.

Because he would. If anything happened to her I'd make all the other men I'd threatened for her look like a doozy.

I had done checks on all of Alisha's old dates. All of three.

Including Matteo DuPont, the pretty boy billionaire who technically wasn't a date, but I didn't discount it.

The first two were in other relationships so I needed to pay DuPont a visit. Not that he seemed like the type to fuck with women seriously, but maybe I just wanted to *talk*.

And maybe Gabriel will finally get out of the icebox of his heart.

Pigs had a higher chance of learning to fly than both of those things.

While Evie flagged every negative comment on Alisha's social media, I went to pay DuPont a visit.

Alisha had no idea the level of oversight I had over what everyone did. Evie had swan-dived into Alisha's privacy without a single regard since I'd asked.

I'd also messaged Gabriel.

As someone who dabbled with the darker stuff than me, and had the stomach to handle it, he would know what to do while I took my time off with her.

I was aware if Alisha didn't let me move her into my apartment, located in one of the most secure buildings in the city, I would need to assuage her fears and let her stay in hers. *For now.*

I wanted to get her out of there sooner, but I knew Alisha wouldn't want to leave. I didn't know how to convince her to stay with me.

Because until she did, this was going to be brutal for both of us in different ways.

I logically couldn't afford to split my time between Titan, her potential note problem, and Alisha.

Not without stretching myself thin and while I didn't mind doing that, I knew I couldn't be the man I needed to be for her at fifty percent operating capacity.

I finally had a piece of her and I didn't want to lose that person to anything. I had known all the pieces moving in my mind of finding out who left the note.

None of which I told her I was doing. Or visiting Matteo DuPont. I walked into the office Downtown where I knew DuPont was working out for the time being.

DuPont owned a luxury sports car company, and specialized in working specifically with race cars.

The entire center of the structure was a vast, open area, with high ceilings and industrial lighting that illuminated every corner.

It was a hive of activity, with cars in various stages of completion scattered throughout. The air was filled with the sounds of machinery, the clank of metal on metal.

In stark contrast to the raw, industrial feel of the warehouse, DuPont's office was a study in sleek, modern design.

Located on the top level overlooking the production floor, the back wall of the office was encased in walls of glass, allowing natural light to flood the space. I strode through the sleek warehouse, taking in the sight of car parts being meticulously assembled and the people dressed to the fucking nines.

I had dressed the part today.

Donning a tailored black suit that felt foreign against my skin. On my wrist, I wore a watch borrowed from Gabriel, a timepiece that could probably fund a small nation. I hated playing dress-up, but Gabriel told me I couldn't set foot on DuPont's turf without looking the part.

House rules.

I tugged at the goddamn tie, feeling it constrict around my throat. Gabriel didn't mind it. I didn't see the point. I already had the cash and nothing to prove.

I lacked the pedigree of a wealthy family to fall back on like Matteo did.

As I walked, I noticed DuPont's secretary, a middle-aged woman whose eyes lingered on the tattoos that peeked out from beneath my sleeve, her gaze a mixture of curiosity and intrigue.

I kept my face impassive thinking about how Alisha had loved to trace them with her tongue.

Earlier this morning I'd dropped by before coming to see DuPont. I wasn't expecting her reaction. I had an entire closet of tailored designer suits I didn't bother with. I had wanted to see her.

She'd been walking out of her bedroom half ready. *"Kellan, I need to —"* She'd come to an abrupt stop, her eyes raking down my clothing choice. Her eyes went wide.

"Clean up nice, hm?" I had asked not understanding.

Kellan smirked at her expression. I'd barely gotten it out of my mouth to Kellan that he should go see if the sun was out today. The other man had gotten the hint and beat feet as I'd all but picked her up.

I'd never seen my girl so frantic for me to get inside of her.

I could still feel the sting of Alisha's nails on my back as I'd taken her against the wall so hard I'd knocked over a few pictures and Alisha had assured me it was fine.

To not stop. I couldn't let my girl down.

Out of all the reactions in the world, that was not the one I had been prepared for.

I'd put this shit on more often if it gets you like this.

Alisha's body had moved, her hips working, struggling to take me and ride me, settling for a grind that I knew bumped her clit every time.

Take it from me.

Reed...I can't— I need—

She was uninhibited and wild. I fucking loved it.

I replaced her fingers on her nipples with my own, pinching them, and driving my hips up to help my girl out. She came apart within seconds.

Oh God, Reed, harder.

I had pounded deep through her orgasm only bringing me closer to mine. I fucking loved the way she sighed as I came.

Such a good cum slut, taking me so deep.

Her head lolled in a nod as I said it. And didn't that make my ego stand ten feet tall.

I think I like you fuck drunk on me.

I was depraved, but Alisha met me every step of the way.

I think I might keep you tied up to my bed and fuck you whenever I want. Her pussy clenched. Hard.

She murmured her agreement into my lips as she kissed me after.

Now the scent of roses and honey lingered all over my suit and my skin, her taste in my mouth, hazelnut and Alisha all over being. I wanted to hold her to my heart and keep her with me everywhere I went.

I didn't remember how I got to DuPonts office.

I moved on autopilot, shaking memories of Alisha out of my mind.

It was the only way to calm myself as I entered Matteo DuPont's office, watching him rise from his desk with feline grace.

At six foot three, he was a lean tower of coiled muscle, his navy suit impeccably tailored to his athletic frame.

Despite being a few years younger than me, he exuded the charm and confidence of a man who had never known struggle.

He looked so young. His face, untouched by struggle.

Those electric blue orbs, rimmed in black, marked him unmistakably as a DuPont.

They gleamed with mischief and something darker, standing out in stark contrast to his clean-cut appearance.

With his artfully tousled ink-black hair, his grin in place, he was the quintessential playboy. *He likes Alisha.*

I grasped his hand firmly, pushing thoughts of Alisha to the back of my mind.

But they lingered there, taunting me.

Her screams of pleasure, the way she clenched around me, her pleas for more as I drove towards my own release.

The knowledge that Matteo had openly declared his crush on her years ago only fueled the fire in my veins.

"Mr. Whittaker," Matteo drawled, his light accent adding to his air of sophistication. "I received a call from Gabriel Monroe at three in the morning. I'm aware that I cannot refuse. To what do I owe the displeasure of meeting one of his operatives?"

His smile was sharp, canines flashing in a dark expression that suggested that Gabriel's late-night call had been far from pleasant.

"Did you date Alisha Malhotra?" I asked bluntly, dispensing with pleasantries.

My mind was a whirlwind of emotions, jealousy, fear, and a burning need to protect Alisha from the unknown threat.

The thought of her staying with Kellan, relying on someone else for safety, twisted like a knife in my gut. It should be me by her side. And I couldn't do that for her.

Matteo's aqua eyes widened briefly before he muttered a curse in French. "I missed a lunch date with a supermodel for this?"

His nonchalance only fueled the rage simmering beneath my skin.

"I'm not going to repeat myself."

Matteo's playful smile never wavered. "I guess she wasn't exactly *that* type of model. But what can I say? I'm not picky."

His cavalier attitude pissed me off.

Reminding me of Nate on his worst days. My mind was clouded, my thoughts far from clear.

In a flash, I had him pinned against the floor-to-ceiling window, my hand wrapped around his throat.

"Are you threatening my girl?" I growled, not giving a damn that I was on his turf.

Matteo laughed, his eyes gleaming with amusement. "Why would I do that?"

I searched those alien blue depths for deceit but found only entertainment. If anything, it grated on my nerves more.

"You've been openly crushing on her for years."

My grip tightened.

The memory of his declarations of affection for Alisha haunted me, taunting me with the possibility that if not for me, she would be with him.

Matteo scoffed, another laugh escaping despite his predicament.

"*Reed* Whittaker," he said, shoving at me with unexpected strength. "I'm not interested in Alisha. As beautiful as she—"

"Watch your fucking mouth."

"*Or you can watch yours,*" a deep voice interjected from behind me, accompanied by the distinctive click of a safety being turned off.

I'd been so consumed by Matteo, so blinded by my own turbulent emotions, that I'd forgotten about the tricks up his sleeve.

This entire building was like his cars, sleek and shiny with hidden compartments.

I never heard him move.

"He's friendly," Matteo said with a grin tipping his head to the side, tendrils of his hair moving to the side. He was unsurprised by the other man...or the apparent weapons in the room. *Everyone had secrets.*

Matteo was addressing the man behind me. I felt the gun at my neck pressing into it.

"You should pick your friends better, *Teo.*" His voice was clear and strong.

135

No accent.

I didn't even feel him in the room.

I released Matteo and turned, blinking in surprise at the sight before me, minus the barrel of a silencer on me. Glancing back at Matteo, he grinned like a madman at my expression.

"You have a twin?"

Standing behind me was someone who could have been Matteo's carbon copy, but upon closer inspection, I noticed slight differences.

He's as tall as me.

I took in the newcomer's lean, muscular build and the coiled, savage energy that rolled off him in waves.

Dressed in a sleek black ensemble, his wild blue eyes shone brighter than the other DuPonts, a fierce intensity burning within them.

Matteo's grin widened.

"Non," he said, as the other DuPont lowered his gun at Matteo's gesture.

This DuPont was unlike the others, his speech devoid of any accent.

"Not a twin," Matteo clarified, straightening his tie.

But they were related.

This DuPont was even more striking than Matteo, a fact I hadn't thought possible.

His eyes, brighter than any I'd seen, studied me like a tiger stalking its prey through the grass.

His black hair, tousled and falling over one eye.

He doesn't make any noise. He's trained.

"He's family," Matteo said, the words carrying a significant weight.

I was only aware of two DuPont brothers, and no one else possessed Phillipe DuPont's distinct eyes and that jet-black hair.

It didn't escape my notice that this man had never shared his name.

Matteo's family member, reluctantly backed off and sauntered to the couches on the other side of the room, observing Matteo and me with a calculating gaze.

His entire profile screamed something darker than me.

"I have nothing to do with your Alisha." Matteo stated calmly, as if the last few minutes hadn't happened. "I'm happy she is happy, though you are not what I expected."

No, I wasn't what I expected either.

He paused before adding. "However, if she is being threatened, we can always offer our assistance."

He tilted his head towards the other DuPont with the gleaming eyes sitting on the couch, who looked less than thrilled about his help being offered.

"I got it," I forced the words out.

"Then why did you come here?" Matteo's smooth smile was in place even as his eyes took me in, having adjusted his suit and leaned against his desk. "If you have no need for my assistance, and you knew before you walked in that I have never dated Alisha, what was your motivation?"

DuPont was a ruthless businessman, and just as I had been assessing him, he had been assessing me.

I didn't answer his question, seeing in his eyes that there was nothing there. He wouldn't be the type to go after Alisha.

It wasn't his style.

"If I wanted Alisha, I would have her," he said softly. "I enjoy flirting with her, like all women. But I would not defile someone so lovely."

The odd twist in his words gave me pause, a flicker of uncertainty in my already turbulent thoughts.

I saw the DuPont on the couch stretch back with a wicked grin on his lips, sharing a private joke.

Matteo DuPont was not the culprit.

I was nowhere close to finding out who had done it.

"You can borrow our assistance, for Alisha."

I'd threatened the man, and he was still offering his aid. Part of me knew it was because he *had* liked Alisha.

Who wouldn't?

But he hadn't gone after her. I didn't give a shit why.

I only cared that she was mine for the taking.

CHAPTER 20
ALISHA

When Reed told me I'd be getting a bodyguard, the tall, blonde man sitting on my couch, eating cereal and watching Sabrina The Teenage Witch, from my childhood, was not what I had imagined.

Kellan walked into my apartment wearing a ball cap and jacket over his hoodie, his blonde hair tousled and a heartbreaking grin on his face.

When I told Kellan to make himself at home, he really made himself at home.

Taking off his letterman jacket and wearing a long sleeve underneath stretching his broad shoulders and muscles.

His blue eyes were delighted as he smiled at me bringing him the entire box of cereal and more milk.

Adorable.

I spent my days working from home, visiting local shops, and snapping photos.

It wasn't until my first outing with Kellan that I realized how dangerous he was.

When a few men recognized me from my social media and tried to touch me, Kellan nearly snapped one of their arms, his expression ferocious, blue eyes wild as he glared them down.

It was the first time I caught a glimpse of something other than an easy grin. After apologizing and giving me a sheepish smile, I noticed him scanning the area, a muscle in his jaw tensing.

That day, I realized something crucial about Reed's world.

Deception was a fundamental part of it.

I had no doubt that the letterman jackets and adorable smiles were merely a disguise, concealing someone who could have easily been much more dangerous.

And smiled that adorable grin while doing it.

"What's it like working at Titan?" I asked one day, sipping green tea while Kellan watched me scroll through social media on the TV.

Reed had gotten a smart TV that allowed me to connect my phone or laptop to the screen, enabling me to view everything on a larger scale.

"Mr. Whittaker's good," Kellan said in his drawl. "He's been nothing but helpful. Everyone there is. I suppose Mr. Monroe can be a little scary, but everything has balance." *Gabriel Monroe.*

Reed's best friend and pseudo-brother.

I smiled as he glanced at the screen, where a video of a brunette dancing to salsa music played.

"Miss Alisha—"

"*Alisha.*"

"Can I ask you a question? Would you like Mr. Whittaker if he were younger than you?" I pondered the question. Kellan was my age.

"I would. I like him for who he is. His age wouldn't matter." But I had a feeling this wasn't really about me. "Is there...someone you like who might be older?"

He nodded, his eyes watching as I stopped scrolling, landing on a video of a storm. My mind drifted to Reed.

"What did you like about him, if not his age?"

I flushed, realizing that Kellan had been watching me intently, his eyes wide and undoubtedly thinking about his particular woman.

"Kellan, why don't you just ask her out?"

"I did." And she said no.

"Are you asking me why she said no, or what you can do to convince her to say yes?"

He looked all of like a teenager as he said with a light shrug. "Both."

Adorable. "How old is she?"

He hesitated before answering. "Twenty-nine."

I mulled over that information. I had friends who were closer to thirty than I was, and one of them had always said. "Does she want to get married and have kids?"

I would have laughed at his expression if I hadn't been serious.

I explained. "She's twenty-nine, which means for many women, it's a time when those without kids feel this pressure. Maybe she thinks that if she doesn't have children with you, there's no point. Or the promise of something more. You're twenty-five, but to a woman who wants children..." I watched his expression closely. "She might not just want to have a fling, but something serious..."

Kellan stewed over that, a noise leaving him. I quickly smoothed that out. "I'm not saying she doesn't like you. You seem like a really nice man, but you should make your intentions clear. I also think that instead of trying to convince her, it might make your case stronger if you're simply there for her. It's like she's a scared cat—the nicer you are to her, the more suspicious she'll become. But if you happen to leave food out on your porch and walk away..."

His ocean blue eyes widened. "*Gatita...*"

"I beg your pardon." *What language was that?*

Kellan's brows had slowly risen while I talked.

"She'll say yes," he said it like it was the magic answer.

I grinned at his expression. "She may consider it, yes."

"Miss Alisha—"

"*Alisha—*"

"Thank you." He smiled at me around his cereal.

Do not ruffle his hair.

I laughed. "Finish your breakfast. We have a few dates today."

As we visited homeless shelters throughout the day, I made sure to note their needs and began sending packages filled with sanitary pads and soap. Kellan accompanied me, taking in everything as we walked around.

"Why do you do this?" he asked, glancing around one of the shelters where people watched me uneasily, wondering about my presence.

"My parents ensured that my sister and I understood how fortunate we were to have all that we do," I explained, looking at a thank you card addressed to me. "My Mum wanted us to never forget that while we have everything, others don't. It was her way of keeping us humble, no matter what we did."

Kellan gave me a soft look. "That's really sweet of you."

I let out a shaky breath at the compliment.

"Is it? My Mum always said the world thinks kindness is a rarity, as though we should congratulate ourselves for every good thing we do

140

for others." I handed him a box of cards that I liked to keep. "It isn't. It should be given out freely."

He took the box, seeming stunned by my words.

"Do you not think what you do is special? I think you're making a huge difference for people."

"Perhaps," I said as we walked down the hallway to exit. "But am I doing anything special? Isn't kindness for other people the bare minimum?"

"Not in our line of work. We only ever see fucked up shit—sorry, Miss Alisha."

I laughed. "It's just Alisha. You can say fucked up shit, Kellan. I'm not a dainty woman."

"No, ma'am, I didn't think you were."

His grin told me otherwise. I shook my head ruefully.

"Being kind is the bare minimum to me. I don't know these people or what choices they made in their lives to be in a shelter. But I do know if the roles were reversed, I would want someone to give me a chance. I hope the work I do gives anyone out there a chance, you know? What do you call it? I don't know the American expression—"

"Pay it forward?" We stepped into the sunlight, and I burrowed into my coat. In the fall, New York could be unforgiving some days, but today was a rare sunny day.

"I think so. I hope I can pay respect to my Mum and do good unto others, but also hope someone out there sees it and finds solace in it."

"That's real sweet of you, Miss Alisha."

"Alisha."

He nodded, his wide easy grin still in place. If he was a deadly spy, he fooled me with that aw-shucks personality.

After our fourth visit, Kellan was curious. "Why don't you hire an assistant?"

"I had some in the past," I admitted. "But my life isn't as hectic now as it used to be. Sometimes things calm down for influencers occasionally. Life isn't always go-go-go. So right now, my life feels like it's settled a bit, and I don't need the extra help."

But I would once I launched my brand. I should really put out a notice.

"Miss," a staffer from the shelter approached us. "I'm sorry, but there's been an incident. Would it be okay if you came back another time?"

I was about to say of course it would be fine when a faint popping noise came from the distance. I frowned, wondering what it was. I didn't have time to ask. Kellan had me in his arms a second later, hauling me out the door and into the street.

"*Don't.*" His voice broke no room for argument, sounding flat and different, far away from the southern guy he was. "I have to get us out of here."

But as he did, I heard the sounds from inside the building spill out onto the street. I turned my head as Kellan swore. New York wasn't as insane as people made it out to be. Once every few years, something insane happened, and people used it as gossip fodder to steer others away from the city I loved.

Across the street, there was a lanky man wearing low-rider jeans, holding quite possibly the largest gun I had ever seen. It was bigger and longer than the one Reed had, and he was firing into the street. From behind me, Kellan shoved me onto the ground, and I heard the sound of a click.

"*Don't move, Alisha.*"

I felt my face burning on the ground and I bit my lip tasting blood, and I looked over my shoulder at Kellan, wondering why he'd reacted that way.

I stilled at the look on his face. Oh my...gone was the golden retriever, and in his place was a man hellbent on killing. He had snapped into that part of him I'd seen in Reed. This was his life.

This is what they do.

His expression was ferocious, his jaw tight. Those calm blue eyes were molten and bright. I understood that Reed had always struggled to introduce me to the life he lived.

He never said it, but some part of me knew he was at war with himself—the darkness he existed in that made him cold, like Kellan on top of me right now, holding his own weapon.

I didn't even know Kellan carried a gun.

"*Do not move.*" He didn't have to tell me twice.

"Reed will kill me if anything happens to you."

I felt the panic clawing into my throat.

Shots fired off around us, and Kellan dropped down on me, covering me with his body.

Sharp glass shattered everywhere. And suddenly, I didn't think at all.

CHAPTER 21
REED

KELLAN'S WORDS SLAMMED INTO ME. ALISHA, *HURT*.

The icy vice-like grip in my chest stayed until I got home.

Entering the apartment, I wasn't surprised to find Selena's dark head bent over Kellan, shirtless and bleeding as he leaned on a barstool, tending to his arm.

His face was cut in some places. Evidence of their interrupted medical treatment littered the island. I'd clearly barged in on something, but I couldn't bring myself to care at that moment.

"Where is she?"

Selena indicated the hallway with a wordless tilt of her head, not daring to meet my eyes as she focused on cleaning Kellan's arm. I found Alisha huddled on her bed, and I was on her in an instant, hands roaming urgently as I pressed fervent kisses along her shoulder, her neck, any exposed patch of skin to assure myself she was safe.

A mottled bruise marred her cheekbone, no doubt from being shoved. I was trying not to be angry with Kellan; he had done his job well. Dried blood caked her split lower lip.

She was here, in my arms, and that was all that mattered.

Her eyes remained glassy, unseeing as I nudged her gently.

"Tell me what happened."

Kellan had already given me the rundown over the phone, but I needed to hear the events from Alisha's lips, to let the truth sink in no matter how much it made my blood boil.

As she haltingly recounted her terrifying ordeal, my control stretched thinner by the second.

First that note, now this?

"It's just another one of those weird things that happen in the city," Alisha dismissed with a wavering attempt at nonchalance.

She couldn't possibly believe her own words, not with the bone-deep weariness lacing her tone. Not when the very thing I worked tirelessly to prevent had happened.

Pulling her deeper into my arms, I murmured the only reassurance I could offer. "I won't let anything happen to you."

Alisha's composure shattered with a muffled sniffle.

"That was scary," she whispered brokenly. She didn't cry loudly unless I edged her in bed. No, Alisha hid her sobs against the curve of my neck, and that quiet vulnerability cut me deeper than any blade. I clutched her closer, kissing her wherever I could reach.

As Gabriel would say, I wasn't a *normie*. I didn't even pretend to be.

Long moments later, when the adrenaline finally bled away, Alisha drifted into sleep in my arms.

Pressing my lips against her hair, I inhaled the faint scent of roses. Of her. Calming me down. I needed to talk to Kellan. Task Selena. Along with the other things in my day. But letting go of Alisha asleep in my arms went against everything I really wanted.

Slowly, I untangled myself, drawing the colorful quilt over her, then the comforter, making sure she was snuggled in her bed. Quietly, I made my way out, snicking the door shut, and walking down her hallway towards her kitchen.

I'm going to find who did this.

I rounded the corner to find Kellan leaning into Selena, his forehead resting against hers as she gripped his uninjured arm. He had her cornered between him and the counter.

You've got to be fucking kidding me.

"Can you two get it together?" I bit out, uncaring of how harsh the rebuke.

Fury was rapidly reshaping me, honing my focus to a singularly destructive point. Selena pushed away, looking abashed as she turned away from me, dark hair shielding her face.

Darkness encroached on the edges of my vision. I simply didn't have bandwidth to spare on them, not with more pressing priorities demanding my full attention.

"Were you followed all day?" I demanded, rounding on Kellan. I already suspected the answer, but I needed to hear it from his lips.

To his credit, the man composed himself swiftly. Swiping at a hint of pink on his lips as his gaze slid reluctantly away from the brunette cleaning up the remnants of the medical supplies.

"No," he responded. "Everything was clear until we got to the last shelter. I made sure of it, every time. I didn't see a tail."

"The shelter was an appointment?"

He nodded once,"Someone knew she was going to be there." I'd already placed my bets on that.

"I'll check the camera feeds on the street. In the meantime, Selena, talk to Giroux at NYPD. Make sure he keeps his guys out of this." Selena's eyes narrowed on me.

I didn't miss how red-rimmed they were as she spoke in Spanish, and I translated quickly in my head.

Is there anything else you need to say?

A muscle ticked in my jaw as I considered her probing question. "No. Nothing else for now."

She looked like she wanted to argue but wisely held her tongue in the face of my current state.

And because she was Selena, she added. *"Your girlfriend pissed someone off. And you won't say who?"*

Alisha had enraged someone, and it was my fault.

"I'm not telling you, because it wasn't Alisha."

I exhaled slowly, gritting my teeth against the impotent rage simmering beneath the surface.

"It was me. This is happening because of my failures. I put her in danger, and I'm doing everything in my power to make sure she doesn't end up in any more."

Selena's eyes widened fractionally as the unspoken truth hung heavy between us. She wanted to ask, I could see it burning behind her concerned stare.

But my expression must have warned her against voicing it.

"I'll find the Lieutenant," she stated flatly in English, as she avoided meeting Kellan's questioning look.

He hadn't taken his eyes off her.

I was keeping them all at arm's length with my secrets, yet still demanding their trust and loyalty.

It made me a special breed of monster.

But I would do anything to protect Alisha.

CHAPTER 22
REED

"Is there a reason why I just had Miss Tavares warn me off the shooting on 10th Street?"

Lieutenant Cameron Giroux's words carried a weary resignation.

He'd served in the same Navy SEAL unit as Gabriel years ago.

Now, he was just another cop with the NYPD, hating the job yet always eager to help Titan in any way he could.

"I gave her one of the bullets from the scene, but even still, there are hundreds of weapons out there. Could be any of them."

I knew that already. But I was good at finding things, at piecing together clues until the full picture emerged with lethal clarity.

"Call me when you get me something useful to work with," I stated, not bothering to answer him. He didn't need to know shit.

He sounded distantly interested when he asked. "Is Tavares single?"

Grinding my teeth, I resisted the urge to hurl the phone across the room.

"Why don't you ask Kellan Watts?" I hung up, irritated beyond belief at the utter uselessness of our exchange.

If Cameron Giroux hadn't been loyal to Gabriel, providing us an inside line at the department, I would have cut him loose long ago.

But it paid to have assets strategically placed.

"Reed?" Alisha's soft voice broke through my thunderous thoughts.

I looked up to find her petite frame swallowed by the folds of a tiny black robe, the delicate detailing accentuating the golden hue of her thighs.

She looked impossibly young and fragile at that moment, delicate features slightly rounded, wide eyes regarding me with naked vulnerability.

The overwhelming need to shelter her, to protect this precious creature from all the world's realities, slammed into me with staggering force.

I wanted to lock her away, keep Alisha in my bedroom, utterly mine in every sense of the word. I ached to claim her fiercely, to lose myself in her warmth and soft curves.

"Come here, Angel." Moments later, she was cradled in my embrace, her slight frame molding perfectly against mine.

"You look angry," Alisha murmured, worry creasing her brow.

Did I? I needed to wipe that shit off my face. Not because I doubted her ability to comprehend the harsh realities I grappled with daily, but because the sins I routinely committed to ensure her safety and peace of mind would utterly change the way she saw me. *Not her. Not now.*

Alisha didn't belong to the world I inhabited. I refused to dirty her light by drawing her into its shadows. All she needed to know was that I would move heaven and earth to take care of her.

To keep her light shining. To avoid becoming split like I was.

"Just got a lot on my plate, that's all, baby."

The lie slid off my tongue with disturbing ease, yet didn't faze my conscience in the slightest. I was too preoccupied with shielding her.

"How do you feel?" I asked instead, nuzzling into the crook of her neck and drinking in her comforting scent. She smelled like dessert.

"A little shaken up, but I'm okay," she replied, those pure, intelligent eyes studying me intently. "You're staying tonight?"

God, she was fucking cute.

Sending Kellan home had been the obvious call. He needed to recover while I stood sentry over my Angel's safety.

"Try and stop me," I murmured against the sensitive skin just below her ear, delighting in the full-body shiver that rippled through her petite frame. "Why do you—"

It had been on the tip of my tongue to ask her why she asked. And then I saw that look in her eyes. The one she gave me before begging me to sink in deeper. *Well, fuck.*

"I can't fuck you with bandages on your face, Angel. That hurts me too."

Her lips curved in an indulgent smile a whisper away from my ear. "It hurts more if you're not in me..." She trailed her fingers down my arm. Alisha loved the sleeve. "We could do that party trick you like so much…"

Well, fuck.

I was shaking with need now.

Alisha had been too embarrassed to call it squirting, so I'd started referring to it as a party trick because it made her laugh.

There was only one thing I liked more than fucking her, and that was making her laugh.

I closed my eyes, trying not to laugh about creating a monster.

"Or should I handle it myself?"

My eyes popped open. A low growl left me. I saw the gleam in her eyes.

"You trying to tempt me, Angel?"

"I don't know, is it working?"

It fucking was. Little minx.

She was over my shoulders, squealing with delight, seconds later.

I left the part of me that felt guilty at the table.

I HELD HER CLOSE TO ME LONG, LONG MOMENTS LATER.

"How did you know I was inherently good?" she whispered, breathless. "When we first met."

I inhaled the scent of her hair, the roses and cardamom scent filling the space. I was drowning in it. In her. I couldn't get enough.

I should take her out on a date.

Get her some candles. Something Selena would know more about than me. But right now in this moment, feeling her breath against my chest while she laid there catching her breath.

I could hit up Selena and ask or just find a nice place on my own. I knew a place that had opened a few weeks ago that had great reviews. I wondered if Alisha would like Indonesian food. Or even going to Indonesia. Singapore.

I would take a break and take her everywhere with me.

That didn't sound like a bad idea.

For a moment I forgot she asked me a question. I was so blissed out at the idea of her going anywhere with me away from our problems.

"The same way I knew you were into me."

I let her tangle her legs with mine, I needed to clean her up eventually. "Your eyes."

She looked up at me, bright and cheeks flushed, lips red from my kisses.

Sweet, beautiful girl.

"I spent my life in intelligence. After a while, no matter how good someone is at hiding it, the eyes always give people away."

I let her absorb what I said. "Have you ever heard of people eventually reflecting who they are on the inside as they age?"

She nodded. "Mum used to believe bitter people would show with their age. I always thought it was a little judgmental."

Perhaps but to me it wasn't that simple.

"In my line of work, it saves lives. Watching people. Taking them in. Absorbing who they are. Let's switch it around, what did you think when you first saw me?" Her eyes collided with mine and for a moment I knew. I knew *everything*.

I could see it in them burning in the hazel, dark passion, warmth and kindness. Everything good that I lacked, she had, it was soaked in the fiber of her DNA.

Her lips parted without a noise, and I smiled. "Yeah, that's what I thought. Should I tell you what I saw when I looked at you?" This was before I had even looked into her years ago.

She nodded, unable to look away from me.

I didn't break her gaze. "I saw a woman, the most stunning...I'd ever seen in my life. Hair the color of midnight. You were wearing this blue dress. All I saw was...your skin, and the light against it and..." I shook my head. It felt like just the other day I was utterly enraptured.

Her eyes widened.

"And I shouldn't have wanted you as much as I did. I was supposed to drop in to meet Lara that night. And instead, I stayed behind for you."

I remembered that night. I told her about it.

"That's Alisha." Lara's dark eyes glimmered with delight. Despite being dressed in lacy nothings, she hadn't attracted my attention like the woman sitting on the second level of the club. She stood out. I couldn't take my eyes off her. And neither could half the men in there. "Do you want me to introduce you guys?"

"I met you that night."

I shook her hand and introduced myself with Lara in tow. And since then whenever I'd dropped by she'd been there by some *coincidence*. *Lara*.

I'd lingered. More than I usually had. I liked Alisha. There was something about her that got under my skin.

"I stayed wherever you were. I didn't know *what* it was. I didn't know you were...a celebrity. It didn't matter if you were." Lara had explained to me, she wasn't available.

"Boyfriend?" I didn't catch a ring.

"Sister." At my expression, her eyes while delighted, she chewed her lip. *"Her parents passed away and she's got a younger sibling she takes care of. She isn't looking."*

As in, she didn't want anyone. Just to do her.

She doesn't need me. In any way.

"I understood that about you from the start." My voice was low as I brushed her hair back. Raven locks running through my fingers. Alisha didn't need me.

She wanted me, which made me want her to need me in some ways. So I made myself useful.

"Every time I saw you, you were teasing your friends. Making sure no one ever got too drunk, picking up the tab for Gemma when she indulged a bit too much. Taking photos and engaging with other girls. You always handled it all with grace. I admired you, you never lost sight of Avani, creating your home. But you worked to make sure you could take care of her and you."

I should have stopped there, but the words kept tumbling forth as I traced the delicate contours of her face, bright hazel doe eyes watching me.

"You're the nurturing person in your social circle. Always present for everyone, giving off this warmth..." I could taste her sunshine from miles away, see it infusing the golden hue of her skin with this inner light. "Between the work with charities, the constant stream of kindness you extend to everyone around you...I liked you."

So did half of the population it felt like.

"You are inherently this good person," I murmured, the husky words seeming to hang heavy between us. "I saw that light in your eyes from the moment we met. Your heart is incorruptible, everything mine is not."

Everything I could never be, no matter how much I might wish I was.

That first night, I'd wanted to pull her into my embrace, to lose myself in the warmth of her welcoming curves. To take that sunshine into my skin. Hold it close. Pretend like it was mine. For so long.

"I told you I'm not a good man, nor will I pretend to be." The words rasped out in a confessional whisper.

"When it comes to you though, anything goes. I don't deal in definitions of black and white. I would do anything for you, every single time."

There was only gray. Draped in designer suits and veneers of legitimacy. I didn't care about following protocol or adhering to laws. The depths of violence I would eagerly tap into to keep Alisha *safe*, and by my side knew no boundaries of legal or ethical *constraints*. Constraints were a myth.

Nothing is going to stop me.

"I don't think you're corruptible," she whispered, stubborn hope ringing in each soft syllable. I closed my eyes against the searing ache her blind faith caused.

"No, Angel? What am I then?"

"An opportunist," Alisha whispered with a slight tease in her voice. I couldn't help the wry grin tugging at my lips in acknowledgment. She wasn't wrong. I *was* an opportunist of the highest order.

"I would be *anything* you needed me to be. I would be anyone you wanted me to be. Especially if it's just yours."

I felt my heart cave open for her. "*Give me a chance*, beautiful girl. I just got you, I don't want to lose you."

Even if it felt like the inevitable danger was looming in the future. My instincts were screaming at me. Telling me nothing was a coincidence anymore.

I couldn't lose her.

CHAPTER 23
ALISHA

IT HAD BEEN WEEKS SINCE REED HAD COME INTO MY LIFE.

Even after dinner, he would often retreat to his computer, his brow furrowed in concentration.

Despite the long hours he put in, Reed always made time for us.

He had said he was working out of Midtown because it was easier, but even then, he brought it home.

I went about my daily routines, Kellan by my side, his easy grins and constant snacking providing me a welcome distraction.

Kellan had a younger sister, Becca, and I thought he regarded me like he did her, which was sweet.

One afternoon, Kellan and I found ourselves at Teasers, the lush garden space now lit up with sunlight and seeming much larger than it was during the night.

The scent of the familiar white sage tickled my nose, and memories of my first night with Reed in this very place skated through my mind. It had been a long time since then.

I watched as Kellan's eyes widened at the sight of the girls practicing their routines on the massive stage, some half-dressed and some naked with nothing but pasties.

A smile tugged at my lips when one of them did a routine spreading her legs open naked in the air. Kellan turned to me.

"Miss Alisha—" he breathed, his cheeks tinted pink. "You come here often?"

I laughed at his expression, as if he was seeing me for the first time. "Alisha. Not often, but enough. I met Reed here."

Kellan blinked several times, keeping his eyes averted from the stage, and I wondered if things had gotten serious with his crush.

"How is your crush?"

He gave me a bashful smile as he told me my advice worked. I beamed as we made our way to the back and up to the second floor where Lara's office was located. I hesitated, not wanting to burst in on my friend who often paraded around in nothing, unsure if Kellan could handle the full blast of Lara.

Before we could get to Lara's door, a stunning blonde woman, whom I recognized as Gianna May, Lara's understudy, was walking down the dark hall.

In daisy dukes and a completely see-through crop top that clearly showed her breasts, Kellan looked at me a little wide-eyed. I grinned at his expression.

"Oh hay, Miss Alishaaa, Miss Lara's in a meetin' did ya'll need her?" Gianna's thick southern twang was always delightful. As she got closer, she beamed.

"No problem, we can wait," I replied easily, shooting Kellan a reassuring look. Only his slight frown and flickering gaze towards Lara's office door gave me pause.

"She should be just about finished. I'll just knock and let her know..." Gianna raised an elegant brow, her wide blue eyes taking us in, Kellan looking at the door curiously.

"No!" I blurted, trying to halt her approach, but the blonde bombshell's hand was raping sharply against the wood.

"Miss Lara!" Her thick, sugary accent rang out. "You got your best friend waitin' on you. *Can I come in?* I've been wanting to talk to you 'bout the damn heater. I swear if that handyman comes back, and tries to sleep with me one more time, I will hit him over the head with a crowbar! I swear that bastard couldn't get laid in a monkey whorehouse with a fistful of bananas."

I clapped a hand over my mouth, desperately trying to stifle my shocked laughter. Kellan simply blinked, his jaw dropping.

Gianna whirled back towards us, eyes wide with sheepish realization.

"I'm sorry, y'all," she rushed out. "It gets colder than my nana's tits in here. My nipples get so hard, I don't even need tape. I just put my gems on and it hurts yankin' those babies off at the end of the night!"

I couldn't hold it back any longer as peals of laughter burst forth as I doubled over.

Kellan leaned heavily against me for support, his deep laughter shaking our joined frames as tears of mirth streamed down our faces.

The office door abruptly flew open, revealing a tousled, red-faced Lara hastily tugging her dress in place.

"I'm gonna start callin' you Uncle Tater instead of Sunshine," she growled at the hapless Gianna, who sputtered uselessly.

Lara's dark eyes landed on me, widening further as she raked a hand through her mussed hair.

Her lips were pouty and swollen in a way that made my gaze instinctively drift...right to the masculine figure slowly emerging from the shadowed interior, tugging down his shirt with nonchalance.

Tall and lean, he walked over from the shadowed office interior to stand at Lara's side with casual grace.

Kellan's laughter abruptly ceased.

Lara's guest leaned on an elegant black cane.

His jet-black hair was deliberately disheveled, giving him a rakish, rock star aesthetic that perfectly complemented his chiseled cheekbones.

Clad in a white band shirt that clung to his well-defined physique, his arms were adorned with intricate tattoos.

His eyes took us in, hunter green and dark, sparkling with a hint of roguish mischief behind his dark-framed glasses.

"Guys, this is Liam," Lara introduced, her voice uncharacteristically soft. "He's the new head of security over Teasers from Titan."

Wickedly handsome, he adjusted the frames of his glasses, his gaze flickering over to us with a considering sweep.

It landed on me, pausing for a moment as if trying to place me, before moving onto Kellan with equal intensity.

"Liam Sullivan," Kellan murmured, a hint of surprise coloring his tone.

"Kellan Watts," Liam replied, his rich baritone sending a shiver down my spine. "Good to finally meet you in real life."

"Liam, this is my best friend Alisha," Lara said, her voice still unusually gentle.

"Alisha," Liam acknowledged, his tone deep and equally soft as he inclined his head towards me.

"I thought you were a ghost," Kellan quipped before I could respond.

"Something like that," Liam grinned wickedly, and I caught a flash of a tongue piercing. *Good Lord.*

As Kellan explained Liam's new role in Titan's security team, I caught Lara watching him with the same intense expression he had given me earlier.

Liam's eyes drifted back to me, and I felt the weight of his stare.

I was used to people staring, a side effect of my social media presence, but there was something different about the way he looked at me, as if he recognized me from somewhere.

"Do you have any family in the States?" Liam asked me quietly.

"I have a younger sister," I said without thinking.

His smile was soft as he watched me. "Pleasure to meet you, Alisha." Considering the redness of his lips and Lara's slight squirming, he wasn't checking me out, but he might've recognized me from my photos.

"I have to head out," Liam said smoothly, his eyes landing on Lara, who turned pink but nodded. As he moved past us, motioning to Gianna that he would take care of her handyman problem, I saw the blonde woman's eyes wide as dinner plates. Kellan shifted me out of Liam's way. I barely noticed, too focused on Lara's dimmed megawatt smile as I took her hand.

"What was that?" I whispered, searching her face for answers. She shook her head and glanced at Kellan, silently communicating that now was not the time. I nodded, understanding her reluctance to discuss it in front of him.

And then Kellan, distracted by the array of sex toys lining the wall, wandered over to inspect a section more closely.

Lara had bounced back to her usual self, entertaining his questions about butterfly clit suckers and g-spot massagers on her wall.

~

I RETURNED TO WHO I HAD BEEN BEFORE THE NOTE. GEMMA OFFERED TO handle the charity work while I tried to pretend I wasn't still thinking about the way things had changed.

I was trying to sit through another meeting at Poppy.

As Gemma's soft voice drifted through the room, enthusiastically outlining the new projects we were undertaking, my pen scratched across the paper, the ink bleeding into the fibers as my thoughts wandered to Reed.

His scent lingered on my pillows, a constant reminder of his presence in my life.

The way his eyes heated before he plunged into me, his easy grins as he handled me with care. The memories sent a shiver down my spine, my thighs tightening in response. I liked him.

And should have terrified me. But what terrified me the most was the idea of losing Reed.

Losing my parents had been the hardest thing I'd ever faced, especially when they hadn't lived to see my success.

Raising Avani had been hard earned, but worth it, and she was my world.

Avani and I had always been there for each other, making safe, secure decisions that didn't allow for risks.

We lived within a carefully constructed net of focus, never stepping a foot out of line. Reed felt like a risk.

One that, if I wasn't careful, would lead me headfirst into the same dark place I'd found myself in after losing Mum and Dad.

Shifting uncomfortably in my seat, I tried to focus on Gemma's words as she outlined her latest initiative for our Poppy outreach efforts.

Kellan sat beside me, having ditched his Letterman jacket. Instead in a navy sweater that brought out his bright eyes, his messy blonde hair looking for all I knew like a poster child for an Ivy League school.

He'd grinned easily, talking to me about his crush who was doing great.

I had recommended a few places for him to take her.

While I teased him, his wide grin remained in place, in turn catching the eyes of several of the women around me who thought he was my assistant, not my guard.

Kellan was listening intently as if he were a part of the organization, and the sight brought a fleeting smile to my face.

Every so often when someone else would speak, Gemma cast glances over at the imposing Viking that was Nate, slouched casually in his suit, tucked away in a corner of the room. Nate maintained a facade of stoic indifference.

I made an effort to redirect my attention towards the meticulously designed pop-up shop templates Gemma had prepared, admiring the striking creativity and thoughtful details she'd poured into the layouts.

Yet for all my concentration, I couldn't seem to dislodge the persistent sense of unease rippling through me.

A sensation clawed at the periphery of my thoughts, scattering my focus into fragments.

I looked outside the meeting and noticed a police officer standing outside the door. Had Gemma asked for security? Given the way paparazzi still hounded her, it made sense, but it made me uneasy.

"I need some air." I murmured, mostly to myself.

"Anything I can do?" Kellan was at my back in an instant, his well-practiced attentiveness a welcome distraction.

I caught Nate's gaze flickering over to us, and not wanting to make a scene, I let Kellan help me up.

His steady hands supported me as we took a break, and I motioned to Gemma. She nodded understandingly.

I felt my breathing ease as I stepped out, and Kellan led me into a quieter room.

He tucked me into his chest as I closed my eyes, but my anxiety had reached a fever pitch.

The weight of my unease pressed down on my chest, making each breath a shallow, labored affair.

My thoughts raced, tumbling over one another in a dizzying cascade of worry and fear. The sensation of something being off clung to me like a second skin, a prickling, persistent feeling that refused to be shaken.

"Reed mentioned you have anxiety," Kellan said softly as he rubbed circles on my back. "It's okay if you need to take a breather sometimes."

I nodded. "I'd like to go home."

Kellan simply called a taxi while keeping me steady. Something just felt off.

He texted on his phone, and I focused on taking breaths, feeling something in my stomach uneasy. My heart tightened, and I couldn't shake that something was wrong. I got a text on my phone as Kellan led me home.

> Watts said you're not feeling good. I'm coming home soon.

He called my home, his home.

My mind focused on Reed.

His voice whenever I freaked out, the way he pulled me into his lap and cuddled me.

Reed insisted three years of waiting for me to even see him as more than just the guy who made sure I was home safe was a long time.

He had stepped into his role with ease. And now I need him.

He came with me to any social events I had when he could, and worked from home in his setup on the island. I couldn't say no.

Not after the long week he spent for days loving me. I felt like he'd broken down all my resolve.

He stayed over more times than not, his clothes hung with mine, his toothbrush, his deodorant, and his house slippers. I caved and bought him a pair.

After the note, things had died down, while things were heating up between me and Reed.

Nights spent with him were indulgent without making me feel like what I wanted was wrong. Some nights he'd just get food and set it up for me after showering.

I'd put on a movie or show, and recently we'd been binge-watching mystery comedy movies. And I got to see a different side, his easy laughter, his kisses all over my face as he cuddled me to him.

In turn, I was falling for him. Just a little more.

Reed was a fan of anything that remotely resembled *Clue*. It made his brain work.

I would lean back into him on the couch until I woke up in bed the next morning with Reed gone.

He made an effort to communicate now, switching me to an app he used to text which he said was more secure. He didn't have social media, and I never posted him, respecting his privacy.

Since he was big on cybersecurity, he'd gone on my phone and added several apps, switched tracking off, and done a bunch of stuff to it with a little frown knit between his brows while he worked.

And afterwards, I'd been so turned on watching his tattooed self work at the island, I had shown him exactly how appreciative I was.

Life began to resume as normal as though it had never happened.

I couldn't shake that something was going to go awfully wrong.

Or maybe that was my imposter syndrome. My issues.

My inability to appreciate the man that had swooped into my life.

But when I got home, I tucked into a ball in bed, hiding underneath the blankets.

I couldn't shake something being wrong.

Kellan had appeared next to me, with ocean eyes full of concern, but I let him know Reed would be home soon.

Kellan could go home…to his life.

When he switched with Reed, Reed curled around me.

He didn't say a word as I curled into him, letting his warmth seep into my skin. *Safe. I'm safe.*

I just hoped it stayed that way.

CHAPTER 24
ALISHA

IT TOOK ME ANOTHER WEEK TO INTRODUCE REED TO AVANI.

"*Didi!*" My sister hugged me, and I forced myself to focus on her instead of the man currently taking a quick shower before meeting her. I liked that he let me express everything.

I inhaled the scent of honey; the feel of her in my arms always comforting and grounding.

"You look pink," she said. "Is everything okay?"

I nodded eagerly and led her into the living room. She wore what I called her 'school uniform': an A-line mini skirt with stockings and a black turtleneck.

Though younger than me by seven years, at seventeen, Avani was more stylish than I had ever been.

She favored our mother, her cinnamon-colored hair cascading down her back, longer than mine.

Her dark eyes were luminous as she beamed at me.

"It's so good to see yo—" She trailed off, and I knew exactly what she was looking at.

"I'm Reed. It's good to finally meet you." He smiled warmly as he approached, pressing a quick kiss to my hair. "I ordered dinner already. Alisha said you like Japanese food, so I got some takoyaki and a handful of other things I thought were remotely Japanese."

I turned over my shoulder, and my abdomen clenched at the sight of Reed, eyes bright as he took her in.

Devastatingly handsome as he smiled at Avani. "Is that all right?"

I couldn't even laugh at the way my sister sputtered at his easy smile. He was devastatingly handsome like this.

Adorably playful and deceptive in his tee shirt.

I looked at my sister, and her expression was still stupefied.

"Yes, you're—that's lovely."

He grinned and winked at her as the doorbell rang again. "I'll get that, Angel."

My sister's jaw dropped as he walked away. I bit my cheek to keep from laughing.

Avani squealed as she floated to me. "That's him?" I nodded, not hiding my smile. I could see the curiosity and excitement in her eyes—she knew I liked Reed a lot.

Even Avani had been curious about Reed, occasionally making sure I got home safe.

I mentioned him briefly once, and it was enough for my sister to guess.

Her eyes went wide as Reed walked back in his house slippers with the food.

"Oh my God, look at his tattoos." She looked back at me. "I can see our governess crying."

I laughed. Growing up prim and proper, it was no surprise we were drawn to someone like Reed.

"I know," I felt her hand tighten around mine. "Wait until you get to know him."

Reed and I talked alone all the time, so I thought I knew him. I thought I knew a lot about him. But that night, I realized I knew nothing.

I had no clue who Reed was around my sister. He was utterly charming, engaging her in questions, asking her about her hobbies, digging into her interests.

He finally narrowed her down to her favorite thing to do as his eyes drifted around the apartment.

"I like reading," Avani admitted shyly a flush tinged her cheeks, and I bit back a smile.

She didn't *like* reading. My sister was a bookworm who devoured books.

If she could, she would read all day, every day.

I had seen Reed sifting through copies of a popular fantasy series from Avani's piles.

Her entire room was covered in books, in drawers, on the floor, all around me.

And I bet her dorm was no different.

"I recently started a new series..." Reed listened avidly about the fantasy series Avani was reading, nodding along like he understood.

I felt disarmed as he easily engaged my sister in conversation while I helped him set out the food. It had become our thing.

I didn't think it was because we were homebodies so much as selfish with our time together.

Reed liked to eat while holding me close or watching something. Those were some of the few times he wasn't engrossed in his phone.

This time, Reed sat with some space between us to avoid making Avani feel uncomfortable.

He ate quietly, only pausing to ask her questions.

I had never seen my sister speak so easily as she did now. Nobody else could get her to open up like this.

As the night went on, I realized he was trying to understand her too.

It had been a huge hurdle for me when dating; most people weren't okay with how important she was to me.

She was my only family, and I loved her deeply, practically having raised her during her teen years.

She did everything with me. She was my *everything*.

Reed grinned at something Avani said, his canines flashing as his tongue darted out between his teeth, making my sister turn beet red.

"You never have to apologize to me for being excited about something," he said warmly. "Mochi?"

I bit back a sigh as he passed her the entire tray.

I felt like a fool for waiting this long.

THE LONGER I WATCHED REED INTERACT WITH AVANI, IT GOT HARDER TO breathe around my emotions.

I found my thoughts and heart racing. I needed some space.

Excusing myself, I caught Reed's eye and I looked away as I placed a hand over my heart.

Emotion bubbled inside me watching the easy way Reed and Avani interacted.

I had been so afraid of introducing the wrong man to Avani, I didn't want her to think men were...bad, but I had to be careful to set a good example for my sister.

He had mentioned there was a young girl his best friend, Gabriel, had adopted years ago.

Reed spoke of Gabriel highly.

Privately, I suspected Reed was adept at talking to Avani, thanks to his experience with Gabriel. It didn't change my heart beating rapidly watching him.

Arousal had blossomed as he casually leaned back, his hair messy from his shower, and his lips red from me.

He had no idea the way my stomach fluttered watching him smile easily. He was charismatic.

But he had to be.

When I returned, Avani was showing Reed photos on her phone, having moved closer to him on the couch.

She said something to him quietly that made him raise a brow and grin, but I noticed how he maintained enough physical distance to ensure she felt comfortable.

"That's *Didi*, two years ago at a Christmas party."

"Send me that." Reed grinned, looking at the photo.

"Are you two going to team up against me?" I teased them, despite the warmth that filled my insides as I watched their interaction.

Approaching them from behind the couch, I leaned in and gasped.

"When did you take that photo!" Avani moved too quickly for me, pulling her phone away.

Her eyes widened, and she gave me a reproachful look. "*Didi*, you said I could take photos that night."

"When did I put a mustache on?" I couldn't recall who had brought the fake mustaches, but I had found them adorable at the time. "Why is there an enormous mustache on my face?"

"You were two drinks in, and I thought it would be funny."Avani explained, looking at the photo. "You're still really cute." Her accent hit the t's harder.

And mine came out when I was upset. "I look like the Monopoly man."

Avani held her phone behind her back, away from me, while I stared aghast. Her expression was wide and pouting.

"At least he didn't see the one with the monocle and top hat!" My eyes widened, and my mouth dropped in horror.

Avani winced, glancing at Reed. "*Oops.*"

I whipped my head towards Reed, who had his fist covering his mouth, his eyes gleaming with amusement as he watched our exchange.

His shoulders shook with the effort to contain his laughter. Avani shot me a guilty expression, looking at her phone.

"Uh-oh," she muttered.

What?

"Don't be mad. You know when Reed asked me to send him your photo?" I covered my face and nodded. "I accidentally shared the entire album."

My mouth dropped open.

"Wonderful, Reed. You can now witness all of my humiliating moments in full pixelated resolution."

I let out a breath, my fists clenching at my side. "I left something in the restroom. Excuse me."

I need to get out of here.

"*Didi—*"

"*Angel—*"

"I'll be back!" I didn't want them to see me like this.

I walked out of the room before I could say something that might make my sister cry, unsure of what was happening to me.

I felt a profound urge to break down.

My throat constricted, and I couldn't think straight. I had never reacted like that before.

I blamed Reed. He threw me off.

I had spent a lifetime making myself perfect, and it was never enough for my parents.

So, I had tried to be perfect for the world. And while it was enough...It required me to hide parts of myself, to lie to everyone, and to cultivate an image that wasn't real.

It was *exhausting*.

Avani was the one person around whom I could be myself because she was my safe space. Reed is your safe place.

I hurried to my bedroom, closing the door and making a beeline for the massive closet.

I went straight to the back, my secret thinking spot, and slid down to the floor.

This corner of my closet had witnessed many anxiety spirals, especially after my parents died.

I never broke down in front of my sister, refusing to show her that side of me. I filtered parts of myself, even from her.

My mind spun with confusion, a dizzying whirlwind of emotions I couldn't untangle.

What did it matter if Reed saw a silly photo?

What did it matter if he saw me like that?

But fear coiled tighter around my lungs with each shallow breath.

What if he didn't like me anymore?

What if that wasn't the woman Reed wanted?

Insecurity clawed at my throat. I hated the way I felt, hated being upset with Avani.

She didn't know better.

And yet, I couldn't shake the sheer vulnerability that ran through me at the thought of Reed knowing anything about me outside my carefully constructed comfort zone.

The pressure of the expectations of perfection I'd carried since childhood weighed heavily on my chest—the need to be everything for everyone.

The perfect daughter, the perfect sister, and now the perfect girlfriend. I'd worn so many masks that I didn't know who I was beneath them anymore.

And the thought of Reed seeing behind them, seeing the real, flawed me? It sent my heart racing with panic.

I tried to breathe through it, to calm the anxiety buzzing under my skin. But the thoughts kept coming, an endless barrage of fears, doubts, and old wounds.

I was drowning in them, my head pounding, my breaths coming too fast. Lost in the maze of my own mind.

A gentle knock shattered my spiraling thoughts.

"Angel?" Reed's voice was soft, laden with concern. The door creaked open, and I tensed as it closed, the click of the lock echoing in the quiet space.

I heard him moving, and I knew he would know where I was hiding. But he didn't open the door.

Instead, I heard him sit down outside, his silhouette barely visible, giving me space.

Somehow, that small gesture of understanding made my eyes burn.

"I'm fine." I whispered, my voice cracking. "I just need a minute."

"You're not." His tone was gentle but firm. "I know what you're going through." I took a shuddering breath, trying to find my voice.

But I didn't have to. Reed filled it for me.

"When I was a teenager, my stepfather differentiated between me and his son through everything. Food, housework, school, jobs. Adam got accepted to an internship for some medical program, while I worked at a grocery store. Initially, I got bullied at school for the way I looked. Gabriel, my buddy at work now, was two years older than me. We met and he realized I was getting picked on, so he taught me how to fight. He kicked my ass for a long time, but he also helped me get a job at a mechanic that paid more and taught me actual skills."

He paused, and I wiped my eyes, lost in his story.

"For the brief time he was in my life, before he joined the military to get out of his own situations, he was the only man who believed in me and wanted better for me. It was after he left that I shot up in height and started packing on weight, but it didn't make living there any easier."

"So they..." I couldn't say it. They'd tried to *stab* him.

"Yeah," he let out a breath. "But Gabriel left me with a lot of skills, and I realized I would never really be comfortable being something I wasn't by putting on clothes I couldn't afford to please people who didn't like me. I still can't. Only now, I can afford the clothes. I just don't care. I knew then what it felt like to be vulnerable, alone, afraid, and nobody accepting me. I was so scared of judgment that if I hadn't let Gabriel in, it wouldn't have saved my life."

And now, they ran a billion-dollar company together. Because he'd allowed himself to be vulnerable.

"Because I didn't let my fears swallow me whole, one day, I met this woman who dressed nicer than me and smiled a lot more than I did. She lit up a room when she walked in. I didn't have any of those skills. And she was—*is*—intelligent, funny, warm, kind, and *everything* I am not."

My breath caught, knowing who *she* was by his tone.

"I told myself I couldn't do relationships because women didn't understand me, my lifestyle, my needs, nor give me enough of anything. My last relationship was about as warm as an ice cube."

I felt the sting of jealousy imagining Reed with anyone else but brushed it off because he was with me now.

"And then, this woman let me be myself. Vulnerable. Open. She lets me show up late, stay out to do my job. She's understanding and tolerates all my quirks—"

"She sounds fantastic. " I croaked, feeling my lips quirk reluctantly.

He chuckled. "I'll tell her you said that."

For a moment, we shared a laugh. He felt like warmth across my chest, a balm to all the parts inside of me that stung. That ached.

"I'm so afraid you'll think I'm not enough." I whispered. "I'm not perfect."

"I don't want you to be. I just want you to be you." Emotion roughened his voice.

"Avani told me a little bit about your parents. I didn't know this, but she said you scored your deal with EllaBeauty, and they never got a chance to see it. I bet that made you feel awful, like they died before you could make them proud. I hope you understand they would be proud of you, just like Avani is now. I'm proud of you. You're a thousand times better than me, and I have no idea why I deserve you—"

I frowned. Did he really believe that?

"But damn if I ever fuck that up. Lish, if I woke up fifty years down the line next to you, you're still going to be the most beautiful woman I have ever seen. I don't care if you gain weight or chop your hair off. I don't care. My love has never been, nor will it ever be, conditional. I don't want the curated selection. I want Alisha. I wanted you three years ago as badly as I want you now. I told you, you aren't going to scare me away. Try harder, Lish. I'm not going anywhere."

Reed's words didn't wash over me.

They slid into every crack of my insecurity like a balm to a wound, melting into my skin, searing into parts of me I didn't know ached. I felt warm listening to his voice, rough with emotion, wrap around me. I felt the sincerity in his tone, the way it hummed through my chest, settling deep in my bones, chasing away the chill of self-doubt.

I inhaled deeply, breathing in his clean, comforting scent, grounding me in the present.

His presence was solid. *Steady.*

If I woke up fifty years down the line...

My love has never been, nor will it be, conditional.

A tiny ember glowed in the depths of my heart, growing brighter with each word of commitment. Tears pricked at the corners of my eyes, but for once, they weren't tears of sorrow or fear.

They were tears of relief, of being seen. And for the first time in what felt like forever, I allowed myself to believe, to trust, to hope. That maybe, just maybe, I had found someone who would like me for any and all of me.

"I like you." I confessed. "A little too much."

"Welcome to my world." Warmth and humor laced his tone, and a small laugh bubbled past the lump in my throat at how my chest expanded at that.

"Do you want to come into my super secret lair?"

"I'd be honored."

Slowly, I heard the door open, and I uncurled my body as Reed pushed the clothes back to see me. His eyes, bright in the dark space, were full of warmth and...love. Just calm.

In a moment, I was in his arms, feeling the tension begin to seep out of my body. His strong embrace held me close, and I melted into him. It was as if his touch had the power to chase away all the doubts and fears that had been swirling inside me.

"I'm not going anywhere." Reed stayed where he was, but I could hear his breathing and smell the sea and spice.

I could feel the warmth radiating off him, an anchor in my sea of emotions. He laced our fingers together, a silent promise.

Bit by bit, the tightness in my chest eased. His words from earlier came back to me.

"Only fifty years, huh?"

I felt his smile. "Wishful thinking, Angel."

My heart skipped a beat at that. "Let me know when you're good so we can talk to Avani. She was upset—"

I gasped, pulling out of his hold. "I *forgot* for a moment. Let's go."

Reed held out his hand, helping me stand, and pulled me in for a quick brush of his lips.

As we both left the closet like teenagers playing seven minutes in heaven, I asked him.

"You really wouldn't care if I gained weight?"

"Not at all, I've thought about you all pregnant and round, asking me for help with everything."

I almost tripped as he said the words, and I heard the smile in his voice as he caught me. I didn't dare look at his expression.

"I bet your face would get rounder and you'd look cute as fuck." *Oh my.*

"Is that so?" I tried to sound cool and composed. Instead, it came out breathless as I walked to the living room.

"Wishful thinking, Angel."

I didn't get a chance to say anything the moment I saw Avani's head snap up when she saw me, and I almost cried again seeing her eyes all big and watery.

"*Didi.*"

"Oh, *darling, you're* all right." I could never be mad at her. As I held her close to me, I tried to not let myself lose it over how good it felt for Reed to be right beside me holding us both. *Like we were a family.*

Fifty years from now...I've thought about you all pregnant and round....

I gripped my sister close to me as she apologized, shushing her again.

When she finally let me go, I brushed her hair back, amazed at how Avani had shown me something important tonight as well. She had seen Reed for who he was when I hadn't.

To my surprise, Reed, who had an arm around me, pulled her into his side.

"Come here, kid." My sister turned pink, and I beamed at how he handled the situation. "Your sister thinks we should have a Halloween party."

Oh, I knew he was paying attention to my conversations.

But I liked that he was distracting her.

I watched Avani sputter, utterly charmed. I bit my cheek to keep my smile contained.

"It's all right." I teased. "Reed volunteered to be one of those fairies from that fantasy series you like so much."

I winked at her. At my sister's shock and awe, I laughed, knowing full well what she was imagining. Then she looked at Reed with appraisal, and he turned pink.

"Which one?" Avani's eyes were curious, and I burst into laughter.

"Ladies, what kind of fairy are we talking about?" Reed asked, and I knew he'd find out soon enough. "Shit, it's late for you."

He looked down at Avani. "You don't have to go tonight. You're welcome to sleep here. It's more your space than mine."

Do not kiss him. Do not maul him like a wild bear.

Avani's eyes widened as she looked at her phone again. "I have class tomorrow, but..." I sensed her hesitation.

I didn't think she wanted to leave us, which was a good feeling.

"It's super early. Otherwise, I would stay."

He nodded as though understanding.

I started. "You can't go back alone this late. I'll take you." She'd mentioned the two missing grad students. I didn't want to leave her alone for a second.

Reed stepped in. "I can call someone. My guys are solid." I didn't argue having spent time with Kellan, and my sister looked surprised that I'd agreed. Twenty minutes later, a stunning brunette appeared, her sharp green eyes focused on Avani.

"I was in the area," she said to Reed in a Latin accent, explaining why she'd been so quick.

Then she focused on me. She was stunning, like a pageant contestant dressed to the nines with thigh-high suede boots.

I recognized the bottoms as a designer that was hard to come by.

What the Hell did these people do?

Avani was stunned as well.

"I'll be taking you home, si?" She smiled politely at my sister and I laughed at her expression.

"Please drive *Paloma* reasonably." Reed looked at her and she frowned, looking adorably young in that moment.

I bit back a smile. As soon as I bid my sister goodbye and the doors closed, Reed turned to me. "What kind of fairy am I dressing up as?"

I laughed. "Come on, I'll show you."

Reed's expression was comical when he saw what Avani was reading.

"That's not a fairy. That's a fucking man with wings, he's got abs *and* wings? What kind of workout would you even do to get that—"

I fell back onto the couch as I laughed hard while Reed tried to comprehend the gymnastics of training your core with wings. Warmth burst in me.

I felt lighter around Reed.

Tonight felt different, something blossoming in the space that had previously been left unfilled.

When I opened my eyes he was staring at me.

"What is it?" I rose up on one elbow.

His eyes glittered. "Fairy man's got a girlfriend."

And then he turned his phone around to show me the scandalous outfits of the female character in next to nothing but gossamer fabric.

"Hang on—" he looked at the photo again. "Is *this* the inspiration for your clothing line?" He swore. "Tell me you're going to make *this* real."

"I can see her nipples from here." *And her entire body.*

"I think *that's* the point." He looked back at the dress and held it up to my face. "In red."

I flushed imagining that dress on me in his favorite color. I caved. *It would be so pretty.*

"Tell you what, I'll design that gown personally and wear it for you." I gaped as he held the phone to his heart and pretended to fan himself, completely out of character for Reed.

Oh, he's...he's meeting me where I'm afraid.
And in turn I was a little less afraid.

CHAPTER 25
REED

ALISHA HAD NO IDEA WHO OR WHAT SHE WAS IN BED WITH.

During the day, I controlled everything, but when I came home, I was just hers.

And because I was hers, I had a lot of responsibility on my shoulders to do this right.

To do right by Alisha.

Which is what led to me showing up at Avani's college. I had never gone to college, and yet here I was.

Seeing Alisha's relationship with her sister made me think of my half-brother, Adam, and the lack of relationship I had with him.

Did I understand that Adam had been just as much a victim as me?

Adam had been younger than me.

I was still grappling with not speaking to him for over a dozen years, not reaching out. I had seen his emails regardless of Evie thinking she got rid of them. James was dead. Adam just wanted to reach out, and I couldn't bring myself to email him back. And say what?

I couldn't let the memories go, feeling betrayed he hadn't helped me.

Bitterness at the thought of him in me, warring with the sensible notions that Adam had been just as much of a kid as me.

Gabriel had become more of my brother over the years.

We'd become closer, with Evie between us turning us both into parents for her.

Nate's teasing became unrelenting, calling us a married couple with Evie as our kid.

Neither one of us gave a shit because we both loved Evie.

Alisha loved Avani.

Today, I had some housekeeping to take care of with Avani. After I met her and analyzed her down to her center, I had everything I needed to know confirmed.

She was the most important thing to my girl—she was *automatically* to me.

So I went to see her in person to give her my offer.

While the sisters shared similar mannerisms and expressions, Avani's cinnamon-hued hair and mocha eyes set her apart. But that was really the only difference in color.

Avani's gaze held the same innate warmth and spark that I had come to associate with both sisters.

Avani's bigger brown eyes were her mother's. I waited outside the building where her class was in, having her entire schedule down.

Any moment she'll come out—

When she did, it was with a girl with bright pink hair done in a ponytail.

When she saw me though, her face lit up similar to her sister's. I grinned back.

"*Reed!*" I could see parts of Alisha in her expressions, and I hadn't expected myself to warm up to her so quickly.

Avani was infectiously warm and soft-spun, a little different than Alisha.

There was an innocence about her which I attributed to being raised by Alisha with no male figures in her life. Gabriel had done his best to set an example for Evie.

I wanted to do the same for Avani.

God help the man who tried to ask her out in the future.

They would have to go through me first.

As she said goodbye to the magenta-haired friend, she walked over to me. I noticed despite her age, she dressed pretty much like Alisha who wore those mini skirts with stockings.

Avani only wore her black turtleneck. Her hair flowing down her back as she held her books to her chest. Her face devoid of any makeup and her skin glowing with transparency.

My girl raised this girl. And I was so proud of Alisha.

"Is everything all right?" Avani's accent was a mixture of the proper British cadence mixed with her soft voice and enunciations. I could see her reading for hours in her crisp tone.

173

I smiled, hoping to take some of the edge off me.

She's softer and younger than Evie.

"Yeah, I was wondering if you were free. I'd like to talk to you." She nodded, but I already knew she had no more classes for the day.

A short walk later, where I asked Avani about her last class, we sat in one of the cafés on campus.

It was sprawling and had lots of couches that were overflowing with students, but I preferred to sit somewhere in the back. As we walked in, I noted the posters of two missing girls on campus. I made a mental note to talk to Giroux since Avani went to school here and I wanted to make sure she was safe.

"How did you know I liked this?" She said after she'd taken a sip of the coffee I'd gotten her.

I drank mine black with some butter. Alisha had watched me like a criminal committing an offense, but I knew Alisha liked it with hazelnut flavor and whole milk.

"Your sister." I kept my voice lowered, learning from Gabriel who did around Evie.

Avani wasn't an operative, so she couldn't take all of the intensity I came with.

"What did you want to talk about?"

I liked that Avani got straight to the point.

Despite her being an English major, I noticed she didn't beat around the bush. She was direct in a soft way.

"I heard—" *No, you fucking snooped.* "I know your sister pays your tuition. Your books. You live in the dorms out of your own accord."

Here it goes.

"I have a proposition." I took a deep breath. *Why am I nervous?* "I paid your tuition in full. If you need books, I created a way for you to pull money from me."

I slid the black card to her. "That's mine. But you're welcome to use it for emergencies and whenever you need *anything* at all. I also got the go-ahead to move you into a place by yourself. So you can focus on school and not your shit roommate."

Her eyes widened exponentially as she looked at the card and then at me.

Her mouth opened. "W—hat- Why?"

"Here's what I'd like in return." I put the card down in front of her. "In exchange, I'll have an operative shadow you on occasion if I need to. No questions asked from you. I'd like to take the weight off your sister's

174

shoulders, so she doesn't have to worry about you. I can take care of all of it. Both of you."

Without a single worry on where my money came from or how often.

Avani's large eyes grew wider, her brows rising.

"And more importantly, I'd like to take care of you. I understand without parents both of you haven't had it easy. A lot of that weight falls on Alisha, I want to take some of it off her. I'm not trying to replace her."

That was an understatement. Both girls were fiercely independent and floundering in their own ways. Alisha struggled to accept me and Avani desperate to seek out some freedom and space to not be in her sister's way.

They needed someone to ground them both, give them security to be able to exist as they should. Someone who would be a rock. I could do that.

Avani's eyes watered. "I don't know what to say—"*Say yes.* "I have to pay you back."

That runs in the family. "I thought you might say that, which is why I have two acceptable forms of payment."

I bit back a smile at her nodding at me eagerly like I would've ever asked this teenager to pay me back.

I'm going to be there for both of you.

"One, you have lunch with me once a month so I can make sure you're alive and well and away from your sister so I can get to know you. I intend on being in her life longer than she realizes and even if I can't—"

Which I didn't want to think about.

"I'd like to still be there for you."

She didn't have a family save for Alisha.

I imagined if anything happened to Alisha, even if the thought twisted my gut, Avani would be alone and I would never let a single thing happen to either woman. I swore my life on it when I began my relationship with Alisha.

"And the second form of payment is you tell me first when shit happens to you. Not Alisha."

Her eyes widened even further. "Not because I want to keep secrets from her, but because everything can be resolved at my level. You can tell her, but I'm asking you to let me fix it first. Anything. Leaky ceiling. Taxi rides. Tickets to a concert in Dublin. Just give me a heads up if you ever do. I don't want Alisha waking up at three am panicking when I

can send a SWAT team to get you, does that make sense? I would rather be able to know both of you are good, then— *oomph.*"

A grunt left me as all five-feet six inches of the brunette leapt and hugged me.

I was cut off in surprise as I slowly wrapped my arms around her. Her honey vanilla scent was all over me. I held her tight to me.

This was the other softer scent in Alisha's house.

"Where did you come from?" She pulled back her eyes now fully in tears. "Yes, I accept your terms."

She lowered her voice. "I know you're in love with Lish, but this is a lot too for me."

I nodded, my chest tightening at the words coming out of her mouth and me agreeing to it.

Her wide grin was infectious like Alisha's. "I can't wait to tell her." And then there was one more thing. Her smile fell at my expression. "I can tell her...can't I?"

I shook my head. "I don't want you ever telling your sister about our arrangement."

I knew she'd be confused.

"If your sister likes me back—" which I know she does. "I want her to like me for me. Not anything else. You can't tell her about our little deal." Her brows furrowed. "But what about when she asks about my tuition—"

"You have a scholarship."

"And the books and everything else?" She bit her lip.

I raised a brow. "She only knows what you're willing to tell her. Alisha didn't go to college. Neither did I, so I'm not judging, but until I looked into everything about yo—*college* I didn't know either." She gaped.

"Tell your sister about class. She had your tuition on autopay, that's been replaced with my account. She'll never know if you don't say a word." I was asking her baby sister to lie to her for good reason.

"You want me to keep this a secret?" She looked hesitant like she couldn't. Because ethics or morals or whatever compass motivated people.

"I don't want her to worry about you any more than she already does."

She bit down on her lip. "This is already killing me."

I knew. Both of them were cut from the same cloth.

Which was why I had to protect them. Both of the girls were genuinely sweet people.

I didn't want them to hurt.

"But you want to take it." She nodded. "I shouldn't feel like this though. It's not proper."

There it is. "True, but if you keep a secret at the expense of not hurting someone it isn't so bad is it?"

I kept my voice soft. Her honey eyes, intelligent, took me in. "Is that what you do for Lish?"

I was carefully composed when I answered. "I would do anything for your sister. And that umbrella of care extends to you. So what do you say, deal?"

A beat passed. Another.

Loyalty always warred with sensibility.

She took the black amex off the table. "Deal."

CHAPTER 26
ALISHA

I QUICKLY LEARNED THAT DATING REED WAS GOING TO BE AN EXERCISE IN patience.

Sometimes his job called him away just as mine did. I was attending an event tonight, and plans had changed. After my shower, Reed snapped his phone shut and looked at me with regret.

"I'm sorry, Angel. I don't think I can make it tonight." His hands played with the ties of my robe. "Got a text from Gabriel. I need to head to the office."

I frowned. "It's so late. Can't he handle it on his own?"

Reed's eyes filled with something I couldn't identify. "No, baby. I promise I'll try to be back as quickly as I can."

Which meant all night or worse, days.

I didn't know where Reed went for so long, but I knew when he came back, he crawled into bed with me exhausted. I didn't know what was so urgent; I had this event on the calendar for a month now.

"Alright," I said with an exhale. "Just text me when you're home safe. I'm guessing you're switching with Kellan?"

He nodded, but his eyes darkened as he began thinking about his meeting, or whatever it was.

I didn't understand the realm of security, just as Reed didn't understand why I needed fifty shades of brown lip gloss.

I had to be flexible with Reed, just as he was with me.

When Kellan showed up, though, he wasn't alone.

Gone was the letterman jacket, replaced by a crisp white button-down and dark slacks.

He looked more like himself, his hair styled back and his eyes darker.

The contrast between the golden retriever persona and this man standing in front of me was a little jarring.

Kellan's transformation paled in comparison to the woman at his side.

She was the dark-haired supermodel who had helped Avani.

Recognition dawned on me as she gave me a friendly smile.

I remembered her faintly from the day I had been caught in a shootout, but I had been too shell-shocked to pay attention. And then again, with my sister.

I didn't miss the way Kellan looked at her, his eyes filled with a mixture of admiration and longing.

Was this...her? *His crush?*

Nor did I miss the way she scowled in response, a faint blush coloring her cheeks. The interaction between them was endearing, and I bit back a laugh.

"You must be Selena," I said warmly, extending my hand in greeting.

"Sí," she replied, her eyes sparkling with warmth and mirth as she took my hand. Her silver floor-length gown shimmered under the lights. "We're going to a party? I thought this dress might be good."

"It's beautiful. You both look fantastic," I assured her, meaning every word.

Turning towards the bedroom, I called out. "Reed! Selena and Kellan are here!"

Before heading to get dressed, I glanced back at Kellan, unable to resist teasing him a little.

"You look so different without your jacket."

Kellan grinned, his signature wide smile lighting up his face. He cast a sidelong glance at Selena, who turned an even deeper shade of pink and muttered. "*College football,*" under her breath.

I laid out my black mini-dress on the bed. Selena's spaghetti-strapped silvery gown was the stuff of dreams, but I was too short to pull off that high of a split up my thighs.

I finished putting on my stockings over my panties, sans bra. Pushing all my hair to one side, I added pearl clips to it, just as Reed walked out in all black, looking less than pleased.

Until he saw me.

Over my shoulder, I watched his eyes take in my lingerie-clad form in shoes and hair and makeup done. No bra. No clothes.

I paused while pushing in the second clip as he closed the small space between us.

"*Don't* move." Reed's voice was guttural. "Don't fucking move."

He quickly walked and locked the bedroom door. "I thought I was going to wait until you came home to fuck you."

He undid his pants as he all but lifted me onto the vanity I had.

"We have guests." I was already panting.

"They can't hear anything," he whispered, already kissing his way down to my nipples. "Trust me, Kellan won't be paying attention to us."

It was on the tip of my tongue to ask why but I let out a faint moan instead when Reed slid two fingers under my stockings and into me. I gasped at the stretch and sensations running through me.

"You're *soaked*," he whispered over my lips as he began curling his fingers into me, working me into a frenzy. "Come for me. I need something to think about tonight."

I didn't get a chance to ask him why when he began a rhythm that drove me insane. *Fast.*

I pulled him up to kiss me to hide my screams as I did.

As I calmed down, with his other hand Reed, drew his cock out and I hungrily fell to my knees to his shock.

This wasn't the first time I'd gone down on him.

It was the first time I'd been this bold.

I loved going down on Reed.

"I would like to do this more often." I whispered, watching the way Reed's head tipped back and his proud thick stalk jutted out.

I was salivating at how hot this was. The first taste of him I lost it.

Trapped against the vanity, I felt his hand fist at my hair helping me, his faint growls sinking into my skin.

I loved when Reed let go. I felt the heady scent of him mixing with the taste and I moaned around him. I fisted his girth struggling to take him deeper.

"You're so fucking beautiful, look at you...all over my cock."

I hummed with pleasure, adding to the moment of getting caught and trying to be quiet.

I managed to swallow him until my nose hit his stomach. For a moment I didn't move, I just absorbed the feel of him closing my eyes.

Above me, Reed swore and growled. "*Suck*, Angel."

I obeyed, bobbing my head, and furiously using my fist until he was a groaning mess.

There was no way they couldn't hear us. And the fact that I was working him into a frenzy dressed in little to nothing.

I never felt more wanton and *wild*.

"*No*," he growled, as he swelled in my mouth.

Faster than I thought possible, he yanked me up, spinning me around and bending me over my dresser.

The rip of my stockings followed, and I gasped from the force of his thrust. I immediately struggled.

"I need—I can't—" I protested. I couldn't even wrap my mind around how overwhelmed I was at the moment. Stretched full. Hot and heavy inside of me.

"Shhh," he pushed his hand over my mouth letting me scream when he shoved *deeper*. "You *can*. You have."

He pushed in so deep, if I hadn't been in heels I would've been on my tippy toes.

I stopped thinking as he began to pound into me.

"I come inside this little pussy. Buried in you."

Yes. It was a sensory *overload*.

He continued to growl filthy things as he fucked into me. "Good girl, clench down on my cock."

Our eyes locked in the mirror.

Oh God, I look...

My breasts bouncing, Reed's body contrasting with mine, the size of him so much bigger as he cupped both of them and worked my nipples.

I arched my head, unable to look away as his lips moved on my neck.

"You're so beautiful," he licked his lips as he moved. "Look at you taking me." I was. I couldn't look at anything else.

"I want you to remember me when you go out *tonight* when every man in the room stares at you wishing they could see you just...like... this."

I would've screamed had I not seen the look in his eyes.

"I—I don't want anyone else," I panted.

My makeup was ruined and my hair was a mess as he slowed his thrusts just enough at my confession. "J—just you."

"Just me reminding you every night that I'm the only man who gets to see this."

"Yes, Reed." I loved it when Reed's body moved like this.

It was long slow strokes that did me in the sweetest.

I was in heaven with every thrust and I realized this was the part of Reed he kept tucked away from others.

The part that the others had whispered to me about.

Reed pounded into my body possessed with nothing, but red hot need.

"This little pussy needs to be reminded who owns it sometimes. You're going to let me come deep in you, aren't you, Angel?" His eyes were watching me in the mirror. His intent was clear. To fuck. To *take*. It was every part of his bloodstream and he couldn't stop. I nodded under his spell.

"*More*," I whispered, my eyes meeting his in the mirror. "Fuck me like they're watching. *Take me like I'm yours.*"

His eyes flashed wildly.

His booted feet kicked my legs open as he bent over the dresser, one hand on my back, the other at my hips as he began to *fuck*.

I stood no chance.

My cries were muffled against my fist, objects rattling, bottles tipping over as he gripped my neck forcing me down.

I was losing it, flushed, my nipples diamond hard as they bounced with every thrust raking against the vanity.

I came apart covering my mouth so I wouldn't scream.

My legs began to tremble and I felt the orgasm quaking through me. Reed used my orgasms as fuel.

I knew he wouldn't stop until I was a puddle of mush and he had drained me of everything.

He adjusted to push both my legs wider.

Oh God, I'm not going to make it.

It felt impossible to survive the pleasure coursing through my body as Reed pounded into me.

I muffled my scream at the adjustment.

Each thrust he hit a place so tender, he moved his hand over my mouth as I screamed obscenely into his palm.

My eyes locked on us, my breasts bouncing, the image of us seared into my brain until I felt another wave slam into me.

This one ripped through me leaving nothing untouched, my fingers clutching until my knuckles turned white, as his brutal thrusts dragged the sensations out of me.

I was sobbing incoherently as he pulled me away from the vanity, stopping for just a moment.

Just enough to catch my breath. He moved me a few steps, until I was face down over the bed, never leaving me.

I scrambled to grasp the comforter tightly as he held my hips on either side and took what he needed from me.

It was the slap of skin that grew more furious with every thrust in this position, Reed hit somewhere so deep there was a sting of pain. I inhaled sharply as his hand drifted around to my womb.

"I can feel myself right there," he growled. "Is that how deep I am?"

I nodded, closing my eyes, feeling my teeth clink as he shoved in particularly hard. And yet I arched my back asking for more. *I loved that.*

Reed grasped both of my ass cheeks and spread me wide. This wasn't the first time he'd played with me, but there were people outside waiting for me. I gasped at the obscene sensation of that as he was stretching me open.

"One day, you'll let me take you here." I gasped as he sank his thumb into me and the stretch and burn left me breathless. My eyes rolled back.

"*Yes.*"

A pleasured hum left his throat at my inability to say no to him.

I was just an object for his desires as he pounded them into me.

All I could was *take.*

Objects broke, the furniture slammed into the wall, there was no way for them to not know I was absolutely being destroyed here.

And I love it.

"Scream for me when you come. Let them know you're mine, that your man fucks you like an animal."

I felt like a supernova went off in my womb. Reed never did anything in half measures. The pressure in me crested so hard, I couldn't *breathe.*

White spots lit up in my eyes and I squeezed tightly aware I was screaming into the sheets.

Behind me I felt him groan as quietly as he could as he emptied himself into me.

I felt the heat in my womb, seeping between my legs, dripping down my thighs.

Moments later, Reed slipped out from me, helping me clean up, and adjusting my dress. I needed to redo my hair and makeup.

"Did you mean any of what you said?" It was on the tip of my tongue.

"Every word."

CHAPTER 27
REED

I HELD ONTO THE MEMORY OF ALISHA WHEN I WENT TO MIDTOWN THAT night.

I didn't have a meeting with Gabriel. The lie burned on my tongue as I told Alisha I did. I wasn't here for Gabriel. Not exactly. It was about him though.

I held her warmth close to me even as it faded on the drive to "work."

Whatever it was tonight. My thoughts strayed to her the entire short trip. She was addicting. Her laughter light around me.

I inhaled her every chance I got.

It was never enough. I felt like every time I was with her, I was absorbing her warmth. In turn, it was melting parts of me I didn't know existed. Once I tasted her I knew she was what I was craving.

An escape.

I came to the office in Midtown to think and put pieces together but I couldn't think when my thoughts drifted back to this morning.

Days with Alisha flew by.

We'd disagree and bicker about little things, but damn if the make up sex after it wasn't the best.

I fucking loved when she caught a little bit of that attitude I saw underneath her soft persona. I ate it up.

I'd just fuck her hard enough to feel her pussy squirt all over me when I did set her off. I bit back a grin at the last time I'd done that to her.

I learned if I teased Alisha and got her hot and bothered, she'd come harder. And that shit was good for me.

Go on, Angel.

Give me that attitude and see what I do with it.

And I was a thorough man. She'd screamed so much I'd all but crooned my praise in her ear as she trembled and shivered all over.

You're my little slut, aren't you? I make that pussy squirt for me and only me.

Y—yes, Reed. I'm yours.

And then I proceeded to fuck her through it until she'd cried and all but blacked out.

I hadn't gotten much sleep but thankfully with Alisha, I could sleep in and wake her up with my tongue between her legs.

She did this adorable thing right before I made her squirt that drove me fucking nuts. She tried to get away. From. Me.

Are you going to try that little stunt on me?

She always screamed no, and apologized. But I was a ruthless man. I was a storm taking everything around me and one of those things was her. And I fucking *loved* it.

I pulled up to Titan Midtown which Gabriel rarely bothered coming to.

Even then, he liked the house up north.

I liked the steel city.

I sat in my car waiting for the black town car to pull up.

The platinum blonde who stepped out was who I was going to meet tonight.

Guilt burned in my throat at keeping this a secret from Alisha. From Gabriel. But what they didn't know was good for them.

Both of the people I cared about the most in my life were going to hurt themselves if I didn't intervene. If I didn't *try*.

Lucy Devereaux's elegant form walked to the Maserati, holding a handbag that cost what most people made in a lifetime.

I liked Lucy, not just because she was my spy. She didn't beat around the bush. She got the job done. That was exactly what landed her in hot water. *Every* damn time.

I had asked Nate to contact the only legal jewel thief we knew, someone who knew enough about everyone to stay out of their way. Lucy was *invisible*.

As she slipped into the passenger seat, her rounded cheeks and feminine curves filling the space, she fixed me with a pointed look.

"My brother better not find out about this, Reed. Lucas has been extra nosy lately, and I went through hell to get you what you asked for."

She explained how she had laid low before bringing the item to me, careful not to attract suspicion.

"I gave you my word," I assured her, my voice soft as I scanned our surroundings. "That's why we're meeting here."

Lucy's cornflower blue eyes narrowed. "Instead of your office?"

"You scavenge for a living," I reminded her, choosing a more diplomatic term for her line of work.

Lucy was known for her ability to acquire diamonds and priceless artifacts from third-world country leaders, a skill that made her invaluable.

She'd been working for me for the last few years discreetly. Gabriel was aware, but he kept his distance, too pissed off at her entire family for their existence.

He'd be livid if he found out I was meeting Lucy Devereaux out of all people for his fucking family heirloom.

But I had no choice.

He was also the biggest reason I couldn't bring her onto the team.

She adjusted her coat, the weight she had gained since college making her look healthier and more youthful.

With her long blonde hair and bangs framing her big blue eyes, her cheeks rounded, she could easily pass for someone much younger.

It was easy to forget that she was close in age to Evie, a testament to how life could shape people in unexpected ways.

"You said it was urgent."

She nodded, her eyes lighting up. "I think I found what you're looking for."

She began to take off her jacket. I already felt the ice invading my insides.

I turned my phone around to not look at Alisha's smile.

For the first time, I realized how much it weighed as it sank into my chest.

I'm sorry, Angel.

CHAPTER 28
ALISHA

As a former brand ambassador for EllaBeauty, I had been invited to attend the launch event for their new makeup line, despite having stepped down from my commitments a year ago.

The event was held in a private room within an immersive art exhibit, and as I stepped inside, I was greeted by a whimsical display of pink popup lips and photo booths.

Lots of lighting everywhere for the best shots, a bright pink bar serving all sorts of wild drinks by the looks of the menu.

I tried to focus on the glam around me and not the way Reed had kissed me before he walked out.

Throughout the entire ride here, I had been clenching down on the toy Reed had placed inside of me.

It felt illicit, knowing that no one else was aware of its presence, but it also served as a reminder of Reed's possessive claim over me.

As I took in the colorful surroundings, a familiar figure caught my eye.

Gemma, her cheeks flushed from the alcohol, practically launched herself at me, enveloping me in a tight hug.

I couldn't help but laugh as I returned it, steadying her slightly wobbly form.

"Lish! So good to see you!"

Behind me, Kellan, who knew Gemma, didn't brace as much as Selena did. The Cuban beauty all but eyed Gemma like a target she needed to pounce on.

Sonya Amin, a Turkish diamond heiress and long-time friend of Gemma's, stood in an elegant floor-length black dress behind Gemma, an amused expression in her bright green eyes. She smoothed her sable hair back, grinning at me.

Beside her stood Nate, his usually rugged appearance replaced by a more polished look. I had to do a double-take to ensure it was really him.

"Nate?" It slipped out of my mouth.

Selena walked up to him and pulled him into a hug, her affection for her friend evident in the way she held him close.

"How are you, *muñeca?*" Nate asked, his navy eyes softening as he looked at Selena. Kellan stiffened next to me.

In my ear, Gemma, still hugging me mock whispered, "I didn't think you would make it!"

Sonya, her voice soft and teasing with her faint Turkish accent, interjected.

"Of course she would make it. Where else would Alisha witness you avoiding your bodyguard?"

She tipped her head towards Nate, who was now scowling as he handed Gemma a bottle of water, his glare fixed on her once he'd released Selena from his embrace.

Gemma, her words slightly slurred, admitted in a fierce whisper. "I hate him...he just follows me everywhere, brooding, on his stupid motorcycle. Him and his abs."

I pressed my lips together, struggling to contain the laughter that threatened to escape.

"How many drinks has she had?" I asked, glancing at Sonya.

"Four?" Sonya guessed, rubbing Gemma's back.

"Five," Nate corrected, his tone exasperated. Kellan watched the exchange with a hard-set jaw.

Weren't they coworkers? I wondered, puzzled by the tension in the air. Nate approached me, gently prying Gemma off and handing her the water bottle. I'd never seen Kellan look so angry.

Sonya leaned in close, whispering in my ear. "Gemma used to avoid Nate when she would come to Teasers with us. Now I am seeing why."

As intrigued as I was by the dynamic between Nate and Gemma, my attention shifted to Sonya, whom I hadn't seen in ages.

"It's so good to see you," I said warmly, pulling her into a hug.

Kellan stood behind me, a reassuring presence, while Nate momentarily paused his argument with Gemma to glance at Selena.

She smirked at him, saying something in rapid Spanish that everyone seemed to understand except for me.

"Really, Lena?" Nate grinned, a mischievous glint in his eye. "You wanna do this here, *muñeca?*"

Kellan's voice cut through the air, sharp and possessive. *"Don't call her that."*

Selena's head whipped towards him, her eyes wide with surprise. Gemma blinked, her blue eyes round as she took in the scene.

Nate, on the other hand, laughed, seemingly amused by Kellan's reaction.

Kellan's jaw was clenched, his eyes narrowed, while Selena seemed caught off guard, her usual confidence replaced by a flicker of uncertainty. Her eyes were on him.

Sensing the rising tension, I intervened. "It is so lovely seeing everyone. Why don't we all just get some food?"

"Exactly." Sonya chimed in, her hand squeezing mine tightly. "Gemma refused to let me wallow tonight when she knew everyone would be here. Lara will be joining us in a moment, and until then, I'm sure we can all be civil, yes?"

She turned to me, her eyes conveying her concern. "It's good to see you."

I noticed Sonya's gaze drifting towards Selena, and I knew where her thoughts were heading.

Eager to diffuse the situation further, I extended my free hand to the brunette in her silvery gown.

"Selena, did you know Gemma speaks Spanish?"

Selena, still looking a little wide-eyed from the exchange between Nate and Kellan, seemed grateful for the distraction. She took my hand.

I sent Gemma a glare to *come here.* Her opal eyes widened as she obeyed. Kellan's posture was rigid as he watched Selena interact with us, but he seemed mildly calmer.

Nate, for his part, remained close to Gemma, but his attention was divided between his charge and the silent battle of wills between him and Kellan.

Selena turned pink as Gemma slipped into soft Spanish. Whatever she said made Selena smile.

Sonya pulled me aside, her voice low. "I'm going to keep an eye on your lady bodyguard to make sure she's going to be all right when those two Neanderthals fight over her tonight."

Kellan's eyes sought out Selena, who met his gaze with soft, questioning glances throughout the night.

She opted to stay close to me, while Nate remained dutifully by Gemma's side.

Selena is Kellan's crush. And they're together.

Sonya leaned in, her eyes glinting with mischief. "I think he likes Selena."

"No." I shook my head, recalling Reed's words. "Reed said they were strictly professional. Siblings, almost."

Sonya knew Reed and I were together.

While Selena didn't seem to reciprocate Nate's feelings, I couldn't help but notice the touch of familiarity in her eyes, no doubt a result of their years working together.

Sonya eyed Kellan discreetly. "Definitely not a sister to him."

I quietly explained a little about Kellan's crush. Sonya's bright eyes filled with understanding.

"So Nate is stirring the proverbial pot."

"Do you think Nate—"

"I *do*." Sonya interjected, her eyes gleaming with excitement. "He watches Gemma like a hawk and won't let her dance with anyone. Besides, he's exactly her type."

Yet, Nate's attention seemed divided between his duty to Gemma and his apparent interest in Selena. *This was too complicated.*

"Why does everything always get interesting when I wasn't paying attention?" I mused, shaking my head. Sonya laughed softly at that.

"I'm sorry," I touched her elbow. "I should've called sooner."

"No, don't apologize." Sonya was the oldest one in our group and a dutiful friend at that. We'd all met at a charity function, and thankfully, her husband had not been there that night.

"How are you?" Her eyes warmed at the sight of my expression. "This is not the best place to have this chat, no?"

"No," I whispered. "But we can all go back to my place after?"

She nodded eagerly. "I'd love that. But, I'm a free woman now and I happen to have my very own place that definitely needs some margaritas and love."

She gave an uncharacteristic twist of her lips. "Michael's grandmother passed away. I was never very close to her, but I knew she liked me. Enough to leave me everything in her will."

Michael Devereaux's family, her ex, had been wealthy for centuries.

I'd heard about his grandmother passing but I didn't know if Sonya had any relationship with her.

"Everything. It makes what my parents had look like child's play. Michael is *so* angry."

Years of abuse at the hands of a man who had taken her for granted had led to Sonya becoming a shy, thin, sheltered woman who had yearned for the security of her own.

"Chicaaaas," All of us turned as Lara, for once, showed up sans wings and wearing what on *her* was demure: a skintight mini black sheath with elaborate cut-outs.

Her inky hair was tied in two space buns, her bangs framing her impish grin.

At the sight of Lara, who Selena seemed to be familiar with, we formed a circle with Kellan and Nate on either half. Kellan stood behind Selena and me, watching both of us, his fingers brushing over her hips every so often.

The rest of the night turned into a bit of a party with all of us catching up, enjoying the event. I missed Reed and I wished he could've met all of them at once.

At some point during the night, though, I felt the vibrator in me turn up just a little.

I excused myself politely, and by the time I reached the bathroom, I was grateful I left when I did. I locked myself into a stall, leaned against the wall, and texted Reed.

> A warning would be nice.

I could imagine his grin.

> Are you alone?

> I am now.

AND THEN THE VIBRATOR WENT WILD. I CLAPPED A HAND AROUND MY mouth squeezing my eyes shut. I felt it against my clit and somewhere sweet inside of me where Reed teased me mercilessly.

I bit back a scream as it grew to an intensity that would've brought me to my knees.

It's not the same as you.

My fingers shook as I tried to get it across.

Thank God I was alone in here. He called. I answered on the first ring.

"Say my name."

I let out breathless moans and whimpers biting them back as I gripped the wall behind me.

"You're so close aren't you?"

"Yes, it's right there, Reed, it's—"

"Not fucking deeper than me." *No, never.* I moaned softly. "When I come home tonight, I want you bent over on all fours for me, would you like that, Angel?" I moaned, rocking my hips.

If possible he increased the vibrations to an intensity that left me breathless, I would've cried out had I not clapped a hand over my mouth squeezing. "Let me hear you—"

"I'm *loud*—"

"I know," he crooned. "Let me hear it. If you don't give it to me now, I'll take it from you later and we both know you want to walk tomorrow, don't you?"

I rocked my hips letting those little cries escape and when it came, I held nothing back, crying his name loudly aware I sounded like a woman possessed and clearly getting railed.

I whimpered, sinking down to the ground as the vibrator continued and he worked me through it, lowering it slowly, talking to me like he was right there.

"Such a good girl, I'm going to come home and reward you so well tonight. God, you're probably pink and pretty right now without me and I hate it. I miss you, Angel. I can't wait to taste all your orgasms tonight."

Who needed love poems when you had this?

I moaned as it finally relented and he continued to tell me all the things he'd do to me tonight.

"Do not take the toy out. Keep it in there, I need you tonight. And I'm not going to go easy."

He didn't have to tell me twice.

CHAPTER 29
ALISHA

It was evident that Selena didn't get much girl time.

Gemma took to her almost immediately, introducing her to people and offering to have her come over to her place sometimes as a girl-friend. Lara handed Selena a tiara from her purse.

And girls' night was…a really wonderful feeling after the last few weeks.

When I got back to Kellan's side, he looked ready to fight someone again. Nate's expression was dark.

Had something happened at the party?

Later that night, the five of us sat around Sonya's brand-new kitchen island in her recently purchased townhouse.

The sleek, modern space was a testament to Sonya's impeccable taste, with its high ceilings, large windows, and an open floor plan that seamlessly connected the living room and kitchen.

Soft, warm lighting from the pendant lamps above the island cast a gentle glow on our faces as we sipped the piña coladas Lara had whipped up.

The aroma of the drinks mingled with the faint scent of violets from the scented candles Sonya had lit earlier. Selena seemed to relax a little more as she was led away from Nathan and Kellan.

She looked amused at us, each out of place in our own way. I had given up on trying to be comfortable with a vibrator inside of me and took it out after cleaning up in Sonya's bathroom.

I knew I would face Reed's punishment tonight regardless. There was something in his voice that told me he needed more, that something had happened.

Lara began looking at me, wiggling her eyebrows. "Now that Reed is in love with you, I think we should take bets on when Gemma fucks her bodyguard."

Gemma promptly choked on her drink as Selena clapped her on the back with the force of an Amazon. "I see the way Nate looks at you, *chica.*"

Gemma batted her lashes at Selena. "Did you…and with Nate?" Selena's eyes went comically wide, and she said something that sounded like a complete denial in Spanish before switching to English.

"We are just work partners. Only. Promise."

Gemma flushed, looking oddly grateful for Selena's words. "I'm not interested," Gemma said, turning pink at the dubious glances everyone gave her.

Lara chided her while I looked at Selena's blush, keeping close to me, figuring she'd prefer that.

Lara crowded closer on Gemma's lap like a cat, while Sonya grinned at their antics.

"Kellan is very interested in you," I lowered my voice, aware that the two men were in the dining room, the housekeeper fawning over them and feeding them real food. Copious amounts of it. Safe to say, the canapés had not satisfied the two men towering over us.

Selena squirmed in her seat, her cheeks blooming with a rosy hue that made her look even more stunning.

For a fleeting moment, I caught a glimpse of vulnerability in her eyes, a crack in her usually confident, femme fatale façade.

"He seems fond of you." Sonya chimed in, her voice laced with a knowing tone. I hadn't realized she'd been observing the interaction so closely. "Has anyone ever told you how gorgeous you are? You could do pageants."

Gemma nodded, taking a sip of her piña colada, the icy drink clinking against the glass. Selena's deepening blush spread down her neck.

"The wise elder sister speaks," Lara declared dramatically, her eyes sparkling with mischief at Sonya. "Golden boy out there looks like he would do unspeakable things to you and your cookie."

Her words dripped with innuendo, causing Selena to turn an even deeper shade of crimson.

"Seriously, *chica*," Lara continued, switching to Spanish, her words flowing. It made Gemma turn pink, and Selena all but covered her face.

"What did she say?" I asked Gemma, curiosity getting the better of me.

Gemma shook her head, her own cheeks flushed with a mix of amusement and embarrassment.

"Kellan looks like he could tongue fuck her pussy into a coma," Lara translated, taking a nonchalant sip of her drink as Sonya and I nearly choked on our own.

"Lara!" Our voices blending into a chorus of laughter that filled the room, bouncing off the walls.

"Is she always like this?" Selena asked me, her eyes wide with a mix of shock and admiration.

I nodded, grinning at Lara's shameless audacity. "Always."

Gemma leaned forward, a mischievous glint in her eye.

"Don't think I don't know about you and a certain somebody," she teased, wiggling her finger at Lara accusingly. Lara's cheeks turned a rare sight of pink.

"Are you guys talking about Liam?" I asked, putting the pieces together.

"His name is Liam!" Gemma exclaimed, clapping her hands together gleefully. Lara's blush deepened to a beet red, while Selena's eyes widened.

"You're dating Liam?" Selena sounded floored. Lara covered her eyes, as if trying to hide from the attention, while Gemma pelted her with candy, the colorful treats raining down like confetti.

"Nate is quite rugged," Sonya mused, her gaze drifting towards Gemma.

It was a smooth attempt to steer the conversation away from Selena and Lara, who both looked grateful for the reprieve.

"After Michael, I think I'm done with the fraternity lawyer accountant types. Maybe it's time for a daring man on a motorcycle, with unkempt hair and sexy stubble. I never thought I'd find facial hair so attractive. What do you call them again?"

"*Bikers*." Lara supplied, shuddering in mock disgust. "*Yick*."

She shook her waves, her nose wrinkling at the thought.

Gemma's shoulders tensed as she said. "You can have Nate."

Sonya caught my eye, a knowing smile exchanged between us. *Well played, Sonya.*

Selena leaned close to my ear and whispered. "Reed has been crazy about you for so long."

I felt heat blossom in my chest.

Her next words were even softer, barely audible above the laughter and chatter. "You compliment him very nicely."

I hadn't had too many interactions with Selena, but I realized that despite her exterior, her quiet intelligence was evident in those sharp green and gold eyes.

I watched her laughing with my girls, and I couldn't wait to meet the other Titans, especially the one Reed considered the most important to him: *Gabriel*.

That's where Reed was tonight.

"You work with Gabriel?" I asked, leaning closer. Selena's eyes lit up at the mention of his name. "What's he like? I know Reed considers him a brother."

She made an appreciative noise. "He's wonderful. Gabriel is..." She went on to say highly complimentary things. That was good to know. "I'm not close, but he's good to me, not as much as Evie—"

"His sister?" I clarified, and Selena nodded. "Anything I should know before I meet him?"

She thought about it for a moment. "No, he's very sweet. I'm his assistant, and Nathan is—was Reed's."

"Like assistants?" I asked, and she considered it before nodding. "That's clever. So who replaced Nate as Reed's—" I broke off, seeing the answer in her eyes. *Kellan*. It was written all over her face.

I absorbed the information for a moment until Lara's blender went off, bursting the bubble and Sonya telling Lara to use less alcohol, otherwise it was just a giant coconut rum bottle instead of a piña colada.

Gemma looked at Selena shyly, and the other woman just seemed happy to be around girls.

And suddenly, everything felt normal again.

Just a girls' night with Lara putting tiaras on us and Gemma turning bright red whenever she screamed that we were dirty little sluts.

By the time the night drew to a close, I was pleasantly buzzed, the room swaying gently around me as Selena and I stumbled arm-in-arm back to my apartment.

Kellan wrapped his arms around us both, steadying our steps as we climbed into the waiting taxi.

Selena, I noticed, was glued to his side, their bodies molded together like two puzzle pieces.

Now that I knew the truth about their relationship, it felt almost intrusive to be in such close proximity.

"I know, *Gatita*, let me handle it this time," Kellan murmured, his voice low and soothing as he responded to something Selena had said. He pulled her closer, nuzzling his face into her hair.

I didn't remember the rest of the ride back, but the fresh air combined with the giddy sensation of a good night with the girls left me on a blissful high.

As I walked upstairs to my apartment, I thought about texting Reed, until I paused.

Was it my imagination, or is my door open?

I felt my giddiness blip out like a bubble floating in the wind. I had locked it before I left. Kellan had checked it.

All the happiness left my body as dread slithered into my spine, settling deep within me.

I must've made a noise, something coming out of my throat as the realization hit me.

"Let me," he was there in an instant, gun drawn, eyes hard, behind him Selena looked like a lioness as she approached me.

I watched my heart beating out of my chest as Kellan opened the door and I cautiously stepped in, unsure of what I might find, Selena at my back.

Nothing was out of place in any of the rooms I had been through. Except for my bedroom.

The door was ajar and I saw Kellan who didn't see me with his back turned taking photos of my room.

Why was he— I stilled. And then I screamed.

CHAPTER 30
REED

"Where did you find it?"

I held the necklace in the palm of my hand.

"There's a market in Senegal, where I had a few people on the ground. The short story is, it's yours now," Lucy replied, her voice tinged with a hint of something I couldn't place.

But my mind was torn between lying to Gabriel, lying to Alisha, lying to Lucy—and well *everyone*.

I bit back a sigh. I flipped the necklace over, pausing at Gabriel's name on the back...*Monroe*.

"And the long version?" I pressed, my gaze fixed on her. "I need to know if you pissed off a warlord."

"No warlords, I swear," she insisted, though something in her expression made me wonder if she was being fully truthful.

She muttered something about one angry woman.

I believed in keeping the enemy close.

Not that Lucas was.

But Gabriel would disagree.

Especially if the 'enemy's' sister was the five-foot-four blonde who had a penchant for riling up people in countries she really had no business being in. I didn't mind intermingling loyalties and Lucy was a good operative.

I rescued her out of a situation in Colombia years ago.

She stayed loyal to me and did whatever I asked her to do. And no one was any wiser.

Why don't I believe her? I mused as I looked at the necklace trying to open it. It wouldn't budge.

Shelving that concern for now, I asked. "How does it open?"

Lucy motioned with her chin, her eyes narrowing.

"A key, I'd guess. I tried picking the lock, but no dice. Didn't want to risk setting off a booby trap or something."

I arched an eyebrow, my voice laced with skepticism. "A booby trap?"

She shrugged, her tone defensive. "I'm just trying to look out for you. Are you going to let me in on why you need this necklace so badly?"

"No." My reply was curt, leaving no room for argument.

Next to me, Lucy sighed, frustration evident in her tone. After a moment, her quiet voice filled the car. "I know this has to do with Gabriel."

I looked at her, my eyes widening in surprise.

She shrugged. "What? I know things too. Lucas doesn't hate him, but Gabriel hasn't exactly made life easy for my family."

No, Gabriel was out to destroy you guys.

"I will continue to keep your name out of anyone's mouth and your identity a secret from your father and Lucas. And you will do what I ask. No questions asked. That was the deal you made with me." I looked at her with no break and no room for argument, my voice low and intense. "Is that clear?"

She let out a shaky breath, her eyes wide with a mix of fear and resignation. I could tell sometimes Lucy was in over her head. She didn't have the same spine that Selena had. But if she had the proper training, she would. She could.

I had debated it. But I knew Gabriel would lose his fucking shit at hiring a Devereaux.

Lucas thought she was a fucking archeologist. And the world didn't really know her. Lucy was good.

But I couldn't tell her anything. I didn't even know myself.

"Yes, sir," Lucy replied, she looked down at the necklace.

"This is the only one of its kind?" I pressed, my voice urgent.

"The only one I know of." She was telling the truth, her tone earnest. "It's custom-made and he obviously purchased it for someone special."

I traced the designs bordering the heart-shaped pendant, my mind racing.

"I think it holds something valuable inside."

Why else would Gabriel go through the trouble of acquiring it? The question is...what the fuck was it?

The heavy piece gleamed under the light, and I couldn't help but ask. "How much would something like this cost?"

"Conservatively, between three and five hundred dollars," Lucy gave me a wry smile, her voice tinged with amusement. "Chump change, right?"

For Gabriel? *Yes.* But what was he doing hunting for this?

I eyed her curiously, my voice low and probing. "Did you actually buy this, or..."

Lucy's gaze slid away, and she fidgeted with the sleeve of her coat. "I didn't, exactly..."

"Lucy." My voice was a warning, my patience wearing thin.

"It was just sitting there!" she protested, her voice rising an octave. "I had to take it for you."

The earnest look in her eyes both touched and exasperated me.

"Right..." I said dryly, meeting her gaze with a skeptical one of my own.

She grumbled, sounding an awful lot like a teenager rather than the twenty-four-year-old who cavorted around the world stealing.

"Do you know who it belonged to in Monroe's life?" She asked, despite my earlier warning about questions.

I bit back a sigh, my voice firm. "I don't know." I'd already guessed it was a woman's. "That's all the questions I'm willing to entertain for the night from you, Lucy. I'll reach back out to you should I need anything else."

"Yes, sir." She wasn't happy but she didn't have to be. I held all the cards now.

I had one more phone call to make as Lucy left the car.

Because he was the only other person actively looking for something for Gabriel.

Aidan O'Hara.

"It's late," the deep rumble sounded wide awake compared to his greeting.

"I found it." I heard a rustle and Aidan adjusting. "Gabriel had you searching for the necklace too."

Who did it belong to?

A long moment passed before Aidan sighed and spoke. "I don't know. I know parts of the story like you do. Seems Gabriel won't tell anyone the truth."

No, he'd take his secrets to the grave.

"He had to tell you something, you've been around him long enough. He's dragging everyone down."

"Including yourself?" His voice filled with humor. "Is your girlfriend aware of what you do?"

I bit back a biting reply. I wasn't surprised. We all kept tabs on each other. "What's Kieran doing buying up a former hotel?"

"He's in his twenties, currently discovering women," Aidan said as a matter of fact. "He doesn't believe in dating."

Kieran was twenty-four and having the time of his life away from his family.

Once I knew what he was up to, I saw why Aidan had asked Gabriel to keep an eye on the kid. Aidan and I had a complicated relationship. I didn't *not* like him, I just knew it was a slippery slope being friends with him.

On a scale of darkness, Aidan was Hades. I preferred to pass through on my journey through Hell. If there was a room for me somewhere down there, it would be a suite. Aidan had an entire throne in his kingdom.

He'd been ruthless in taking over his father's empire with Gabriel's help, and the initial start had been a bloodbath.

Aidan was juggling everything on a tightrope. It reminded me of someone else I knew.

Aidan's voice broke me out of my thoughts."How much does Gabriel tell you about his past?"

Enough for me to know he had more secrets than he should.

"I'm guessing he's told you?" I huffed out.

"I have a few contacts in the government sector." If he could feel my judgment through the phone he tagged on. "A man needs his hobbies. I had one of them look into Gabriel. A deep dive."

I had already done that. "He's clean."

Aidan gave me a sardonic reply. "Is he? Because they couldn't find anything on him. He's a ghost."

I knew that, I played a part in that years ago.

"You think this necklace has something to do with the Agency?" My brain was working. "Are they watching Gabriel?"

"You think they'd let someone like that walk away?" Someone who had been the golden boy. Gabriel had made a name for himself, a former Navy Seal advancing through the CIA. And he'd walked away without a word.

"Do you know why he walked?"

Aidan sounded surprised. "I was hoping *you* would out of all people.

Besides that one assignment Gabriel said had gone wrong? No, I didn't *know* him. A far cry from the teenager I had known.

Gabriel wouldn't have started a security firm to stay loyal to the same people he despised.

Unless...The necklace, the key, the agency, the secrets—*He's working the mission himself because he doesn't need anyone else finding out about it.*

Because the less we know the better.

Because the trip to Africa was a suicide mission.

I was going to kill him.

"*What* is it?" I didn't know what it all led to. It was almost hurting my brain to think about it this late with the week I had.

"I think we've been asking the wrong question. Not what."

What did he just say?

I closed my eyes as I exhaled. What would Gabriel need so badly, only Aidan could help him. Nobody else could know. I wracked my brain. Something about the necklace.

I had been asking the *wrong* question.

I'd been looking at the puzzle all wrong.

From the wrong perspective.

Before Aidan had taken over, his father had been trafficking girls. Gabriel and Aidan had cut all that shit out of the clan like a tumor.

"When you took over, Gabriel got involved with the trafficked women your father ran—"

"He asked me to keep tabs, searching for particular traits, but I found no one who matched."

Aidan had different intelligence, the criminal underground had more answers than questions. Gabriel wasn't looking for what. He was looking for a *who*.

As he said. "I suspected, but you confirmed it—" *I fucking knew.*

"Gabriel is looking for a woman." It was never about the stupid necklace.

I felt it leave my lips. "And this necklace is hers." She was the reason for all this. I had no fucking clue who she was.

"I suspected, but he would never tell me..."Aidan passed me more information. Enough that he could.

"Did you know who she was?" Because no fucking way she was alive. Not with the way he acted.

"No, he never talks about himself." I wasn't even sure I knew him right now.

When Aidan and I finally hung up I got a moment to myself. I was shaking with frustration.

Why is Gabriel looking for a woman?

I needed mine. I messaged Alisha when I started messing with her vibrator. I called her. I needed to hear her voice. Needed to remember her.

Only after she'd come screaming I felt hard as iron but I wanted to go home to her. I need her.

As tempted as I was to go talk to Gabriel I realized why I was left in the dark. It wasn't about need to know.

In the world we came from, the wrong information could get you killed or worse…who was she? The woman Gabriel was hunting for.

Until I knew how many players were involved I needed to regroup. I stayed there processing everything I needed to do.

All the new things that the necklace unlocked. My thoughts racing. I needed to catch my breath and take a second to hide it all. Bury it deep where it couldn't touch her or me.

I needed Alisha like my next breath after tonight.

I breathed deeply, aware that finding the necklace didn't unlock answers so much as more questions. I sat there for so long I didn't know where to start.

Alisha was my anchor.

Despite knowing things about me I had never told anyone, I still confessed things to her as it fell from me without any issues.

I wish she was on my lap right now doing that thing where she threaded her fingers through my hair.

I just needed her until she became an all-consuming thought.

And then I got the text from an unknown number.

Jupiter. BravoCon. Venus.

We operated off the Alpha to Delta codes. Bravo was the elevated threat stage. The danger being *imminent*.

I called immediately.

I heard sounds in the background, Kellan's voice.

Was that Alisha crying? Fury laced through me.

"What the fuck happened?"

As soon as Selena said it, I knew what I had to do. Alisha's wishes be damned.

"Take her back to K2."

CHAPTER 31
REED

K2 WAS A BUILDING I HAD DECIDED TO PURCHASE AND MAKE INTO MY own domain.

Over thirty floors of luxury apartments at a fortune that people scrambled to get thanks to security, privacy, and safety being huge factors.

Moreover, I liked being left alone on the top floor.

The entire suite was mine, with a private elevator, gym, study, office, and multiple bedrooms with their own bathrooms.

Gabriel joked it was my version of a castle, fortified with a moat and alligators in the form of security guards and state-of-the-art features that allowed tenants to have peace of mind.

K2 was built and constantly updated with the most up-to-date security features, and the people who lived and visited valued privacy and security over everything else.

The rent was exorbitant and only meant for people who wanted in, and I did well enough for myself that I could retire and never worry about living again.

One of the more secure places to live in the city. And it was mine.

A far cry from sleeping in the backseat of my car waiting to escape my hell. I had named it after the most difficult mountain peak to climb in the world.

Nobody was getting in here.

With Alisha there, though?

I wanted to lock down the entire building, but I didn't think my tenants would appreciate that.

I walked through the marble floors on edge. The rage I had felt at Selena's voice letting me know what they had found in Alisha's bedroom, combined with photos? I was livid.

He left one of her panties on her bed with a note. I was going to find the person who did this...She wasn't safe in her home.

She wasn't safe anywhere but with me.

The moment I walked in, I took in Kellan. Easily one of the best I could have hired.

He had the all-American good boy role down pat.

He tipped his head to the living room where I saw Alisha wrapped in a blanket with Selena sitting on my coffee table across from her, looking out of place like a disco ball in my dark room.

Her eyes met mine with concern.

She stood, closing the distance. "We are going back to her place to gather her things."

Selena would go with Kellan as backup, and both would be back later.

I slowly approached Alisha, taking in her ashen skin, her eyes unfocused as she covered up with a patchwork quilt I noticed from her couch.

When her eyes met mine, I saw the way her lip quivered. She was in my arms a moment later, a muffled sob leaving her throat.

Every single sob infuriated me more. I knew I had cameras installed, but I left them turned off for her privacy. Now I didn't give a damn, having turned them on the moment I walked into K2. I was going to find him.

I let her, my hands stiff as I adjusted her on my lap and let her sob.

I felt my heart clench and my blood boil at the threat of her life being in danger. I wouldn't let her leave my side.

In the meantime, I processed all the ways I was going to protect this woman and figure out who was doing this.

Her spine was stiff, and her hands were cold as she let me go. The color in her face was leeching out as they drifted behind me.

I recognized fear when I saw it. Losing her parents. Fear of losing her sister.

Being attacked for finally living.

Losing her home. I knew how much that place meant to her.

"I'm going to find who did this to you." I didn't care about beating around the bush. She just needed to realize that.

"I can't go home ever again, can I? Is this my fault?" Her voice broke. "Why is this happening to me?"

I didn't know. But damned if I wouldn't get down to the bottom of it.

"It's not your fault." *It was mine.* "Come on, let me get you cleaned up."

She dumbly nodded, and I hated how shaken up she was.

Part of me wanted to get Gabriel and find the person who did this and ensure he never breathed.

Another part of me forced it all down to tamp the rage in me and help her. I carried Alisha into my bathroom. It was state-of-the-art, black and navy chrome and silver finishes.

I reached for her coat, and then her dress, tugged it off, and even as I stopped myself from doing anything remotely intimate. This was about her.

When I finally got her out, she was all but falling asleep in my arms, as I passed her a spare toothbrush, drying myself off as she brushed in my robe.

She looked half asleep as I ended up carrying her into my bed. Watching her collapse into the sheets I had dreamed of her waking up in was not the way I wanted things to go. As I stayed with her while she slept, I knew I couldn't. Not yet.

There were ninety things I needed to do. I needed to put an operative on her sister.

Because there was an ugly feeling in my gut that there were things to the picture I was missing. The entire picture was messed up.

I just needed to figure out what to do while protecting all the pieces on the board.

I slowly crawled out of bed, slipping into black on black as I prowled back to the kitchen to plot. I needed to work and get into the mindset of working. Because I had a stalker to find.

∽

My mood was black by the early hours of the morning. Nothing had improved. I hadn't slept.

The necklace burned a hole in my pocket. And Kellan had come back with Selena to explain that the stalker hadn't shown on any cameras.

"Tell me everything."

Kellan broke it down. I didn't miss the way he tucked Selena close to him.

I set up that camera outside Alisha's door myself. I made sure it was in line to catch everything. The fact that it hadn't was infuriating. He had come through the back.

But he had left the door open from the inside...He was messing with me.

And I was livid.

They dropped off enough for her, clothes, bath products, essentials.

Selena had brought more items from her house and put them around my living room. The colorful items looked out of place in the cold black interior.

That would have to change.

Kellan shook his head. "No prints. I don't know how he got in. I checked everything, and we both scrubbed the place. Nothing."

I racked my brain sitting with Kellan on the kitchen island.

Alisha was in the bedroom, far away from all this. It gutted me to see her like this.

"I checked, and I made sure to go back to the fire escape to—"

I cut him off. "What?"

The fire escape? Did I forget it was there?

"In her sister's bedroom." Kellan looked between me and Selena. "There's a fire escape, but it's easy to miss next to the bookshelf. It's New York. I figured he got in through there, so I tried to find a nearby camera. And I found a few suspects, all of whom I'm checking out."

I shook my head, putting my hand out for the suspects on his phone. I ran through five of them one by one.

I only stopped on one.

"It was him." I pointed at a man with a cap pulled down, in all black. "If we run this image against all the cameras within a ten-mile radius, we find him, we find our guy." And I deal with him.

Kellan looked surprised as he nodded. "How did you—"

"Face covered, hands away hiding gloves, avoids all the cameras in the area most likely because he's familiar with the layout of the place. I'll see if I can get him on any security cameras for the people living in the area."

I just needed someone's doorbell cam to catch him. Maybe he hadn't hid from them.

"Yes, sir."

I pulled out my laptop quickly, pulling out all the stops.

I would work from home for the past few days while Alisha recovered. I did exactly what I told Kellan I'd do.

It didn't take long. I just took the physical image and ran it against a program that matched it to similar entities for the local area for the date and time range.

When I pulled it up, I turned my screen around.

"Tony Lopez, thirty-five, lives with his mother, did a few years for aggravated assault against his girlfriend. And guess who just got out last week?"

Kellan looked impressed. "Want to pay him a visit?"

CHAPTER 32
ALISHA

THEY BROKE INTO MY PEACE.

Devastation was the lowest word to describe how I felt. Ripped to pieces at leaving my home.

I had lived in my apartment for so long it had become a piece of me. Avani and I both had started over and furnished it with all the things we could want.

It felt as though the unknown dark specter that had done this to me was laughing at my situation.

I missed it so much.

Nothing had been touched nor had anything been taken. But he—wherever he was—had been in my space. Defiled my clothes. Me.

He was sending a message.

And I had heeded it.

I wanted to scream and cry.

Throw something. I knew Reed was doing his best to find out who had done this to me.

Instead, I had become a zombie walking outside to Reed's spotless living room and crying as I saw boxes of my old life piling up over the course of the next forty-eight hours.

A man named Garrett, the size of a Goliath, had replaced Kellan to drop off items, checking my old furniture and putting what I wanted into storage.

I didn't know who had done this to me.

I was surprised when I heard a familiar voice at the apartment door that night, and the bell going off. The ring cut in through my thoughts as I walked tentatively up.

Reed had told me the building was secure which meant the only people come to see me would be –

"Is it all right if I come in?" Gemma asked softly, her voice filled with concern.

I bit back a sob and nodded, watching as Gemma walked in, her blonde hair pulled back into an elegant chignon that contrasted sharply with my disheveled appearance in Reed's shirt.

Nate, his suit impeccable as always, followed close behind her.

As he shut the door and entered the code, it dawned on me that Reed's inner circle was well-acquainted with his penthouse.

We made our way to the guest room, where Gemma and I settled into the bed crawling in, Gemma drawing the deep blue comforter over us curling and facing me.

I felt my body sigh at my best friend having a moment like this even if it wasn't in my house. It had been some time since I'd seen her or the girls, not since the night of the party.

"I'm so sorry." Gemma whispered, her opal eyes filled with sympathy as she took in my fragile state. "I feel like such a bad friend. I never should've let you go home that night."

"What? No, none of this is your fault." I protested, my voice cracking. "If anything, it's mine—"

"Are you joking?" Gemma interrupted, her expression incredulous. "None of this is your fault. Not a single bit of it. Whoever this is, I'm sure Reed will catch him."

She shook her head vehemently, as if the very idea of me being at fault was absurd.

"Is this because you feel like whoever this was only came after you slept with Reed?" She paused, her gaze searching mine. "Or is it that you blame Reed for this happening? For letting him in?"

"I don't blame Reed." I clarified, feeling hot tears prick at the corners of my eyes. "I just feel like I let my parents down by bringing this to my doorstep. To Avani. How could I have put my sister in danger?"

Gemma's expression softened with understanding. "But you didn't. You didn't do anything. You're still the best sister in the world. Avani couldn't be luckier."

She reached out, her hand gripping mine inside the comforter. "You know, I checked up on her, and she said Reed assigned someone to watch over her."

I blinked in surprise. I hadn't even asked. I had simply texted my sister, letting her know that I had moved in with Reed because of the incidents I'd told her about earlier.

She'd been devastated, but understanding.

"She didn't tell me," I murmured, feeling a pang of guilt.

"She didn't want to worry you. And she said you might blame yourself if she had."

Gemma curled her arm under her cheek, her gaze earnest. "I know you blame yourself and put all this pressure to live up to the expectations of your parents. But your parents are not here anymore, and I know that hurts to hear, but you know who is? Reed. Avani. You. You're still here, and you can't keep blaming yourself for the things you cannot control."

Gemma's voice was soft, filled with compassion. "I think whoever hurt you wants to get under your skin."

She lowered her voice, her tone conspiratorial. "Nate also thinks that it has nothing to do with you specifically, but you might be the target of someone who gets off on doing this to other women too."

"What?" I gasped, my eyes widening. "How did he know?"

"You didn't hear it from me, but I think Reed and Kellan are working on it. I overheard Nate on the phone with them."

My mind reeled. Reed hadn't told me. Now he was out somewhere, doing God knew what.

"Nate...he caught me outside the door," Gemma admitted, her cheeks turning a delicate shade of pink. "But that's beside the point. He told me that it's just a hunch, but Reed will be gone tonight. I offered to come visit you and stay with you tonight if that's all right." It was.

"Is there something going on with you two?" I watched as Nate kept eyeing her. I kept my voice down but it felt like he knew.

She looked away too quickly. "Nothing at all."

On cue, a knock came twice, and Nate stepped carrying two cups of tea.

His eyes widened slightly at Gemma laying under the covers with me.

I watched that look vanish just as quickly as it came. Gemma ignored him.

"I have dinner on the way, Reed said he wants to make sure you're eating."

I pretended not to notice the way he put a hand on her as he set the cup down. "Let me know if you need anything else, Duchess."

I saw the way Gemma's eyes lit with fire. He knew exactly what he was doing.

I saw her lips pursed with displeasure as his jaw tightened.

For a moment the electricity crackled in the room between them.

"Lish, will you excuse us for just a moment?" Even as I heard Gemma and Nate's voices in the apartment grew distant, I knew something was wrong.

CHAPTER 33
REED

MY PHONE WAS BLOWING UP.

I got home from trying and failing to find Lopez at his address listed. No dice.

I hated seeing Alisha like that.

I had asked Gemma to keep Alisha company while I had since I knew it was better for Alisha to have company than none at all.

I could feel the buzzing in my back pocket.

There were ninety thousand things I had to do. I wasn't getting any sleep tonight. Between Titan and this?

I could do it all and then some, but Alisha was my main focus.

Slowly, I untangled myself from her picking her up in the guest room bed, and carrying her to our bedroom.

I hadn't even bothered turning on the light, just the dim glow of the floor lights lighting the way.

Once I put her there asleep, I closed the door and walked to my office, the furthest place in the apartment. I called only one number back.

"Any updates?"

"None you're going to like," Gabriel was all business. "Giroux can't find Lopez anywhere so I called Killian, Aidan's brother. He got you an address that would work. I checked and Lopez has no relation to Alisha, so it doesn't explain why he'd target her."

"Something's wrong. That doesn't mean he didn't try anything."

I had already filled in Gabriel about the note and the shootout.

"Was she really a virgin?" He sounded impressed.

"*Gabriel.*" Now was not the time.

He grumbled. "It might explain why Lopez is so overzealous. Ripping panties up, leaving demented notes on her door? He's in love with her and he wants her as his." It soured my stomach. "But my question is…how did he know she was with you that night?"

I had been wondering that as well. "I took her home from Teasers. But we didn't—" I racked my brain. I couldn't think about who would've seen us. But there was one reason why Gabriel was asking. "You don't think…"

"No, he got out last week, remember? Which means—"

"Alisha has two stalkers?" I swore. I could *hear* Gabriel thinking.

"Why now?"

"Because of me. I slept with her. They probably—" Oh fuck. "Gabriel—"

He was on it. "I already ran that angle. Lopez and you have no connections."

"But that doesn't eliminate the first guy. What if that's the person who does have a grudge against me?"

Gabriel made a noise. "It doesn't make sense. None of this does. I need to think. I'll call you when I figure out why there's pieces in front of me, and it feels like something is missing. I think we're looking at this wrong. Do me a favor, don't try to figure it out. You're too emotionally connected to this." A beat passed.

"How serious are you about her?" I heard him clicking around.

"Do I seriously need to answer that question?"

I had been in love with her for years before I met her. He didn't give a shit about it before.

"No, that was the answer I needed." After a beat he laughed low. "Evie was right about her. I thought she was exaggerating."

That she was gorgeous?

"Evie made a whole slideshow about her you missed." I swore I heard him say under his breath that he did miss it.

"It's good you finally have a girlfriend who has a stalker."

"Gabriel," I growled. "I don't need you taking enjoyment out of this."

"I'm not. I'm thinking about how much fun it'll be to deal with him. I just bought a chainsaw."

Only Gabriel could talk about murder and hum about dismembering bodies.

215

"First dibs," I mused as my brain worked on what the fuck I was going to do.

He switched the subject.

"Why did you hire Liam Sullivan?" Conversations with Gabriel were an exercise in mental gymnastics, because he liked to switch and fast, and when he did, I knew he was trying to mess with someone's head.

Gabriel liked to disarm people.

"Are you asking me, if I knew about his leg, or if I knew it would set you off to have him here?"

"Both."

"Both." I knew it would trigger him so I kept Liam out of sight but not out of mind. I was playing my hand, tired of Gabriel being frozen.

He swore. "Why are you like this?"

"Because it's the only way to talk to you." I was aware sometimes *why* Nate made fun of me and Gabriel being a married couple.

"Call me when you get an update."

Because what Gabriel didn't know wouldn't hurt him. The necklace was hidden in my closet.

When I hung up, I looked at the time and realized I needed some shut-eye as well. I didn't subscribe to staying up late and ruminating like he did, and as hard as it was?

I showered in the guest room and curled into Alisha, I realized sleep was a lot easier with her in my arms.

The next night I was going to Lopez with Kellan who pulled me aside. And stumped me.

"I can't let you do this right now," he'd turned and looked at me with hard eyes for once. "I can't let you. You're going to kill the man and I can get answers out of him you can't."

"Are you questioning my ability to do my job?"

"Yes, sir." He said it with such confidence I felt my nostrils flare. "But out of sheer respect. I don't think you should do this."

"And what do you think I should do while my girlfriend is threatened by some low life?" It was a rhetorical question. "If it was Selena what would you do?"

His eyes went dark at the mention of the Cuban. I wasn't a fool. I knew they spent every second of the day together now.

"I respect you. But right now your woman, she doesn't need you to go killing people. She just needs you to stay home with her."

I felt my heart clench tightly as I realized what he was saying.

Kellan stepped up and I realized how big the kid was. "Don't do this.

216

Let me do it with Selena. Go back to her. Don't let this shit take your time and your soul any more than it already has."

His eyes were pleading with mine.

"We can handle Lopez. It's easier to attract flies with honey so we're going out to a local bar to get a feel for him. I will get back to you with what I find."

"Watts, I need to find—"

"You need to go back home to her. She needs you more than she even knows. And there is no substitution for that."

His words hit me then, and an unfamiliar emotion entered my chest realizing what Kellan was doing.

I was being handled. But it wasn't out of manipulation or fear or control. I recognized somewhere deep down I picked people off characteristics I had wished I had as a teenager. *As a kid.*

"I know you love her. I can see it all over your face. Let me do my job. Please, let me prove it to you."

He was asking me as a partner. As a teammate. I tipped my head. A deep exhale left him.

"Sweet," he grinned wide, looking like a college kid again. "*See ya, Jefe.*"

I blew out a breath and I shook my head.

What the fuck am I even doing?

CHAPTER 34
REED

WHEN I GOT HOME SHE WAS IN THE BEDROOM. FAST ASLEEP. NAKED.

She needs you more than she even knows it.

I closed the distance between us, stripping my clothes off along the way and crawling into bed.

Loving the way she immediately responded to me. Turning on her back and sighing, melting into my touch. I didn't want to talk tonight.

I didn't want to do anything but crawl inside of her and hold her down and make her mine.

"I need all of you, Angel." She moaned softly as she was waking up. She was half asleep and already moaning my name.

I fucking adored this woman.

She's so beautiful like this, soft and pliant.

I bent my head to her ear, devilish with intent. "Were you dreaming of me, Angel?"

She moaned, spreading her legs.

"Is that why you went to bed naked knowing I'd find you like this?"

I moved over her settling against her center immediately groaning at the feel of slick heat against me.

"Look at you, already wet and ready for my cock."

I felt her quaking breath as her eyes fluttered open. "You came home."

Even with my cock hard as steel, my chest pounded at her words.

Go home to your girl.

"I came home, baby." I gently cupped one of her breasts, squeezing gently, loving her moans.

My hands trailed down her body. I smiled as she tipped her head back, her entire expression looking out of it. Drugged with me. The way she moaned my name. I could see it all over her face. Because even if she said one thing, she was grinding on me, gripping my shoulders, and moaning my name.

"Should I taste all of you?"

Everything about her captivated me. It wasn't just her beauty but her passion that drew me in. The way she wholeheartedly loved, the peace she brought to any place she called home—these were what I desired.

Despite being a recognizable figure, she remained humble, always taking photos with fans and stopping to greet screaming girls who adored her. She was constantly surrounded by admiration. Warmth. Love.

So much profound love. I realized why I wanted Lish more than I needed anything else in the world.

I wanted to be swallowed by her *love*.

Take her in and feel her melt against me. Taste her until the scent of her and her arousal flowed through me. I'd let her do whatever she wanted to me just for a fraction of what she was.

The more I got to know her, the more it grew that my intuition had been right about this woman.

I bent my head taking one of her nipples into my mouth massaging the other loving the loud raw moans coming from her. Spreading her legs I worked, kissing down her body, curves in the right places, the softness of her stomach as it quivered and my breath met over the center of her. So soft and beautiful, her pretty pussy creaming.

The long moan that escaped from her lips at my first lick made me grin.

Nothing made me happier than knowing Alisha was a screamer. I ate her pussy like a man starved for the honey that was in her body. I felt her thighs shaking around my face and I wrapped my arms around them and spread them wider growling as she bucked her hips.

My name left her lips in whimpers and sobs, her hands tangling in my hair as she gave herself up to me.

I lifted my head up, pausing to watch her reaction to flicking her clit.

Tears of pleasure streamed down her cheeks as she gasped at the position.

"Should I stop?" She was too gone to say anything but tug on my scalp. I sealed my mouth over the top of her clit and sucked. I loved the way her breasts shook as her body trembled. *Guess not.*

No one had ever been with her like this.

The beast within me wanted to see her come apart.

No one else will get to see her like this.

I was driving her up the precipice so much, when she fell she'd scream my name and remember me. Because she was mine. I reached up to tug at her nipples, playing with the soft globes as she came apart in my mouth while I sucked on her clit.

I growled my pleasure as she screamed my name, her legs threatening to close around my ears, her face contorted in pleasure.

"Reed."

I would never get tired of my name falling from her lips in the breathless abandon she gave me all the time.

I lost all control then, as I rose up above her.

All it took was that and I was unleashed. I wanted to taste her lips, ruin her for life, plant myself so deep inside of her she wouldn't know where I ended up.

Be a part of her forever and keep her in my home, in my bed, where she wouldn't have to think of anything else but taking me. Over and over.

I was depraved and just as deadly as everyone suspected, but I'd be damned if I gave a fuck if I was good enough for this woman.

I was hers.

My cock was throbbing with my pulse as I rose up above her bracing myself over her in the most ancient way to take my woman.

Her ethereal beauty glowed under the moonlight, like a fairy I'd found among the lush greenery of Teasers, innocent and sweet and life itself while still being the most seductive creature I'd ever seen.

I wanted to decorate her with jewels, spoil her beyond any measure, and take care of her until she didn't have a single care in the world.

Her skin glowing as she wrapped her arms around my neck, her legs spreading open, her body accepting me as hers as I leaned down and captured her pretty pout in my mouth.

Thrusting my tongue deep I felt my cock drag against her slick folds.

A groan escaped my mouth as I took control, wanting with every fiber of my being to make it last for as long as possible.

I'd taken her with such ferocity the first few times I needed to savor her.

Just once, even if she wanted me to be an animal, I wanted to drive her mad with need.

Just like she'd driven me for so long.

I didn't want to taste her or touch her, but have her take me into her soul.

Let me rest there for a moment while I caught my breath and made love to her under the moonlight.

"Open for me." I couldn't recognize my own voice as I grabbed her thigh, bracing myself with one hand and feeling the tip of me slipping into the tight confines of her body.

I groaned as I slid in, stretching, still feeling her moan as she clenched around me. *"Such a good girl."*

A soft sigh escaped her, her eyes widening as I took up more and more space.

Lust darkened my voice. "This is the only way you'll listen to me, isn't it? Stretching you until you can't think."

She was biting her lip as she sobbed, nodding when I slid in so deep I couldn't think. I lost a bit of my control at that admission. Nothing in the world had compared to this. To her. Anyone I had before her faded out to nothing but a memory in the dust.

I kept my voice smooth, not wanting to give away the effect she had on me. I was a man drugged on that pussy. "Tell me who this pussy wants."

"Gods, I'm yours. I want it." Alisha's moans became wild as I bottomed out. *"I need you."*

The desire in me was fanned by her whimpers and moans as she adjusted. Her head was thrown back, never looking as beautiful as she did until that moment.

Licking the column of her throat I felt her pussy clenched tightly around me, the haze of lust taking over.

Her body instinctively recognizing its master. *Who* it belonged to. And she was *mine*.

I hadn't realized I said it out loud, but her admission spilled out in a cry, as sucked on her pulse. I savored her, not moving. Just feeling. Long moments where I inhaled her scent of roses into my lungs.

"I'm going to take my time with you." I whispered. "I'm going to

221

drive you insane like you did to me. I'm going to make you scream until you lose your voice, until you pay for the sweetest frustration you are."

I sighed as she squeezed tight around those words.

"Teasing me in those tiny skirts, stockings, heels, I'm going to make love to you, for a long time. The only word I want to hear on your mouth is my name." I gasped, dragging my cock out. "Say yes, Angel."

It was an easy one.

"*Yes.*"

A smile lit my face as I thrust back in loving the way she cried out.

I bent finding her nipples hard as diamonds, sucking one of the hard tips into my mouth as I fucked into her with steady easy thrusts designed to drive both of us over the edge and insane.

I was a man starved on a mission. I was a fucking beast in bed with this woman. I wanted to provide for her in more ways than one.

In ways Alisha couldn't even understand.

I wanted a ring on her finger, a collar around her neck, her entire body would be mine.

The feel of her skin against mine was heaven, smooth silk against my own hardness.

I felt the telltale clenching of her pussy and I sucked harder. "*Reed.*"

So *close.* I could fucking feel it.

The hot grip she had on me was impossible to ignore.

I groaned as I gently bit down as I sank deep, feeling myself pressing down on her clit while hitting that spot inside of her I knew drove her over the edge. She shattered.

I held onto her, as she cried out in intensity.

"*That's my girl.*" I pulled my hips back. "I'm not done with you yet."

CHAPTER 35
ALISHA

WHEN REED SLAMMED BACK INTO MY ALREADY SENSITIZED BODY I WAS LIT up from the inside.

I couldn't think with his dark whispers in my ear, whispering naughty things and promises while he worked inside of me.

When his mouth covered mine for a hot moment, I ceased to think altogether, simply becoming pliant with pleasure and taking him in with ease.

His groan as his thrusts grew nearly ferocious, struck somewhere low in my gut.

I whimpered his name breaking off my mouth.

"You're close again, aren't you?" The dark wicked look in his eyes never faded, as I nodded.

"*Yes.*" Reed abruptly stopped, pulling out of me leaving me breathless as he turned me to my stomach, drawing my hips up. I was breathless as he plunged back into me hitting that spot *hard*.

A scream left me as I gripped the sheets in my fists. "*Reed.*"

It ignited something sweet within me, all coherent thought escaped as his growls caressed my ears, promises of ecstasy from his lips.

"*Fuck.*" His voice was gravel as he growled and thrust deeper than I thought possible.

A squeal left my lips as he held onto my hips, setting a pounding rhythm that I knew would make me come.

And I knew why he wanted to do it too. "*Let me see my fucking party trick.*"

I shrieked as my orgasm slammed into me harder than the others as Reed split my legs wider and fell over me, fists on either side of my body. Pinning me, forcing me to accept every exquisite stroke. Rational thought fled as animalistic need consumed me.

Unintelligible noises left my lips. I was so close, the intensity felt too much. I would never survive it. Helpless and at his mercy my entire body centered down to the powerful drives of Reed's body into me.

I'd never done it while he'd fucked me like this.

It felt *too* much.

I felt my body bucking against his, some primal instinct fighting even as I surrendered. It was too much, the intensity threatening to shatter me.

Through the haze of sensation, I heard his voice, dark with possession and something like anger.

"Did you just try to fucking run from me?"

As if I could escape this, escape him.

He pinned me down, forcing me to take every punishing thrust, until I was nothing but a creature of instinct and need, lost to the pleasure and the pain.

As though it was *unacceptable.*

My eyes rolled back as he drilled that spot that never failed to make me explode until the embarrassing force of my orgasm exploded from me.

"Ohhh, fuck, fuck." I screamed into the sheets as I came over and over as I felt him groaning above me.

"Fuck, squirt all over me. "

I was. I was shrieking into the pillow.

Delirious with pleasure, he pounded in and out of me, hot warmth pulsing in my womb from his orgasm as he emptied himself into me.

"That's it, Angel." His words brushed against my skin as he trailed kisses down my neck, teeth grazing my pulse point. "Work that pussy on me."

I felt myself squirming on him. Struggling, like I was fighting it.

"Come on Angel, I know you're *right* there. Such a *good* girl. You're going take every drop of my fucking cum. Say my fucking name—" I didn't have the energy to scream anything other than his name.

My body felt like it was no longer my own. *"Reed."*

Reed pressed in deep as I felt my body react gushing long and hard. Wild noises and animal sounds left my lips into the sheets, as I worked myself on him, taking from him what I needed.

Coherent thought slipped away, replaced by pure sensation as he pressed deep, wringing every last shudder and spasm.

I collapsed onto my belly as I shook wildly, my awareness dimming and feeling lightheaded.

Reed kissed every bit of my skin that was exposed.

"I love you." His voice was gruff. "You don't have to say it back. I just want you to know I love you. I would move mountains to bring you the moon if you asked. I know your head is going to lose its mind when you calm down, so I want you to hear me say it over and over when you do. *I love you. I love you. I love you.*"

CHAPTER 36
REED

I LOVE YOU.

Those words from my mother had only been uttered when I was a child.

As I grew older, when my stepfather took control and my half-brother Adam realized he was the favored son, exploiting that advantage, I was no longer loved.

Not through any fault of my mother's, a woman from the wrong side of town, financially dependent on the man she was with. I didn't blame her.

No, I blamed him for putting her in a position where she had to choose her favorite child to survive.

Gabriel had told me my stepfather died, so Adam either lived back home or disappeared into his own life. I had never gotten back to him. I didn't want to. Not right now.

My mother passed away the year I began working on Titan.

As devastating as it was, it reminded me of all those years of lost love. Not saying the words I needed.

I'm sorry.

I understand why you chose yourself and Adam.

I don't hate you.

I just didn't want to show up broken for Alisha.

Working on mastering myself had always been my goal. To be effective, you had to know your strengths and weaknesses.

She didn't have to say it back.

I knew it in her eyes, in the way she held me. I knew I scared her. She didn't want to lose me. She never would.

The house slippers she gifted me, the way she said a shirt would accentuate my eyes, how she handed me coffee as I worked. There was something soft about feminine energy that I craved more and more as I grew to appreciate it.

Her soft, musical laughter in contrast to my deep, booming laughs whenever Alisha said something amusing.

The way she threaded her hands through my hair when I dozed off on her.

Her need for chick flicks, trading me for my mystery movies, and munching mochi donuts to decompress after a busy day. Her wiggling her manicured toes in my face until I licked her everywhere. The constant flow of color across my couch when she went to shower.

Slowly, she made herself at home. I loved her. And she loved me. I lifted her head, stilling for a moment at the sight of her beauty.

Pleasure-hazed eyes, her head lolling onto my shoulder, lethargic and no doubt exhausted. For a fleeting moment, I took her in—inhaling the scent of roses and Alisha's essence, her soft raven hair spilling over me. My lips found her temple, and I couldn't recall the last time I had been like this with a woman.

Her soft eyes met mine. I kissed her again.

"I need you." She whispered. "Please, fuck me. I need you."

Alisha's sex drive outmatched even mine, and didn't I fucking love that. Gabriel knew I wasn't coming back for a few days and he had understood slipping into the old operative he had been and not the vampire in his lair.

It didn't matter where he was personally, professionally he was still the man who would do his job.

I made love to Alisha. She didn't want to talk. I didn't want to say anything. I knew there was one way to communicate with her and that was through orgasms. So I did. I kept her tied up in my bed as promised. I fed her. Fucked her. Bathed her. And rinsed and repeated.

I recognized halfway through the sessions I needed this just as much as she did. With every bit of contact I felt her coming through.

As soon as she was fed, I'd push her back down to the bed.

I fell on her loving the cries as I slammed in deep. I realized my mattress springs bounced her while she was stuck between my cock and me until I was withdrawing to my tip and slamming into her with the motion. I sank deeper in that position.

Brutally, hitting her so deep.

Oh holy fuck that's so good.

Her squeals and screams made me love it even more.

"*I promised you, I will destroy that little pussy.*" She screamed wildly with every slam until she was shrieking her orgasm. I filled her and her pussy flowered open for me with the help of multiple orgasms. I groaned she was already clamping down on me post-orgasm. "Greedy little pussy's already milking my fucking cock."

I let her adjust to me as she trembled, breathing wildly under me. "That's it, you can take it, can't you?"

I pushed *deeper*, loving the way she moaned, her eyes glassy, her body shaking. "Oh God, Oh God, oh God, *please let me come.*"

It was my turn to groan with her as I slammed into her over and over wondering to myself why I didn't do this sooner.

That if this was the only way she would stay by my side, I would keep her like this forever.

Keeping her in bed for days was a dream.

Until Alisha begged me to stop teasing her and just take her the ways I wanted to. I teased her all day about taking her ass, I'd stretched her with toys and lube. I knew how to take my time. I was a patient man.

And this is what I'd been waiting for.

Possessing all of her. Every hole. Every bit of her was mine. I held fast, buried deep in her. It had taken me an eternity and she'd adjusted to every inch. Now she was clenching on me. A tight smile curved my lips.

Bracing myself above her, I held her face. *She is so beautiful.*

"Tell me when you're good." I brushed back dark strands of hair. "Say when, and I'll make it better."

Just a little bit more.

I took her lips then, devouring her slowly, as I slid in the last bit.

Her strangled scream in my mouth shooting straight to my cock pulsing in her. She was incredible.

Hot wet heat wrapped around me.

"You're tinier than I imagined, Angel."

"It feels different," she whispered.

I locked eyes with her for a moment. "Better?"

"Not sure," she held me tighter. "But you feel bigger."

"I don't want to hurt you," I moved my lips over hers. "I'm trying not to tear into you."

She exhaled as I reached down for her clit, giving her those slow circles she loved.

"Keep your eyes on me, Angel. I want to see your pretty face when I fuck your ass for the first time." And that pink flush over them. Then long moments later, blissfully, she uttered the words.

"Oh, that feels a lot better." *Don't have to tell me twice.* I was shaking with the effort to not slam into her over and over again, but I knew she'd need to adjust. I couldn't take her like a fucking animal. *Yet.* I drew back and held her face as I watched her expression as I sank back in.

Her lips curved into an. "O."

Her eyes rolled back and her entire expression blissed out.

"That feels good, Reed." She looped her arms around my neck. "Just a little more."

Where had she been my entire life?

I didn't hold back. I didn't mind fucking her hard and fast, but I'd also learned sometimes, having precise accuracy over mindless thrusting was better.

"*Harder.*" She cried, those beautiful eyes pleading with me. "Right there, please."

I groaned, ducking my head to kiss her hungrily.

I opened her legs wider and settled in pummeling that little spot inside of her I knew would drive her crazy, giving her all of my strength in every thrust.

Under me she was wild, a sobbing mess of tears and cries and I absorbed all of them in my mouth.

"*Come for me,*" I commanded, bracing myself on either side of her arms still tight over her.

She cried as she did, tossing her head back looking glorious and beautiful. I groaned at the tight sensations around my dick.

Manic words fell from my lips, unable to stop them.

"*I own you.* Every fucking *inch* of this body. Every hole is *filled* with my cum. *You are mine.*" *I'm depraved.* And yet, I already knew the answer.

"Y—yours." Oh fuck, I wanted to groan in pleasure as she tightened with every word. I was going to blow.

"That's it. Keep going. I can feel you." I groaned into her neck, my hips moving with utter abandon.

For her pleasure. For mine.

Her eyes rolled back with my thrusts, and I waited for her to come back to me.

I never gave up and faltered, only deepening my strokes. I knew my girl could have multiple orgasms. I fucking loved pushing her through them. I groaned then, feeling the tightening reach its peak. I reached down between her legs and found her clit, pressing down against the swollen nub.

"That's it. Come for me, Angel."

I pounded her through it loving the way her pussy grew exponentially wetter and the hard slap of me against her added to the symphony of sex.

She sobbed in my mouth as I pummeled that little part of her.

That's the fucking spot, isn't it?

I grabbed her throat as I fucked loving the way her eyes rolled back. I slowed down just enough to let her come back to me. When she did, I squeezed her throat tighter.

"Again, Angel. I'm not finished with you."

A dark chuckle left my lips as I saw her shake in denial.

"No, p—please." I love when she begged. "I'm too—" I pushed deep and squeezed loving that little groan she gave.

"*Sensitive*, hm?" I was fucking gone. "You can take it. I can feel your ass clamping down on me again. Any minute now you're going to squeeze down like a fucking vice. And you're going to take me with you."

She cried out into my mouth as I began a brutal rhythm neither one of us would make it through.

I was swearing. Praising her.

Giving it to her hard, dropping my weight on her and *drilling. That. Spot.*

"Oh God, oh God, *Reed*." Listening to her scream my name and clutch my back made me groan, as she raked her nails down my back I lost it. *Faster. More.*

"Such a bad girl." I rammed my cock in deep. "Taking my dick like a fucking champ. Is that what you needed tonight?"

I slammed in not giving a fuck if she was sensitive because whatever she had started, I was determined to finish.

"That's it, Angel, I'm going to fuck you until come. Over and over again. You're going to beg me to stop by the time I'm done with you."

"*Yesyesyes*."

I felt the moment she tipped, her asshole squeezed so tight I almost lost my breath and my hips faltered thrusting deep.

That was it.

I tipped over just like that, and she shrieked as she followed me.

I grabbed her tight as I came into her body. And she took me every thrust.

I held her steady through it.

Such a good girl.

The words and more praise left my mouth over and over as she calmed down and I continued to pump through until every bit of come was in her.

Hugging her tight to me I panted slowly, kissing her everywhere aware I had let her breathe.

I needed to cuddle her and give her some warmth after this. As I pulled out she winced as she let out a groan.

"You took me so well, Angel. I'm going to run you a bath."

Her mouth covered mine and to my surprise, she tugged me back on top of her. Kissing me with intent. Long and slow and so unlike Alisha, I curled into her.

I never wanted to leave.

CHAPTER 37
ALISHA

I WAS SORE EVERYWHERE.

Places deep in my womb ached, sensitive from the battering ram of Reed's cock.

I could feel the aftershocks, his size stretching me, filling every inch of space.

I had no idea sex could be like this.

I craved Reed, over and over.

Something warm bubbled in my belly every time I heard the sound of running water where Reed had gone to clean us both.

Is this what you needed, Angel?

It's gonna feel like the first time, every fucking time with you, isn't it?

For once, I awoke before him.

He looked adorably grumpy in his sleep. His brow furrowed as I kissed the little crease in his forehead.

I wanted to stay in bed with Reed.

But I had avoided responsibilities for a week.

I left him sleeping and dressed in the other room to head to Poppy.

A twinge of guilt nagged at me for not waking him. Reed had gifted me house slippers when his apartment lacked carpet. I made a mental note to ask his thoughts on rugs.

His place smelled wonderfully fragrant—sandalwood in the bathroom, bergamot candles in the living room.

No plants or other signs of life. I wanted to get him a cactus or something living. The touches of a housekeeper were everywhere when he was away.

The apartment lay dark in the early morning hours as I left, the sun just streaming in.

Not my home, since boxes from my old place cluttered the living room.

But it was Reed's.

I walked to K2's concierge, pleasantly surprised that while Reed occupied a private section, the rest offered full amenities. A pool, an enormous gym, and dark elegance all throughout.

The receptionist, Stephanie, smiled as I passed her.

"Miss Malhotra," she smiled back. "I have a letter for you."

Anxiety churned in my stomach—I hadn't ordered anything or changed my address to Reed's. I thanked her and frowned at the envelope.

"Who dropped this off?"

She looked concerned at my expression. "I'm sorry, Miss. It was just on the desk. Should I toss it?"

"No, it's alright." As I left, I saw her on the phone, likely busy. Kellan waited down the hall.

I texted Reed, figuring I'd be home before he awoke, and then Kellan and I headed to Poppy's.

I told Kellan about the letter when we arrived. He immediately recognized the note, and his face fell. "Did that note get dropped off at K2?"

I nodded, hands shaking. Reed had been sleeping.

Kellan took it, opened and scanned the page. "*Motherfucker.*"

He rarely swore. *"I need to take you back."*

"What?"

He swallowed hard. "Alisha, he's going to be angry."

I read the note.

You can't run from me.

Chills ran down my spine. I knew this was some demented mind game by a crazed fan.

To think they'd come to Reed's building? Initially afraid, my fear hadn't helped.

I couldn't let this person scare me anymore.

The past few months, they'd just sent weird letters and broken into my house.

Whether shaking up my life or forcing discomfort, I squared my shoulders, taking a deep breath.

I refused to break down over this any longer.

"No." I held Kellan's arm, meeting his concerned ocean eyes. "Reed hasn't had a decent night's sleep since I brought this to his door. It's just a note. I live in a fortified tower. It can wait until we return. Whoever it is won't do anything in broad daylight."

Kellan looked ready to fight me on it. "*Lish—*"

"It's my choice."

This was wrong, but I cared more about Reed's well—being than a stupid note. "It can wait a few hours."

"He's going to be angry."

~

IT WAS MUCH WORSE.

When Kellan and I returned, I sat Reed down before we broke the news to him. Kellan and I both looked like naughty children.

Reed hadn't even looked up from his tablet, wearing a black long-sleeve shirt he had rolled up to his forearms, revealing an arm full of the tattoos I loved. He listened, not looking up once.

I am in so much trouble.

And for a long moment, he looked at the note, and he didn't speak.

"Kellan," he said quietly. "Did Miss Alisha give you the idea that you couldn't wake me up when her life was being *threatened*?"

Reed hit some keys as though occupied. My life hadn't been threatened per se but I got the gist.

"No, sir, it was my fault."

Indignation flared through me. "No, it was *my* choice. I told him it could wait."

Uh-Oh.

Reed's eyes were stormy as they flashed up to Kellan. He closed the screen on his tablet not before I caught him reviewing surveillance.

Reed's eyes never left Kellan.

"You should know Stephanie tells me everything that makes it into my building—" His *building? Reed owned the place?*

"*Especially* any packages addressed to my girlfriend."

"*Yes, sir.*"

"What will you do from now on?"

He stood to his full height, and I watched Kellan take a step back. Towards me.

Which made Reed's face turn to granite.

"Report everything to you." He hung his head, unable to stay looking at Reed.

"Head home."

As Kellan turned, I made a move to leave with him.

"Not. You."

I winced.

"You live here."

He sounded positively seething. Kellan didn't dare turn back as he quickly walked out.

Leaving me alone with one very pissed-off Reed.

"I'm going to give you a running start."

His voice was deceptively soft, but I knew what he was planning. I knew him.

"When I catch you, you will *not* come tonight. You won't sit for a week. I will do everything in my power to make sure you hurt to walk."

When. Not *if.*

I took off running.

CHAPTER 38
ALISHA

"Don't run off without me." Reed said smoothly, a hint of warning in his silken tone. "I don't need Gabriel scaring you out of all people."

Run? A scoff escaped me.

"Thanks to you, I can't walk."

Even now, a dull ache lingered as evidence of his recent claiming.

Reed had carried me from the garage to this spectacular mansion, my steps unsteady in the aftermath of the depraved acts he had put me through days prior.

Acts that I had reveled in.

"I don't even know how you got a hold of half of those..." I trailed off, flushing at the memories.

"The wand or the ginger—" Reed prompted, a wicked gleam in his eyes.

I squirmed, unable to meet his heated gaze.

"I never want that ever again. I have nightmares about ginger. I didn't even know it could go there."

After he had caught me, pinned me with a blend of dark intent and infinite patience, he had worked me over relentlessly.

I hadn't come all night.

And when he'd finally worked into my shaking body? I'd died a little.

He smiled at me. "I'm glad I got my point across." Had he. I wouldn't be keeping anything from him again.

"Is Gabriel fond of being frightening?" I asked, ignoring the dark, lust-filled looks Reed leveled my way as he observed my wince of lingering tenderness when rubbing my abdomen. He wasn't even sorry.

Reed chuckled low, the sound raising goosebumps along my sensitized skin.

"Gabriel's fond of a lot of things that the general population wouldn't approve of."

I nodded mutely as we entered the enormous white grand manor that was Titan's headquarters.

"This place is like a fairy tale castle. It's so beautiful."

Reed smiled faintly as we continued down the deceptively vast interior.

"Don't you have an office in the city as well?"

"I do," he responded, his voice holding an undercurrent I couldn't decipher.

We strolled down the hallway, chestnut floors gleaming beneath our feet, stunning artwork adorning the walls.

"But the team likes to camp out here. Liam sits in the one in Midtown sometimes." I had met Liam, but not Evie.

"Evie is Gabriel's ward."

"She's an adult now," he smirked at that, though the expression held no true mirth. "Although Gabriel would disagree."

Reed had convinced me to accompany him to Titan's Connecticut headquarters as a means for me to remain by his side while he checked in on work.

I realized I needed to get myself together. I had meetings and Ella-Beauty functions scheduled over the weekend before Reed informed me of this sojourn.

We had an art gallery event that evening, and I wanted to ensure we arrived on time.

But first, Reed wished to stop by this office.

His hand squeezed mine as he led me towards the back of the house.

The entire ambiance shifted, the theme becoming distinctly more feminine as we approached our destination. The doors leading into where we were going were extremely feminine.

As Reed opened the door, I caught sight of a petite woman with deep mahogany hair cascading down her back, reaching her waist.

She was dressed in pajamas and working at a standing desk, surrounded by an array of monitors and an abundance of plants.

Vines and large trees filled the space around her, creating a lush, verdant atmosphere.

She didn't look up from her desk as she typed, a stuffed cactus perched beside her.

She resembled a tiny tech fairy.

"Selena's outside murdering one of your new hires," she said nonchalantly, her voice contrasting with her delicate appearance.

"Which one?" Reed responded without missing a beat, shooting me a humorous glance as I raised my brow.

"Quarterback." I bit back a smile. *Kellan.*

In the light, her long hair shimmered with a deep cherry hue, strikingly beautiful against her honey-colored eyes. She didn't sound like one though.

He shook his head looking far from the man who'd held me in bed hours ago. "I told you guys to play nice."

The woman looked up then, her eyes widening in excitement.

"Ohmigosh!" She rushed around her desk with surprising speed.

"I'm Evie," she introduced herself, bouncing her way towards me.

I couldn't help but laugh as she rambled on, wide-eyed and reverent, about how she had done her research on me and created slide shows.

"When Reed was always stalking your pictures, I knew—"

"Aw, you're adorable." I couldn't resist the urge to hug her drawing her closer with a grin. This certainly wasn't a spy.

"Aaaannd that's enough, kid." Reed interjected, his cheeks turning two shades darker.

He didn't blush often, but when he did, it was cute.

Before Evie could utter another word, a shout rent the air.

Both Reed and Evie turned their heads, and I followed as they jogged outside to the yard.

Two figures darted into view in the backyard, and I recognized them as Selena and Kellan.

Kellan came flying across the backyard as Reed stepped in front of me protectively.

Landing with a groan, a volley of Spanish followed from a feminine voice, accompanied by a few chuckles.

Selena's tall strikingly gorgeous form dressed in a tight black outfit she looked every inch the badass she was, dark hair pulled up in a ponytail.

Behind her, someone else watched.

A Goliath of a man with a small smile on his face.

I knew he was only an inch or two taller than Reed, but with his short blonde hair, cropped close to his scalp and hard green eyes, he looked a little mean. His eyes landed on me.

Reed gently nudged me behind him. He blew a whistle with his teeth.

Both men froze, head snapping up. Selena did not since he'd blown the whistle when she'd moved her leg.

With a feminine growl she hooked her leg around his.

I winced as Kellan hit the ground again with a groan.

Beside me Evie made a noise of pain. "That's gotta hurt."

Selena grinned for all of two seconds before Kellan did something with his legs hooking them around hers, and had her on her back again.

Only she didn't go down on the ground. He caught her in his arms and pinned her to the ground. Evie looked away.

I looked at Reed who showed no emotion. It was the Goliath who spoke. "*Watts.*"

The Goliath behind him all but hauled Kellan off who was grinning. Selena was pink. I cannot believe I thought I had sexual tension.

"Now you know why Reed will stand you up frequently on your future dates," Evie whispered it in a sotto voice, and I looked at Reed.

His scowl at Kellan and Selena changed into a brief second of regret. "Cut the shit. I need you two in my office."

Kellan's eyes darted to Reed. I knew Reed was still slightly angry at Kellan for listening to me.

Kellan stopped smiling. Privately I wondered if Reed had brought me here to show me a glimpse of his life.

"Evie, take Alisha back inside. I gotta go talk to the kids."

I didn't get to protest as Evie turned to me and said quietly. "I don't think he wants you to see him all scary."

Reed didn't look at me, his expression cold and shutting himself off as he walked to the group heading inside.

This is his work.

"Sorry," Evie explained as we came back to the sun room she worked out of. "Want me to get you something while you wait for him? Gabriel got me cake, Reed says your family's from the UK, want some tea?"

I blinked at the girl who looked barely old enough as my sister.

Her eyes were wide as she offered me English Breakfast or Earl Grey. She batted an enormous plant out of the way as we walked back from the chill of the autumn air.

"Are you a spy too?"

239

This was a little unreal when I processed what these people were.

"No. I just sit at a desk," she said glumly. But somehow I didn't think so. "Everyone else is important. Reed's training me so I can be good at both. But with Gabriel as his shadow..." I gathered that.

Gabriel had been a slight point of contention between me and Reed. An unspoken point.

I understood Reed would run and help Gabriel who was like his brother no matter what it was. What it cost.

I didn't mind so much because there was always another dinner or function for us to attend. But he only had one brother.

That's what I considered Gabriel.

Even though Reed avoided the subject of meeting him. Now, I was here in his home.

And didn't I know how important it was.

I hadn't met the man but it seemed like everyone else had.

"I'll go get us some tea, that always makes me feel better."

But I was curious. "Is Reed always busy because of this?"

She smiled. "Reed's been trying to get Gabriel to hire replacements for the last year. This way someone can take over so we can get a break. But Gabriel..." She drifted. "He didn't want that, but somehow Reed got his way. And Reed gets a tiny breather."

How long had it been since Reed got time off?

"How much do you guys usually work?"

Evie's brow furrowed as she scrutinized her screen. "It depends. Since you have your current situation, I've been monitoring your social media and your apartment for the last few days."

What...

She glanced up, registering the confusion that must have plastered across my face.

"It's not bad," Evie smiled at me. "I like it. Your fans are really funny, and all the princes who hit on you drive Selena to tears. But the creepy comments? I flagged them for Reed to check out when he got a chance..."

As her voice droned on, the room seemed to constrict. *"What do you mean..."*

Panic gripped my chest as the weight of what Evie was saying crystallized.

"Wait..." I cut her off, struggling to draw breath past the lump of horror in my throat. *"Are you...spying on me?"*

Evie looked uneasy all of a sudden.

"Reed was the one who got in your network. He has access to anything you do…" Evie explained in a small voice. "He always has. We can see whatever you can see."

I don't know why I felt the disbelief and anger blossoming in me.

As a way of protecting me. Without telling me?

"How much can you see?"

Evie squeaked, those eyes of hers wider than before.

"I'm sorry! I just knew you had a stalker and oh…I'm not good at this."

"Reed gave you permission to spy on me?" My head spun a little. I was so angry that he was gone.

What's all this stuff you're installing?

Don't worry about it, Angel.

Someone I had never met. Who seemed like a nice girl. Had access to all my accounts and my phone and—

"Wait, did you say you can see my apartment?"

Evie said softly. "I never watched you guys. He made sure there wasn't—"

I gasped in horror, but there were cameras in my apartment.

Oh God, the things I'd done with him.

Humiliation and embarrassment flowed through me.

When had he put them there?

How much did Evie know that she didn't want to tell me? What *other* secrets is he keeping?

My jaw dropped and my heart dropped into my stomach.

"No, Alisha please—" I held up a hand to stop her from continuing as I processed the violation of privacy this was.

"Please don't be angry. I swear it's just your old apartment. We didn't see —"

"We?"

"Gabriel sees the feeds—"

Good Lord.

I've never met the man and he's seen me naked. "Oh my God!"

"I promise he didn't see you and Reed. It wipes daily—" I couldn't hear a single word she said.

Reed wasn't bad at communicating.

He was bad at telling me the truth.

How much had they known about my life that I thought was private?

"...Let me go get you a cup of tea and some cake, I promise, it'll be okay."

I looked at the girl who was all of fifteen herself. "How old are you?"

"I just turned twenty-three." Barely older than my sister and surrounded by all this.

"It's okay." She smiled easily, her soft spun hair around her. She had a classically beautiful face with big doe caramel-colored eyes. She's just a kid in her cloud pajamas. "Gabriel tried to tell me to get a normal job, but I wanted to help him with his." *She's his ward.*

I nodded dumbly, still processing that I had no privacy this entire time. "Gabriel is your brother..."

"Gabriel's got a heart of gold. He would die before he hurt you or let anyone hurt you. He didn't see you."

She made a staying motion. "But he isn't in a good mood right now so just stay here. Reed will come back for you. I'll go get cake and we can talk about boys or something. It's good to have another woman around."

I gaped at how quickly conversations switched here and how Evie had handled me freaking out as a normal occurrence.

Because this was his life.

This is normal for Reed.

Evie quickly jogged away down the hall, her dark red waving behind her, and I stared around me at the way in a moment's notice my life had not completely flipped upside down.

Leaving my heart racing, my stomach bottoming out at the sheer nonchalance these people had to things that left me shaken up.

I looked outside at the pristine manicured lawn feeling utter confusion and rage brewing at Reed.

How could he keep so much from me? I felt utterly out of control.

I needed some semblance of it back.

Evie could see my entire life splayed open, but did that mean he could?

How much did he know? Is that why he knew how to be everything to me?

He was incredible...but now it all felt like a lie.

Standing there I felt out of my element.

I needed some air and not anywhere near Reed. I needed some space.

As I stepped out in the same direction Evie had gone, I found myself at a loss as I walked down the hallway.

Should I turn left or right?

With no clear guidance, I chose a path, hoping it would eventually lead me back to the front of the house.

However, with each step, my frustration grew, and I began to regret not following Evie. The deeper I ventured into this place, the more I realized I was utterly lost. And a little terrified now.

Something was off about this place...

Despite its beauty, the house was clearly designed for a family, with its sprawling hallways and numerous rooms.

I wandered aimlessly, turning into one corridor after another, feeling as though I were trapped in a maze.

I walked down another hall.

Reed had mentioned that this was one of the larger turn-of-the-century mansions, warning me not to get lost.

I should've listened to him.

As I pressed on, the atmosphere of the house seemed to shift, growing darker.

I didn't like this at all.

The Titan manor held secrets, and I had no desire to uncover them right this moment. Not when I felt my anxiety growing by the second.

A noise echoed from somewhere, causing me to turn around, not wanting to disturb whoever it was.

In my haste, I accidentally bumped into something metal, sending it clattering to the ground several times, and nearly giving me a heart attack.

A scream burst from my lips. Then, a sound, a dull thud, like something heavy striking the ground.

"Drat!" I was clutching my chest as I rushed away from the source of the sound.

Desperate to find my way out, I walked towards another hallway, only to be greeted by nothing but another hall.

This wasn't the right way at all. A suffocating feeling crept up my throat as I felt increasingly trapped.

With each step, I seemed to be wandering further into the depths of the house, the atmosphere growing colder, until I hit the darker halls.

My heels clicked quietly on the marble.

I was not going down the right way.

I could turn back. But how?

How do I find my way out?

It was *freezing* here.

What the hell was this place?

CHAPTER 39
ALISHA

"I should've listened to Evie."

I looked around, stopping, finally letting out a breath. "How on Earth does one get out of here?" I pulled out my phone.

"How do I not have a signal?"

"We have Wi-Fi."

The dark silken voice that came from behind me scared the crap out of me.

Another scream tore from my throat as I dropped my phone, startled by the sudden voice that seemed to come from nowhere.

As I whirled around to face the speaker, the temperature plummeted, and I found myself staring into the coldest blue eyes I had ever seen.

In gray slacks, and a white dress shirt, rolled up his forearms, he was striking and large. A little terrifying.

Clutching my hand to my chest, I struggled to catch my breath as I took in the breathtakingly beautiful face before me.

He looked like an angel, but one who was utterly bored with his existence on Earth.

However, as his gaze settled on me, that bored expression shifted, his eyes widening slightly in recognition.

Instinctively, I scrambled backward, my phone forgotten on the floor between us.

I glanced at it briefly before returning my attention to the man before me.

If Reed had exuded an aura of potential danger, this man was the embodiment of it. *Gabriel.*

True to his namesake, he looked more like an archangel than a human, radiating an aura of power and authority.

Wheat-hued locks fell across a noble brow, framing eerily pale blue eyes.

A regal bearing exuded from every inch of him, his presence swallowing me in its chill. You're in danger. I couldn't move.

I was frozen.

"Isobel." It was a whisper.

I didn't like the way he looked at me at all. Like he could devour me. His eyes took me in. My face.

Like he knew me or I was familiar.

"No, my name's Alisha." I managed to choke out, my voice trembling slightly.

"Reed's Alisha," he stated, emphasizing Reed's name with a hint of amusement. Indeed. Swallowing hard, I tried to regain my composure.

"You scared me," I said, immediately regretting the words as they left my mouth. "I'm going to grab my phone now." I didn't move.

"Did I?" He shrugged nonchalantly not looking surprised nor sorry. "I'm trying to be better."

Tipping his head, his eyes on me he added. "I guess I need to try harder."

His deeper voice was silken smooth.

As he bent down to retrieve my phone, I felt dwarfed by his towering stature. He was taller than Reed.

With broad shoulders tapering to a trim waist, an imposing physique that commanded the space around him in his white dress shirt.

With a polite smile playing across features that could have been chiseled from marble, he extended my phone.

In that moment, the world seemed to still as I found myself staring at Reed's best friend and brother.

"You're Gabriel." I stated, but he remained eerily silent, studying me with those penetrating eyes.

"I would take your hand, but I'm a little filthy right now," he said at last, a hint of wry amusement coloring his deep voice as I gratefully accepted my phone from his outstretched hand.

The lighting in this part of the house cast a streaky glow on the device's screen.

Had he moved closer while I was distracted?

"Were you...gardening?" I asked, finding it difficult to imagine this imposing figure puttering amongst flowerbeds.

"Planting daisies," he replied, and I could have sworn I detected a glimmer of dark humor flickering in his eyes.

I recalled reading once that the most handsome angels fell from Heaven, and I was quite certain Gabriel was surely one of them.

Somehow, I doubted that gardening was how he spent his free time, but at least he had a hobby.

"Can you show me the way out?" I ventured, hoping to escape the increasingly unsettling atmosphere that seemed to thicken the very air around him.

The air dipped several degrees. His head tipped ever so slightly to the side, and an inscrutable gleam appeared in his strikingly blue eyes.

"Are you running away?" He sounded like an outraged king.

As he took one prowling step closer, my blood turned to ice in my veins. I noticed then the dark stains marring his dress shirt, previously obscured by shadows.

While he adjusted his cufflinks in an almost casual manner, his voice dropped an octave, resonating through me.

"That's not very smart of you."

In this dim alcove of the sprawling manor, the shadows seemed to swell and envelop us, yet his eyes glowed with an unholy light. I gripped my phone tightly, my heart thundering as his penetrating gaze raked over me.

"Gabriel—" I began, but he cut me off, his expression softening into something alarmingly tender.

"You look so much like—" He started, then broke off, dipping his head faster than I could react. "Hold still."

And then he stamped his lips over mine. Opening my mouth for a second in shock, I felt the gasp leave me.

He used that as leverage, wrapping his arms around my body pulling me flush against him, and for a second, I felt his tongue brushing mine, plunging into my mouth.

It was only a moment. But I tasted him, unwelcome, *not Reed*, a soft sob escaping into him, as he walked me back against a wall.

His hand on the back of my head stopped it from hitting the wall, before he gently retreated.

I fell silent as he made a sad noise, something I never expected from him. When he pulled back, his eyes looked lost.

247

Haunted. Especially for a man who had just stolen a kiss from me.

"It's not the same," he murmured, voice pitched low as he unconsciously swiped his tongue over his lips.

"Why are you running?" he asked disarmingly, his gaze piercing through me, his hand still holding my face, and I didn't know what to do.

I had two options: run, which seemed foolish considering whose arms I was in. An apex predator. Or stand up to him. My gut told me he wouldn't hurt or kill me, so I decided to be honest. The worst he'd do was kiss me again.

I struggled to keep my voice steady. "I'm not running. I needed some space."

Even then, I sounded breathless.

"There's plenty of space here," he replied evenly. I gathered that.

"Can you help me find my way out?"

"Perhaps."

"Will you let me go?" I tried a different tact, fighting not to squirm against the masculine heat surrounding me.

His lips tipped up. "Perhaps."

He likes to play games.

And I was walking a thin line.

Wait a minute! He had kissed me. What was I going to tell Reed?

I needed a different approach.

"Do you kiss all your best friends' girlfriends?" I growled at him, trying to ignore the warmth of his body pressed against mine.

"Should I do it again?" He drew me tighter against him, as if to better gauge my reaction dipping his head lower again.

"That hurts." I blurted out, pulling back.

Instantly, he loosened his grip, and I realized I was several inches off the ground. *Oh, bloody hell.*

Then, I remembered he had been spying on me. Shoving him, I felt a sense of satisfaction when he released me and set me down.

"I don't care if you run this place or if it's your home." I spat, my voice quivering with the intensity of pent-up emotion. "I got lost, and all I need is to find my way back out."

I wasn't finished, the words tumbling forth in a torrent.

"I am utterly fed up with people keeping things from me and making decisions without consulting or informing me. It's one bloody stalker. I am perfectly capable of taking care of myself."

I took a breath. "And frankly, I couldn't care less if you're trying to frighten me by being an absolute brute. It's not working."

Taking a deep, shuddering breath, I felt a sense of relief wash over me.

Gabriel blinked slowly, then straightened to his full, towering height.

His eyes glinted with something feral, as his hands gripped my shoulders, pulling me closer into his gaze. Cold.

My heart pounded a frenzied staccato as a new tension.

"That's what we do. We take care of problems nobody else can. There isn't just blood on my hands. They're all over Reed's. Don't scream. He'll come running the moment you do, and I've decided I like you too much to help you find the way out of here."

His low rumble reverberated through me as I registered the threat underlying the words.

I was powerless against him. His massive frame even more imposing, more predatory up close.

Bigger and scarier than even Reed.

"I don't care what Reed is." I countered, channeling every ounce of conviction I could muster. "I never have."

The words resonated within me.

Gabriel's voice lowered to a rumble. "Reed likes you so much he's hellbent on tearing my unit apart for you to get some downtime so he can be your full-time hero."

I stilled, my breath catching in my throat.

"He's my brother." Gabriel continued. "And he loves you. You've got fire, I'll admit that. But you're stubborn, like me. And if you're not careful, you're going to lose Reed."

I could see it then, a flicker of genuine emotion lurking behind the icy facade of his eyes, a glimpse of the profound concern he harbored for his brother's wellbeing.

"Why did you kiss me?" I whispered. "If you know he loves me."

The question tumbled from my lips before I could rein it in, curiosity overwhelming in the face of his brutal honesty.

"To see if you tasted like someone else." His response was as blunt. "You don't."

He continued, seemingly unfazed by my stunned silence.

"I heard about your stalker. Those things don't usually end well. Reed would die for you. And it's going to hurt so bad when he does." When, not if.

"When?"

Gabriel's presence was centimeters away from me. "When Reed's dead, it'll tear you apart. Turn you to ice. It's going to ache when he takes a bullet to the chest—"

I slapped him reflexively, my hand stinging from the impact as I viscerally rejected the thought of losing Reed.

Losing Reed was not an option, could never be permitted to become reality.

"Stop talking." I growled, anger and fear coursing through my veins.

I channeled every ounce of those chaotic emotions into shoving him with all my might, watching his eyes flare.

"One, you infuriating arsehole, I need to process things. Unlike you, I'm not a bloody spy. I'm a regular woman. I can't just adapt to your stressors like you can't adapt to changing into an evening gown after wearing a bikini."

I shoved again, frustration mounting with each impassioned word. "Why would you expect me to adapt to your world when I don't expect you to adapt to mine?"

Gabriel looked thrown at the thought of an evening gown to swimwear.

Clearly, he didn't understand fashion.

Undeterred, I continued. "You don't get to speak to me that way. Ever. You don't get to say horrible things like that. I couldn't give a toss where you live and what your world is like. I won't let anything happen to him. Do you understand? As long as I can, I would do anything for him."

A gleam entered his eye as I advanced.

"Because you love him," he stated, his glacial eyes glittering with a smug sort of satisfaction that irritated me.

Why does that bastard look so smug?

"Yes." The realization crashing over me like a roaring tidal wave. "I love him. I love Reed. So bloody much. Every part of him. Because he isn't the sum of his sins! *I don't care what he's done.* I am pissed off at him for planting cameras without telling me, taking away my privacy."

My accent thickened as I continued. "I needed some air after I found out just the sheer extent of information he has."

I was on a roll.

"Oh, and the fact that he does nearly everything while you stay here like a bloody vampire."

His eyes widened a little at that and I was relentless. "Are you the reason why he doesn't come home for days at a time? Are you the reason why he runs off in the middle of the night out of my bed and to you?"

He opened his mouth and I shut him down, snapping. *"I'm not finished!"*

He shut his mouth quickly looking at me wide eyed for once. *Good!*

"Do you have any idea what it's like when you're the *other* woman in your own relationship?"

He looked surprised by me.

'That felt good." I whispered surprised myself. *I must be getting my period.*

For a moment I thought he'd lose it on me. I was ready to run for it screaming bloody murder.

But then a slow smile spread across his lips, transforming his harsh features into something wickedly handsome for a fleeting moment.

"Bloody hell, you're not going to kiss me again, are you?"

Dear God, that would prove...difficult to explain to Reed, to say the least.

Gabriel's smile widened in apparent delight, his sharp canines glinting like fangs as he rumbled. "You love Reed."

"Yes." *Why was he so smug?* "Were you dropped on your head as a baby or something?" If anything, he looked even more insufferably pleased.

"You're just angry with him for being a secretive dick?"

"Not exactly those words." I huffed, but his wolfish grin remained firmly in place. "I don't even know how to tell Reed about meeting you."

"You just did." I froze, breath stilling in my lungs, then Gabriel's pale gaze slid over my shoulder toward something, someone, behind me.

"There's your answer. Don't ever say I didn't do anything for you."

I never heard him.

Slowly, I turned, locking eyes with a stormy, all-too-familiar gaze burning with a host of roiling emotions.

"Gabriel kissed you?"

CHAPTER 40
REED

"WHY WOULD YOU KISS HER?"

Raw, unfiltered fury coursed through my veins as those guttural words tore from my throat. "Gabriel!"

He was my oldest friend, my confidant, and yet in this moment, I couldn't see past the red haze of anger that consumed me.

Nothing could stop me, not even the voice of reason.

"Reed!" Alisha's desperate plea sliced through the blinding fog of rage.

Her hands clawed frantically at my back, desperately trying to anchor me, to pull me back from the brink. *"No! Don't!"*

She was hauling at me with all her strength, but my eyes were locked on Gabriel, who lifted his head with regret etched into his features, a stark contrast to the icy facade he usually wore.

"I'm sorry," he said, his deep voice heavy with remorse that did nothing to dull the blistering edge of my fury. "She's beautiful."

Damn straight she was.

And she was *mine*.

The fact that he was my friend, the one I'd moved mountains for, was the only thing keeping me from choking the life out of him.

But Alisha?

"Don't apologize to me," I growled, a dangerous rumble as my fingers curled mercilessly into the fabric of his collar. I shoved him against the wall with brutal force, the impact reverberating through my very bones."

"What the fuck is wrong with you? Are you out of your fucking mind!"

"Reed!" Alisha's voice broke on a desperate, pleading cry. Her fingers scrabbled at my sweater, trying in vain to pull me away from the smoldering precipice of madness yawning before me. I was livid, every muscle rigid with the intensity of my rage.

Are you serious about her?

This is why he asked. Because he liked her too.

My grip on Gabriel's collar tightened remorselessly until my knuckles strained pale, the fabric groaning in protest under the force of my punishing grasp.

Ice invading my veins as Alisha tugged at me, her touch a distant sensation compared to the all-consuming rage. Gabriel had the decency to look away, unable to meet my gaze.

"Jesus fucking Christ, Gabriel."

I shook my head, disbelief and anger warring violently within me while Alisha's persistent, frantic attempts to tear me away never ceased.

"What the fuck is wrong with you! Why are you so fucking hell bent on fucking up *every good thing you have!*"

He looked away, his expression pained. I didn't care anymore. I was his best friend. He was my brother.

But he kissed my girlfriend.

"Figure out your fucking mess. *I'm done.*"

I released him, watching as his eyes changed, a flicker of something unreadable in their depths. I turned then to Alisha, who looked utterly shaken, her eyes still trailing over Gabriel's imposing figure.

Without a word, I pulled her away from him, feeling the weight of his stare on my back as we moved.

She stumbled, and I swore under my breath, the urge to protect her overwhelming as I scooped her up into my arms, carrying her down the hallway that led to the spare rooms.

I knew she would get lost in this fucking trap, but I had hoped she wouldn't bump into the vampire of the manor, as she called him.

We reached the farthest room, and I closed the door behind us with a resounding thud.

In an instant, I had her pressed up against it, my emotions a swirling mix of anger, jealousy, and frustration, the intensity threatening to consume me.

I told her not to get lost in this fucking place.

The thought was a bitter reminder, fueling the fire that burned within me. My mouth pressed urgently against hers. Emotions ran high as we frantically reached for each other's clothing. Alisha was trembling as much as I was.

"I need you." I rasped in a voice that didn't even sound like my own, my hands tugging impatiently at my pants as I drank in every breathless pant, every whimper of yearning that escaped her lips.

"I'm sorry," she gasped, breath escaping in ragged bursts as she hiked her skirt up in a silent invitation.

"Why did you run off?" I wrenched my shirt off over my head, flinging it aside as I pinned her again with my scorching stare.

"You lied to me," she panted, still struggling with the fastenings of my pants.

"I didn't lie," I bit out, the words emerging breathless and ragged as I pulled her flush against me. "I installed those cameras *after* your place was broken into."

I lifted her with ease, pinning her against the door as my aching cock found her center. "I swear, I would never hurt you like that. They've never seen anything."

And then I speared into her with one driving thrust, sheathing myself to the hilt in her welcoming heat. She gasped.

"Evie can see...everything," she forced out in a breathless whimper, her fingers digging urgently into my shoulders as I shoved deeper.

I wasn't gentle. I couldn't be.

I was as primal and ruthless as my intent as I arched and shoved deeper, swallowing her screams against my lips.

"That's it, open up to me, Angel."

I pumped deep, staking my claim over every quivering inch of her with each powerful thrust. "I know you're tender, I know it hurts, doesn't it?"

"Just a little, Reed," she whimpered, and God she looked transcendent in that moment, ethereal with passion and deliciously, unrepentantly mine. "Why didn't you tell me?"

I leaned in, licking at the tears that spilled unbidden down her flushed cheeks, savoring the salt sting of her distress.

"It auto-scans and flags anything we need to look into." I stilled then, buried to the root, allowing her to pulse and flutter around me, possessing every bit of space, every gasp and tremble.

"She doesn't see anything else."

I had told Evie not to, unless I asked her.

"Show me where it hurts, baby," I demanded in a low growl.

One hand curved possessively around the swell of her ass as I hitched her higher, allowing myself to sink even deeper.

Her breath escaped in a shuddering exhale, as she reached down to flatten her palm against her stomach.

I captured her lips again, devouring her.

Alisha once told me my eyes reminded her of an impending storm.

Now I *was* the storm.

And she was the island I would take my anger out on. I drew out before slamming back in.

A sound, part whimper, part gasp, spilled from her lips.

"Stings?" My voice had taken on a darker, more dangerous timbre. Her throat worked as she nodded, resting her forehead against mine as our breaths mingled.

"Why did he kiss you?" My voice went dark. "And so help me God, if you try and lie...I will keep you here like this, taking me over and over until you admit it."

And she knew I would.

"R—*reed!*" I loved it when she said my name breathless, like a prayer. As though I would heed it.

My hands gripped her ass, holding her tight as I fucked into her setting a pace that I knew would have her coming apart.

I didn't care if people came by and heard us. I didn't care who knew. Or *saw*. She was mine.

"I didn't let him. I *swear.*"

"Say it," I was a demon inside this woman. "Say it again." I locked eyes with her.

"I love *you.*"

Was it possible for my heart to explode?

"*Keep going.*" I was going to fuck her like this. "Let me make it better."

"*Reed,*" she sobbed. "I'm loud. He'll hear..." She turned a brilliant red.

"Good, *let him.*" I didn't give a shit *who* heard me fucking my girl. At this point I *relished* Gabriel hearing her. "Hold onto me, Angel."

I waited until she wrapped her arms around my neck and then I took her off the door and groaned as she sank lower on my cock. In this position, I could slam her up and down on my length, the entirety of it.

"Does that get you excited, my little cum slut?" I worked her on me driving myself insane as well. "Knowing everyone will hear your pussy getting demolished?"

"Y—yes." She admitted, looking so fucking beautiful her hair tossed back, the waves moving as she shook her head and her eyes closed tight as she bit back another moan. "Oh God, that's so good, so deep."

My growl was wicked. "Let them hear you. I want them to know I'm breaking you in."

They wouldn't hear a thing in this room.

"Tearing up my little fuck toy." Alisha bit down on her lip suppressing another moan. But if it got her hot and bothered? I slammed her down a couple of times testing out the angle, and when she started squirming, I knew I had her. *"Give it to me, Angel."*

I set a brutal pace that even Alisha couldn't stop holding back and I knew listening to those cries I'd never make it.

"Oh God, oh God," she chanted, each cry gaining in frequency until she was crying my name in sobs.

Between my groans and the sound of my skin slapping at her, I wasn't going to make it and neither was she.

She clung to me nearly slipping as we both coated in sweat.

I pressed her against the door, driven by a primal need to be as close as possible. In that moment, nothing else mattered but her.

I licked at her tears. "Say it," I urged. "Say it again."

"I love you," she screamed as she reached her peak. *"I love you, Reed."*

She whispered those three words over and over until I stamped my mouth over her as my own release poured out of me.

Burying deep, I kissed her harder.

I love you.

CHAPTER 41
ALISHA

WE LAY CATCHING OUR BREATH, REED'S FOREHEAD PRESSED TENDERLY against mine, when a sudden knock at the door made me tense.

An accented voice spoke something indecipherable in Spanish.

I mouthed, '*Selena*' to Reed with a questioning look.

He gave a small, weary nod, his eyes closing briefly as if steeling himself against an onslaught of fresh stress. He responded verbally in Spanish.

I watched his eyes soften momentarily before a guarded look returned to his face. A look I realized he fought against.

I cupped his face in my hands and kissed him deeply, feeling him stir within our still-joined bodies.

I was still trembling, and I knew he wouldn't leave until he was sure I was alright. But I couldn't let him go until I knew the same about him.

"How much can Evie actually see?" I asked carefully.

"Just what I've told her to monitor. Negative comments, anything out of the ordinary." Reed's burning gaze met mine. "Do you believe me?"

There was a desperate edge to his voice. I nodded slowly.

"But don't do that again, Reed. I'm not an operative or an assignment—"

"I know—" he started.

"*No*, you kept something important from me. About me. Don't ever blindside me like that again." I couldn't hide the wince as he shifted our position to kiss me again.

His eyes softened. "I'm sorry."

"It's okay, I forgive you. I just—" The memory of what Gabriel had implied sank in. *When not if.* "It's not a big deal. I just want honesty." I knew Gabriel was trying to manipulate me, push me into a corner. I had seen his face when Reed went after him.

He nodded. "I'll do my best. I love you."

"...What are you going to do about.." I hated coming between him and his life. *His best friend.* "I don't think he was actually trying to kiss me..."

I relayed to Reed what Gabriel had said. Reed's eyes narrowed as he processed this, then he looked up briefly, seemingly asking for patience.

"He called me Isobel." I reiterated, watching the emotions play across his striking features in that heavy silence. "Who is that?"

A tense silence stretched out before Reed spoke.

"He wasn't kissing you." He shook his head with frustration. "Fuck my life."

I could sense Reed being pulled away by the demands of his job, the life he led. A life I hated seeing take him from me, and yet I knew his drive, his dedication to his work was part of who he was.

"Reed."

"Yes, Angel?"

"You have to go."

"I do," he whispered, sounding reluctant to leave. It struck me then. It didn't have to be an either or situation. He could find balance.

"Go," I told him softly. "I'll be here when you get back. I promise."

He looked at me with surprise and what seemed like relief. I realized then how much I had contributed to that torn, pained look he often had. I nodded, blinking back tears.

"I promise." I held up my pinky finger to seal the vow. His eyes warmed as he linked his pinky with mine.

"I love you," I whispered fervently.

"I love you. Just stay with Evie." He set me down, slipping out of me and I nodded, kissing him again. Reed and I left for my event an hour later, with Gabriel nowhere in sight, only stopping by my apartment to change.

Reed had changed at Titan into a suit that always drove me insane.

As he smirked, taking in my expression, I changed into a dress I knew would drive him crazy as well.

And when I come out he'd all but growled, dragging me back into the room. I'd laughed it off since we were going to be late.

Days and nights after that Reed and I learned to adapt and find balance in each other's worlds. With my kiss with Gabriel causing a less-than-ideal relationship with him and Gabriel, I felt guilty.

They were brothers.

I couldn't stop hearing Gabriel's haunted voice. Calling me someone else's name…

Kellan updated Reed about things.

I overheard Kellan mention something about someone named Lopez. I didn't know who that was so I sketched and took photos.

Kellan came with me whenever I went to Poppy and the teenagers we ran programs with loved him. He was good company.

And it was always the good days that I least suspected and maybe forgot that my life was still in danger.

One afternoon Kellan and I were at Poppy, I had been ready to ask him about Selena, since he hadn't said a word about her, but came in looking happier.

I figured whenever Reed was around, Kellan had time with her. He was taking a call and I saw the door to the back was open.

I was downstairs where we typically had meetings. In the mini skirt outfit and stockings I was wearing, I felt a bit chilly.

Had one of the maintenance workers forgotten to secure it again?

We kept all doors closed to ensure privacy and safety for everyone in the building.

I moved to shut the door, aware Kellan wouldn't want me venturing outside alone.

But then I saw the doorstop.

I quickly stuck my booted foot out to push the door open wider, my eye caught sight of the dumpster outside.

What I almost missed in my rushed motion made my scream catch in my throat. I froze, until strong arms yanked me back inside.

"Alisha." Kellan's gruff voice sounded as he pulled me away from the door viciously.

My scream was muffled inside Kellan's chest as I shook wildly, unable to get the image of the bloody woman next to the dumpster.

Even though I knew, she was *dead.*

∾

I DIDN'T CRY. I WAS TOO SHELL-SHOCKED.

I'd never seen a dead body in real life. I didn't have a spine of steel.

Especially not as Kellan told me to stay close to him. He didn't let me go as he called Reed.

I would never get the image out of my mind.

Long moments later, as I sat in the hallway with a blanket wrapped around me, an icy-eyed Gabriel with Reed had shown up wearing masks of nothing but collected rage.

I didn't know they'd been together. The temperature dipped the moment Gabriel stepped into the hallway.

His eyes locked with mine for a moment and I swore I saw regret in them.

Kellan immediately handed me over to Reed.

"I'm taking you home."

Reed had taken one look at me and whisked me away while Gabriel watched me and spoke to Kellan in hushed tones. His recognition in his eyes had flashed.

I reminded him of someone. Someone he must've loved. *Isobel. His girlfriend?* It was impossible to imagine Gabriel with anyone. What kind of a woman had she been?

You don't taste like her.

"Wait." Gabriel growled, his pale eyes blazing with something akin to outraged defiance as they raked over me. "We have to tell her. Now."

"No." Reed looked furious. "I need to get her home. This building needs to be shut down while we take care of the mess outside."

I'd never heard him sound so callous. A dead body was just a mess to him?

I didn't know who he was right there as he looked at Gabriel.

"This isn't the time," he bit out in a tone that brokered no argument.

"Tell me what?" My voice emerged as a tremulous rasp, my body beginning to shake with uncontrolled spasms.

I was shaking wildly and even Gabriel seemed to take pity as he reached into his pocket and pulled out a pair of blue gloves. My hands shook so bad as he handed them to me moving closer.

I didn't miss the way Reed's jaw ticked as he saw me take them quietly.

"What are you hiding from me?"

"Not now." Reed's voice held no argument towards Gabriel. Except I had the scare of my life.

"Now, she needs to hear it. Just rip it off like a bandaid." I turned to Gabriel, and Kellan who looked uncomfortable.

"You're on thin fucking ice, Gabriel." Reed growled in blatant warning.

And I turned to Gabriel letting Reed go. "Tell me."

At that moment I saw something in his eyes. I got a feeling that if I asked Gabriel for the moon he would move it for me. Not me, her. *Isobel.*

I didn't know how to explain that look in his eyes. That realization lanced through me with clarity. He couldn't see me, the real me, at all. I was a ghost to him, conjured from his grief.

He saw her when he saw me.

"Please, Gabriel." I clutched the gloves in my hands feeling unable to even put them on with how bad I was shaking.

"Don't you dare, Gabriel—"

"Mr. Monroe—"

Gabriel's eyes leveled with me. "You have a serial killer obsessed with making you his next kill."

I stood still.

As Gabriel explained it to me stating that's why he was in the neighborhood I stood there stunned and shaking with a frigid blast of ice going through me. I didn't even catch half of what he said too in shock and panic. He explained to me all the haunting notes, the weird obsession, they were common in the way he attacked women he thought were attractive, but would never like him back.

"*What?*"

"It's not a stalker. It's a serial killer. You match the profile of the girl outside." Gabriel's voice was calm. As he continued my head spun.

"We think someone out to get you initially because you were attractive, they had a crush on you from far away. Then, you got involved with Reed. Your admirer began hating you. Resenting you. It eventually always leads to hatred, doesn't it?" Gabriel shrugged lightly. "It's Reed's fault, since he was so distracted with you."

"I'm going to murder you." It was a vicious growl from Reed.

"*No, you will not,*" I said firmly, ignoring Reed's astounded expression. Turning back to Gabriel, I pleaded. "He's the only one who's been honest with me this whole time. Please, continue."

I may have been just a civilian, but I deserved to know the truth.

Gabriel's eyes warmed a little. "I've been looking into your little problem for the last few weeks with Selena and Quarterback here."

I whipped my head toward my bodyguard, feeling betrayed. "You knew about this?"

Kellan shook his head but I saw the guilt in his eyes. "No confirmation, Miss Alisha. It was all just suspicion, especially after the shooting."

Reed stiffened next to me looking pissed at Kellan.

"What about the shooting?" Looking between the three men, hysteria crept into my voice. "That day...it was just a random incident, wasn't it?"

The panic rose in my throat. *"Wasn't it?"*

Gabriel looked the most put together like he experienced this daily. "I wanted to make sure the pieces fit together. We think Lopez was working with whoever is hunting you down, before he went to jail and even after. He's just a patsy. Unlike the rest of the girls in the city who've gone missing—" That name.

The name Kellan had told Reed.

"You fit the description of his targeted victims," Gabriel continued, relentless. "The notes, the break-ins, all the women he's killed reported similar incidents to the police. I just received confirmation from our NYPD contact."

"Giroux talked?" Kellan stated more than asked, seeming unsurprised.

Meanwhile, I felt utterly lost in their coded language.

"What? Wait—this is too much." My voice rose in disbelief and dawning horror. "You think I have a serial killer after me? After me?"

This had to be some cruel joke. There was just no way.

"Is this some sort of sick prank?"

Gabriel didn't give a rat's arse about feelings, but I was oddly grateful he told me straight. "I found Lopez dead in his apartment after Quarterback tried to finesse information out of him. Whoever it is knows what to look out for. He blends in. He dropped the note off at Reed's. This means until further notice you're going to have a shadow at all times."

He raised an inquisitive brow. "Unless you'd prefer to stay at the manor with me?"

I got the feeling I shouldn't do that. Gabriel's eyes weren't cold anymore as he took me in looking a little worried. "You don't look so good."

"She's not fucking good!" Reed erupted furiously. "You just dumped months' worth of terrifying information on a civilian! She's not some hardened operative like us!"

Icy eyes flashed toward Kellan as Gabriel spoke in a steely tone. "You will not speak a word of this."

Kellan's expression went blank and impassive.

Then Gabriel turned to me, his voice unexpectedly gentle, almost tender.

"I'm sorry." I hadn't realized how close he was to me. I got the feeling he didn't apologize often, the words sounding rusty on his lips. "I figured out your problem. I told Reed I just needed some time to think. Aren't you pleased?"

Is he standing closer now?

"Gabriel—"

"Mr. Monroe—" Kellan began, but Gabriel's gaze never left my face.

"You're in shock, but you'll thank me later."

Would I?

I was in shock, that much was certain.

This couldn't be real.

I couldn't be here, with a dead body outside.

I closed my eyes, willing myself to wake up from this nightmare. *Any moment now.*

"We just talked about this." I whirled on Reed, who looked at me with wide, concerned eyes.

"Miss Alisha—" Kellan reached for me, but I brushed him off.

"Angel, I think you should sit down. You look ready to—" Reed's voice held a lacing of worry, but I couldn't focus on his words. Dizziness overcame me, my head spinning. My breath came in short, ragged gasps as I struggled to breathe properly.

"Do not say a word." I turned on Reed, my voice shaking uncontrollably.

"I cannot believe you right now. How many secrets did you keep from me?"

I couldn't breathe normally.

"How could you not tell me?" I didn't recognize my own voice as I started to hyperventilate.

"Lish...baby." Reed reached for me, but he seemed to drift further away.

"Don't baby me!" I snapped, my body trembling violently. I was in shock. I needed to sit down. Get a blanket. *Anything.*

"Panic attacks are good. It usually means she's processing it," Gabriel's voice was oddly softer than usual, almost...comforting.

"I don't think you should've told her all that, Mr. Monroe—" Kellan protested, but Gabriel cut him off viciously.

"Fuck off, Quarterback. She needs to hear it."

"Don't be mean to Kellan!" I cried out, and Gabriel fell silent immediately.

I couldn't get it together. I should've been better composed. I should've—I held my head in my hands, trying to remember what I had eaten today.

Coffee. Just coffee.

I couldn't think clearly as warm, strong arms wrapped around me soothingly.

"Angel—" Reed's voice was gentle, calming, but I put a hand over my eyes, rubbing them vigorously.

The world went dark.

CHAPTER 42
ALISHA

"She has anxiety."

Reed's voice cut through the haze of waking up, laced with thinly veiled menace.

"I told you she's a civilian. You can't talk to her like that. She doesn't understand, and she's not used to this."

As I drifted back into consciousness, the murmur of voices around me slowly came into focus. Reed's words, meant to protect me, only fueled the embers of frustration smoldering in my chest.

The idea that he had intentionally kept me in the dark, no matter how well-meaning, stung.

Gabriel growled irritably. "She handled it well enough when I told her."

"Don't think for a fucking second I am done with you."

Gabriel groaned in the background, a hint of exasperation in his voice.

"She needed to know. She'll never be a part of us if she can't handle a little serial killer."

"Oh, would you cut it out—" A third voice, tinged with annoyance, entered my dreams. "She's exhausted, and she's been running around trying to distract herself with her new life, and you two idiots are making this more difficult. Did you have to fight each other while she passed out...? Oh, look, she's waking up."

Gemma. What was she doing in my dream?

"I will murder you if she's angry with me." Reed growled.

Gabriel scoffed dismissively. "She won't be angry with you, she's a bunny—"

Gemma sounded livid. "I will not ask you again to cease. You are the most rude person in this room. And if you continue again, I will not hold Reed back from choking you again."

Gemma continued firmly. "She isn't used to any of this. How would you feel if you knew someone was out to kill you?"

"I'd be flattered." Gabriel's tone dripped with sarcasm. What was he doing in my dream?

"Reed, please kill him." Gemma pleaded, her hands stroking over my hair with tenderness.

"I will. But she's waking up." Reed replied, his voice softening.

"Gem," I mumbled groggily. "I had a horrible dream."

"Come on, Angel, wake up." Reed's soothing voice stirred me, and I felt a slight weight and discomfort in my head. Then Gabriel's cold tone cut through, devoid of emotion.

"Kellan and Nate just took care of the body. Giroux's tracking what we know."

That got me up.

This was no dream.

I was definitely on the floor in Reed's arms, with Gemma's big blue eyes batting at me in concern. She knelt on the floor while a pair of grey trouser-clad legs stood a few feet away. From down here, Gabriel looked positively cold as I remembered him being, with a bruised eye and purple marks on his neck.

I was up, looking up at Reed. I hated that they had fought.

He sat on the floor, holding me on his lap. A dainty hand came into my field of vision, and Gemma gave me a small, reassuring smile.

"You're all right, darling. Nate went to help Kellan, so I'm staying for now with this..." She looked at Gabriel with disdain. *"Thing."*

He didn't look thrilled at the prospect of being a babysitter.

"I own Nathan," he stated flatly.

She scowled at him with contempt.

I squeezed Gemma's hand gladly, not able to look at Reed even though he held me. "Lish, are you okay?"

No, I wasn't okay.

I whispered, my voice trembling with fear and anxiety. "Can I have a minute?"

I looked at Gemma, letting go of Reed's hand.

Gabriel gruffly extended a hand and helped Gemma off the floor as she brushed her skirt. Gemma ushered Gabriel somewhere far from us, leaving me and Reed. I couldn't look at Reed, while I could envision the concern etched into his handsome face.

I felt a surge of conflicting emotions.

"I don't even know how to speak to you right now." I managed, my voice thin with hurt and betrayal. The words felt inadequate in the face of death.

The fact that he had planned to wait, to keep me in the dark even a moment longer, only intensified the ache all over me.

How could he claim to love me, to want my trust, when he couldn't extend the same courtesy to me?

"I'm sorry, Angel. I was going to tell you—" Reed began, his voice laced with regret.

"When were you going to tell me about the shooting?" I didn't care. I cut him off, anger and disbelief rising in my tone. "When was the perfect time to tell me about a bloody serial killer?"

I couldn't even fathom how much he had lied.

"I may not be familiar with your world, but you didn't give me a chance." My voice grew stronger, fueled by righteous indignation.

"I am allowed to be human. To have different reactions to things than the ones you are programmed to learn. You were allowed to train and grow as a person. You were upset that I waited to show you that note. You punished me and Kellan. But the standard is not the same for you?"

The realization that I was fundamentally different from the people Reed surrounded himself with, from the life he led, settled like a weight in my stomach.

I locked eyes with him, now, seeing his stunned expression. "You told me to give you a chance. To let you love me. But I didn't deserve a chance to meet you at your level in your life?"

The words tore from my throat, raw and bleeding with hurt.

"The point of being in a relationship is to let your partner in. I cannot believe you kept things from me." My voice broke, the image of the dead woman flashing behind my eyelids. "Would you have cleaned up the body and not told me?"

The guilt that flickered across Reed's face was all the answer I needed.

The man I loved, the man I had trusted with my heart and my future, had been willing to hide anything.

Everything.

The betrayal cut deeper than any physical wound ever could.

I shook my head, tears welling in my eyes. "This entire time you wanted my trust. My faith. But I didn't have yours?"

"No, of course I trust you. I love you. I would do anything for you—" Reed protested earnestly.

"Including lie to me—" I retorted bitterly.

"I would do anything for you to keep you safe." His voice was pleading.

We were both not doing anything to keep our voices lowered, and I didn't see Gemma and Gabriel anywhere, but they were likely listening.

"I need some space," I whispered, the words like shards of glass in my throat. "I think a woman was killed because of me...and I think I'm next. I need to lay down."

The exhaustion, the fear, and the overwhelming sense of helplessness crashed over me in waves.

"Angel, don't." Reed begged, his voice thick with anguish. "It was never my intention to hurt you."

No, his intent had been to hide the truth from me as long as he could because he felt like I couldn't handle it.

"You're not going to be next. I won't let that happen. Look at me, please, Lish. I promise, I was going to tell you. I just needed to figure it out."

He clenched my hand tightly, and I saw the vulnerable teenager in him, the young man begging me to listen.

Give me a chance, beautiful girl.

I looked at Reed at that moment, and I saw him truly. For the first time that day, I saw the bags under his eyes.

The way he looked exhausted. I saw that when he had gone to Titan, he was juggling so much. He was handling everything. And me. He was signing up to be my bodyguard when we both knew Reed didn't have the time or energy.

I lived with him now, and I saw how diligent he was. How hard he worked.

Reed worked hard, but he never played hard. As far as I was aware, I wasn't sure of the last time he had a vacation or took a break.

And the longer I looked at him, my heart broke. A little kindness. A little kindness goes a long way.

"I know," I said softly, my anger dissipating into understanding. "I know, but what you kept from me, Reed—this is not the first time. We just talked about this."

I didn't want to fight around people.

"I swear, I was going to tell you," he pleaded, his voice raw with emotion. He was begging me. "Please, Alisha. I love you. I would never hurt you." *No. Not intentionally.* "Please don't leave me. I will do anything."

But beneath the terror and the anger, a new emotion took root within me.

Determination. I couldn't lose Reed.

Gabriel's words echoed in my mind. *When.* Not If.

"You have to start telling me the truth."

WE DIDN'T CONTINUE OUR CONVERSATION AT POPPY WITH GABRIEL AND Gemma nearby.

Instead, Reed whisked me back home. I sat with him, wringing my hands together at what Gabriel had said.

"The truth." Reed's brow furrowed, a flicker of unease in his eyes. "Lish, there are some things —"

I cut him off gently, my hand cupping his cheek, my thumb tracing the line of his jaw. "I know."

The relief in his eyes was palpable, and he nodded, grateful for my understanding. "But the other things, yes, the things you want to get off your chest."

"Like when Selena tries to kill Nate?" He suggested.

A small laugh escaped my lips, lightening the tense moment.

"Or when you know it has to do with me and it would deeply upset me had I not known," I added.

I pressed closer to him, offering my comfort, my support. I know why Reed didn't speak openly. He didn't trust easily. He'd suffered at the hands of people he should have been able to trust. I couldn't even imagine what that did to him. But I also needed him to understand, that I wasn't them.

Reed's arms tightened around me, his chin resting atop my head.

"I need to communicate better."

I understood why he had a hard time.

With his background, his lack of close relationships, his lack of family minus the dysfunctional one he had at Titan—I got it. But understanding didn't mean I could make excuses.

"I think I'd like it if you communicated in general." My eyes searched his, vulnerability shining through."I like everything with you, but we can't just...make love and move on. We have to communicate these things, even if it's in bed."

A shaky exhale left his lips, his forehead touching mine. "I'm sorry. Are you afraid?"

"A little." The admission was hard, the fear a tangible thing, twisting in my gut. "Can you catch him?"

The look in Reed's eyes was fierce, a promise and a vow all in one. "I will. I'll do whatever is necessary."

"Reed, I am terrified. My sister—"

"She's taken care of," he reassured me softly. Gratitude welled up inside me, tears pricking at the corners of my eyes. "Thank you for everything."

His smile was gentle, loving. "I will always take care of you."

And I knew, with every fiber of my being, that he would.

Later that night, as we lay entwined, our bodies close but our minds even closer, Reed opened up to me in a way he never had before. He spoke of his life, his past, the things that haunted him.

And I listened, my heart aching for him, my love for him growing with every word.

"Gabriel thinks, like any serial killer, that whoever it is might be obsessed with you." Reed's words sent a flush to my cheeks. "But he thinks the person might not be. He thinks they might've just thought you were a good person who then started dating me."

A cold realization settled in the pit of my stomach. "You think this person assumed that because we started being together, that...I was no longer good?"

The look on Reed's face was unreadable, but I could see the pain in his eyes, the self-loathing."I think whoever it is thinks you defiled yourself by being with me. And they want to make you pay for it."

Tears blurred my vision, my heart breaking for the man I loved, for the way he saw himself.

"You don't think sleeping with you was...bringing myself...beneath me, do you?"

"Oh, baby, I know it was." The fierceness in his gaze took my breath away. "You were mine from the moment I saw you. I didn't care if I went to hell, so long as I could taste you before I did."

A memory flashed through my mind, our first night together when he'd avoided answering if he thought he was inherently bad. "Do you think you're inherently bad?"

"I don't know." The words were a whisper, a confession. "I just know I haven't done many good things, and you were the best thing I'd ever experienced. I just wanted to keep you for as long as I could."

The realization hit me.

"Is that why you call me Angel?"

His nod was almost short. "I can't stay away from you. I want everything you've got. I want a taste of heaven, just from your lips. I'll do anything to get it."

I kissed him, all but taking over him, crawling into his lap. He immediately brought his hands to my butt, dragging me closer until I brushed into the hard ridge of him, and I ignored it.

"You are not the sum of your sins, Reed Whittaker. You are the kindest man I know, the most generous lover. I would love you until I didn't know what love was. In every lifetime, I would choose you. I feel like I waited all those years for you, and I picked you because I thought you were inherently good...I love you. For all that you are. I love you." I kissed him hard.

I felt him groan under me, and a heavy sigh left him.

"Goddamn, Angel. Do you have any idea what I want to do to you right now?"

I smiled against his lips, reaching between us.

"Maybe." I gripped the length of him and stroked the thick stalk of flesh, loving his moans. Reed helped me shove my panties aside, and I gasped as I felt myself sinking onto him.

"Maybe I just needed to help you think straight tonight." I whispered in his ear what he had said to me. "The only time you listen is when you're inside of me."

I felt his groans increasing as I worked myself on him in a way that Lara had whispered to me on one of our meetings she knew drove men crazy. I worked him inch by inch, which was easier for me to take anyway. Just the tip at first, and then sinking up and down until the entire length of him was buried in me.

For long moments, I kept my legs wrapped around his waist, and he sat still, as though he might snap.

"Being inside you is the closest to heaven, Angel," he rasped, his voice thick with desire. I wanted to not cry, but it felt impossible.

I kissed his chin, his jaw, working my way to his lips. "I love you, Reed Whittaker. I'm your girl."

Reed's hips moved then, slowly inside of me, and I was lost to the pulsing pleasure that I knew would follow.

For long, searing moments, I felt more than I ever imagined.

And when Reed and I finished, I felt something else, something new blossom between us.

"I love you," he murmured, his voice reverent. "I love you, Angel."

CHAPTER 43
ALISHA

REED HAD TALKED TO ME ABOUT A LOT OF THINGS. TITAN. GABRIEL.

Telling me from start to finish about my stalker/serial killer. Which sounded insane to me.

When he did make love to me, it was so gentle, and different. He kissed me and apologized. Over and over. His touch, usually so assertive and demanding, was now tender and reverent, as if he were worshipping every inch of my body.

The contrast left me breathless, my heart aching with the depth of his love and the weight of his secrets.

One morning, several days after the incident, I woke to the sound of Reed moving about the apartment.

The clink of dishes in the kitchen, the muffled sound of his voice from his office.

No doubt he was busy handling what he had to. For long moments, I lay in bed, luxuriating in the silk sheets that still held the scent of our lovemaking.

The memory of the night before, where Reed had taken me to new heights of pleasure, made me warmer. I slowly got up, my body aching deliciously, the bruises on my skin evident.

You're all mine. Every part of you. Every hole, mine to suck and fuck and fill up.

I was at the kitchen counter, lost in thought, when a knock at the door startled me.

I knew Reed had said not to answer the door without him, but this was K2. Surely it was safe.

When I opened it, I realized my mistake.

A stunning blonde woman stood on the other side, her curves stretching her athletic outfit, her blue eyes darker than any ocean I'd ever seen, her lips pretty in pink.

"Good morning," I said, suddenly acutely aware of my disheveled appearance, my hair a rat's nest and Reed's shirt barely covering my body. "Can I help you?"

She held two cups of coffee, the aroma wafting towards me.

"Sorry, I think I have the wrong apartment."

Except her coffee cup said *Reed*. I felt a burning in my chest, my throat constricting as I looked at the beautiful woman ready to leave.

How could she have the wrong apartment?

Reed's apartment took up the entire floor. There was only one way to get here.

Which meant she had a key card.

"Are you..."

"You're Reed's new girlfriend." *New.* Which meant...she was the old one?

"I'm Lucy. Will you let Reed know to get in touch with me? It's urgent. I felt so bad, I didn't want to bother you."

She wasn't mean, but I could tell she saw how I looked. I had never felt jealousy like this, a hot, sickening feeling that twisted in my gut as I took in the other woman.

"Is there...I'm sorry." Why was I apologizing. "Is there something I should know?"

"No," she shook her head, but I could feel the lie in her words, the way her eyes flickered away from mine. "It's not like that—"

But I could feel she was hiding something from me. Was Reed cheating on me? The thought was like a knife to my heart, a pain so acute it took my breath away.

"Will you tell him it's urgent, please? Tell him Lucy came by and she says, Charlie and Iris are going on a date."

Charlie and Iris are going on a date?

Was that some code for Reed's current girlfriend while she stopped by with coffee for him?

She smiled as she left, holding her coffee. And his. And I stood there like an idiot, my mind reeling. *Go talk to him.*

One part of my brain assured me that after last night, Reed would never cheat on me. But he was a man. And he was allowed to have had flings in the years we hadn't been together.

He hadn't been celibate like Lara.

Another part of me couldn't help but think that Lucy was his type. Tall, blonde, stunning.

The kind of woman who looked like she belonged on a runway. *Talk to him!*

I found my legs moving of their own accord, shutting the door and walking to Reed's office in the massive apartment. I stopped at the door when I heard Reed raising his voice.

He never did that. He sounded angry.

I knew better than to eavesdrop, but my curiosity was piqued after Lucy's visit. His voice was too muffled to make out.

Until I heard. "Alisha's asleep. After the stunt you pulled the other day? No...no she doesn't know. Why would I tell Alisha about Lucy?"

My heart plummeted, a sickening feeling washing over me. What was he talking about?

"And she's not going to find out..."

Good Lord.

I leaned in, pressing my ear to the door despite the guilt churning in my stomach. Some deeper instinct compelled me to listen, to find out the truth, no matter how painful.

I pressed my toes into the floor, straining to hear him better.

My ears against the door, I felt like I was betraying him, but I couldn't stop myself.

"What do you want me to say? Yes, I met with Lucy..."

I froze, my chest tightening in shock, ice flowing through my veins.

"...My arrangement with Lucy...I did you a favor. I missed out on Alisha for your bullshit and games?"

My entire body went numb, a wave of nausea washing over me.

I wanted to cry. I wanted to scream.

That night he hadn't come to the event with me, I remembered the look in his eyes.

Oh God, how long had he been with her for? I was so stupid...Hot tears burned in my eyes, blurring my vision.

"...I should have been more careful?" I stumbled back, my mind reeling.

What was going on? There was an ugly pause, and for a moment, I thought Reed might catch me.

But then he said. *"...Is that what you want to hear?"*

Yes. I didn't say a word.

I slowly walked back, staring at the door like it was a monster.

Like he was a monster. He was darkness. He was dangerous. And he had broken me.

CHAPTER 44
REED

"You went behind my back with a Devereaux for the fucking necklace." Gabriel's voice was dark, his tone accusatory.

I fucking knew he would be mad I went to Lucy.

But Lucy was the best at what she did.

Only he would have the audacity to call me at this ungodly hour and interrogate me.

"You kissed my girlfriend." I shot back, my anger rising.

Thank fuck, Lish is asleep.

"If Alisha hadn't told me why you did it, and even then – I fucking hate you."

I was seething, furious that I had to leave the warmth of Alisha's side to entertain his bullshit.

"You don't trust me at all." I had a migraine, and all I wanted was to slide back into bed with Alisha. "I hired Lucy to find your treasure in Senegal."

I was livid.

"I've been feeding you information from her fucking lips for the past three years. I gave you all the ammo you needed against the Devereaux's. And you have the gall to ask me why I kept it from you? Kept secrets from Alisha? Listen to yourself. I don't even know why you want the necklace—"

"Did she have it?" Gabriel interrupted, his voice urgent.

I couldn't believe what I was hearing. *"What?"*

"Did she have it?" he repeated, his impatience palpable.

"You knew I met with Lucy, but not if I had the necklace?"

"I only knew because Lucas called me." He muttered something about showing up to his office with Garrett. *Oh shit.*

"Does he know? Did you kill him?" Gabriel was one straw away from breaking everyone.

Gabriel sighed. "No. Someone's trying to kill him, and he talked."

He proceeded to explain how Lucas Devereaux had been attacked in his garage, cursing him out under his breath. Someone was trying to kill Lucas fucking Devereaux? What the fuck.

Lucy never told me...is that why she'd been nervous about the necklace?

This was getting ridiculous. *"And he thinks it's you?"*

Gabriel broke off, muttering about that *one time,* but he stopped quickly. "Do you have it?"

I sighed heavily. "Yes."

I heard his exhale from the other end of the line. "Do you have the key?"

A pause. "I don't have it."

"What? Where the fuck is the key?" I demanded, my frustration growing.

"You thought I had the key the entire time?"

"I fucking thought you were the key!" I shouted, and both of us swore. Heavily.

"Gabriel, from now on, when you go on your fucking fantasy quests and you've got your questions, please, do it after nine am."

Gabriel continued as if I hadn't just asked him for space. Typical work wife he was.

"Lucas is a fool if he thinks people don't want to shoot him. I'd shoot him for free." Gabriel muttered, saying something about target practice.

"You'd shoot the entire population of New York for target practice," I retorted.

"Sensitive bitch."

I grimaced. "Entitled snob."

Silence.

"When can I have the necklace?" Gabriel asked, his voice insistent.

I groaned.

"Goodbye. I have a woman in bed, and as I remember correctly, you do not."

He grumbled something about being a work wife.

"I will give it to you. But you're going to tell me who the woman was and who Isobel is."

And if it's the same person. Because I didn't know her.

"Fine," he agreed grudgingly. "Do you know why Evie is avoiding me? She's seeing someone, I know it."

"She's got a brother who dismembers people in his basement. Let the kid try to live a normal life." I swore he said, *absolutely not.*

"I'm leaving." I didn't wait for his response, hanging up the phone. It wasn't even nine am.

I walked out of my office and into my room where I saw the sheets rumpled.

I smiled at the memory of Alisha curled into my sheets last night, exhausted and begging me to stop. And then to not stop. I walked into the bathroom to see if she was there taking a hot bath.

I meant to run her one this morning and get her some food before finding out how sore she was. I wanted to lick it better.

"Lish?" I called out, an uneasy feeling settling in my gut as I noticed how quiet the apartment was.

Something was wrong.

There was no way someone could have broken in and taken her while I was on the phone.

Frowning, I searched the closet where she often looked through the designer clothes Selena picked out for me to play the part. She wasn't there.

I checked the library and the kitchen, but still no sign of her. "Alisha?" She wouldn't have left without a reason.

As I walked towards the door, a chill ran through me, the house feeling cold and empty. My shoes, which I always kept organized, looked off.

One of them was on its side, and her shoes were missing.

But there was no way for Alisha to walk out unless—*Why would she leave?*

And then, it hit me.

I remembered the prickle at the back of my neck when I'd been going off on Gabriel. I hadn't been quiet, but my office was on the other side of the apartment, far away from the bedroom.

Unless Alisha came to say good morning. And she'd heard me mention Lucy.

And the night I hid things from her.

Oh fuck, why were all my secrets unraveling around this woman?

And Gabriel. Oh shit, shit, shit.

I picked up my phone and dialed, slipping on my shoes.

I pulled up my laptop, my fingers moving rapidly across the keyboard until my call was answered by a sleepy voice.

"Hey, boss."

"Kellan, I need help."

CHAPTER 45
ALISHA

As I sobbed into Gemma's shoulder, I was grateful she wore soft sweaters all the time.

I choked out the words. "…And her name, i-i-is L-l-ucy. She was so pretty. She l-looked like a starlet…I'm a potato."

The scent of Gemma's perfume, a blend of grapefruit and lemons, enveloped me, providing a small measure of comfort in my distress.

It was familiar and consistent.

Gemma shook her head, her silky blonde hair brushing against my face as she spoke, her voice gentle but firm. "No darling, you're not a potato."

Despite the hint of a smile tugging at the corners of her lips, Gemma's expression remained serious as she laid with me in the bedroom of the suite I had gotten.

The Primrose, with its charming, old-world decor and plush furnishings, had seemed like the perfect refuge when I checked myself in, seeking solace in the quaint boutique hotel tucked away in the heart of Midtown.

Nate, ever-present and vigilant, was in the other room of the expansive suite, giving me the space I so desperately needed.

"I also don't think you should be running around without protection," Gemma added, her brow furrowed with concern.

"I don't care. Everything is a lie. I was so afraid for so long, and now I feel like I had every right to be."

I could still picture the look on Nate's face when he arrived, the suspicion in his eyes when he noticed Kellan's absence.

The soft glow of his phone screen illuminated his features as he typed out a message, his fingers moving swiftly across the screen.

But I couldn't bring myself to care about what he was doing or who he was contacting.

All I wanted was to be alone, to shut out the world and everyone in it. If there was a killer out there, targeting me because of my relationship with Reed, well, they could rejoice.

I was no longer in a relationship.

My phone vibrated incessantly, the screen lighting up with Reed's name over and over again. Calls. Texts. Voicemails.

I ignored them all, each one a painful reminder of the secrets and lies that had torn us apart.

A knock at the door pulled me from my thoughts, and I watched as Gemma tucked the soft, downy blanket around me.

She rose to answer the door, her movements graceful and purposeful.

Nate's arm reached out, his hand gently grasping Gemma's elbow as he leaned in close. I saw the way she stiffened, her posture rigid with tension.

Nate's gaze lingered on Gemma, his jaw clenching as if he were physically restraining himself from saying something more.

Gemma met his stare unflinchingly, her chin lifted in a silent challenge, a defiance that spoke volumes without a single word being uttered.

"I'll be right back, darling," Gemma said, her voice clipped and tight. She shook her head.

As they disappeared from the room, I burrowed deeper into the covers.

The pain of the breakup was a tangible thing.

Maybe this was what I had been avoiding all along, the inevitable heartbreak that came with loving someone so deeply, so completely.

I had foolishly believed that I could be a part of something important to him, that he would share his world with me in the same way I had shared mine with him.

I never stood a chance.

My phone buzzed again, the vibration a dull, distant thing, barely registering through the haze of my emotions.

I reached out, my fingers numb and clumsy as I fumbled with the device, turning it off and silencing it.

I curled in on myself, drawing my knees to my chest as I tried to make myself as small as possible, as if I could somehow disappear.

The images that haunted me, the woman who looked so much like me, my sister, Reed's broken and bloody body, they played on a relentless loop in my mind.

When, not if. When, not if.

I squeezed my eyes shut, trying to block out the world, to find some semblance of peace in the darkness behind my eyelids.

I wanted to cry into the sheets. I hated this. Hated this.

Distantly, I heard the murmur of voices.

More than just Gemma's.

It sounded like there were others, their words indistinct and muffled, filtering through the haze of my grief like radio static.

I couldn't bring myself to care who they were or what they wanted. All I wanted was to be left alone. But I was curious.

The plush carpet was soft beneath my bare feet as I padded towards the door, each step a monumental effort.

As I reached for the handle, my hand trembling slightly, I heard the unmistakable sound of Reed's voice, low and insistent, filtering through the heavy wood.

"...Let me see her."

Gemma's response was swift and unyielding, her tone regal and uncompromising. *"Absolutely not."*

Her voice as sharp as a knife's edge. "I won't let you hurt her anymore. This is the *second* time *you* have made her cry like that. *I haven't seen her like that in ages—*"

"Gemma, one way or another, I will see her. Did you forget who's in the room right now?"

Everyone was under his thumb. Everyone, that is, except for me.

I mustered up enough strength, grateful Gemma had brought clothes for me, and I walked out of my room.

I would not let him have his way anymore.

CHAPTER 46
REED

I KNEW THE MOMENT ALISHA CHECKED INTO THE PRIMROSE HOTEL. As I strode into the room, unlocking the door and leaving Kellan outside, my footsteps muffled by the plush carpet, I was met with Nate's navy stare. Gemma was here.

His eyes, usually so calm and unreadable, were filled with a quiet intensity that stopped me in my tracks.

"I can hear her crying," he said, his voice low and heavy with unspoken accusations. Nate's jaw clenched, his distaste for women in distress evident in the hard set of his mouth.

"What did you do this time?"

I brushed past him, my focus singular and unwavering. "I need to see her."

Nate's hand shot out, his fingers wrapping around my arm in a vice-like grip. His touch was familiar, but the intent behind it was foreign.

"She doesn't want to see you," he said, each word deliberate and weighted.

I whirled on him, my patience wearing thin. The loyalty I had always counted on from Nate now felt like betrayal.

"Since when are you so fucking protective of my girl?" I snarled, the words tasting bitter on my tongue.

Nate met my gaze head-on, his eyes boring into mine with a quiet intensity that spoke volumes.

The silence stretched between us, taut and fragile.

"Get Gemma out of here. I'm going to see her, if I have to break that door down."

And he knew I would. My eyes locked on the door to Alisha's room, my mind already calculating the force it would take to splinter the wood.

Nate's jaw tightened. A muscle twitching in his cheek as he knocked on the door.

A moment later, Gemma appeared, her regal bearing and icy blue eyes a formidable presence.

"Absolutely not," she said, her voice low and unyielding as she stared me down. "You cannot see her."

She positioned herself in front of the door, her slender frame a seemingly fragile barrier between me and the woman I loved.

"Step aside, Duchess—"

"I am no longer a part of my family," Gemma hissed, her eyes flashing with a fierce protectiveness that caught me off guard. "And I will not let you tear apart what little family I have now."

She crossed her arms over her periwinkle blue cardigan, the delicate fabric a stark contrast to the steel in her spine.

"Gemma, I swear to God, let me see her—"

"Not bloody likely. I won't let you hurt her anymore..." Her words were like a slap in the face, a painful reminder of the damage I had caused.

I barely registered her words, my focus narrowing to a single point.

"One way or another, I will see her. Did you forget who's in the room right now?"

"She isn't yours." Gemma raised her voice, her words laced with a quiet fury that seemed to radiate off of her in waves. "She stopped being yours the moment you decided lying to her and going behind her back—"

"It wasn't about her—" I tried to interject, but Gemma was relentless.

"You keep hurting her—"

"I would *never* hurt her."

The words tore from my throat, my voice rising in a way that was foreign to my own ears.

The moment it left my lips, Nate moved, his body a blur of motion as he positioned himself between Gemma and me, his back blocking her from my view.

"I will take anything for you," he said, his voice low and steady. "But not a word against her. You hear me? You got something to prove, you'll go through me."

I was stunned at the look in Nate's eyes, a mixture of defiance and unwavering loyalty that I had never seen directed at anyone but me.

"I'm going to explain everything to her," I continued, my voice softening slightly as I thought of Alisha.

"When were you going to do that?" The sound of Alisha's voice, raw and broken, cut through the tension like a knife. "What was Reed's master plan?"

I looked beyond Nate and Gemma, my eyes locking on Alisha's slender frame as she stood in the doorway of her room.

The soft light from the room cast a gentle glow over her features, highlighting the dark circles under her eyes and the tear stains on her cheeks. She looked exhausted, as though she had been crying for hours, and my heart clenched painfully at the sight of her in her pale pink pajamas.

She looked so young, so vulnerable, and I felt a wave of guilt wash over me at the knowledge that I had caused her this pain.

"Lish," I said, my voice catching in my throat as I took a step towards her. "Please let me in."

She hesitated, her eyes flickering between me and the open doorway, and for a moment, I thought she might refuse.

But then, she stepped back, holding the door open for me to enter.

I could feel Nate's eyes on me as I moved past him, his gaze heavy with unspoken warnings.

Gemma looked as though she wanted to protest, but Nate shook his head, his hand resting gently on her waist as he guided her away from the door.

"Thank you, both," Alisha said. "If it's alright with you, I'd like to speak to him alone."

Gemma looked as though she would rather do anything else, but Nate took her elbow, his touch gentle but firm.

"We'll be outside," he said, his eyes meeting mine for a brief moment before he turned and led Gemma out of the room.

As I stepped into the room, Alisha closed the door behind us, the soft click of the latch echoing in the sudden silence.

The room was dimly lit, the curtains drawn against the bright afternoon sun, and I could see the rumpled sheets on the bed where she had been lying.

I turned to face Alisha, my heart racing in my chest. She wouldn't meet my gaze, her eyes fixed on the carpet at her feet, and I could see the tension in her shoulders, the way her hands crossed over her chest.

She took a shaky breath, her eyes finally meeting mine, and I could see the pain and confusion swirling in their depths.

"Are you...are you the person doing this to me? So you could manipulate me into trusting you? Letting you into my life?"

If I could crawl on glass, it would've been less painful than hearing that question out of her mouth.

It was agonizing.

"Angel, I would never have done something to you like that—" I started, my voice rough with emotion, but she cut me off with a sharp shake of her head.

"Don't," she said, her voice breaking on the word. "Don't call me that. Not now. Not after everything."

Tears streamed down her face, her delicate features crumpling under the weight of her emotions.

"You've hovered over me for years. You had plenty of time to get under my skin. You keep secrets from me—"

"Not you," I cut her off, my voice firm and insistent. "It was never about you."

"I heard you!" She raised her voice, a rare occurrence that sent a shiver down my spine. *"I heard you this morning. What won't Alisha ever know?"*

The realization that she had overheard my conversation with Gabriel settling heavy in my stomach.

"Who is Lucy?"

I closed my eyes, the weight of my secrets pressing down on me like a physical force.

Nobody save for Nate, who had called her up on occasion, knew how far my working relationship with Lucy ran.

I had long suspected that there was something more between them, but I had never cared enough to ask.

When I opened my eyes again, Alisha was shaking, her eyes glistening with unshed tears as she studied my face.

"You can't even tell me, can you?" The pain in her words was like a knife twisting in my chest.

My voice was low. "If I tell you, you will never look at me the same way again."

I couldn't meet her eyes, the shame and guilt weighing heavily on my shoulders.

"It's not what you think," I said quietly, my words sounding hollow even to my own ears. "Lucy works for me in many capacities."

"Is that why she showed up this morning at your door?" Alisha's question hit me like a bolt of lightning, my head snapping up to meet her gaze.

"What?" I breathed, my mind reeling at the implications of her words.

Lucy wouldn't have shown up at my door unless something was wrong, unless there was a reason for her to break our carefully established rules.

Alisha continued, her voice steady despite the tears that still streamed down her face.

"She came this morning. With coffee for you. And I didn't even think that you were with her—"

"I'm not!" I insisted, my voice rising in frustration and desperation.

"I came to your office to ask you why a woman showed up at your door to bring you coffee, looking more comfortable with your apartment—" Alisha's words trailed off, and I swore softly under my breath.

"She isn't. She knew better."

"You lied to me. I heard you on the phone." Alisha's voice broke, the sound like a knife to my heart.

I couldn't resist any longer.

In a heartbeat, I was in her space, my palms pressed against the wall on either side of her head.

She raised a hand to her mouth, trying to muffle the sobs that tore from her throat.

"Why did you skip that event? What was so bloody important that you couldn't tell me the truth if you weren't seeing her!"

"I was—" I broke off, the words sticking in my throat. I can't even get the words out. "Lish—"

Honesty was a foreign concept to me, something I had never had to navigate in any of my relationships.

"Then show yourself out!" Alisha snapped, her voice sharp and unyielding. *"You can't tell me the truth, you're sneaking behind my back, you're either seeing someone else or not. And you know what, Reed? None of that matters! Because just when I thought I could trust you, I could be a part of your world, you lied to me."*

"Lish—" I pleaded, my voice breaking on her name.

"No! You don't get to call me anything," she growled, her accent thick-

ening with each word. *"You've lied to me so much during this relationship. I don't even know if you're the man I—"*

"You what?" I interrupted, my heart pounding in my chest. Because I knew she still loved me. She had to. "Say it, Angel."

"No," she said, her voice low and fierce. "I am not yours anymore."

I felt nothing but resignation as the words left my mouth, the carefully constructed walls I had built around my secrets crumbling to dust at my feet.

Everything I had worked so hard to protect was falling apart, slipping through my fingers like sand.

And as I stood there, watching the woman I loved pull away from me, I knew that I had no one to blame but myself.

Tell her. You're going to lose her.

"Lucy works for me," I dipped my head, inhaling the scent of her mixed with my own from earlier this morning. "I was on the phone with Gabriel because I lied to him. I lied to both of you. I had Lucy find something for me."

"What was it that you needed to lie to me about?" She wouldn't believe it unless she saw proof.

"You're not going to believe me, but...it was a necklace." It sounded so stupid now that I said it out loud.

"What?" I smiled at her soft tone, her eyes blinking, taking me in. I pulled out my phone and showed her the photo.

"You had Lucy...get you that? Why?"

"I don't know. I told you you wouldn't believe me, but...Gabriel has been searching for this for the last year. Lucy, she procures artifacts. That night I got a text saying she had it in her possession and I needed it."

I looked down at the photo. "Somehow Gabriel found out I was working with her to get it first—"

"Wait...why is Gabriel looking for...this?"

"I don't know," I admitted. "I can't even figure out how to open it. It's got a key pair to it and I have no clue."

"Then why..." Alisha shook her head, her frustration palpable in the way her hands clenched at her sides. "Why do you keep so many secrets?"

The absurdity of the situation hit me then, a bitter laugh bubbling up in my throat. I had asked myself the same questions countless times, the weight of the secrets I carried like a physical burden on my shoulders.

But they weren't my secrets to tell. It was *all* Gabriel's.

I struggled to find the words, to explain the complex web of lies and half-truths that had consumed Gabriel for so long.

He was heading towards a darker place than I had ever been, a place that terrified me more than I cared to admit.

I don't want to lose my brother or you. And I am trying so hard.

How could I tell her that I had found the necklace with the help of someone Gabriel hated, that I had intertwined myself in a game that I barely understood?

"Because half of this isn't mine to tell," I said finally, my voice low and resigned. "I know that this necklace belonged to someone in Gabriel's life. I know he wants it badly enough—"

"Because he loved her," Alisha interrupted, her eyes fixed on the photo that lay between us, our argument momentarily forgotten. "It was his girlfriend. He's been searching for a woman. Is it Isobel?"

Isobel. I nodded, the name a whisper in my mind. "I don't know who she is. We just know her name."

I had done a deep dive into Gabriel's past, searching for any clues that might lead me to the truth, but I felt like I was missing something important, something that was right under my nose.

I had found an Isobel.

But she wasn't his girlfriend.

Just a woman who had been on the last assignment Gabriel had been on.

I had seen her name on the file.

Isobel Santos.

Right next to Liam Sullivan.

I didn't know how to ask Liam since Isobel Santos was dead.

It didn't make any sense.

Why would Gabriel have a relationship with someone he supervised under him?

It wasn't like him.

It was a feeling that left me unsettled, a constant itch at the back of my mind.

"I think Isobel looks like you...he loved her, and got this necklace for her. That's why he kissed you," I said, the words tasting bitter on my tongue. "I figured Gabriel would snap out of whatever funk he's been in if he had it. For closure. That was it."

Alisha's voice trembled with a mix of confusion and anger."If it was just about the necklace, then why didn't you say so?"

She paused, her brow furrowing. "And why would Lucy want me, of all people, to give you a message?"

I froze, my heart skipping a beat at her words.

"What?" I breathed, my mind racing with the implications of what she had just said. Alisha's eyes widened at my expression, the color draining from her face. "What was it?"

The energy in the room shifted, the air growing colder and more charged with each passing second.

"Lish, what was the message?" My voice was different, the words coming out sharp.

She swallowed hard, her unease evident.

"Alisha, I know you won't believe me. But Lucy works undercover for me. She's a professional thief. If she's giving you a message, it's because she's in danger. And she trusted you enough to give it to you because she knew you were—you are a part of me. Which made you safe."

The words tumbled from my lips in a rush, my desperation bleeding through into every syllable.

To my surprise, Alisha nodded, her eyes wide but steady as she met my gaze.

It was a small thing, but it gave me hope that maybe, just maybe, she still believed in me on some level.

"Something about Charlie and Iris...who is that?" she whispered.

I closed my eyes, my worst fears confirmed.

"I was afraid of that. Did she say what about them?"

Alisha shook her head, confusion etched into every line of her face. "She said...they were going on a date."

I felt the blood drain from my face, my heart pounding in my chest.

Charlie was code for escalated trouble, a reference to the military scale used to measure the severity of a situation. And Iris...Iris was Lucy's call sign.

Whatever message Lucy had tried to pass along, it was clear that she was in trouble. Deep trouble.

Never-ending chaos.

I didn't tell Alisha about Lucy. She didn't know how much danger Lucy might've been in to come to K2.

And I had been on the phone with Gabriel.

"It means she's in trouble. That's what going on a date means."

I had set up codes with her to talk to her, but the fact that she delivered it at my door...I explained the rest to Alisha, who looked at my wide eyes.

"Did she have a bag with her?"

Alisha looked at the floor as though remembering. "It looked like a gym bag."

She's in trouble. It wasn't a warlord Lucy pissed off trying to get that necklace.

I nodded. I can't catch a break.

"There is nothing romantic about my relationship with Lucy Devereaux."

She and Nate have an arrangement. For a moment, it looked like Alisha was processing that.

"Lucas Devereaux's sister is Lucy?" How the fuck— "Lucas used to date Gemma, I met him...just what exactly is going on?"

"I don't know," I shook my head. "I'm trying to figure things out as I go, but I'm not used to ever letting anyone in. I handle it all alone. Even this—"

"But I was yours."

I fucking hated this. "You still are. You never stopped. It was a misunderstanding. I didn't think you'd find out what I was doing because it didn't matter if you did. Gabriel wanted to leverage my feelings for you against why I had kept his ex-girlfriend's necklace a secret."

"Why did you!"

I sighed as it spilled out of me. "Because Gabriel hates the Devereaux family. All of them." I proceeded to explain to her the cold war between my best friend and them. Why I kept an eye on Lucy.

Gabriel managing Lucas's entire empire from afar. Making sure they didn't fucking hurt anyone anymore.

"I cannot tell you why. Half of me is all of Gabriel's secrets. I told you he used to work for the CIA. There are things I cannot tell you. Half because I don't know the truth, and the other half because if I did, it would change the way you see everything."

And because it wasn't mine to tell. Some things I couldn't say.

"I never wanted you to be a part of my world," I said, my voice cracking. "You're the only light in my life, Alisha. Coming home to you, feeling your warmth...it was the first time I ever felt normal."

I ran a hand through my hair, frustrated. "I thought I was protecting you, but I was just being a coward. I was afraid of losing the one good thing in my life if you saw the darkness in me."

I kept going because I couldn't stop it. "It was never my intention to lie to you and hurt you. I wanted to keep you safe."

She was every bit of sunshine as I was darkness.

Even now the shadows swallowed me while Alisha stood in the glow of the warm lamp.

"You realize that none of this matters," she stood with her hands against the wall, palms pressed flat as though she had to stop herself from touching me.

"You lied to me, you repeatedly kept things from me under the guise that maybe it could protect me. But when these problems showed up at my doorstep, at yours, you couldn't keep it a secret anymore. You had no intention of ever telling me anything."

She shook her head. "None of this mattered—"

"The fuck it didn't," I was on her, done resisting. She was in my arms a second later.

"It meant everything,"my lips found her throat and her erratic pulse. "You are my everything. I swear hurting you was the last thing I ever wanted. Please, Angel, please don't let me go. I'm afraid of who I'll become without you."

Even now the ice and darkness swallowed me whole. I was in a losing game. And she was the only anchor I had.

"You – we can't do this anymore," her voice wavered as her hands gripped my shoulders. And then she did something I never thought possible.

She pushed me back. "No, Reed. Stop."

I did. I yielded to her. Always.

"Please, Lish—" I was desperate. "I can see you're hurt. Let me—"

"No, because even now I know you're holding things from me. I can see that look in your eyes, the one you taught me about." Her words stung because I had taught her that. "You're hiding things. And that's what it's going to be. You keep secrets, coming home with lies, and me finding out only when I'm blindsided. How does that work, Reed!"

She was pissed, I knew so and I took the brunt of it as she pushed me back with her palms.

"When do I find out that your secrets are unraveling? With another dead body at my door!"

"No," I growled. "I will protect you if it's the last thing I do."

I was crowding her in again, her eyes flared. "I won't let anything hurt you. Do you understand me? Secrets be damned. I will always love you. No matter what you say or what you do. For now and forever. It's always been you. I might hide things but don't think for a second it changes how I feel for you."

"I don't believe a thing you say," and it cut into me as she said. "How do I know any of it was real?" *Any of it?*

"How do I know you didn't lie about everything and use me?"

"Because I fucking love you!"

We both stilled breathing hard as though we'd been physically fighting.

"Because I love you. I always have. I always will. Every time I close my eyes it has always been you. I tried to convince myself that if I hid you from the darkness I wouldn't take you with me. And I worked so hard—"

"You are not a bad person!" She was in my face now, and I caught the little wince.

I growled and picked her up all but hauling her back to the bed and setting her down.

"I hate seeing you in pain," I swore as she sat there looking so small. *Because of me.*

I knelt on the floor in front of her, bringing myself to eye level with her.

"You still let me touch you, so I know deep down you know I'm telling you the truth. You know I am. Lucy isn't my mistress and you are the only woman I have ever loved. I will only love you. Since the day I saw you, I've never felt warmth like I did from you. I have never known love from people in my life, my family, but with you? For the first time, I hoped to everything I'd be able to give you anything you needed to feel your love. I'm sorry I kept things from you, I lied. I know you hate me right now. But please just come home, baby."

It gutted me to know she couldn't look at me. It hurt like a lance in my chest digging deeper as she closed her eyes pulling away from me.

"No."

And I felt it in my chest. I did.

"Are you going to stay here?" I looked up at the pretty feminine hotel celebrities and models stayed at. Alisha fit right in. Unlike me, I'd stood out like a sore thumb the moment I walked through the doors.

She nodded. I let out a deep exhale.

Oh, I fucked up.

I felt it leave my lips. "I'll keep Kellan with you, until I get to the bottom of what's going on. I can keep you in on everything. But if you need anything, I'm a call away, a text away. I'll always protect you."

Her eyes were glossy as she nodded.

"When I move into my new place, I'll take the rest of my stuff."

I felt the panic in my throat. Lodged in like I swallowed something bad. She couldn't go. Not when she'd made the cold apartment where I lived in her home.

"I would give you whatever you want," I whispered, feeling like gravel was in my throat. "Whatever you ask for—"

"Except the truth."

I hung my head. I fucking hated the ice that threatened to crack inside of me.

The darkness itching to protect me. And I didn't want it anymore. I had felt agony for the last few hours and something told me it wouldn't compare to what was coming.

"Angel, there's a lot of things I don't know," I swallowed, hating the way my vision blurred. "All I'm asking is you give it time to think about what I said. Please don't let me go."

I wasn't opposed to begging nor did I think it made me less than.

I'd begged my mother for her love. My stepfather not to kill me. My brother to protect me. Gabriel to see some sense. I wasn't opposed to saying it.

"Storm." It hit like lightning in my chest. Alisha never used her safe word.

But she knew what it would do to me.

Leave Reed. Go away.

Nobody wants you. We don't want you.

I let the ice slide over me, the darkness coating my insides like an old friend. "Anything for you, Angel."

I stood then unable to look at her and my vision blurred. I couldn't even see as I felt my heart ripping out of my chest at her feet as I walked out of the room.

Nothing hurt as bad in my life as losing Alisha. Not a single thing. Not being stabbed. Not shot. Not my family. Nothing but her.

The air was silent outside and I was grateful to have a few moments to compose myself since everyone else was outside. I took a moment to myself. I never cried. Not when all the horrific things had happened in my life.

Not a single fucking time.

The door outside opened and Nate looked at me closing it. I averted my face by running my hand over it.

He didn't need to see this shit.

"It was for Gabriel, wasn't it?" I gave a tight nod.

"Reed," He looked kinder than usual as he always stood by me. "I mean this with the most respect, I know you're working your ass off. You need to go home to your apartment and take a break."

I couldn't. "Not with the monster harassing her on the loose."

"Then let that be the only thing you focus on. Not working yourself to death." He paused as he took me in. "Do us a favor and stop destroying everything around you for the sake of someone as lost as Gabriel. Nothing in the world can bring back what he's lost. Not even for all your trying."

I let out a shaky breath. Is that what I had been doing?

"You're trying so hard to keep everyone together, we can see you're falling apart. Go home. Take a break. We got it from here." Nate's eyes were kind as always as he looked at me. "Quarterback is still outside, I'll bring him in. Depending on how long this lasts it'll be hard for him."

I knew.

I knew I was asking a lot of Kellan. I had nothing else that mattered save for finding out who was threatening her.

For the first time, I listened.

CHAPTER 47
REED

She's not eating or sleeping.

THAT WAS THE TEXT FROM KELLAN.

I was in the office in Midtown. I had been for a week now. I was waiting for a video call with my therapist.

I hadn't gone home.

Her clothes were everywhere, the scent of roses all over my apartment. Memories of us on every surface. It was freezing.

I'd packed a bag, unable to look away from the way the colors that had made my house and closet more vibrant. I couldn't think straight.

Alisha had always been afraid of losing the people around her.

Enough that at the beginning of our relationship, I worked hard to ensure she would understand I wasn't leaving her. I worked hard to earn all of her trust. And then I'd left her shattered.

Completely. I hated seeing her so broken. So hurt. Not being able to take care of her? It gutted me.

My therapist had once said, the thing about being in a relationship was not that you would never get triggered.

It was the fact that it would in fact trigger you. All your insecurities. All of your moments that made you–*you*.

I was triggered.

I don't want you.

My mother had cried brokenly as my stepfather smirked. Mom.

The word didn't make it out of my mouth. I felt a searing pain at my back as my mother clapped a hand over her mouth. An animal noise left my lips as Adam screamed at him.

Distantly I remembered Adam moving. I never did reply back to his emails.

But I just saw my mother turning away.

As her husband attacked me.

As my life was at stake. She'd moved away.

It had been the one time Adam had defended me. Had it mattered to him? At all?

I knew Alisha was not the same. She was letting me go and turning me away because I fucked up.

It was only after my long session with my therapist that I realized the only person who had given up was me. I had treated Alisha with a repeat of what I imagined I should've done with my parents. In return by trying to prevent it, I had made it happen.

I felt ice coating my veins as the memories warred with each other. My stepfather's voice contrasted with Alisha's.

You're not my son.

I love you, Reed.

You don't belong in this house.

Are you coming home tonight? Stay away from my family.

Avani and you are my family.

I focused on my therapist's voice in my head: Don't let your triggers run the show, Reed. Focus on a point. *Focus on the truth.*

What is the truth?

Nobody ever loved me like Alisha had. Nobody wanted me the way she had. And I had fucked up so bad.

As I leaned back in my chair long after my session was over, I was interrupted with the banging on my office door.

I grabbed my gun. Nobody should be here this late.

"R—Reed?" My thoughts were interrupted at the sound of a crying voice. I knew that voice. She was hysterical.

"Evie?" My sister was in my arms moments later. "What's the matter?"

She shook her head in my chest feeling smaller than usual as she sobbed wildly.

"Sweetheart, talk to me."

Brokenly, Evie mumbled something. Stunned, I held her close to me. Her wild sobs tore at me. I'd never seen her like this. I needed to sit her down and talk to her.

"Tell me everything." I could fix it. Or I could kill him. Either way she'd be fine. She puffed out hard breaths of air and shook. She was seeing someone. I wanted to hurt this son of a bitch. "Evie, just tell me his name."

"No," she wiped her eyes. "I never want to see him again."

A sentiment I felt for her. As she spoke to me and asked me questions I answered, still rubbed raw after my therapy sessions. This was the most honest I had ever been. Until she reached the point where she knew Gabriel would kill whoever it was. He would.

But while we talked about Gabriel.... I waited until Evie's crying eased, long moments later.

"Did Gabriel ever have a woman in his life?" She was his sister. She had to know.

"I mean, he definitely—he's not a saint." I knew that. He was just discreet about it.

"No, I mean...in a serious relationship."

In all the times I knew him, he had never been in one. Evie blinked, her expression shifting to one of surprise. "You mean besides Isobel?"

The name hung in the air between us, a heavy weight that seemed to steal the breath from my lungs.

"Isobel?" I repeated. Isobel Santos. There she was again.

Evie tipped her head, her eyes searching my face. "My sister. They were married. Isobel passed away. I thought you knew..."

Everything in me ground to a halt, my mind reeling with the implications of her words.

Gabriel was *married*? To Isobel Santos? What the fuck...

I shook my head, trying to process what she had just said. "You and Gabriel have *different* parents?"

I had never bothered to look into Evie or Gabriel's past. She had been here before me, and there had been no reason to question their relationship. Because they were siblings. I just thought Evie needed therapy after losing *their* mom.

Evie's smile was tinged with a sadness that I hadn't noticed before.

"We aren't related at all. Not by blood."She paused, her eyes growing uneasy. "He was my next of kin. My real last name isn't Monroe. It's Santos. Isobel married Gabriel when they were in the CIA."

Every part of my body froze, the pieces of the puzzle suddenly falling into place.

Isobel. Santos. Evie was the missing piece. The answer had been under my nose the entire time. I tried to speak, but the words came out as little more than a puff of air.

Evie's eyes widened, concern etched into every line of her face.

"I'm sorry...I thought you knew. Gabriel was in charge of her. I know it's frowned upon, but Gabriel didn't give a shit. You guys always spar, and he's got her name tattooed on his heart. I thought...you knew..."

He's got her name tattooed on his heart.

My real last name is Santos.

Isobel had been on the file with Liam, from the final assignment Gabriel had been on. *Oh. Motherfucker.*

His last assignment. Where he lost his team, save for Liam.

Where...he lost Isobel.

I had hired Liam with the intent of giving Gabriel a reminder of his old life, hoping that maybe Liam would be good for him. As a reminder of hope.

Something more. But I wanted Gabriel to go to Liam naturally, and so far, he hadn't.

I need to talk to Liam.

I fucking knew Gabriel lived with guilt.

Liam and Gabriel never spoke, and I didn't force it. I just told the team to leave Liam alone.

Gabriel hadn't said a word.

I hadn't put it together...It was like the file had been scrubbed, like someone had tried to bury it before me.

It had taken me ages of digging through shit, but I had fucking found it recently, in the hours I spent pining for Alisha.

Isobel Santos was Gabriel's wife.

The necklace. Gabriel's obsession with finding it. The tattoo. His darkness since he left...She wasn't just a fucking teammate.

She's his wife...

I was reeling, my mind racing with the implications of what Evie had just told me.

"Reed, I thought you knew...you know everything about everyone." Evie's voice was soft, apologetic.

But not everything. Not this.

"I'm sorry...Gabriel's going to be so angry..." The idea of losing Alisha, of having to move one foot in front of the other without her by my side, felt impossible. And yet, Gabriel had lived with...his wife had been dead for years. I was reeling.

"Why is he—" I cut myself off, the words sticking in my throat. There was no way Evie knew he was looking for a dead woman. And then, the question filtered through my mind. Gabriel wasn't looking for a dead woman.

He was looking for the last memory of her. *Monroe*. His name was etched into the necklace...not just a necklace anymore.

Gabriel was a widower?

Shock reverberated through my system.

"Isobel died years ago on a mission he was...in charge of. He feels guilty. Like it was his fault. He keeps himself locked away in the manor. He never leaves. I feel like he's haunted by her. He found me when my mama died."

Evie drew her finger in patterns across her dress, her eyes distant. "Don't tell him I told you. He doesn't like it when people talk about her. He was different...you know? A long time ago."

Seven years ago. I did know. But something had changed in him. Even Evie, with her gentle nature and kind heart, wasn't a fool to how much he had changed.

Iced out. Different. *Dark*. I was losing *my* brother in turn.

"Do you have a picture of her?"

She nodded, her hand already reaching for her phone. "He keeps all her photos in a drawer, but there's one on his dresser."

She scrolled through her photos, her fingers trembling slightly. "Gabriel had lots of photos of her, but this one is my favorite. His too."

Evie drew up an album, scrolling through the photos with familiarity. She stopped on her favorite. *His favorite.*

In the photo, a younger and strikingly handsome Gabriel had his arm around a woman clad in a slinky red dress. A woman's secret weapon.

She was beautiful. Her dark mahogany hair cascaded down her back in waves, shimmering under the light. Like Evie's but darker.

Gabriel, my fucking best friend, looked a decade younger.

Unrecognizable, in his white shirt crisp and clean against his tanned skin. Someone had clearly said something funny because the woman's lips were split open in a wide grin, her eyes sparkling with mirth. And his eyes were nothing but pure, unadulterated adoration.

I had never seen Gabriel look like that.

And suddenly, something deep in me ached. I had never seen him look like that before. How had I not known my best friend had a wife?

The question burned in my mind, but I couldn't dwell on it for long.

My attention was drawn to the necklaces around their necks. Isobel Santos wore the necklace.

The one I had hunted the world for. And Gabriel...he wore a necklace too, but his was different.

It was a key, unusual in its pattern. Unique.

Gabriel loved puzzles.

I zoomed in, my heart racing. He doesn't have it anymore? So what happened to the key?

"Evie, can you send me a few photos of your sister? I want to show Alisha." Evie didn't know. She couldn't know. I felt like Evie was talking about a stranger, a man I had never truly known. She was oblivious to my inner turmoil, smiling at the photo with a fondness that made my heart ache.

"She kind of reminds me of Alisha," she said, her voice soft and wistful.

My heartbeat sputtered, my mind racing with the implications of her words.

"They look a little bit alike."Evie held up the photo, and I *really* looked at young Isobel Santos. She would my age now if she were still alive. Her eyes were darker than Alisha's, but I could see what Evie meant. The bone structure was similar, almost identical. Not exactly.

I knew my girl off the bat. But I could see how Gabriel saw Isobel the first time in seven years the moment he saw Alisha. Not exact. Just similar.

Alisha's eyes were hazel, warmth radiating from them like the sun.

Her hair was darker, and she was shorter than Isobel. But Isobel's eyes...they were mischievous, like she was hiding a secret or teasing Gabriel. She is why he doesn't laugh.

Evie continued, oblivious to my revelations as she scrolled through more photos. Some showed Gabriel and Isobel together, others were of Isobel alone. Someone had been with them.

"He took photos of her all the time. Sometimes she didn't know—"

"Stop on that—" I said, my voice rough with emotion.

It was a photo of Isobel, the sun hitting her eyes just right, making them glow. She looked ruefully at whoever was taking the photo, the teasing in her eyes apparent.

"She looks like—"

"Alisha," Evie finished, her voice soft. "I think Gabriel thinks so too. He was really shook up after she left, and I saw her photos years ago. I think that's why he was happy for you. Maybe he sees Isobel in her too.

I imagine if Isobel were still alive, she'd be a lot like Alisha. I think Alisha could help the team move on and heal. I know you work really hard, but I think Alisha's a good balance for you, to put your energy back into you. And not always us. I met Avani the other day, and we talked...I'm in a group chat now."

I held Evie's hand, my mind racing with the implications of what she had just told me. I was happy for her, for the connections she was making outside of our little world.

But my thoughts were consumed with Gabriel, with the secrets he had kept hidden for so long.

"I'm happy for your group chat, kid," I said, my voice sounding distant even to my own ears.

I was lost, my mind reeling with the implications of Evie's words.

If Isobel were alive. The thought hit me like a physical blow, the air rushing from my lungs as I tried to imagine what I would do if Alisha was dead.

The idea made my heart bottom out, plummeting to the pit of my stomach.

For years, I had been fighting the chill that encased my soul, the darkness. Every night, when I sank into Alisha's warmth, she saved my soul a little bit more, pulling me back from the brink.

If I ever lost her? For good?

I'd be a fucking ghost. *I'd be Gabriel.*

And suddenly, with a clarity that took my breath away, I forgave him.

I had been holding him kissing Alisha over his head, a grudge that seemed so petty in the face of what he had lost.

If Gabriel brought a woman into his life who was the spitting image of Alisha, I knew I wouldn't be able to look away.

I had his wife's necklace, probably the last physical piece of her that he had.

Would I hunt the world for a last piece of Alisha, if I were in his shoes?

I would. I'd burn the whole fucking world to the ground to find anything of hers.

And I wouldn't let Avani go.

Now, holding onto Evie made sense. She was the last bit of Isobel he had. Nothing would ever—

She will never know pain.

303

I turned to Evie, my voice low and urgent. "Did you tell anyone else about Isobel?"

No fucking way she knew about Liam.

She shook her head, her eyes wide and earnest. "Gabriel doesn't like talking about her. I just thought since you're our brother, you knew."

Because I was his fucking brother.

Her phone pinged, the sound jarring in the heavy silence that had fallen between us. She quickly muted it, her fingers trembling slightly as she tucked the device back into her pocket.

I realized then, with a sinking feeling in my gut, that I had been wrong.

So very wrong. The weight of my mistakes pressed down on me, a suffocating burden that made it hard to breathe.

I had made decisions without Alisha, keeping secrets from her and hiding important things. Things that she deserved to know, that she had every right to be a part of.

The hard knot in my throat was difficult to swallow as I watched Evie's eyes light up when she talked about her sister.

It was the same way I felt about Alisha, the same way I had always felt, even if I hadn't always shown it in the way she deserved.

I fucked up.

"You okay, Reed?"

No. I wasn't okay. I was so far from okay that I didn't even know where to begin.

I stayed with Evie for a bit longer, making sure she was doing better after the current situation she found herself in.

God help the idiot she was with if Gabriel ever found out.

But it looked like I wasn't the only one keeping secrets from everyone, a realization that only added to the weight on my shoulders.

A part of me was tempted to march straight to Gabriel, to confront him about his past and demand answers to the questions that now burned in my mind.

It had been the one thing he'd asked of me when I'd promised to help him out, back when we were just two kids trying to survive in the shits together.

He'd wanted an aspect of his life left alone, a door that remained firmly closed.

But now, with Alisha's pain still fresh in my mind, I understood how she felt.

The betrayal, the hurt, the sense that the person you loved most in the world had been keeping a part of themselves hidden from you.

I knew. I got it.

Now I wanted to search for Gabriel's other half, and figure out what other secrets my best friend had been hiding from me for the last few years.

Because I felt like I didn't know him anymore.

Which was how Alisha felt about me.

CHAPTER 48
ALISHA

MY HEAD WAS A MESS.

I spent my days and nights crying at the Primrose, terrified and breaking apart.

Kellan, who I had initially teased about being the girls group chat, was now bringing flowers and chocolates and in the room next to mine.

I feel so bad, he doesn't get a break.

He stayed with me all the time as the best brother a girl could ask for. Deep down, I knew he was keeping Reed in the loop about me.

I saw him look guilty whenever he did.

I saw my sister's name flash on my phone.

She had texted and called and I didn't know what to say texting her that I wasn't feeling too good.

Avani still thought I lived with Reed. I didn't have the heart to tell her it didn't work out between us.

That was my worst nightmare after introducing her to him and it only made me cry harder.

Memories swamped me of my time with Reed.

I sifted through the shirts until I found one. And then padded into the shower. I was never going to stop being amazed.

As I walked, the motion—activated lights on the floor I'd seen last night switched on.

Reed's apartment felt like a nocturnal presidential suite. Everything was made in his image.

The oversized suede couches, the enormous coffee table, the black granite kitchen island and countertops. It was decked out. There was no way he'd even have this place if he wasn't – well off. And then there was Reed, in a pullover and sweats looking like he belonged there sitting on the kitchen island with a half—eaten bagel, and a cup of coffee as he worked on his laptop.

He looked up for a moment taking me in his clothing.

"I'm borrowing this."

His smile was soft. "For as long as you like. What's mine is yours."

"I think we're doing this backwards."

"I think we're doing all right...come here baby."

A FEW DAYS INTO MY STAY AT THE PRIMROSE, I RECEIVED MY FIRST visitor.

Dressed in a custom gray suit that likely cost more than my entire wardrobe, Gabriel radiated a dark, magnetic presence. His blonde hair was styled, not a strand out of place, and his icy blue eyes bored into me with a look of utter disdain at the mere act of knocking, as though it made him lesser somehow.

I would never have expected him to leave his manor. I only let him in because I knew that if I didn't, he would find a way in, shutting down the entire hotel and threatening the staff in the process.

Kellan had all but scrambled to get out of his way and exit the room.

Only then did I speak, my voice trembling. "If you kiss me again, I'll scream."

I didn't realize how hoarse I'd sound from crying. My entire being trembled. The black robe I wore felt flimsy compared to his tailored suit.

Gabriel's lips curved into a soft, predatory smile, a glint of dark amusement dancing in his eyes. "I just might. Since you're single and all now."

If I thought Reed was a storm, Gabriel was a force of nature on his own.

The temperature plummeted the moment he stepped inside and closed the door behind him with a decisive click. The closer his looming figure advanced, the more arctic the air became, as if he extinguished all warmth in his path. I saw his eyes roaming over me.

"Do I remind you of Isobel?"

He stilled, his eyes snapping to mine with an intensity that stole my breath. He took in the robe I wore and the slip Gemma had lent me.

"You don't look surprised to see me."

"Should I be? You're the reason Reed keeps lying to me." I understood that Reed had his loyalties to his team and to this man, but I couldn't forgive him for what he'd done.

If Gabriel had any shame, he didn't show it. He simply walked over to the large creme couch, undoing his jacket, and settled in the center of it.

Gabriel looked out of place among the polished coffee table strewn with some beauty products and perfume.

The artwork of half nude women, glowing signs in script, gilded mirrors, combined with the fresh roses Kellan had got me, created an airy romantic space. For me.

He looked comfortable.

I inhaled something that was inherently masculine and expensive cologne as he settled.

He looked around, his eyes taking in every detail, even the elegant warm lights all around him.

"This is...very you," he said finally, the barest hint of a smile playing across his lips.

I didn't say a word as I took a seat across from him, the coffee table between us, feeling like we were in a meeting where I was severely underdressed.

He carried himself with the grace of an angel doing business with a mortal.

I was aware that even in darkness, the first time I had met him, he had looked too handsome to be real. If he tried to be civil, women would fall at his feet.

The room was frigid with him, and I tucked my hands together, a motion he noticed immediately. He withdrew a pair of light blue gloves and set them on the table. I hesitated, unsure if I should accept them this time.

"Why do you carry around gloves?" I asked, my curiosity getting the better of me.

"Why don't you? You're the one that's always cold." *How did he—*
"Goosebumps," he said, answering my unspoken question.

He stood so fast that I inched back, startled by his sudden movement.

"Does this place have a—*oh yeah, there it is.*"

He adjusted the temperature, the room slowly warming to a more comfortable level.

When he returned to his seat, his eyes were softer, almost gentle.

"I'm not good at small talk, so I'll cut the bullshit. No, Reed doesn't know I'm here. No, you can't tell him once you forgive him. And no, I'm not here to convince you to do that."

Well, that was my first three questions.

His lips quirked, and his eyes lit up, and I realized how devastatingly handsome he was when he did that. Almost human.

But he had missed one question, the one that had been burning in my mind since the moment he walked in.

"Who was she?" I asked, my voice steady despite the fear that churned in my stomach. "You loved her so much that Reed hunted down her necklace. To kiss me and pretend like I was her."

Gabriel leaned back in his seat, appraising me with a gaze that made me feel like I had said too much. Reed's gaze was like a patient, friendly wolf, but Gabriel...was an apex predator of the highest order.

He lurked in his white manor home, hidden in the shadows, scaring people away like the predator he was.

When he looked at me lazily, his pale blue eyes bright, I felt the urge to run.

It was the exact opposite of what you were supposed to do if a shark was coming at you. I remembered seeing a video that said you just needed to gently push a shark down when it came at you.

How did one do that now?

"Did Reed give you that much?" His voice was always soft, belying the threat that lurked beneath the surface."I'm surprised. He usually keeps things to himself."

Didn't I know that?

"Tell you what, I'll answer five questions. To give you clarity. On one condition."

"And what's that?" I asked, my heart skipping a beat. This felt like a trap, a deal with the devil himself.

"You tell me why you love Reed."

Silence permeated the air, thick and heavy like a blanket.

"This feels like a trap," I said, my voice steady despite the unease that coiled in my gut.

To my surprise, Gabriel smiled, his eyes alight with a dark amusement.

He's enjoying this.

"This is the most fun I've had all year," he said, his voice low and smooth. "It's only a trap if you renege on our deal. I won't be pleasant then." I believed him.

But this was my chance, my opportunity to get the answers that Reed couldn't give me, to uncover the secrets that had been kept hidden for so long.

"What will you do if I don't answer your question?" I asked, my heart pounding in my chest.

This is not the kind of man you toy with.

His eyes cooled, leveling at me with an intensity that made my breath catch in my throat. "I'll kiss you again."

CHAPTER 49
ALISHA

My heartbeat sputtered.

"But you said I didn't taste—" *Like her.*

Something was chucked my way, an orange ball wrapped in plastic landed in my lap. "Is that toffee?"

"Butterscotch."

Why had he—

"Now you do."

I clenched the candy in my fist. All he wants to know is why I loved Reed. I could do this.

"Why did Reed hide the necklace from you?" I asked, my voice steady.

Gabriel leaned back, his posture relaxed but his eyes sharp. "He didn't want to tell me why he was working with Devereaux because he knew I hated them. Still do. "

The way he said Devereaux, it was like he was talking about a particularly disgusting insect.

"And he didn't want me to know he had found it so he could get to the bottom of it and spare my feelings if it wasn't what I thought it was. "

"Which was?"

He raised a brow, his expression almost mocking. "A family heirloom."

Somehow, I doubted that was the whole truth. I opened my mouth to ask another question, but Gabriel cut me off.

"Careful. You have three left."

"Why do you hate them, the Devereaux family?"

He looked bored, as though I had wasted my breath on something so insignificant.

"I'll pretend that one wasn't a real question. Don't waste your breath on mongrels," his voice was low, dangerous.

I realized then that I would hate to be on the receiving end of Gabriel Monroe's anger.

But I was beginning to recognize something in his answers, a pattern that I couldn't quite put my finger on.

"And the necklace Lucy found for you..." The family heirloom.

"Was for someone I loved." Loved. Past tense. *It is Isobel's necklace.*

I was beginning to realize that the game with Gabriel led to more questions, and if he saw me piecing it together, his smirk only grew. Whatever Gabriel had been in a past life, it had been formidable.

"You have two left," he said, his voice a low rumble.

I couldn't resist. "Actually, I have three...the last one wasn't a question. You just answered it anyway."

I felt a smile tug at my lips, a small victory in a game that seemed rigged against me. *He's not used to that.*

His lips curved upwards, his eyes filled with mirth, and if possible, he looked even more frightening. Wicked.

There was something off about Gabriel, a darkness that seemed to seep from his very pores. It surrounded him like a cloak, spilling out onto the couch, into the room, until it enveloped me completely.

"Why did Reed lie?"

At that, he looked bored again, shrugging a shoulder as though the answer were obvious.

"Imposter syndrome, like you? He thinks if he takes on the weight of everyone else, he can make them happier. He doesn't realize some crucibles are others to bear. Some people need to handle shit on their own. He wants to protect you from your own head and feeling too much of the shit we deal with. And then he wants to protect the team from falling apart, and the fucking list goes on."

He tipped his head back as he spoke, his eyes fixed on the ornate ceilings. "Two left. Please make it count."

But I could tell he was anything but bored. He was hanging onto my every word, his attention laser-focused on me.

Deep down, I realized why he was here.

This was his way of apologizing, of trying to mend the rift between

Reed and me. He couldn't say it outright. His pride wouldn't allow it. And he knew I wouldn't care even if he did.

Because at the end of the day, Reed and I weren't together anymore.

I realized then that everything Gabriel did held a double meaning, a hidden agenda lurking just beneath the surface.

Simple conversations were like mental mazes, puzzles that led to traps no matter which way I turned.

Because if I didn't know any better, I'd say he knew more about me from the questions I was asking than I knew about his answers.

I understood why Reed had said he didn't know much. How could anyone, when talking to a sphinx? I was piecing him together, just enough to know that he liked this.

That was why Reed didn't know.

I realized then why Gabriel and Reed were friends, why they balanced each other out so perfectly.

This entire time, I had thought Reed struggled with darkness, but in reality, the darkness was sitting right in front of me.

The darkness in my room, the darkness that was Gabriel, was what kept Reed tethered to the world he lived in. And Gabriel needed Reed.

Because he loves Reed too. I had been joking about being the other woman.

But in some ways I was.

Because my relationship with Reed had been torn apart by Gabriel's secrets. Reed had protected him.

I saw him watching me, his eyes searching my face for something I couldn't quite name.

"Are you cold?" he asked, his voice softer than I had ever heard it.

"No," I said, realizing that the temperature in the room had risen since he had first arrived.

He nodded, as though my reply satisfied him in some way.

An odd look crossed his face as he asked the question, and I realized then that I still had two questions left.

Two chances to ask him anything, to uncover the secrets that had been kept hidden for so long.

"Why did you kiss me?" The real reason.

Gabriel stilled, his body going rigid as though my words had struck a physical blow.

He wouldn't meet my gaze, his eyes fixed on a point just over my shoulder. He's nervous.

Nervous around me? I knew then that he was looking at me like he was seeing me for the first time, like he had finally found me.

"You look a lot like my wife," he said, his voice low and rough with emotion.

The owner of the necklace was Gabriel's wife. Not his girlfriend. And he'd lost her. I inhaled deeply, trying to steady myself.

"Isobel," I said, the name feeling foreign on my tongue. "Her necklace was taken from you?"

His eyes swung to me then, sharp and intense. "Is that your final question? Because that would be a waste."

Think fast. Why do you love Reed?

"Why is Reed your best friend?"

The question seemed to catch him off guard, his brow furrowing as though he had never considered the answer before.

He answered with zero hesitation. "I admire the way he never became what I am. We have the same background, but he never let it consume him like I did. Both of us have shit stepfathers, people who failed us. I became a villain. Reed...didn't. Same values, different outcomes."

His words were heavy with a weight that I couldn't quite comprehend, a darkness that seemed to cling to his very soul.

But a part of me wondered what the difference was.

Why had Gabriel become a villain?

But my questions were up.

I had none left.

"You need Reed just as much as I did."

"You still do." He leaned forward, his eyes boring into mine with an intensity that made my breath catch in my throat. "Why do you love Reed?"

I thought about it, my mind swirling with memories of us together. *Why did I love him?*

My love has never been, nor will it ever be conditional.

Give me a chance, beautiful girl.

It's always been you.

I love you, Lish.

I looked down at the candy in the palm of my hand, the bright wrapper crinkling under my fingers.

"I haven't seen these since primary school," I whispered.

Gabriel didn't make a sound, but I could feel his eyes on me, waiting for my answer.

314

When I spoke, I spoke from my heart, my words ringing with a truth that I had never been able to put into words before.

"Reed saw me. For what I was. Not what I pretended to be, not the masks I wore. He saw someone in me that was inherently good, and I saw the same in him. Reed always was my rock. He was always there, and he did everything to stand by my side. He knew what he wanted..." And he'd gone after it. Me. He hadn't ever stopped, no matter what obstacles stood in his way.

I don't scare easily.

Fifty years...with you.

My eyes watered, tears blurring my vision as I stared at my hands.

"I love him," I whispered.

"Yet you gave up on him." Gabriel's voice was sharp, cutting through the haze of my emotions like a knife.

My eyes shot up to meet his, narrowed and intense.

"He lied to you to protect you and me, and our stupid feelings," he spat the word out like it was something distasteful. "He kept secrets from me. I forgave him in a heartbeat. It's Reed. It's all he asks to make sure we're good. He can see you. Could you see him?"

The thought had already crossed my mind, a nagging doubt that had been eating away at me since the moment I had walked out of our apartment.

Why did Reed lie?

He doesn't tell anyone anything.

The realization dawned on me then. "So nobody would see Reed for what he truly was..."

Gabriel gave me a tight nod, his expression unreadable. "Reed's been training my sister to fight. You've met her already once."

His eyes warmed significantly as he talked about his family, a softness creeping into his voice that I had never heard before.

"He thinks I don't know. He gets cakes for her and presents all the time. Her desk and computer setup is entirely built by hand by him. He teaches her everything he knows. After her mom died, he made sure she got to therapy and took care of her like she was his own." He began ticking off his fingers, listing. "He takes care of Nate's lady problems whenever they arise, time and time again."

He rolled his eyes at that, as though it were a common occurrence.

"He treats Selena with all the respect she deserves, and never gets and gives her what she needs as an operative. Space. Time. Energy. He juggles everyone in the company, along with the rest of the agents we employ. He's hired several others to take over so we can get a break."

Gabriel paused, and I realized that this was the most I had ever heard him speak.

"And in the middle of it all, he decides to go for you."

He set his fingers down, his point made.

It occurred to me then that there were things Reed had kept from me, secrets he had held close to his chest while he carried the weight of the world on his shoulders.

I had been his only break from everything, his one respite from the chaos and darkness that surrounded him.

There were a hundred questions on my mind, a thousand things I wanted to ask Gabriel.

But at that moment, I knew that none of them mattered. Because Reed...Reed was the only thing that did.

"You never came here to get me to forgive him," I said, the words coming out as a statement rather than a question.

Because I already had.

The moment the realization hit me, Gabriel's expression remained impassive, a mask that I couldn't see through no matter how hard I tried.

"You just wanted me to understand." I tossed the candy back at him, the wrapper crinkling as it flew through the air.

He caught it deftly in one hand, his fingers closing around it like a vice. "Don't tell Reed I came here."

"No more secrets," I frowned, shaking my head. "What does it matter if he thinks you care about him and his relationships?"

"It's not about me caring about them," his gaze was unwavering, his eyes locked on mine with an intensity that made my breath catch in my throat. "There is so much you don't know. I'd rather keep it that way."

I realized then I would never understand Gabriel or why he was who he was. No matter what I tried.

As he stepped up, I followed, watching his eyes stare at my features.

I watched him take in my expression then and he blinked as though snapping out of it.

For once, I looked at him. At the man rather than anything he was pretending to be. Did I see Gabriel? He was Reed's brother.

And I took him in as he watched me. Inhaling him in. There was a profound sense of loss and solitude to him now with his confessions.

Is he lonely?

In that moment Gabriel seemed almost...fragile.

Like a man who had the world ripped away and never found his way back from it.

Is that why he was who he was?

Did he push everyone away after losing his wife?

But where my walls were a defense mechanism, Gabriel's had morphed into something harder, crueler.

A sharp edge that lashed out at anyone who dared to get too close.

A means of ensuring he would never have to endure that kind of heartbreak again.

The revelation of Gabriel as a widower was jarring, so at odds with the cold, unfeeling demeanor he projected.

Yet, it made a tragic kind of sense.

When he kissed me I saw it, that haunted expression.

Was that the first time he'd seen her...in me in years?

I didn't know anything about Isobel Monroe. I just knew enough from his eyes.

Self-preservation against being hurt again. After her.

Did his loneliness consume him day after day?

My nerves were still frayed from the mental gymnastics of our tense conversation, but I found myself extending a hand towards him, an offering of connection in spite of...everything.

He's alone. Even with his team...he's alone.

Reed turned to me at the end of the day.

Who did he go home to?

"I would like to be your friend," I said, the words tumbling from my lips before I could stop them. "I think we should start there."

His brow rose, he looked at me for a long moment, his expression unchanging. It was like he was looking through me.

"A friend," he repeated softly, the word sounding foreign on his tongue.

"Not your best friend. I wouldn't take Reed's place. Or hers. But I don't think you have anyone else in your life to talk to, and at this rate, you're going to burn Reed out. And then I'll be angry."

I held my hand out, a peace offering that hung in the air between us. "We can have brunch. What do you say?"

A little bit of kindness.

That was all it took.

When I was younger, I remember reading a story about a lion with a thorn stuck in its paw.

Gabriel reminded me of that lion, wounded and angry and lashing out at the world.

But the thorn in his paw wasn't one that I could remove, not with a simple act of kindness.

What kind of a woman was she, to have brought Gabriel to his knees?

And what happened to her?

When Gabriel looked at my outstretched hand, an indecipherable expression crossed his face.

It was like he was battling with himself, torn between the desire to accept my offer and the fear of letting someone in.

Slowly, he reached out and took my hand, his fingers wrapping around mine like a lifeline.

His hand swallowed mine.

I almost blinked at the warmth of his skin, the heat that radiated off of him like a furnace.

He must have been boiling the entire time he sat there with me, his body temperature rising with every word we exchanged.

He turned my palm up, his eyes closing for a moment as he bowed his head.

His lips pressed against my wrist. Neither one of us moved.

Without another word he walked out.

MY SECOND VISITOR ARRIVED LATER THAT SAME DAY, AND I SWEAR IT would have seemed planned had I not known better.

If Gabriel hadn't wanted me to tell Reed about his visit, he wouldn't have told anyone else either.

When I opened the door, I was surprised to see a familiar face standing there, looking nervous and unsure.

"Evie?" I said, my voice laced with confusion.

The young woman stood at my door, her dark cherry hair swirling around her face in the gentle breeze, making her look like a wide-eyed fairy.

She was dressed casually in jeans and a long-sleeved henley, as though she had just come from class.

Her hands were clasped in front of her, fidgeting nervously as she shifted her weight from foot to foot.

"Can I come in?" she asked, her voice soft and shy.

I didn't know what to say, my mind still reeling from the events of the day.

Kellan, who had been standing guard, took a step back and nodded respectfully to Evie, a silent acknowledgment of her presence.

He looked exhausted too.

And I let him nap and didn't go anywhere.

I didn't need to ask if he was with Selena since I saw her photo on his phone. He was always texting her.

As I stepped aside to let her in, I couldn't help but wonder what had brought her here.

This visit wasn't about Reed, that much I knew.

"I didn't know Reed had you staying here," Evie mused as she stepped into the room, her eyes taking in the plush furnishings and elegant decor.

Her words caught me off guard, and I realized that she didn't know I had moved out of Reed's apartment.

In fact, I wasn't sure if she even knew that I had moved in with him at some point.

"I came because Reed said you'd be the right person," she continued, her words coming out in a rush as though she had been holding them back for a long time.

I listened intently as she spoke, my eyes widening with each word.

A part of me warmed at the thought of him sending her my way, even in the midst of our own turmoil.

"Is this about a boy?" I asked, already knowing the answer.

Evie nodded, her expression turning somber as she began to tell me what she needed.

As I listened, I couldn't help but feel a sense of excitement building in my chest. "I would love to give you a makeover."

Evie beamed at me, her face lighting up with joy and relief.

As I led Evie further into the room, my mind was already brimming with ideas for her makeover.

I motioned for Kellan to come sit with us after a while.

Evie's excitement palpable in the air around us, I couldn't help but feel a sense of gratitude towards Reed.

Even when we were apart, he still knew exactly what I needed.

CHAPTER 50
REED

I HAD BEEN WORKING OUT OF THE OFFICE IN MIDTOWN FOR DAYS.

I lost track of time.

Gabriel had taken the necklace, retreating to his lair. Just not the key.

I told myself it was because it was a lasting memento of the woman he used to know.

And while I was in Midtown, I was trying to find any connection to Alisha's would-be stalker while digging up information on Gabriel, cautious of what Aidan had said.

I was using every private network I could get into and I searched up info on Gabriel. Aidan wasn't wrong.

There was next to nothing on Gabriel.

He'd vanished. He was real to me as my best friend, but on paper?

He was a ghost.

I felt guilty after my conversation with Alisha.

I told myself I was here because it was an easier commute.

Not because the Primrose was two blocks down and to the left. That's what I told myself.

Not because I knew everything Alisha was doing and that she was safe.

I felt guilty since my mistakes were costing Kellan sleep, and Selena would take my head off if he didn't come home at some point.

But when I walked in that day I almost had a heart attack.

Initially, I thought it was Alisha, if she had lost more weight than she should have and changed her hair.

Around Lucas fucking Devereaux.

His blonde hair messy now, navy suit straight from work. Who was kissing her cheeks, her lips. I lost my shit.

I realized I'd made a noise, and Lucas ripped away from—"Oh shit," I breathed, taking a step back. "Evie?"

Only it didn't look like Evie. Alisha did a damn good job.

Gone was the shy girl who wore clothes that made her look like a teenager or borrowed Selena's wardrobe.

Instead, in her place dressed in an outfit that reminded me of my Alisha, meshed with something perfect for Evie with boots that were so much like Selena's sans heels.

The only thing that made my blood boil was her eye makeup now leaking dark lines down her cheeks.

I was a storm then as she wiped them frantically. "What the fuck did he do to you?"

I was advancing on Lucas in a second. This fucking idiot. I would end him.

"Reed, stop," I felt her smaller hands trying to keep me away but I was on him.

"Why is she crying?" I demanded, my voice shaking with fury.

But Lucas's eyes only darkened, pupils eclipsing the blue as an inhuman growl ripped from his throat.

In an instant, he had me by the throat, murder in his eyes.

What did he do to her?

Instead of looking the least bit guilty, something happened, Evie was screaming. And something shifted in Lucas's blue eyes.

It was like the pupils swallowed his eyes, going black.

An inhuman growl left him as he grabbed for me two seconds after his back shook the walls.

Holy PTSD, I knew that look.

Lucas was in a killing mood.

Grateful I still knew how to hold my own, I took him on. "No, you son of a bitch, you look at me."

What the fuck was going on?

"Reed, let him go." I couldn't though.

Lucas was gone. In his place was a man who had experienced too much too young and didn't know how to cope with it. "Lucas, stop! He's my brother!"

At the sound of her voice his arms trying to still get a chokehold on me, broke off, and looked at her.

Evie was crying.

Pulling at me to get him off me.

I realized their relationship was more complicated than I gave myself credit for.

And from the looks of it he was in hot shit. When the fuck had Lucas Devereaux gotten into the office and into Evie?

I was going to ruin him. "What the fuck is going on with you two?" But she wasn't looking at me. "And how the fuck did he get in here?"

He shouldn't have known about this place. I looked at Evie and suddenly pieces were forming in my head.

"Is he the reason you were crying the other day?" And then another ugly question reared up.

"How fucking long have you been sleeping with your brother's enemy?"

I shoved Lucas back as he shook it off looking at Evie.

"Lucas, stop!" And he stopped. For her. I gaped.

"I didn't know who he was!" she sobbed, tugging at me.

"I'm sorry Evie," Lucas panted. "I knew if I told you—"

"—that I'd know my brother hates you?" she finished, her voice rising to a near shriek.

I had never seen her like this.

"Yes!" He yelled.

"What the fuck is going on?" My brain was working overtime, trying to make sense of the chaos unfolding before me.

Evie's eyes flashed with righteous anger as she spat. "Why don't you ask Lucas Devereaux, or should I say, Luke Delaney?"

The pieces clicked into place, and I turned to Lucas, my voice low and dangerous. "You knew she was his sister, and you..."

I couldn't even finish the thought.

"Oh, fucking hell. Gabriel isn't going to kill you. I am."Another realization hit me like a ton of bricks. I whirled on Evie, my voice rising. "He is the guy you've been seeing?"

"Not anymore! I didn't know!" she cried, her voice cracking. Lucas looked at her, desperation etched into every line of his face.

"Doll, please," he begged, and even though I hated him, a small part of me understood the anguish in his eyes. It was the same look I had when I lost Alisha.

"Evie, look at me—please," he implored.

322

"I'm not sleeping with him," Evie choked out, her eyes brimming with tears.

She met his gaze, her voice hardening. *"Do not call me Evie. Only the people I love call me Evie."*

Lucas stood there, stunned and broken. He looked worse than I felt. I turned to him, a pang of sympathy cutting through my anger.

"You need to leave," I said firmly.

"No need, I'm going home," Evie said, locking eyes with me. "Please do not tell Gabriel."

I gave her a look. There was a lot of shit I could keep from Gabriel, but this was not one of them.

"Evie," I warned.

She doesn't know.

She can never find out who Lucas really is.

"I am begging you," Evie pleaded. "No matter how much I dislike him right now."

She motioned to Lucas, who was trying to compose himself, straightening his suit and hair.

"I know what Gabriel is capable of. He will not stop with just hurting him."

She paused, her next words cutting me to the core. "Gabriel will kill him."

This wasn't just some secret.

If Gabriel ever found out Evie was seeing Lucas Devereaux behind his back, he would burn half the city to the ground.

And I would help.

"On one condition."

"Anything." Evie breathed.

"You'll never see him again. Ever. And he never shows his face around the Titans," I pointed at Lucas, who looked ready to throttle me. "I can't protect you from Gabriel if you do. It makes my job that much harder."

Lucas was shaking with barely contained rage.

"Evie, please," he begged. "I can take him—"

No, he can't.

"You don't know why Gabriel hates him. But I do," I cut him off, looking directly at Evie. "Say the words, and I'll never tell Gabriel. Ever."

Lucas was desperate. "Evie, I am begging you, I can protect you—"

Not from Gabriel.

Evie's voice was raw with betrayal. "You lied to me. You knew who I was for so long. And you let me think you were someone else."

She turned to me, her eyes pleading. "I didn't know who he was. I swear." I tipped my head, understanding. She was still so young.

"*Evie—*" Lucas tried once more.

Evie was breaking, and it killed me to do this to her. But he was a Devereaux. And Gabriel was going to kill Lucas if he ever found out. I couldn't stop him. He barely tolerated Lucy.

She tipped her chin at me, her voice steady despite the pain in her eyes.

"Yes. I will never see Lucas Devereaux again."

As she turned to leave, I didn't miss the way Lucas looked at her.

It was the same way I'd looked after Alisha kicked me out.

The look of a man who had just lost everything.

"I heard someone's been out to kill you recently," I said softly. "Is that why you thought it would be Gabriel? Because you suspected he knew you tried to seduce his sister?"

Lucas sat in the seat in my office, and I prayed to fucking God Gabriel didn't show up here.

"How long has this been going on?" I asked Lucas, who was currently sitting with an ice pack on his cheek.

His blonde hair was in disarray, and his molten blue eyes flashed at me. For a man hitting his thirties, somehow he looked like he was in grad school.

"Luke Delaney?"

He let out an exhale. "It's my mother's maiden name. I don't use my real name most of the time..."

"When did you start lying to Evie?" Because that's what she'd screamed. And I believed her.

"I can't go into a fucking meeting like this." He'd been a grump ever since Evie had walked out, looking like he wanted to follow after her, but he knew better.

"Yes, you can. You're the CEO. You can do whatever the fuck you want." I continued. "Answer the fucking question, or you'll have more than a bruised face."

"Months." He said it after a moment of thinking. "I met her months ago by accident."

He shook his head. "I was at a...it's a convention for people who like these board games, and Evie was there—"

I held up a hand. "You met Evie at the Annual Board Game Convention?"

Lucas turned a shade of pink I couldn't help but grin at. "I just needed to process that you're a fucking nerd."

"Says you? You think I don't know you're the biggest fucking geek in Titan."

I was. But I kept that shit under wraps.

I motioned for him to go on.

"I knew who she was the moment she said her name. How many fucking Reeds and Gabriels are there? I knew Gabriel hated me. I tried to get as much info on him, but—I couldn't find anything. Gabriel is a ghost." That he was. With good reason now.

"But I knew when she would talk about him. I didn't expect to like her, let alone want—" He broke off at my narrowed eyes.

I couldn't believe I was having this conversation with Lucas fucking Devereaux.

"Do I need to ask the obvious?" I saw it in his eyes how much he liked her. Even now, he couldn't get the lipstick off his mouth, so it made his lips redder than normal.

It was a little outrageous when I realized Evie was sleeping with the man Gabriel hated the most.

"She was my sub, if that's what you're asking." I closed my eyes.

I was a dominant partner, but I didn't like the whole lifestyle of contracts and collars. I liked Alisha and to please her, but I liked the concept of it. Gabriel was more into it than I was, considering Isobel's necklace. And Lucas? I knew enough about him to know he was head-first into it.

The whole nine yards. Not my style. The idea of fucking Alisha in front of people was hot, though.

Then he said something that stumped me. "Why exactly does Gabriel hate me so much?"

I wasn't going there. I couldn't. Not without hurting everyone.

"He would hate you now for having sex with his sister."

I could imagine Gabriel coming up with ways to torture Lucas. No more pretty boy face.

Sitting there looking regal and prim, those blue eyes of his were honest. Sometimes I forgot Lucas was Gabriel's age, but they'd chosen different paths in life.

"Between your familial issues and your PTSD, though, I'm not surprised you don't know why Gabriel hates you."

"I tried looking up why but—" he broke off. "Did you have to hit me that hard?"

"You made my sister cry."

I went easy.

I looked at Lucas and actually looked at him for once. "Why didn't you hit me back?"

He'd served in the military; he could fight.

He was in for a few years during the worst of the covert wars in Africa, and it showed.

I heard his unit got lit up a few times. And he had nasty scars and PTSD.

Evie was with him? Why the fuck—

He didn't look at me.

"Because you're her family."

I looked at Lucas for a moment with a different level of understanding. He's nothing like his family...

Evie had more humanity in her soul than a person should be allowed to have, and it was odd considering her brother was a psychopath.

They aren't related by blood. Now it makes sense.

Despite being close to my age, Lucas had been spoon-fed success through his parents' company, taking over at a young age and building an empire.

"Tell me who's trying to kill you." He looked surprised. "Didn't you just tell me to stay away from Titan?"

"From Evie. I don't need your problems finding their way back to her. Gabriel isn't in a good mood."

He was never in a good mood.

I didn't care if Evie told me she'd never see him again. Lucas had never and would never give me the same word. Plus, if he'd been her Dom, he wouldn't let her go.

I kicked my feet back and listened as he spoke, all the while imagining Alisha next to me, taking notes with that fluffy pen she had, and analyzing Lucas with me.

Lucy goes missing...and someone's trying to kill her brother...What were the odds?

I didn't even bother to understand why it felt right to want to tell her about what I had been through today. I want to tell her.

Halfway through, I had gotten hungry, and rather than ordering food, I ended up walking with Lucas down the street to a local café.

I thought the entire place reminded me of a place Alisha would have liked to check out.

I did that a lot nowadays, finding things that I knew she would like. Missing her so much that I slept in the office.

"You come here?" He looked around. "Evie would love it—"

I silenced him with a look as we placed our orders. I paid for him. It was the bare minimum, as Alisha would've said.

When we sat down, I heard musical laughter drift in through the shop.

My head turned and I stilled.

Alisha.

She was gorgeous in a red coat that brought out her dark hair, Avani next to her laughing at something Kellan had said.

I had told him to ditch the jacket now that the team trusted him. His wool coat blended in with the cityscape.

I had skipped my lunch with Avani, given the shit going on with her sister, which made me feel like the worst.

Her guard wasn't with her during the day, only when she was going out.

Unless Kellan was with her.

Then Avani didn't need one since Alisha went to get her all the time. She was covered.

Avani noticed me first and smiled at me.

Kellan glanced my way immediately after, his eyes sharpening, taking everything in.

Alisha was the only one who didn't notice; she looked tired, out of focus.

Turn your head, beautiful girl. Just a little this way.

As though she could hear me, her head moved, turned, eyes locking with mine. She stopped moving. I hadn't realized how starved I was for her until I caught myself moving, ignoring Lucas's stare. Walking to her.

"Alisha."

"Reed."

She looked like she hadn't gotten an ounce of sleep, her eyes slightly red and exhausted. Next to her, Avani looked between us.

"We should get some cupcakes." She dragged Kellan away.

"You look beautiful, Lish."

As her throat worked, I saw her eyes well. Her shoulders shook a little with the effort to keep from crying.

I couldn't resist. I reached out for her. I hated the way her eyes watered and how uneasy she looked.

Cuddling her close was second nature.

"Reed," it broke my heart. "What are you doing here?"

"I had a meeting. I haven't seen you in forever. Are you taking care of yourself, Angel?"

She didn't look like she was, which meant it had hit her as hard as it hit me. I was on her; I didn't care where we were, even if my instincts told me otherwise.

I dropped my voice, pulling her close. "I know you're scared. I'll be here when you need me...when you want to come home. I'll be here."

I wiped her eyes. "I'm always going to be your home. Just like you'll always be mine."

For long moments she didn't say anything, and the noises around me blurred. I felt Lucas's eyes on us.

"I just need time."

She was coming around, though. Somehow, someway she was.

I felt the ice in my body crack as she said the words.

My eyes burned into hers as I dropped my mouth to hers, pressing tight for a second.

She let me kiss her.

"Take all the time you need, Angel...just come home to me when you're done."

When I got back to Lucas, he looked at me with confusion.

"Why did you let her go? She's gorgeous." I eyed him with a look. "Relax, you're already invested in my life with Evie. I happen to know Alisha. And she doesn't date anyone."

At my glance, he explained. "She works with the DuPonts. I went to school with Matteo, and I used to date Gemma—don't start—It was one date. She's just a friend."

I devoured the sight of her.

She looked warm and cozy, even if her eyes were a little sad. Kellan sent me updates from time to time, but I wasn't expecting to see her here.

"Did you sign a contract with Evie?"

His eyes didn't meet mine. "No."

That was surprising. My eyes drifted to Alisha.

"Is Alisha yours?" She was. *She still is.*

I never stopped thinking about her. I just made sure Kellan got my updates to her. I owed the kid big time.

And Selena.

I knew what Alisha was doing and where she was at and that the person doing this shit to her had gone quiet, which gave me plenty of time to brainstorm over it.

"I didn't let her go." I said softly, my eyes finding her in the line with her sister.

As if drawn by the tether between us, Alisha looked over her shoulder at me, her eyes meeting mine.

"She's still my girl."

CHAPTER 51
ALISHA

Open up, Angel.

I GOT THE TEXT LATER AT NIGHT.

I reached for my robe and then decided to pad to the door naked. I knew who it was.

The room was lit up by moonlight when I opened the door. I had been the one to text him earlier.

I need you.

He'd been at the cafe today and I had seen him for a brief moment, my eyes hungrily taking him in.

Stormy eyes locked with mine. He exhaled shakily, taking one look at my body. *"Angel."*

He was on me, tugging off his jacket while kissing me. The door shut behind him.

His mouth was hungry, all over me.

I felt my fingers ripping at his pants. He was half carrying me, half dragging me back to the bed.

Coming together in a tangle of urgent kisses, and grasping hands.

"You need me." I did.

I was taken down to the bed, my legs falling open, Reed settling, I felt him hot and heavy between my legs.

I was wild, lost in sea and spice, the tip of him pushed at my body, untried for the last few days, but still dripping for him.

The moment he speared into me, I cried out.

Reed pressed his lips to my collar letting out a breath, fisting the sheets on either side of my head, and urging me to take more.

Reed pressed his forehead to mine.

He didn't move. He sighed as he kissed everywhere he could reach. I wanted to cry. He didn't say a word. I ran my hands down his shirt, the white cotton soft under my fingers and raked my nails down his back. A low hiss left him as his hand came up squeezing my throat.

He growled in the darkness. "I can feel how soaked you are, and yet you're still struggling to take me."

He squeezed tighter and I moaned as he slid in inches deeper. I gasped, nodding quickly, tears in my eyes from the intensity of *this* alone.

"I need something tonight from you too." His voice dripped with a dark promise.

"I want you to call me sir." I clenched at that, and his breath hissed through his teeth. "I felt that."

I was ruining my sheets. His dark silk murmur caressed my skin.

"Are you going to open your pretty thighs wider for me?"

"Yes, sir." A flood of warmth rushed into my womb.

His fingers trailed down my throat to my clit where an animal noise left me feeling him gently rub that little bud of nerves promising to get me off.

"Such a good girl." I bit back a sob at the praise. "That's my good girl, opening wide." *That felt so fucking good.*

"I'm going to fuck you for hours," he whispered and I all but screamed at the thought of that. "Until this little pussy remembers how to take my cock."

He didn't let me respond. Stamping his mouth over my mouth, he fucked me with everything he had. Weeks of frustration were delivered into my body with the kind of thrusts he only gave me when he was angry with me.

I relished *every* bit of it.

Even as it stung the deeper he worked, I gripped his back, lower to his ass pulling him deeper.

A ragged groan left him.

"Goddamn, Lish, you feel like heaven."

When he bottomed out, he groaned like an animal, muffling my screams in his hand.

Even if I sounded like I was being murdered, the only thing he was destroying was my pussy.

"*Try* to run from me now, my little cum slut," he hissed.

I was *wild* after a brutally hard thrust.

"You can't run from me here. Not *anymore*."

As my orgasm hit I was shrieking, and Reed was groaning, the bed slamming into the wall, and the sounds of sex permeating the air.

His grip on me tightened as he growled feverish promises in my ear, demanding my total submission.

I responded with equal fervor, clutching him closer, needing to eliminate any space between us.

Oh God, this was so good.

He punctuated his filthy words with his thrusts working me through the intensity of it. I exploded. It felt endless as I shook and bucked as it became too much. And he fucked *harder*. He was inhuman.

"Take my come. There you go, Angel, look at you taking me deep." I was depraved but so was he.

"Is this what you needed, buried deep in your pussy?" He growled it into my lips.

"*Reed*," I was sobbing.

"*Fuck*," he hissed his pleasure. Letting go with him felt blissful as he came.

The way he accepted what I liked. "I love you." His lips were at my ear. "*I will never stop loving you.*"

He repeated it as he pulsed in me, over and over until I silenced him with my mouth. Slowly he licked at my tears.

"Call me whenever you get like this," he whispered. "I don't care how busy I am. I'll come and take care of you."

My eyes were streaming and as I shivered with the intensity of my orgasms, he continued to kiss me.

When I nodded, he smiled softly against my lips, aware of the energy changing. I wrapped my legs around his waist tighter.

"I need to fire Kellan," he whispered. "I could've fucked you six ways to Sunday and he wouldn't wake up."

"Don't you dare," I said, feeling my eyes closing as sleep came over me. "He already left when you came into the hotel."

Kellan had gone home to Selena needing some much needed rest.

I didn't miss how exhausted my bodyguard was becoming. Reed's quiet laughter and soft kisses lulled me to sleep.

And when I woke up in the morning he was gone.

CHAPTER 52
REED

THE DAY AFTER I MADE LOVE TO ALISHA LIKE A DEPRAVED MAN, I GOT A call from Nate asking me to show up at Gemma's place.

As I entered the Upper East Side townhouse, I found Nate with an uncharacteristic pissed off expression.

"Gemma's on the phone arguing with her fucking family, so we're good," he said, shaking his head in disbelief.

He led me to the living room, where he had set up a murder board. His intelligent eyes, now a murky blue, focused on the board as he delivered the news that made my blood run cold. "Selena's missing."

I gaped at him, my headache intensifying. "What do you mean she's missing? Ping her cell."

Nate's frustration was palpable as he explained. "I haven't seen her lately. No threatening texts about taking my balls off. Kellan hasn't heard from her either."

His eyes met mine, a question lingering in them. "You knew about those two?"

"I don't care what they did so long as it didn't hurt anyone," I replied, my mind already racing with possibilities about Selena. Nate nodded, his voice dropping as distant shouting echoed from inside the apartment.

"Evie and I took a look. And it does matter. I know Selena. She was my partner for the last five years, until you moved me," Nate's tone laced with anger.

Change was never easy, but I had my reasons.

"If you don't like being a Titan, quit. I don't have the fucking patience to explain to you why I make the choices I do. I know my team. You might be angry about Selena, but she's the best operative we have. If she made a choice—"

"Because of Kellan—" Nate interjected.

"She has free will!" I snapped, my patience wearing thin. "She was trained by some of the best in the Agency when she was in Havana with weeks of training. Gabriel brought her to Quantico because he believed in her. She can kill us both with a fucking stiletto. She kicked your ass from day one. Kellan and Garrett follow her. They move with her. As a unit!"

Nate growled. "You put me on a security detail gig."

"Because Gemma is your former girlfriend, and I fucking *figured* she would trust you more than some random *idiot* off the street."

"You knew?" Disbelief etched on his face.

Of course I fucking knew.

I ran a hand through my hair, exhausted by the constant need to explain myself.

"I'm going to say this, and then you're going to speak with your ex-girlfriend."

Nate's eyes widened as I continued, my patience wearing thin.

"I asked Gemma if she would prefer a friend or a fresh start, and she said given her current situation, a friendly face would be helpful. I figured her *summer crush from Capri* would be a good break, since you were out of it, holding Selena back, getting into more issues than you should've, and fucking around like I wasn't going to know."

I was on a roll, and I didn't care about the shock on Nate's face.

This was why I hired new people, why I wanted a break in the team, and why I was in charge.

"Now, where is my fucking operative?"

Nate's voice was quiet as he replied. "Evie can't find her either."

His eyes looked away.

"How long has it been?"

"Sixteen hours of no contact," Nate's eyes held a glint that made the situation even more damning. "She knew something. About your girl."

I tried to force calm, but too many things were spiraling out of control.

"Evie says Selena's images on cameras go missing. They just crap out after Selena gets Downtown. Evie's canvassed security cameras up and down. Can't find her. Just what the fuck is going on?"

I shook my head, my mind racing.

"I need to think. Selena is alive."

I knew her. Years ago, Gabriel had brought a bright-eyed Selena to the team. She'd been highly trained and capable.

She wasn't the type to rush into anything without thinking. Something was wrong.

Nate's question hung heavy in the air. "I know she is. But what condition would she be in if she was investigating your girl's stalker?"

The door behind us opened, and Gemma entered, her blonde hair flowing behind her, her cheeks flushed. "Reed, you're here."

I glanced at Nate, who shook his head. Gemma's cornflower blue eyes were wary as she took in the scene before her.

"Everything all right?" Her gaze drifted to the murder board. "Oh, is it time?"

Time? What was she talking about?

Nate's expression softened as he looked at Gemma. "It's time, Duchess."

Gemma turned to me, a glimmer of hope in her eyes. "We solved your case."

I didn't even have it in me to give a shit right now, but I motioned for her to continue anyway.

"It's a cop." Nate began to lay out the evidence, his brow furrowed in concentration. "The neighborhood Selena's tracker pinged at was this place. Selena said something felt off to her about the missing girls and Alisha."

I nodded, having had the same thoughts about each incident.

Nate continued. "Selena was investigating Alisha's stalker because you asked her to go to Giroux, and she discovered a disturbing pattern. The victims all looked similar—women of color, under five-foot-eight, from different walks of life. It wasn't just a coincidence."

I leaned back on the arm of one of Gemma's many couches, my eyes narrowing.

Nate kept going. "Selena realized that the stalker had to be someone with access to Alisha's life, someone who could blend in and go unnoticed. Most of his victims were street walkers, women of low income, no notice. Gone in a flash. We started looking into the security personnel hired for the events Alisha attended and the staff at her apartment building. That's when we found a match."

He pointed at a photograph. "Detective James White. Recently divorced, with a history of domestic abuse. His wife took their kids and left him."

Nate's expression turned grim. "White worked on most of the missing persons cases involving the victims. And his superior? Lieutenant Cameron Giroux, the NYPD contact Selena had been meeting with. That's how Gabriel started digging."

"She didn't tell me—" I began, but Nate cut me off. Kellan hadn't gotten anything from Lopez.

"Neither her nor Gabriel were certain yet. She had a suspicion after the dead body, it was one of the girls who was talking to her. She saw Lopez meeting with a cop. Except that cop has nothing to do with Lopez's parole."

The pieces started to fall into place.

"White was threatening Lopez, using him to get to the girls."

Nate nodded. "And then those girls would call the cops. White would show—"

He didn't finish his sentence, his gaze breaking to Gemma.

Gemma wiped her eyes. "Apologies, please continue."

She wasn't an operative, but...Nate had made her his partner. *His equal.*

My jaw clenched. "Giroux didn't know?"

"It gets worse," Nate continued, nodding at Gemma. "Gabriel asked, so Giroux looked into it and discovered that White had a history of racism and misconduct. He'd been reprimanded multiple times for unlawful arrests and discriminatory behavior, but he always managed to escape serious consequences. Giroux told Gabriel that just a few weeks ago, White was caught harassing some high school girls during a patrol. The school reported it, but the precinct let him walk."

I swore under my breath.

Nate's voice dropped lower. "Giroux said White had a hard time working with people, and one cop, in particular, told Giroux that White made offhand comments about people belonging to their own race. He wasn't a fan of interracial relationships."

White's obsession with Alisha wasn't just because she was a high-profile target. It was because she was with me.

I had caused this. Gemma gasped, her eyes widening in horror.

"I thought I recognized him! He was there that day, I held the pop-up meeting about..." She trailed off, her voice trembling.

Nate's jaw clenched as he looked at Gemma with more emotion than I had seen all day.

He didn't break his gaze from her as he spoke. "White used his position to gain access to your friend's apartment building."

Gemma nodded, her expression apologetic as she turned to me. "I thought he saw you guys together that night when you went over to her place. Or any night. Gabriel wasn't wrong, I'm sorry Reed—"

She gave me an apologetic look as I motioned for her to continue. "When Gabriel said you didn't pay attention, I realized at some point while you were with Alisha, even if you set cameras, he worked in the building."

He just hadn't been expecting me. Gemma looked at me, her mouth turned down.

I felt it leave me. "He could've had his eye on Alisha for a long time."

That thought made my blood run cold.

"Reed," Gemma said. "It's not your fault. If anything you might've saved Alisha's life since it looks like he was going to do something regardless."

Nate looked uncomfortable as he continued. "We think White went after girls he thought wouldn't have anyone in their lives. Alisha was inevitable after Avani left. And then you came into her life."

"I got it," I said, my voice strained.

Gemma sprung up. "Selena figured it out. She knew the victims looked like her, and she realized White was escalating."

She snapped her finger. *"Then why—"*

I swore loudly, realization dawning on me. "Because she's still a spy and she knew how dangerous White was and didn't want to put anyone else at risk."

Plus, she knew one of the dead girls.

"But now she's missing..." Gemma looked at Nate with an expression that told me, something deeper was there in her understanding of Selena and Nate.

I didn't have the energy to figure it out.

"White has her," Nate said with confidence. "I told Selena not to do anything stupid. I know that's why Kellan fought with her. She was my partner for years. I know how she thinks—" He broke off, enraged, his face a mask of fury. "White has her."

A nagging feeling tugged at the back of my mind.

"Alisha was in places where her sister could have been. Avani used to live with her, she was there that night."

Nate waved a hand. "Probably just a threat to scare Alisha. Avani fits the description to a T as much as her. The grad students are from

Avani's school. And the high school girls aren't too far from there. And you know who else fits it?"

"Selena," Gemma whispered.

Nate looked at me, his expression grave. "He's getting desperate if he took Selena. He has to know she's tied to figuring it out. He's pushing it. Alisha is a trophy kill. He gets her? He feels power. He's been doing this on the down-low for years. Now he's finally got someone like her?"

"But why now?" I asked, knowing something wasn't adding up.

Gemma stepped closer to Nate who spoke. "Giroux said after White's divorce, he's been in and out of the hospital. We think something is wrong with White. And he's trying to get his last kills in. Giroux said a lot of those incidents matched with White being gone."

Another thought popped into my head. "White knows we're onto him. Gabriel said Lopez was killed. He knows we know."

He wasn't a fan of interracial relationships. Nate's eyes were hard as he realized what I had.

"No. He thinks Selena did. She was with Kellan. That's when White saw her."

The night Kellan asked me to take the case. I swore out loud. They had been too wrapped up in each other to notice.

Nate looked at me. "Selena didn't realize until two days ago. She called me when you kept Kellan by Alisha's side for days." I know, I felt guilty for that.

"She's been putting the pieces together. Gabriel was busy with Evie and Titan, and Selena didn't take back up," Nate said.

Kellan and her fought, and so she went in alone.

White was going to kill Selena.

"Where does White live?" I asked, my resolve hardening.

Nate tucked Gemma into his side. "In the same neighborhood Selena went missing, Lower East Side."

CHAPTER 53
ALISHA

"YOU SEEM DISTRACTED, DIDI."

Avani sat across from me, chewing her lip, at the diner we went to for brunch.

The words jolted me from my reverie. Was I that transparent?

I forced myself to focus on my sister's concerned eyes, pushing away the memories of Reed that had been haunting me all morning.

"Is everything okay with you and Reed? You looked a little upset when you saw him."

Avani's words cut through my thoughts, and I felt a pang of guilt in my chest. My sister was too perceptive for her own good sometimes.

"I'm sorry. Yes, everything is fine. I just have a lot on my mind."

I tried to smile, but it felt forced. *Like the feel of Reed slamming into you over and over?* I felt heat rise to my cheeks.

I kept thinking about the night Reed had shown up after I'd messaged him.

The memory of his touch, his taste, his scent–it *all* came flooding back.

I didn't know what I was thinking. But nobody ever said a woman out of love made any reasonable sense. The worst part was, Reed didn't care if I used him for sex.

Take what you need from me.

And I had.

Call me when you get like this.

I'll take care of it every time.

He'd explained what he needed from me. Complete and utter surrender. And I knew I'd give it to him over and over again.

I shifted uncomfortably in my seat, the vinyl booth suddenly feeling too warm.

The retro diner we sat in, with its checkered floor and shiny chrome exterior, was almost too bright for my mood.

The smell of freshly brewed coffee and sizzling bacon filled the air, making my stomach growl with anticipation, but also churning with unease.

My eyes flickered to Kellan sitting on a barstool across from us. His brow was furrowed, deep in thought, his fingers tapping an irregular rhythm on the counter.

Something had been bothering him, but I couldn't bring myself to ask.

I turned back to Avani, pasting on what I hoped was a convincing smile.

"It's nothing, tell me about you. Any cute boys I should be aware of?"

She flushed, her fingers nervously twirling a strand of hair. "I don't think I like college boys."

I mock gasped, grateful for the distraction. "Let me guess, between the chlamydia and drinking binges, it's hard to find a decent man?" We laughed as Kellan choked on his drink, the sound breaking through the diner's background chatter. I knew he could hear us.

"It's not that," Avani whispered, leaning in closer. Her eyes, so like our mother's, held a wistful look. "I just haven't found someone...you know what Mum used to tell us about? The kinds of men in her stories, the kind that sweep you off your feet and love you more than life?"

I did know. The lump in my throat grew larger as I thought about Reed. He was all of those things, wasn't he? But I'd pushed him away, let my fears get the better of me. The realization made my chest ache.

Avani continued, her voice soft and reminiscent.

"Do you remember when Mum hadn't gone back home in ages? I asked her if it made her unhappy. Why did she stay? She said Dad was her home. She had no reason to go back when she'd been blessed with so much."

Her eyes met mine, filled with understanding. "Sometimes I think Reed is like that for you."

My heart clenched at her words. Was she right?

Had I been too blind to see what was right in front of me?

Avani bit her lip, hesitating before she spoke again. "I feel like after

Mum and Dad died, I realized recently you stopped living your life. You stopped being happy. Because of me—"

"No—" I interjected, my voice sharp with emotion.

I would never let her think that. The guilt that had been simmering beneath the surface threatened to bubble over.

"*Didi,*" she shook her head, using the endearment that always made me feel both loved and vulnerable. "You've never looked happier. Even after you became the brand ambassador for EllaBeauty. Reed, he's been so good for you. Good to you. You look healthier."

Her voice softened, filled with gratitude. "I'm so grateful he's a part of our family now. I'm so glad you finally gave him a chance. I wish we hadn't missed out three years."

Me too. The words echoed in my mind as I listened to Avani speak, each one a bittersweet reminder of the time I'd wasted.

The diner's warm lighting cast a soft glow on her face, highlighting the genuine happiness in her eyes.

When she smiled at me, I could almost see imaginary butterflies perched on her shoulders, a flower crown adorning her head—an image of the carefree girl she used to be.

"I'm really glad after everything you've been blessed with so much," Avani continued, her smile widening. "Mum would've had such a huge crush on him."

I wiped my eyes, a watery laugh escaping me at the image of our tiny mother looking at Reed's tattoos and his easy smile, falling for him just as I had.

The thought brought both joy and a renewed sense of loss.

As I reached for my coffee, needing something to ground me amidst the swirling emotions, a glint of rose gold caught my eye.

On Avani's wrist, partially hidden by her black sleeve, was a charm bracelet I'd never seen before. The sight of it momentarily distracted me from my emotional turmoil.

"Is that a...?" I trailed off, leaning in closer to examine the intricate piece of jewelry.

It was a charm bracelet, and not just any ordinary one.

The chain, crafted from a blend of gold and rose gold, sparkled under the diner's lights. I knew these bracelets. Davina&CO was a luxury retailer that custom-designed pieces for celebrities.

Those bracelets were hard to come by. You needed an appointment to get one, and this one was clearly custom made.

The charms on Avani's bracelet were far from the classic designs. A tiny gold bow, a butterfly, a tiny pink heart with an engraved "A" hung off it.

As I examined the bracelet, I felt a shift in the atmosphere.

Avani's demeanor changed, a hint of unease creeping into her expression. She shifted in her seat, watching my reaction closely.

"I have to tell you something," she said, her voice hesitant. "I don't think you'll like it."

My curiosity piqued, momentarily overshadowing the emotional whirlwind I'd been experiencing.

"Anything. I'd never judge you...but you might have to explain why you're wearing a thirty thousand-dollar bracelet I didn't buy for you."

I raised an eyebrow, trying to keep my tone light despite the growing sense of apprehension.

"*Thirty*—?" Avani's eyes went huge, a wild look crossing her face. "Reed said he got it from an antique shop?"

"*Reed?*"

"He said he was browsing antique stores—"

"Reed doesn't go antique shopping," I stated matter-of-factly, my thoughts racing. He would never step foot in a furniture shop. The man ordered his groceries because he had no time to do them.

Avani sat back in her seat, her words coming out in a rush.

"I know you'd know since you're his girlfriend."

I didn't bother correcting her, too caught up in trying to understand what was happening.

"But he told me it was cheap."

For Reed, it probably was. *But why?*

"He paid my tuition." The words hit me like a blow, my jaw dropping in shock. "*All of it.*"

As Avani rambled on about books, cards, brunches, allowances, and dorms, I felt my world spinning. Each revelation was like a punch to the gut, leaving me breathless and disoriented.

"He said he didn't want me to tell you because he didn't want you to like him with any outside influences," Avani explained, her voice soft but clear. "He wanted you to like him for who he was. And he told me to keep it a secret so you can focus on you."

My mind reeled, struggling to process this information.

"But I paid..." I couldn't form coherent thoughts, let alone words. The enormity of Reed's actions was overwhelming.

Avani continued, her eyes watching me carefully. "He said he sent it back and switched it with his account. He said even if things don't work out between you guys, which it won't ever happen, he's paying for me to go to school until I finish my PhD."

My sister's dream of becoming an English professor flashed through my mind.

Reed had made that possible. Reed, who had access to my network, who could see *everything*.

Avani looked at me warily, her voice tinged with concern. "Please don't be upset, I just wanted to tell you since our last lunch he said he wants to take us somewhere nice. I told him we hadn't been back to Calcutta in years….thirty thousand? I have to give this back to him."

I couldn't speak. My throat felt tight, emotions swirling inside me like a tempest.

"Are you okay? You don't look so good—" Avani's worried voice seemed to come from far away.

Suddenly, I felt Kellan's arm wrap around my shoulders.

He knew my tells, knew when I was about to break. As he tucked my head into his side, the dam burst. I started crying, deep, body-wracking sobs that I couldn't control.

Through my tears, thoughts raced through my mind.

Reed doesn't tell people anything.

He thinks telling people what he does will make them think one way or another about who he is.

Expectations he can't always live up to.

My vision blurred as I saw my sister's expression fall and her eyes water at me.

"It's okay. It's all right. I'm just–" I choked out, unable to finish. I had been so worried about Reed.

For three years.

I liked him. I was so afraid to let him in.

And he had defied all expectations.

He did keep things from me, and as stunned as I was, I realized I was more upset that he kept good things from me than bad ones.

I knew why though.

I got it. I did.

He'd taken care of Avani so easily.

Because he knew she was the most important thing in my life. I would do anything to keep you safe. Let me love you, give me a chance. His words echoed in my memory.

She had no reason to look back when she'd been blessed with so much already.

And it was all because of Reed.

As I wiped my eyes, Avani bit her lip, and I saw Kellan shake his head at her, silently telling her to drop it.

For the rest of our time at the diner, Avani didn't mention Reed, and I found myself lost in thought as Kellan took over the conversation.

When Avani left to head to a friend's place and mentioned a party, I declined.

"Do you mind if I call Selena real quick? I haven't heard from her all day," Kellan's voice broke through my reverie.

I nodded dumbly, still overwhelmed by the revelations of the day.

As Kellan stepped away to make his call, the diner now emptied out, I felt a strange sense of unease settle over me.

Then, a text from Avani lit up my phone.

I think I left my scarf.

I glanced over to the other side of the booth. She had.

Should I bring it to you?

Yeah, I'm right outside.

I frowned, a feeling of disquiet growing. That was strange. She'd left a while ago.

Kellan had told me to stay put, but it was just Avani. *I'd be right back.*

He won't even know I'm gone, I rationalized.

I grabbed the scarf and my purse, heading outside. The front of the diner was empty, so I walked around the side.

There was nobody there.

"Avani?" I called out, my voice sounding small in the quiet street.

A cold feeling slithered down my spine. Something wasn't right.

I heard a crackling sound behind me and gasped, thinking maybe Kellan had followed me after all.

Suddenly, black obscured my vision. I screamed as an acrid, sour scent assaulted my senses.

Panic surged through me as I fought and kicked, but my attacker was too strong.

Sheer terror coated my lungs, making it hard to breathe.

In another second, darkness claimed me, and I was out.

CHAPTER 54
REED

THE CALL CAME AS I WAS LEAVING GEMMA'S, MY MIND ALREADY RACING with plans to confront White. Kellan's breathless voice on the other end of the line sent a chill down my spine.

"I had her, she was right here—"

"What happened?" Fear clawed at my insides. Any rational thought fled my brain as I raced to my car, my heart pounding in my chest.

As Kellan explained, his words jumbling together in his panic, I felt my world tilting on its axis. Alisha.

My Alisha. Gone.

The fifteen-minute drive to the diner felt like an eternity.

Every second that ticked by was another moment Alisha could be...*No.*

I couldn't let my mind go there.

I had to stay focused, stay in control. But the fear, the rage, the helplessness—it was all threatening to overwhelm me.

I'd already called Gabriel, the words spilling out of me in a rushed, frantic tone I barely recognized as my own. He'd issued the task order to recall everyone. He was in the city.

He'd be on his way. But would it be enough?

The diner came into view, and I was out of the car before it had fully stopped.

Inside, Kellan was with the manager, reviewing security footage. The look on his face—guilt, fear, desperation—made my stomach churn.

"There's a blind spot," the older gentleman explained, his voice trembling slightly. "She walked out to where the servers usually take smoke breaks."

Rage boiled inside me, hot and vicious.

I turned on Kellan, barely containing the urge to lash out physically.

"And nobody fucking saw her?" I snarled, my eyes narrowing as I watched him step out of frame on the footage, leaving her alone. *"Where the fuck were you?"*

Kellan's face paled, making the dark circles under his eyes stand out starkly. "I'm sorry, I left her for a minute—"

"Are you fucking kidding me? Did Selena teach you nothing? Anything could've happened to her—" *By now.* The words hung in the air, unspoken but heavy with implication.

It took every ounce of self-control not to wrap my hands around his throat. This was my fault too.

I should have been there.

I should have protected her.

I turned back to the footage, my heart pounding as I replayed it, searching desperately for any clue, any detail we might have missed.

"What did you and Selena fight over?"

"Reed—" Kellan's voice was pleading, but I couldn't deal with his emotions right now. Not when Alisha was out there, alone, scared...

"What the fuck was it?" I demanded, my voice raw with emotion.

When he didn't speak, my eyes caught Alisha's movement on the screen.

She'd gotten a text, and then I saw it— her sister's scarf. A chill ran down my spine as the pieces started to fall into place.

Why had Alisha left?

That should have been my first thought.

She knew better. I'd trained her for this.

The only reason she would have gone outside was if something—or *someone*—had lured her out there.

He has both of them.

Alisha and Avani. The two people I loved most in the world, the two people I had sworn to protect.

"Fuck."

The word tore from my throat, raw and desperate. I felt like I was drowning, the weight of my failure crushing me.

But I couldn't give in to despair. Not now. Not when they needed me.

I turned on Kellan, channeling my fear and guilt into determination. "Move. We gotta get our girls."

CHAPTER 55
ALISHA

I HAD A HEADACHE FROM HELL.

"*Didi.*" Avani? Why was she crying? "Please be alive."

I moaned softly, my senses slowly awakening as I became aware of my surroundings.

The musty smell of the basement filled my nostrils, and the cold, damp air sent shivers down my spine.

I tried to move my hands, but the rough texture of the ropes binding them together chafed against my skin.

My fingers and toes felt numb, and I struggled to open my eyes, feeling as if they were weighed down by lead.

"Selena's hurt. Please wake up." Avani's trembling voice pierced through the haze, jolting me awake. I gasped, my eyes flying open as the realization hit me like a freight train.

Kidnapped. The word echoed in my mind before I could fully process the scene before me.

"Avani?"

My heart was in my throat at what I saw. We were in a dimly lit basement, the musty smell of mold and decay permeating the air.

The sound of footsteps creaking above us sent a wave of fear coursing through my veins.

Avani's face was red, streaked with tears. She was tied to something, just like me.

She looked down at the floor to the right, her eyes wide with horror, and I followed her gaze, barely suppressing a scream.

The long heels, unmistakable even in the shadows, were the only way I could identify the figure sprawled on the ground.

"*Selena.*"

Her name escaped my lips in a whisper.

She looked like a broken doll, her body crumpled and lifeless on the cold concrete floor. Bruises marred her skin, and blood matted her forehead, the crimson stark against her ashen complexion.

There is so much blood.

The metallic scent assaulted my nostrils, and my heart began to race, pounding against my ribcage.

"She was already here. What's happening?" Avani's voice quivered as the sound of footsteps echoed above us once more. "We need to find a way out of here."

Despite the tears streaming down our faces, I nodded, determination burning in my chest.

"I'll find a way out of here."

My eyes scanned the room, settling on a tiny window along the far wall.

It was barely large enough for a person to fit through, but...I glanced at Avani, assessing her small frame.

"You can fit if we can get it open."

"No," she hissed, her voice fierce despite the fear etched on her face. "I'm not leaving you."

"You have to," I insisted, my voice rising with urgency. The sound of footsteps grew closer, each one sending a fresh wave of panic through my body. "You have to run when I give you the chance to. Go find Reed."

I knew he would love and protect her, provide her with the safety I couldn't guarantee.

"He's coming!" Avani's whisper was laced with terror.

"I'll distract him. Run, Avani. Look at me," she did. "I love you so much—" I began to cry as I saw her face contort and whimpers left her.

"*Didi—*"

"*Listen to me!*" I snapped. "*Find Reed. Reed will love you so much. Always. I'm so proud of you.* You are the smartest woman I know, and I am so honored to have been your sister. Thank you for making me better. *I promise, I love you.*"

Reed's smile ached to think about it.

"Run for your life. Do you understand me?" She began to cry harder. "*Avani, run.*"

She nodded. *Good girl.* She began to struggle with her bonds. I forced myself not to cry.

I was going to have to be strong for her.

One last time.

My throat felt parched, and I swallowed hard, trying to ease the dryness.

My head throbbed, and every fiber of my being yearned to fight, to protect my sister at all costs.

He had used my sister as bait to lure me out.

Rage and fear battled within me, twisting my gut into knots as the sound of muddy boots descended the creaky wooden steps.

Despite the dizziness that threatened to overwhelm me, I forced myself to focus, to stay present.

I wasn't an operative.

I wasn't some super spy with incredible skills.

Focus, Angel, you don't have to be.

You act for a living. Focus.

I shook my head at my sister, ignoring the migraine from hell that pounded behind my eyes.

The darkness was so thick, I could barely make out the figure approaching us or the object gleaming in his hand. I swallowed hard, my heart racing.

"Nice to see you're finally up." His voice sent chills down my spine.

I blinked, trying to clear my vision. Avani was pretending to be asleep, but I knew she was watching through slitted eyes. *Good girl.*

Bile rose in my throat, and fear clawed its way into my chest. I couldn't see him clearly, but I felt his energy, his presence, and it made my body tremble uncontrollably.

Whoever he was, his smile was psychotic as he apprised me.

"Thought you got rid of me?" I shook my head, my pulse pounding in my ears as I caught sight of the metal object in his hand. A bat. *Get away from my sister!*

"What do you want with us?" I managed to choke out.

His face was grotesque in the dim light, twisted with malice.

"Wouldn't you like to know, Alisha."

He hurt Selena. The thought filled me with a renewed sense of determination.

"Let them go."

He laughed, a cold, humorless sound that chilled me to the bone as he pressed the bat against Avani's head. Every drop of blood in my body turned to ice.

"Stop," I pleaded.

"What's the matter, princess?" He grinned, his yellowed teeth flashing in the dim light. I saw my sister flinch, her eyes wide with terror. "No more Reed Whittaker here to save you anymore?"

Reed wouldn't find me in time. The realization slammed into me. *Oh God, I love you, Reed.* I wanted to sob at the thought that consumed me.

I love you, I love you, I love you.

I would never see Reed again.

My girlfriends, my sister...My eyes focused on the man pressing the bat against my sister's face as he watched me, his eyes gleaming with malice.

"I knew you wouldn't take my threats seriously until I gave you something to think about."

"Why are you doing this?" I demanded, my voice trembling.

"Because you ruined my fucking life!"

His roar echoed through the basement, but a wave of relief washed over me as I realized it would draw him away from Avani if I could distract him.

Panic clawed at my chest, but it didn't matter. I would do anything to keep him away from my sister, from Selena.

"You fucking whore!" He was in my face, his hot breath washing over me, and I couldn't stop shaking. "You always take everything."

What was he talking about?

It doesn't matter. Focus.

Reed's eyes were in my vision.

Focus, Angel.

I could see the confusion etched on Avani's face, mirroring my own. "What?"

He was insane, his eyes wild as he invaded my personal space.

"Don't play dumb with me, you little cunt. You know exactly what you did." He started toward my sister, his voice dripping with venom. "Don't worry, one of you will pay."

As he approached her, Avani abandoned her pretense of sleep, squirming against her bonds, barely suppressing a scream.

Reed's voice was in my head.

Selena's hurt. It's just you.

I'm not an operative, Reed.

What if you don't have to be, Angel?

What if you're just as good?

Think fast, Angel.

"You're right," I choked out, the words tasting like bile in the back of my throat. I would say *anything* to keep them alive.

I didn't even know if Selena was still breathing. "It is my fault. I'm so sorry."

He blinked, surprise flickering across his face. "How could you ruin my life?"

"Please, untie me. I'll make it up to you." I couldn't believe the words spilling from my lips, but somehow, I had slipped into the role of the woman I had always presented to the world. A shield.

A protective outer coating of defense. *Think about it like work.*

Reed's eyes, flashing with pride whenever he looked at me, drifted into my mind like smoke.

I wish I could kiss him one last time before I die. I blinked back tears, steeling myself. "I'll make it up to you."

At his leer, I knew exactly what he wanted. I knew what he had done to that girl. Reed hadn't gone into detail, but there was only one thing a man like him could want from me or my sister.

And it was going to be me.

"Why should I believe you after you slept with Whittaker?"

"I didn't sleep with him."

He was furious at my denial. *"Don't fucking—"*

"I didn't," I interrupted, my heart pounding in my chest. *But I did.*

"He was annoying me."

He's the best thing in the world.

"I don't love him."

I love him with all my heart.

And I hate you.

"Maybe I want you instead."

I hope Reed finds you and kills you.

"I want to be with you."

I bit back the bile in my throat.

"Is that so?" The mad glint in his eyes was back as he tossed the bat to the floor and grabbed me roughly.

I couldn't hide my disgust at his hot, foul breath, reeking of alcohol, sweat, and the stench of someone who didn't believe in basic hygiene.

"Or is it a lie because I already killed one of you bitches?"

My sister bit her lip, but a small, pained noise escaped.

Selena had been her shadow, her constant companion. Avani adored Selena.

Kellan's smile flashed through my mind talking about Selena.

Focus, Angel, get him out of the room.

Reed's voice held me together.

Panic gripped me as his focus darted to Avani. "Untie me. Take me upstairs."

I forced the words out, my stomach churning with revulsion. "Maybe you'll believe me when I'm free."

"No!" Avani screamed, her voice raw with desperation. *"No, take me! You can't—"*

We both started shouting over each other, my pleas for him to focus on me mixing with Avani's cries of protest.

"Shut the fuck up!" he roared, silencing us both. Avani was crying, her eyes locked on mine, pleading and I looked away ready to cry even harder.

"You're next," he snarled, aiming the bat at her in a clear threat.

I felt like I was clinging to a tenuous thread as he made his decision.

When his hands darted out, brandishing a knife, I bit back a cry as he cut through my restraints.

The moment I was free, he gripped my arm, hauling me to my feet. I knew he had a knife now, far more dangerous than the bat. I didn't run. I didn't move. I just waited for my chance.

"You'll pay for everything you put me through," he growled, his voice dripping with malice.

He was delusional, lost in his own twisted reality. And I needed to keep playing along, to buy time and find a way out of this nightmare.

I knew none of this was my fault, that his delusions had led us to this moment. If not for his madness, I would be safe in Reed's arms right now, curled up in bed.

The thought brought hot tears to my eyes, but I blinked them back quickly.

Survival mode had kicked in. He dragged me up the stairs to the first floor, my bare feet and knees slamming painfully against the steps.

I winced and cried out as he pulled me into the house, which looked like a reflection of the man himself.

The only light came from the windows, casting an eerie glow over the broken-down furniture, dingy carpet, and moldy walls.

The entire room was bathed in a sickly sepia tone, a physical manifestation of his demented mind.

"Take off your clothes." I bit back a sob as I shakily moved my hands.

They shook wildly as I tugged off the jacket I'd been wearing.

"Faster, else I'll go back down and finish off the other one."

The sheer thought of that had me tugging off quicker until I was in my bra, and his hungry leer made me want to vomit. I had avoided looking at him directly in the face.

When I did, what I saw made me internally scream.

"Tell me who you are." I tried not to shake and failed. "I want to know the man who…wants me so much."

I was in a photoshoot. That's all it was. I bit back the panic I felt.

"Detective White," he said almost in a condescending tone. "I worked hard to get here. Not that women understand what hard work even is."

I was shaking so hard. Fear gripped my throat. This was it? This was it.

"Why me?" There was that glint of madness again. "Why am I special?" He was a serial killer. Gabriel had said he was obsessed with me.

But I didn't get it. I didn't understand and maybe I didn't need to. He was clearly crazy. I was shaking as I moved to take off my bra, every part of me screaming not to.

"Because you ruined my life, you stupid bitch. You cost me my life." He motioned with the knife. "Get on your knees."

I swallowed hard. "And if I said no, if I wanted to know why you do this?" I added. "You're going to kill me anyway, the least you can do is tell me."

White reached into his pants. *"I said get on your fucking knees!"*

I think I played my luck too much.

Villains don't ever explain their actions; *they just kill because they can.*

He closed the distance between us, ripping my bra off, and I shrieked. I couldn't help it. He was grabbing me, and I tried to stop him, to block him.

I kicked out, shrieked. He slammed my head into the wall, his fist slamming into my head.

A broken cry left my lips. Searing pain. Reed. I saw spots as my vision began to blur.

"You stupid little—!" I felt his hands at my throat. Reed.

It happened too fast. I felt myself beginning to black out—*Reed!*

And then he was gone.

White's head snapped back violently, the glass shattering in the apartment, as he dropped to the floor in front of me, blood everywhere behind him. I didn't understand what was happening.

I hit the floor painfully, crawling back, and tried to tell myself not to black out.

There wasn't enough air.

I was freezing, naked, clutching at the floor. Avani. *Run.*

Something exploded then, a door, something—I heard shouting. Yelling.

The force of the blast knocked me out.

CHAPTER 56
ALISHA

DIMLY, I BECAME AWARE OF PEOPLE'S VOICES, THEIR WORDS FILTERING through the heavy fog in my mind.

The sterile scent of disinfectant tickled my nostrils, grounding me in reality.

"Why isn't she waking up?" I recognized Reed's voice, his tone laced with concern and desperation.

The familiar sound sent a weak flutter through my chest, even in my semi-conscious state.

A calmer woman's voice was soothing him. "Mr. Whittaker, she was assaulted twenty-four hours ago. She needs rest right now."

"Reed, don't—" Gabriel's voice cut through the haze, a warning in his tone.

The unexpected presence of his voice piqued my curiosity, even as exhaustion pulled at me.

A soft beeping accompanied my descent back into slumber, the rhythmic sound oddly comforting as I drifted off.

The darkness enveloped me, carrying me away from the confusion and pain.

I don't know how long I was asleep, but in my dreams, my Mum and I were having a picnic.

The warmth of the sun on my skin felt so real, the scent of grass and wildflowers filling the air.

She knew I had gotten my deal with EllaBeauty.

I felt her push my hair behind my ear like she had when I was a kid, and I was…happy.

For a moment, all the fear and confusion melted away.

But then she started saying things, things I didn't expect my Mum to say. Minor contusion. Risk of swelling. Brain injury.

The medical jargon jarred me, shattering the peaceful illusion.

What are you talking about?

I wanted to ask, but the words wouldn't come.

The dream began to fade, reality seeping in at the edges.

Another time, I felt someone squeezing my fingers, and cold lips pressed against my wrist.

The sensation was startlingly real, anchoring me briefly to consciousness.

The contrast between the warmth of the hand and the coolness of the lips sent a shiver through me.

"He's going to turn into me if he loses you."

Gabriel? What was he doing here?

"Gabriel, she's not waking up." Reed's voice was barely a whisper, filled with anguish. The pain in his words tugged at my heart—urging me to fight through the fog that enveloped my mind.

When I finally woke up, I opened my eyes slowly.

The dim light of the room felt like daggers, and I blinked rapidly, trying to adjust.

Everything felt heavy, as if gravity had increased tenfold while I slept.

A noise escaped my lips, somewhere between a groan and a whimper, and Reed's face came into view.

His bright eyes were filled with worry.

I'd never seen him look so vulnerable, and it scared me.

"Gabriel, get Perla," his voice was low as he leaned over me. "Lish, baby, look at me."

Why is the room so dark?

"Avani…Selena." I remembered them, fear gripping my heart.

The last memories I had of them were hazy, tinged with panic.

"They're fine. Kieran's keeping Avani occupied in her room. She's in good hands."

Reed's voice was reassuring, but I didn't know who Kieran was.

If Reed trusted him, I did. But a nagging worry persisted.

He didn't mention Selena.

"Selena's recovering," he added quickly, but the worry in his eyes told me there was more to the story.

Kellan. The name flashed through my mind, accompanied by a surge of guilt.

What had happened to him?

"Reed," his eyes never left my face, and I saw they were rimmed red. "I was with my Mum."

He was rapidly blinking, his lips pressing together in an effort to maintain composure.

Before he could respond, Gabriel walked back in with another woman, a blonde doctor with stern features but a quiet voice.

She immediately began checking me, her cool hands a stark contrast to the warmth of Reed's touch.

As she explained what had happened, I tried to focus, but her words seemed to swim in and out of clarity.

I had a concussion, she said, but the stress of everything—the breakup, moving, being kidnapped—had caused my brain to shut down.

I didn't even remember half of what had happened, and Doc Perla assured me that it was normal.

Her words were meant to be comforting, but they only heightened my sense of disorientation.

"I've had some people who endure head injuries lose their memories leading up to the trauma because of trauma even prior to that. I don't know what stressors you were under prior to your kidnapping," she said, her clinical tone at odds with the gravity of her words.

My eyes darted around the room, seeking comfort.

Gabriel was a statue on the other end.

Reed's face was dark as he watched Doc Perla, his jaw clenched tightly.

"Your brain scan shows that you have sustained a mild traumatic brain injury, also known as a concussion. When your head was slammed into the wall, your brain..."

I barely understood her, my focus drawn to Reed's stony expression.

The medical jargon blurred together, but the gravity of the situation wasn't lost on me.

"...I let Reed know he should look for headaches, memory loss..."

As Doctor Perla continued, explaining the need for sunglasses and a dark room, avoiding blue light...

"I'm not trying to scare you, and I don't think this will be the case for you. I'm not saying it will happen to you, but I told Reed to err on the side of caution. If you start forgetting him," she teased. "We'd have a problem."

"I can't imagine forgetting him."

Despite my assertion, I couldn't remember what had happened.

One moment I was sitting at the diner, and then...nothing. The gap in my memory was terrifying.

Reed didn't smile as he asked Doc Perla a few questions, his concern evident in every tense line of his body.

My gaze shifted to Gabriel, whose ear twitched as he turned to me.

His face was cold and impassive, but something in his eyes spoke of a deep, hidden emotion.

When Doc Perla finished, I nodded and Reed accepted the medication.

I asked about payment, but Perla and Reed shot Gabriel a glance.

He waved a hand, seemingly annoyed.

As Reed and the doctor spoke discreetly, I could feel his reluctance to leave my side. It wasn't until Gabriel moved that Reed finally looked away, turning his back to focus on Perla.

They had made up.

Gabriel handed me water, his movements gentle despite his cold demeanor.

As I sipped slowly, rising with his help, I found myself reaching for his hand.

"What brings you here?" I whispered.

He took my hand quietly, his grip cold, but gentle as he sat down on my bed.

"You owed me brunch," he said after a beat, his tone holding as much warmth as it could. "I needed to make sure you didn't renege on your promise."

Holding out my free hand, I offered my pinky. "I wouldn't dream of it."

He stared down at my offered pinky, a flicker of emotion passing over his face before he looped his finger around mine.

I tried to pretend I was the one whose hands were shaking. I gripped his hands tighter, and in turn, he squeezed back.

Later that day, I saw my sister.

The relief that washed over me upon seeing her unharmed was almost overwhelming.

Avani's presence was like a balm to my frayed nerves, grounding me.

Kieran, a tall amber-eyed man assigned to her, stood nearby.

His presence was both reassuring and a stark reminder of the danger we had faced.

"It's not Kellan's fault. It was mine." I told Gabriel.

The absence of my bodyguard was painfully noticeable, and worry for Selena gnawed at me.

How is he faring?

I made sure Gabriel took that information to Kellan, not wanting him to bear the weight of guilt for what had happened.

As the full story unfolded, each detail hit me.

Reed finding me unconscious, Gabriel and Kellan rescuing Selena, Avani's trauma...

The reality of what we had all endured settled over me like a heavy blanket.

I held my sister for a long time, feeling her body shake with silent sobs.

There was something different about her, a shadow in her eyes that hadn't been there before.

White had taken something from her, and the knowledge filled me with a deep, simmering anger.

Gabriel explained the situation to us both, his words direct and unflinching. Reed listened silently, letting Gabriel deliver the harsh truths.

Their dynamic fascinated me—two sides of the same coin, balancing each other out.

Despite the pain of hearing what had happened, I noticed how Gabriel softened, especially towards Avani.

When it was time to leave the hospital, Reed helped me change in the dimly lit room.

As I caught sight of myself in the mirror, I barely recognized the woman staring back at me.

Bruises marred my throat, and my eyes held a haunted look that made my stomach churn.

Reed's silence as he helped me was both comforting and unsettling.

As we stepped into the hallway, I was struck by an explosion of color and fragrance. Flowers filled every available space, their sweet scent almost overwhelming.

"Where did all these flowers come from?" I gaped, my eyes wide with disbelief.

Behind me, Gabriel's livid expression at the floral display puzzled me.

Did Gabriel not like flowers?

Odd, considering he was a romantic.

The journey back to K2 felt surreal.

As we entered, I was struck by how different everything looked.

"Is this..." I trailed off, not recognizing a single inch of the space.

The chrome and black had been replaced with warmth and color. Transforming the once impersonal penthouse into something entirely new.

"I made a few changes," Reed said softly, his words laden with unspoken meaning.

A few changes?

He had *completely* transformed the place.

The stark contrast between my memories of the apartment and its current state left me breathless.

Flowers adorned every surface, their gentle fragrance filling the air.

The once-black furniture had been replaced with soft white pieces that seemed to glow in the natural light flooding through the floor-to-ceiling windows.

Despite the abundance of sunlight, warm lamps were scattered throughout.

Everywhere I looked, there were personal touches—throw pillows, vases, books.

His apartment looks like—

"It's your home too," Reed said softly, his words stopping me in my tracks. "Both of you."

"How?" I breathed, my eyes wide as I took in every detail.

Beside me, Avani and Kieran's expressions mirrored my own amazement.

Reed's soft smile held a hint of shyness as he began to unstrap his bulletproof vest.

"I got a new decorator," he said simply, but the weight behind his words was anything but simple.

Avani's voice broke through my reverie as she explored the living room. "I don't think Reed shops at antique stores..."

No, he did not.

As I made my way down the hall to what was now our room, each step felt monumental. I was taking in the new space.

The weight of everything that had happened, everything that had changed, pressed down on me.

My hands shook as I slipped out of my clothes, the fabric feeling suddenly foreign against my skin.

The knowledge that my sister was safe with Kieran, brought a measure of comfort.

Avani was here.

Reed was here.

We were all safe.

I needed to burn my clothes, to destroy any physical reminder of what had happened.

Stepping into the shower, the first spray of hot water hit my skin like a shock, forcing a gasp from my lips.

As I sat there, steam rising around me, the full weight of my situation crashed down.

Mum, I don't remember what happened. And I'm terrified.

CHAPTER 57
REED

I LED AVANI TO THE GUEST ROOM, KIERAN FOLLOWING CLOSE BEHIND.

The space glowed with warm light from the new lamps, and I watched Avani's eyes widen as she took it all in.

Under different circumstances, her reaction would have made me smile.

As I showed them around, my initial reservations about Kieran O'Hara faded.

Despite being the newest Titan member and a former Irish mob associate, he'd proven himself invaluable.

When I couldn't leave Alisha's side, too distraught to function, Kieran had stepped up to watch over Avani.

Gabriel had hired Kieran full-time to keep an eye on him. But Avani's safety my primary concern and I was grateful for his presence.

K2 was secure, but having Kieran as her shadow offered additional peace of mind.

The youngest O'Hara brother stood an impressive six-foot-two, all muscle, with a grin reminiscent of Kellan's.

Compared to his brothers, Kieran seemed the most approachable, the most "normal" of the bunch. I encouraged them to make themselves at home.

I'd gone overboard, buying out nearly an entire store to ensure Avani had everything she might need.

Kieran, too, was welcome to whatever would make him comfortable.

Leaving them settled, I retreated to my own space. With Alisha.

The sound of running water told me Alisha was in the shower, likely washing away the lingering scent of hospital.

She'd been in and out for days, and fear still gripped me.

Perla's assurances that Alisha's body was healing did little to ease my terror. I'd come so close to losing her.

The memory of my breakdown in front of Gabriel surfaced.

"She's not waking up," I'd said, my voice breaking. "What am I going to do?"

In that moment, I'd seen a rare vulnerability in Gabriel's eyes, and a horrifying realization struck me—he had lived through this.

Isobel hadn't made it.

Gabriel had remained silent, but his understanding was palpable.

The guilt of failing to protect Alisha, of not being there when she needed me most, had left me raw and exposed.

In Gabriel's quiet empathy, I found both comfort and a deeper, shared pain.

I couldn't begin to imagine what Avani had endured. She had been mostly awake through all of it.

One moment of carelessness from her guard, who'd assumed she was with Kellan and Alisha, and everything had fallen apart.

As I waited for Alisha to emerge from the shower, the sound of water hitting tiles was almost deafening.

My heart clenched at the thought of what she had endured. I sat outside the bathroom, waiting patiently, minutes ticking by like hours.

When I knew she would be finished, I quietly entered the bathroom, steeling myself.

The sight shattered my heart. Alisha was curled up on the floor, knees drawn to her chest, body shaking with sobs drowned out by running water.

Steam enveloped her like a shroud, turning the bathroom into another world.

I stripped off my clothes and gathered her trembling form into my arms. Her tears soaked my skin as she clung to me, each sob feeling like a knife twisting in my gut. And I couldn't get her close enough.

In that moment, I silently vowed that if White were still alive, I would personally drag him to Gabriel's cabin and make him suffer.

I stayed with Alisha until Gabriel texted.

She crawled into bed in Avani's room, and I checked on Kieran in the kitchen, heating food for everyone, before I left.

Reluctantly, I departed, the weight of the situation heavy on my shoulders.

My team needed me, and with Gabriel's bedside manner being practically nonexistent—I had to be there for them.

Selena's condition was still critical, and as both Gabriel's and my operative?

I felt deeply responsible for her well-being.

Gabriel's texts had been sporadic, but he was keeping me updated. He knew if he didn't, I'd find out anyway.

With a heavy heart, I made my way to the clinic, bracing myself for what awaited me.

As I stepped in front of Selena's room, the scene before me was all too familiar.

Kellan sat beside her bed, his white tee still stained with dried blood. His head was bowed, hands clasped around Selena's limp fingers.

The usually lighthearted operative was gone, replaced by a man I intimately understood—I had been in his shoes mere days ago.

The only difference? My girl woke up.

I couldn't find it in me to be angry with him.

As I watched Kellan, memories of Selena's laughter and sassy teases flooded my mind.

The weight of pain settled in my chest. I knew exactly how he felt, the agonizing wait, the desperate hope.

"He isn't leaving her side," Gabriel's voice materialized beside me, his presence as silent as a wraith.

"I'll handle them. Garrett will switch out Watts when he wants it. Perla has a female nurse, Nisha, when Selena wakes up she'll have someone else other than us."

He had changed out of his black gear and into a suit, but the shadows under his eyes revealed his lack of sleep. I didn't miss what he said: if she woke up.

"She's been through a lot."

I didn't know the details like Gabriel did, and we'd split up tasks like always. I could sense his restlessness, a coiled energy seeking an outlet, and with Garrett switching with Kellan, I knew he was on the prowl for a fight.

I didn't know who he could go toe to toe with. Gabriel's expression remained impassive as he gazed at Selena through the window.

I knew him well enough to detect the slight tremor in his hands, which he had buried in his pockets.

"I'm going to have a talk with Giroux," he stated, his tone laced with a quiet fury.

Gabriel had a lot of political leverage over the years.

I knew Lt. Giroux wouldn't be a Lt. any longer by the look on Gabriel's face.

No, he'd flip over the entire precinct.

Gabriel moved away from the window.

I fell into step with him, our movements silent and precise. He let out a breath, breaking the tense silence.

"I already asked what happened. Watts told me he got into a fight with her." I recalled asking him about that at the diner. "You know what happened?"

Gabriel nodded. And he wasn't mad. Gabriel's mouth turned down and he shook his head.

"I see why you picked Watts. She's stubborn. Watts is good for her. I thought moving Nate would help her. Turns out Nate was the problem this entire time."

And then he explained to me what had happened and I gaped. I didn't know *any* of that. And once I did? My fury was redirected at someone else. Nate.

"I'll settle Nate."

He nodded. "That should have never happened."

Despite his displeasure with the entire situation, I could tell Gabriel didn't blame Kellan. I didn't feel guilty for losing my temper with the young operative earlier, but seeing the devastation on his face, I knew he was in deep.

"Where's White's body?" I asked, my voice low and controlled.

"Killian is on the cleanup." Gabriel paused. "He asked how you got a sniper so fast?"

I stopped breathing. *"What did you just say?"* I turned to him and his eyes were watching me. "What do you mean *how did I get the sniper? I thought you got it.*"

Gabriel's eyes widened and there was a glint in his eyes. I saw his brain working and mine...

"Who wasn't there?" I racked my brain. "Sullivan's disabled, Garrett was here, and Nate was with Gemma."

I looked at Gabriel. I knew his face mirrored mine.

Someone shot White and saved Lish. *Why?*

"Not our guys. Nobody said anything. Killian's guys showed up after." Gabriel let out a shaky breath. Kill shots to the head were precision.

Gabriel said quietly. "Evie found anomalies through her program, the cameras blocking out Selena were wiped."

Something went through his eyes, a haunted look, as he said softly. "They're back in the city." *Back?*

"You've seen this before?"

A chill ran down my spine when Gabriel nodded. He passed me a card. Shiny black with gold claw marks slashing across the center.

"Who is this?"

"I was hoping you'd find out." He paused, I saw the emotion burning in his eyes. "I'll talk to Killian. He should track that, Aidan's keeping him in the city for something else, I'll find out in the next week. Killian wants to know if you want the house torched."

"I'll do it myself." I would relish it. "Kieran's with my girls."

Someone had shot White. Someone that wasn't us. *For us? Or for them?*

Gabriel didn't smile. "I see why Aidan wanted me to keep an eye on Kieran. Matteo DuPont is the investor in Kieran's club *De Nuit.*"

Which means the youngest O'Hara hadn't come to New York for shits and giggles.

Matteo, whom I'd looked into a while ago, hadn't been wrong about defiling Alisha.

The kind of things Matteo was into required a private sex club.

Gabriel explained to me what *Maison De Nuit* was.

The thought of Matteo knowing he was a monster, admitting it, and never ruining something good made me see him in a different light.

"Kieran's close to the DuPonts."

And he owns that club.

Gabriel nodded, focused. "He considers Matteo his brother."

On the subject of brothers, another face entered my vision from weeks ago, someone I hadn't investigated, too preoccupied with Lish.

"Who's the third DuPont brother?" Gabriel raised a brow. No doubt he'd have that information by the end of the day. I could see him mentally noting it.

"A third DuPont." I told him how Matteo never introduced him but I could tell.

He's a mercenary. Silencer on his gun. The clothes he wore. Except we had no idea who he worked for. Gabriel nodded mentally taking notes.

His eyes flickered over to the other side of the hall.

"There is one more issue I need you to handle, the sooner the better." I glanced at Gabriel, whose eyes were cold. "I didn't know Doc Perla hired him. I think because she thought he was related to you, it would be fine. He's at your three o'clock."

I hadn't seen the lone figure standing by the desk, but I knew that face.

Gabriel's voice was low. "I didn't know he worked here. I spoke to Perla, she said you can fire him tonight if you want."

I watched my younger half-brother, Adam, look over at me, so familiar yet so different from the kid I used to know. His dark blonde hair was styled and his eyes took me in.

Adam.

The one whose father hated me for my existence.

The one who'd blamed me for his mischief, and then finally, the one who'd slowly looked confused at me as though he didn't understand why I even existed.

"I'll handle it."

Gabriel nodded, looking different from his usual stern self.

"Evie moved out of the manor." *Oh. Fucking. Shit.* "Did you talk to her recently?" I didn't give anything away.

"Did I?"

His eyes narrowed. "I'm serious."

Really? I couldn't tell.

"I did. She'll be fine."

"It is a boy." He was seething now. *"Who? Is he the reason for all these flowers?"*

The hallway was covered in them, enough flowers that Gabriel explained the nurses had wondered if Selena had an admirer, setting Kellan off.

Bundles of some catering service had come in, where the hospital staff thought they came from Gabriel.

I didn't think Lucas would. I didn't know who sent them. But everyone was pleased with them.

Lucas loves your sister.

And you're going to lose your shit when you find out.

"She's not with him anymore. Let her grow up. Did you open the necklace?" I shifted gears.

He shook his head. I saw that look.

I give it a week before he finds out.

We'd been focused on all the other crises around us. But now?

Nothing would stop Gabriel.

"You should find your jewel thief." For a moment, I said nothing. A multitude of emotions passed in his eyes. *Is this his hell?*

Did you die with Isobel?

I understood him after almost losing Alisha.

We weren't just partners, but shadows of each other.

Two halves of the same coin. He had loved and lost.

He was haunted by the woman who'd never give him peace.

He protected Evie because Isobel, the love of his life, had asked him to before she died.

I would bend over backwards to protect Avani had anything happened to Lish; I would hold her so fucking close.

"I saw a photo of your wife," I said softly. "That's why you kissed Lish. You wanted her all this time because she looked like she was yours."

But Alisha didn't look exactly like Isobel; the faint similarity there was probably overwhelming for him.

Gabriel remained silent, his eyes filled with a pain that I now understood all too well though.

"I forgive you," I said, my voice firm and unwavering. "But she isn't Isobel. And if you touch her ever again, I'm leaving the team. I promise you, I will find the key. But you need to trust me. Is there anything else besides the key?"

"No...I have a lead. You might not like it."

"When do I ever fucking like anything you do?"

Gabriel said nothing.

I exhaled. "Why doesn't the necklace open without the key?"

Gabriel was just as fond of puzzles as I was.

"I had an old operative make the key with her name in a sequence. It's why you can't pick it."

But of course he did.

"What happens if you do?"

His voice was soft as he said it, his eyes faraway. This experience was too much even for him. "The entire thing breaks."

And he couldn't have that.

"Where is she buried?"

He'd never mentioned her grave.

I didn't know if he went to visit her.

"I never found the body. I think they took it—"

I felt my chest and throat tighten as Gabriel never got to bury her.

Because some villains were worse.

Was she tortured like Selena?

Kellan's hell was just beginning.

"I checked for a long time. I think they dumped her body somewhere…"

I could see how much emotion he kept locked away the lower his voice got.

"After…an old contact of mine told me her sister, Evie, their mom, had been terminally ill. I showed up and took her in. It was the least I could do after I failed—"

He failed. I saved my girl. *He can't even say her name.*

"I'm sorry." I couldn't find a pile of bones, but I could try. Anything to help him.

"Why do you care about…?"

Because I think you died with her.

I think Isobel didn't leave empty-handed, she took Gabriel's soul.

I could see the haunted look in his eyes.

He was going to off himself if he didn't find peace. I knew that look.

Emotions burned underneath that I felt I was staring at through a melting glacier.

That was Gabriel.

He loved her.

He has her name tattooed on his heart.

"Just trust me."

After a long moment, he tipped his head in a small nod.

CHAPTER 58
REED

After Gabriel, I had one more bird to kill.

I almost didn't recognize my younger half-brother.

What were the odds he'd be working at this hospital? *On this day?*

I took in his even six feet, dark blonde hair worn a tad long, his features warm and nervous as he glanced at me.

"Adam."

"Reed, it's good to see you again." His voice held a tentative hope, tinged with a hint of something else.

"It's just pure coincidence, I work here with Doctor Perla. I'm guessing by the way your scary friend was looking at me though, I don't work here anymore?"

He ran a hand through his hair, a gesture that reminded me of my own nervous habit.

Gabriel owned a lot of powerful investments, one of which was this standby hospital for emergencies.

I glanced back at Gabriel, who was staring at Selena with a frown.

I remained silent, my gaze unwavering, a myriad of emotions swirling beneath the surface. Memories of our shared past, the hurt, the anger, the longing for a connection I'd never truly had.

Looking as awkward and uncomfortable as I felt, Adam wrung his hands.

"I'm sorry." His honest brown eyes looked into mine, eyes that I remembered differently from our past.

Eyes that now held a depth of understanding and regret.

"After you left, nothing was the same in the house. Mom and Dad—"
He trailed off, but I already knew.

They were dead.

"Stop," I said, my voice sharp and cutting, trying to mask the pain that threatened to resurface.

He pressed his lips together, his eyes searching mine, seeking a glimmer of forgiveness, of acceptance.

"I didn't care then, and I don't care now."

But even as the words left my mouth, I knew they weren't entirely true.

A part of me, buried deep, had always cared.

"Why did you come to New York?"

A moment passed before he answered, his voice quiet, filled with a longing I recognized all too well.

"I thought I'd find you."

"And then what? Work things out between us?"

It was a laughable thought after finding brothers among my own people. But there was a flicker of hope in my chest, a tiny spark that refused to be extinguished.

Adam shook his head, looking all of thirteen instead of what I figured was at least twenty-five.

"I finished med school out here," he said, a hint of pride in his voice. "I thought you might need someone full-time for your team. But something tells me I'd be the last person you'd want."

Correct.

Except I caught the look in his eyes.

I recognized it from Avani when she told me about a new book series she found, and Evie when she'd been happy to be in Alisha's group chat.

When they wanted to show me something they were proud of.

"I finished med school. He'd always wanted to be a doctor. Help people."

I looked at my half-brother, really looked at him.

He looked so much like his father.

And I looked *too* much like mine.

Alisha's words rang in my head.

A little bit of kindness. Reed, just a little bit of kindness.

Time had changed him from the spoiled younger sibling who was doted on by his father to someone who apparently had become a doctor and gone to med school, judging by his ID.

Something caught my eye. My heart stopped a little.

"You changed your name?" *Why the fuck would he do that?*

"James was a piece of shit, I didn't want to be related to him." I blinked in surprise.

Adam Russell was now Adam Whittaker. I swallowed. My Dad's name.

I didn't even know Adam–

"What did he do to you?"

There was no hesitation when he said. "Beat the shit out of me after he lost his favorite punching bag."

The knot in my chest tightened.

My brain worked for a long moment, processing this new information.

I pulled out my wallet.

We had the office in Midtown, Sullivan could get him settled in. I handed him the card with the address.

"This isn't anything official. This is a trial run. Liam Sullivan will be in touch with you. I expect you to be on call. Try not to piss off Gabriel."

I didn't show any emotion at the hope that shone in his eyes as he took the card, but something within me stirred.

A feeling I'd thought long buried.

"It's a start."

He nodded. "A start...I'm sorry, Reed."

"I know, kid."

I wasn't ready to shake his hand or hug him, but this was a start.

CHAPTER 59
ALISHA

"How is she?" I asked softly, as Reed and I sat on his bed, our legs hanging over the side, holding hands.

It was the one time we'd been on the bed not making love.

Reed had come back home from the hospital where I knew Selena was.

"Not good," he admitted honestly.

We'd talked about being more open with each other, not keeping secrets, and working together on being vulnerable.

"When I left, Selena woke up, screaming down the hospital..."

He didn't look freaked out so much as he wanted to find White and kill him several times over.

"Gabriel's not pleased with any of this. White caused more of a mess than he left behind with the other women."

White had been a serial killer.

All of his victims had been women of some minority descent, and some had been women who had trusted him as a police officer to come to him.

The thought of his basement holding their remains chilled me to the bone, especially when I considered the other women he'd done this to, the ones who hadn't made it.

"It's not Kellan's fault," I said, remembering how exhausted he had been in those last few days. It felt like our fault in a way.

Reed nodded in agreement. "What are we going to do?"

With Avani staying with us in the other room, I couldn't help but think about the recent developments in her life.

She'd found out earlier that a request had come from someone with connections in the school board, asking her to be excused and allowed to take classes from home until further notice.

I could practically see Gabriel scaring the crap out of people to get that done.

Gabriel had also scheduled a therapist to help her, and I knew he had her number since she mentioned he'd messaged her.

It was odd seeing Gabriel care for my family as much as Reed had, but both of them split tasks and swooped in, taking out different avenues of issues.

Right now, Kieran was with Avani in her room, both of them watching a movie.

He was taking really good care of my sister, and I didn't want to intrude on them noticing she calmed down around him.

I was worried sick, and after Reed had left, Gemma had stopped by with Lara, who was wearing real clothes this time, and carrying enough flowers to make the entire apartment look like it had been someone's wedding.

At the mention of Gabriel, Reed told me the story he knew. Even the case files he looked up were hidden.

"No wonder he looked haunted," I said, my heart aching for the pain Gabriel must have endured.

Reed agreed. "I'm worried about him. Evie tried so hard to help him."

On that note, I remembered something. "About that..." I began, telling him about going down to get mail after ordering a few things for Avani and myself. "I didn't know Evie and Lucas were a thing."

His eyes narrowed. "Evie doesn't live with Gabriel anymore...Lucas and her are..."

He let out a breath and muttered about Gabriel killing him.

"I still don't know why Gabriel hates the Devereaux's so much," I said, curious about the backstory.

As he explained it to me in bits and pieces, my eyes widened in horror. "You're not joking, are you? This is why you keep all your secrets. Gabriel is going to murder Lucas when he finds out." When, not if. Because Gabriel would.

He nodded again.

"I certainly hope you're not as brutish when Avani finally finds someone who falls for her."

At that, Reed's expression changed. "You like me brutish...I never even imagined Avani dating. She's such a cinnamon roll. I thought she'd stay single forever."

I couldn't help laughing at that.

"She's adjusting a lot better now with a particular someone in her room." I smiled at Reed's eyes widening in realization.

He gaped. "Kieran? He's fired."

"Absolutely not, I adore him. He's so sweet to her..." I told Reed about all the times I'd caught Kieran and Avani together. Reed's expression was one of horror and I laughed harder.

"You cannot do what Gabriel did to Evie, if you want Avani to come to you in the future..."

I talked to Reed for a while about Kieran. Avani. Relationships.

He looked bemused by it.

I smiled distracting him trailing a finger down his shirt. "Now that you've saved the city and got your girl, what's on your to-do list?"

A slow grin spread over Reed's face, his eyes sparkling with mischief and adoration.

"I'm going to take you out on a date."

EPILOGUE

REED

It took time for Alisha to recover.

She experienced headaches and lapses in memory, having no recollection of how she had woken up in the hospital.

The last thing she remembered was the diner, with the entire interaction with White erased from her mind.

Dr. Perla explained that this was completely normal, a form of selective dissociative memory loss often seen in patients who had experienced trauma.

"Amnesia?" I gaped, my heart clenching at the thought of Alisha forgetting our time together.

Perla waved a hand, sucking her teeth. "No, it's not that dramatic. It's just traumatic memory loss."

She went on to say. "A lot of patients forget things. Some of my patients who were victims of domestic violence or child abuse forget a lot of their memories. I've had patients with gunshot wounds and head injuries severe enough to cause them to forget people in their life. The brain has interesting ways of coping with trauma. It really should be explored more..."

As Perla delved into a patient from years ago, I sat there, my mind racing, praying that Alisha wouldn't wake up one day having forgotten our memories together.

If she had, I silently vowed to win her over every single day until she was mine once more.

Days later, when Alisha was a bit better, I took her out on our first real date to somewhere quiet, renting out the entire place for the night.

Even then, she thought it would be a good idea to wear a vibrator without telling me.

When it accidentally slid on in the middle of dinner, I had to haul her into my lap and swallow her orgasms with my mouth.

Thankfully, I had thought ahead and secured the entire place for ourselves.

It had been fun, but we hadn't made it back home. I just took her in the car, and made out with her on the elevator ride up.

Avani was still staying with us with Kieran, and Alisha teased that we were parents who had to be quiet otherwise the kids would know.

And damned if that didn't sound like home. Something I wanted in the future.

Now, back in the apartment, in the privacy of my closet that Alisha had grown to love filling with all her colors, I held her tightly to me, the doors closed so I could make out with her.

"There is one thing I have to tell you," I said, cradling her face in my hands.

I walked over to the case where I was supposed to keep jewelry.

Unlike Gabriel, I didn't have fancy shit, but I had one thing to show her.

Lifting the case, I found the panel underneath and pulled it out, revealing Isobel's necklace gleaming in the light.

Alisha gasped. "He gave it back to you?"

I nodded, explaining the significance of the key and the search for it.

"Gabriel said he trusted me with it, and he wanted the other half, the key, before he took it back. He said it was safer with me."

K2 wasn't easy to break into.

Even if someone did, it would trigger alerts and lockdowns.

Nobody was making it out even if they got in.

"He wanted this so badly, yet he trusted you with it." Alisha marveled at the necklace, understanding the depth of Gabriel's trust. "You're going to help Gabriel find his other half?"

"Angel," I leveled a look at her. "We are going to help find Gabriel's other half."

I paused. "Lucy is hiding, I know it. That's why she said she's going on a date."

"Where do you think she is?" Once Alisha had realized the extent of what I do, she'd accepted it and listened intently.

"You think she'd leave the country?"

"I have no clue. I'm trying to find her, and I'll sit you down and teach you some of the codes we use."

I loved that she looked thrilled. If I had known her eyes would light up at that, I would have told her sooner.

As she kissed me, I held the necklace tight, my mind already working on ways to move forward
. Alisha and I had talked about Gabriel several times, deciding on the best approach.

You said he left his old life? He started Titan with just you and Evie. I think he wanted a family.

After losing Isobel. I don't think he was asking me to come home with him that day at Poppy. Not me...her.

I don't blame him, do you? No. Not anymore.

Not after experiencing the last few days. In his shoes. In his Hell. That's why he held Evie tight.

I would've done the same with Avani who still resembled Alisha enough, amplifying my love for her.

I didn't want Alisha to stay away from Titan because of Gabriel, but I didn't know how to reconcile the two of them just yet.

He needs a friend, Alisha had said, her compassion always leaving me in awe.

She brought up how Gabriel was handling everything for Avani and Selena, making sure Perla checked up on her while he took over both mine and his side of Titan.

It was hard on him—I knew that much.

"Gabriel is still the boy who saved you from being bullied, who found you years ago. And he lost his wife. You didn't see his eyes. He is not the sum of his sins. People are multi-faceted..."

Her words left me disarmed.

She was more emotionally intelligent than I was. It was the kind of answer I'd expect from her.

I held everyone apart—except for her. Alisha was still doing her career. But I let her in more with what I could.

And Alisha had standing brunch days with Gabriel. In turn, he was doing better, mellowing out more around her.

I found it less threatening to my relationship.

I was just happy my brother was healing. Gabriel.

Not Adam. Who I didn't know how to approach.

I talked to Alisha about my other brother, Adam, talking about a way forward with him. If there was one. Alisha stepped in there.

I had laid into Nate, not giving a shit, with everything I knew now about Selena and Kellan. Because there was a lot people didn't recover from.

I was worried deep down that Selena might not come back to the team.

And if that happened, Kellan would follow. I had told Alisha everything in the days when I'd been helping Gabriel.

"This is so exciting!" Alisha's giddy expression was infectious, and I grinned, watching her squeal about a treasure hunt, wherever the treasure was.

I slipped the necklace back under the panel.

"Is the necklace safe here? I mean, with how valuable it is and the entire story behind it, I feel like you should've made a copy of it and hidden the real one, you know, like the two-million-dollar one Ella-Beauty gave me for the film festival I went to."

She chewed her bottom lip. "I know it's K2, but I would hate to find out the answer to that question...Why are you looking at me like that?"

Because she was better than me in every way.

"Because you're perfect," I said, floored. "I was going to wait—" This fucking woman.

I said. "Come with me." I fucking loved her. I loved her. "I love you."

I had planned to wait, but seeing her joy in my trust, my truth, and her never-ending support of my team made me want to share everything with her.

"I had this made in case anything ever happened to my office. Think of it like a bunker...but better."

Her eyes went comically wide as I swung open the wall of part of my closet, revealing the concealed space that mirrored the closet.

"This is your super-secret hiding spot?" she asked in an awed whisper. "This has been here this entire time?"

I nodded, feeling a twinge of embarrassment mingled with excitement at sharing this part of myself with her. "What are we doing here?" she asked, still whispering.

I laughed at her whisper. "There's no one else here, Angel."

Walking around, I showed her my tech center and the boards of things I worked on, including cases I needed to work through, plotting for the team, and some of the future new hires I wanted.

"I was wondering why you'd vanish into the closet..." Alisha looked around, amazed.

My lips stretched wide while she walked around, taking it in.

"I have the office, but it's a bit of a risk. I keep my secrets here." I paused, wondering if I should—*Give her a chance.* "Can you keep my secret, baby?"

I wanted to show her something I'd been working on.

I loved the eager look in her eyes now that I had made her my partner, my equal.

I opened a drawer inside the desk in the room, and she blinked. *Twice.*

"I cannot believe you," she said, shaking her head in disbelief.

"You are right. It was worth a lot of trouble. Why make it easy?"

I had made two copies of Gabriel's necklace.

The one outside was a dud, one I expected someone to come after at some point.

But this one? This was the real one.

Which meant...

She continued to whisper. "You think someone is coming for this?"

Smart girl. I felt my throat work. "I know so."

The key didn't matter. If K2 was ever under attack, I needed a safeguard in all ways.

Something was coming.

They are back in the city...And I didn't know who *they* were. I could feel it in the air, in my gut, the unease didn't stop.

All I could do was hope I was prepared.

Lucy was gone. *No trace of her.*

Someone was trying to kill Lucas Devereaux, according to Gabriel.

I got the feeling this wasn't over. It had only begun. And it was all related to this fucking necklace.

I slid the real necklace into the drawer in this room, my eyes landing on one of the boards holding the black card with gold claw marks on it.

When I turned back, Alisha was looking at the screens. "Is this one big screen or..."

"It can be."

"Do you have cameras in here?"

I nodded, confused by her questions until I saw the look in her eyes. "Baby—" *Again?* My dick was already hard.

This woman was going to drain me and I would love every second of it. I noticed the glint enter her eyes and I knew I was fucked.

When my fingers hit the monitors to show both of us standing there? A shy smile played on her lips.

My breath caught as she moved, her meaning clear even as her dress slipped to the floor. My eyes drifted to the screen as Alisha tapped the side of the screen. "How does it record?"

Oh holy fuck— "I thought you just wanted to watch."

"We should," she whispered. "Later."

I am in love with you. In that moment, surrounded by the hum of electronics and Alisha's intoxicating presence.

"Trying to give me something to think about when I'm gone?" At her nod, I groaned, finding her center.

"And something to come home to." I smiled into her lips. I peered at the screen watching myself move over her.

Her eyes drifted up to it and I felt her clench.

"I'll always come home to you, Angel."

DE-BRIEF

Congratulations…

You've successfully completed your first assignment at Titan Security.

Your next assignment awaits in…

∼

Stroke of Fate
Titan Security Book II

I never meant to fall in love with him...

Dark. Dangerous. Devoted.

I didn't know Lucas Devereaux was a man of secrets and shadows.
I should've known better than to fall for the one man my brother hated most.
Every instinct told me he was right for me—until he wasn't.

I never meant to become his obsession.

His temptation.
His weakness.

As the youngest member of Titan, I had everything to prove.

Love was never part of my plan—especially not with a man whose past was as dark as his soul.

But with every touch, every kiss, every calculated lie, I fell deeper into his web.

Even if I believe love conquers all, will his lies destroy us both before we can discover if what we have is real?

Or will the truth about who he really is destroy everything?

Get Stroke of Fate

AUTHORS NOTE

Thank you so much for getting this far in Stroke of Luck.

I would love to see what you thought about the mystery unfolding in your review. Reviews help authors a lot so leaving one is great!

Lots of Love,

Lilah

ABOUT THE AUTHOR

Lilah Lance writes romance for all the girls who dream of being seen, being *accepted*, and being loved for *who they are*.

Get exclusive content and giveaways by signing up for Lilah's newsletter on http://lilahlance.com where you can get sneak peeks and news before anyone else.